MÂTOWAK
WOMAN WHO CRIES

Joylene Nowell Butler

DANCING LEMUR PRESS, L.L.C.
Pikeville, North Carolina
www.dancinglemurpress.com

Dedication

To the missing and murdered on the Highway of Tears, Highway 16 in British Columbia: "We will never forget."

Acknowledgment

Doesn't matter how many years I've been writing, I couldn't have finished this book without my writing pals, Vicki L. Smith, Keith Pyeatt, and Christopher Hoare. To my beta partners Merilyn Liddell and Monica Zwikstra, thank you. My sincere gratitude to Royal Canadian Mounted Police (RCMP) Cpl. Marion C. Davis (Rtd) Reg. # 35803. Any discrepancies in this story are no fault of Marion's. And finally a very special thank you to my oldest and dearest friend Judi M. Geib for her unwavering support, and to my security blanket for four decades, my husband Ralph Butler.

Blood. So much blood. Pooling on the slate tiles around his head.

Leland—dead?

I always assumed he'd outlive me. Mean people are lucky that way. But maybe that is what's wrong. He used to be mean. After our sons died, he changed.

With my palm firmly pressed to my chest, I still my erratic thoughts. Giddiness overwhelms me. I drop my purse and grip the edge of the countertop. Tears blur my vision. An uncomfortable heat descends upon me, similar to those hot flashes I suffered for ten years. Ohmigosh, now I'm blubbering like a fool.

Leland gone? I don't believe it.

I slip off my ankle boots. Bare feet on cold tiles ground me. The kitchen phone is on the wall next to the breakfast table clear across the room. I can't make it that far. My fingers grope across the marble counter and connect with Leland's cell phone. I detach it from the charger and gawk at its keypad.

A second passes before I'm sure I hear Leland say: *911. Dial 911, you stupid woman.*

Morning light struggles to force its way through a ceiling of black clouds and makes the space around me grainy like salted air. I suck back sobs and, despite the rancid taste of death, take two deep breaths.

"911 Emergency Services. Fire, police, or ambulance?" a male voice asks.

I stare at Leland's body. "Ambulance...and police."

My call is redirected. Suddenly, a woman speaks to me, but the ringing in my ears prevents me from hearing what she says. "Pardon?"

"What is the nature of your emergency?"

"My husband is dead. There is a hole—"

"Your name, ma'am?"

"Sally Warner."

"Are you in your residence, Sally? Your ID is blocked. What's your address?"

My address? I think for a moment and then tell her. The

smell of blood burns my nose and throat. My stomach contents rise. I can't take my eyes off his blood pooling on the floor.

"The police and ambulance are on their way, Sally. Are you okay? Do you know what happened?"

"Happened? No. I was upstairs. I heard nothing. I was getting ready for an appointment downtown. Leland was fine. He was sitting at the breakfast table reading the newspaper. I went up to shower thirty minutes ago—not that I spent the entire thirty minutes in the shower. I had to find the right suit to wear because I've lost a great deal of weight, and well, all my clothes feel so weird because they're stiff and new and—" I take a deep breath, ashamed of my babblings. A gust of cold wind sweeps over me. "The door's open. Where's Digger?" Leland's dead on our kitchen floor, and I'm thinking about my dog?

The operator clears her throat loudly. "The police are on their way. Are you alone? I don't mean to alarm you, Sally, but could there be anyone else inside your house?"

"Inside my house?" The hairs on the back of my neck stand up. I peek around the corner and stare out through the open service entrance to the quiet threshold. My legs tremble. Could I make it to the door? The monitor below the hidden camera shows no one lurking outside. "The service door is open. That probably means whoever did this is gone, don't you think?"

"I'm sure it does, Sally. I'll stay on the line with you until the police arrive. They'll be there soon. We'll wait together."

I stare down at Leland's body, wipe my nose, and shiver. "Okay, that would be good. Thank you."

The smell reminds me of something, but I can't remember what. My frazzled brain registers one word: violence. Violence took place in my home. Violence means rage. "He isn't well liked."

"The police are on their way, Sally," she says in a soothing voice.

"He's only home because he's due in court tomorrow. He always takes a day off to refresh himself and to review the material. Those years he spent in Parliament left him rusty. At least that is what he said when he first got home from Ottawa. But honestly, Leland never does anything half-heartedly."

"Pardon me. Did you say Leland? Do you mean you're *those* Warners, the ones from the government?"

"He's not well liked at all." I cough. I've been referring to him in the present tense; I must stop. "Leland upset the status quo. Before he took the office, he went against the Minister of Defence and urged taxpayers to spend millions on those new helicopters for our soldiers in Afghanistan. It's because of him that Canada had its own spy planes instead of leasing them from the United States. Oh yes—and he made sure our troops received new tanned uniforms. But what choice did he have? Our troops were dressed in jungle fatigues in the middle of the desert. It was humiliating and dangerous. They deserved better."

The operator clears her throat. "Excuse me. Is your husband *the* Leland Warner?"

That is a dumb question. Unless she means...of course. Warner is a common enough name.

But Leland was different. Disparaged. Even so, that is not what I'm trying to tell her. He was hungry for power and justice. A strange coupling. "He hated the world laughing at Canada because we couldn't dress our soldiers properly."

"Are we talking about...the former Minister of National Defence Leland Warner? The one in the news? Your sons..." The operator stutters, "Ah-ah. Okay. Sure. Uh..." She mumbles something to someone in the background. It's now I realize I hear other voices, other operators talking to distressed victims. I'm not the only one whose world is falling apart.

Except, she'd said "Your sons," didn't she? She's referring to what happened to Bronson and Declan. She must be thinking about the night they were murdered. Of course, the whole country knew about it.

"I'm right here with you until help comes, Mrs. Warner. Can you see your husband from where you are?"

"He's on the floor." My heart aches for my boys. "I didn't touch anything. Do you think I should check for a pulse, just in case?" It wouldn't matter; I know he's dead.

I turn my back on him and hug one arm across my chest. The stench rising from his body is quite awful, not vile like the dead squirrel Bronson placed in my bed so many years ago, but smelly like a public restroom.

"Should I shut my door?" I'm afraid to approach the door. What if whomever did this is outside? Waiting for me? That is silly. I press my palm against my chest, but this time it's not calming me down. I need my sweater. Dear God, I can't go through this again.

"Are you using a cell phone?" she asks. "Do you want to go to another room? Perhaps outside? I'll stay on the line with you."

"No. I want..." I don't finish because I'm not sure what I want. Someone to find my dog after they fix this terrible moment. Someone to take away my husband's body and with it the fear, though I know it will stay with me forever.

I swallow and cough up my own sobs. The operator's breathing

on the other end of the line is shallow.
"I just—I want someone to tell me...what do I do now?"

large shadow falls over my desk. I look up to see my boss, RCMP Staff Sergeant Gabriel Lacroix, scowling down at me. Lacroix is French. He's not First Nations, but his stance, size, and dark skin remind me of our chief on the reservation when I was a kid. A no-nonsense man with little patience for the shenanigans of restless boys.

"There has been a possible homicide in College Heights. Dispatch has the particulars. There was no weapon found at the scene. Handle with kid gloves; this one is high priority. I want you to treat the victim's wife as if she were your own mother. Clear?" His scowl deepens. "And no further involvement in your wife's murder. You wait until Surrey call you. Is that clear, Corporal Killian?"

I nod and present my yes-of-course-Staff-Sergeant face. Lacroix, neither satisfied nor more perturbed than normal, walks away.

It's been fifteen weeks since he accepted my transfer in from District, yet, he still only speaks to me when necessary. I'm satisfied with that arrangement. After too many years spent trying to impress the white establishment, I just go ahead and call Dispatch. I check my watch, 9:24, ask them to send the file to my computer, and request they page the Forensic Ident members.

An instant later, I click on the link, read: Victim: Leland Warner—a name I recognize—shot to death in his home. Address: College Heights. Shooter: unknown.

I page the rest of my team.

Constable Stan Carrigan texts to say he's en route. Two seconds later, Constable John Ryan texts. He's less than a block from the address. Ryan has been at many crime scenes but never without our team, though there is a senior officer, along with his junior counterpart.

I call Ryan. "We'll be there as soon as possible."

Ryan says, "I'm pulling in the driveway now."

"Who's there so far?"

"Two patrol cars."

"Page PDS and request their best search dog. Take your time."

"Gotcha," Ryan says. "Anything else?"

"No, just follow protocol." I hang up with him and call Carrigan. "How close are you?"

"I'm passing Costco. ETA ten minutes."

"Ryan's there with a senior member."

"Understood."

Last night, the local weatherman had advised no snow until next week when a system in the Pacific was due to hit. Given that, I slip on my parka, leave my outdoor boots behind, and exit the building via the side door. It's warm enough not to zip the parka.

My car's parked in the lot across the street. The Ident team are in the minivan in front of me at Fifth Avenue waiting for a break in traffic. I pull up to them, turn with them southwest onto Victoria Street. Suddenly, I'm sweating. In the middle of winter.

At the intersection of Victoria and Seventeenth, the light turns red; I crack open my window. Cold air seeps into the car. A heaviness I've experienced off and on all morning pushes on my chest. A heart attack?

Couldn't be.

The light turns green. At Twentieth Avenue, we turn right. I pull my favourite photograph of Angie out of my inside pocket, cup it in my left palm, glance down at her face. My hand shakes.

On our first date, my hands also shook. There was no mistaking the look of surprise on her friends' faces when we showed up at the whites-only party. Angie'd worn white, like a bride, which set off her silky blonde hair and blue eyes. My black T-shirt, jeans, dark skin, hair, and eyes must have stuck out like a raven trying to hide amongst swans.

There was an embarrassing moment at the door where we were greeted by three gawking females, two grinning widely. I had my hand on Angie's back and felt her stiffen. Then one of the girls broke the ice, and said, "No wonder you've been hiding him. He's gorgeous."

The host grabbed my arm and, beginning at one end of the house, introduced me to every person there. Halfway through the room, I caught Angie's eye, and mouthed: *Save me.* She threw back her head and laughed. Later, while we made love, she said, "My friends are wrong. You're nerdy, not gorgeous. And, mister...don't ever forget that."

We were in love. Sure of our future.

Now, six months after her murder, I'm celebrating our seventh anniversary alone.

I place her photograph back inside my pocket. "Happy Anniversary, babe." My eyes burn while I fight not to cry.

A kilometre down Haldi Road I pull into the vic's large circular driveway and park between a patrol car and Carrigan's vehicle to the left of the garage. The minivan is at the back door. The time is 9:41. I pull coveralls and shoe coverings from the trunk, walk to the house's open service entrance door. As I approach, I repeat in my head: *The job. I'm here to do the job.*

Inside the enclosed porch I climb into the coveralls, slip the covers over my shoes, then pull on two sets of nitrile gloves. Inside the residence, it's a short walk down a short hallway to the open space of the kitchen.

The odour of defecation and gunpowder lays heavy in the room. Even after fifteen years, I gag over the film coating my tongue. I was an embarrassment to my staff sergeant back in Surrey's Homicide, who told me early on I had better get used to it. I survey the scene. This is nothing like we faced when I worked the cases off Highway 16. The majority of the time we had only bones to process. No crime scene. No witnesses. No large quantities of blood.

Ident waste no time collecting evidence; brain splatter across the top of the island. I kneel beside the remains of an older gentleman sprawled face-up on the kitchen tiles. There is a puddle of blood under his head. It doesn't appear that he's been moved. There's no bruising on the forehead, no signs of residue on the skin, which could mean he wasn't shot at close range.

Tilting the head gently reveals the bullet had exited the back of the skull, leaving a large hole. Possibly from a 9mm. I stand up, my knees creak, which reminds me that while The Butcher, Vancouver's worst serial killer in two decades, gets life in prison, I'll probably get new knees in a ten years. I look towards the door, the counter, and the kitchen window. Squinting, I make out a small hole in the glass above the sink.

Kneeling again—damn, it hurts—I open the vic's mouth, check the tongue, the cheeks, and thank the powers-to-be for nitrile gloves. Otherwise the thought of sticking my fingers in some dead man's cavities would have me gagging. In front of subordinates, no less.

I check his chest pockets, which can be as scary if the vic had a drug habit and was hoarding old syringes. I rifle through trouser pockets, feel someone standing next to me. It's a young constable, the driver of the patrol car outside.

The kid's baby-smooth face is grey, and there are dark circles under his eyes. Either he partied too hard last night or this is his first crime scene. He stares at the body, blinks, swallows. Hopefully he has the good sense to go outside if he's going to puke.

"You were first on the scene, Constable...?"

"Pinscher. Constable Riley had a blow out coming up the hill, so I arrived first."

"And?"

He opens his notepad. "My ETA (Estimated Time of Arrival) was 9:14. The back door was open, no sign of forced entry. I taped it right off, asked Mrs. Warner to stay with in view, while I came in and checked for vitals. I immediately went back to the door and assisted Mrs. Warner in through the front entrance. She hasn't been back in this room since. I waited for Constable Riley. He checked the vic's pulse, looked for a casing, went to see if there were footprints. He called it in at 9:19. Mrs. Warner said she was upstairs and didn't hear anything. Apparently, only delivery people use the service door. There was no blood on her, no casing. Oh, and—" He sucks air. "The vic's a VIP."

"Yes, the Honourable Leland Warner, retired from the Cabinet of Canada. How old is the widow? What's her condition?"

"Sixty. Constable Riley is with her in the living room. She's upset."

No—really?

I smack my lips together to stop myself from smirking. "Go and stay near her, but give her space. Later when you get back to the detachment, copy your notes and give them to Constable Carrigan."

Pinscher turns to leave. Behind him, Stan Carrigan steps forward. A camera flashes behind me.

"It's true? The victim's our former Minister of National Defence?" Carrigan asks. "Holy cow."

"How long have they been back in Prince George?" I pat Warner's stomach, legs, ankles, and find nothing. I didn't expect to.

"About eighteen months. Warner was Cariboo-Prince George Member of Parliament for a lot of years before taking over as Minister of National Defence after the scandal with the last one. Apparently, he's responsible for suspending use of those Mercedes G-Wagon combat vehicles. He also made sure we got the sixteen new CH-47 Chinook choppers and the seventeen C-130Js for The Sandbox. He may have been a horse's ass, but that one gesture endeared him to a lot of Canadians. He retired and came back to work in his law firm here in Prince. Do you remember the incident with his two sons?"

I nod. Two privileged, rich, white brothers terrorized a First Nations woman and her daughter by kidnapping the daughter and later threatening to kill them both. The First Nations mother was a highly respected English professor from UNBC. The brothers were Warner's sons. If they hadn't ended up dead, they probably wouldn't have done time."

I glimpse Carrigan's face. He doesn't look apologetic over his bias opinion.

"As soon as the Coroner's finished, send Constable Gregory with the body to Kamloops; he'll sign the body out. Have him do the stats for their forensic pathologist. Age, weight, COD (cause-of-death). Fill me in on the back-story later."

"Okay."

"Check the window over the sink. There's a hole in the glass, consider the position of the body, determine whether that's the exit path of the bullet or vice versa. Scan the backyard. Is somebody outback with a search dog?"

"Yes. Chastin and Bandit. They're scanning the neighbourhood and surrounding woods."

I nod. "Good." My knees crack as I stand, and I wince. Damn. If Carrigan heard them crack, there's no indication. Why I care is stupid. Bad knees don't mean I'm not capable of running this investigation.

The Ident photographer steps forward to snap pictures of the counter and floor.

"I want photos of everything," I tell her, "before and after the body's removed."

I point at one of the fingerprint experts. "Pay particular attention to the service door entrance for prints. Since there is no sign of forced entry, our perp might have knocked on the door, pressed the button without gloves, or leaned his hand against the door frame. Or maybe the door was unlocked, and he opened it." I turn back to Carrigan. "We'll need a sketch. And two teams canvassing the neighbourhood."

I look at the counter, stove, prep area, then down at the body, searching for anything out of the ordinary. No one will be able to accuse us of putting low priority on this case. The dead man on the kitchen floor isn't a cop's spouse, or a missing kid from some northern village or the wrong side of Prince George. Former Minister of National Defence Leland Warner was an influential member of society. Those in command will make sure his death is solved. If not by me, then by somebody else.

That should annoy me, but it doesn't. I'll do everything possible to find the shooter. Since Angie's death, securing justice for the victim is what gets me out of bed every morning. I can, and will, and must make a difference to somebody.

Won't say that to the grief counsellor, though. I'm not sure my privacy is safe from the bureaucrats. Sorry, Dad, but white people make me nervous.

This murder looks too neat, void of emotion. The shooter got Warner's attention, and Warner left the table—the newspaper still lay on top. Maybe the shooter directed Warner backward towards the counter with his gun. Or he used the delivery of a package for cover and asked for Warner's signature, prompting Warren to turn to the counter.

I glance at the counter and floors for evidence of a pen or a package.

The youngest member of my team, Constable John Ryan, joins me at the entrance to the kitchen. John is built like a hockey player, fast on his feet, alert to his surroundings. Dedicated. Easy to respect. So far, as I can tell, he's good-natured under all circumstances. Some would say that's a gift. One day I'll ask him where he grew up. Bet it was a long way from the reservation or residential schools.

"You were able to get here fast."

"Yeah, just my luck." Ryan catches himself and injects, "I delivered those papers you gave me, so I happened to be the closest one when you paged."

"What did you find?"

Ryan looks at his notes. "Honourable Leland William Warner, sixty-two, retired. You'll want to see the file on his sons, Declan and Bronson. They've been dead eighteen months. Most say it's why Warner retired before the election. God rest his soul."

I ignore the religious reference. I learned a long time ago that there is no God. Anyone with half a mind should know that. The world is a godless, corrupt, hideous place. Why else would eighteen families be missing loved ones off the same highway? Why else would a woman lose her children, then her husband? Why else would I be celebrating my seventh anniversary alone?

"Any possible suspects?"

"Yes, three. Doctor Brendell Meshango, Declan's English professor, was with Warner's sons the night they died. Last report said she was head of the English Department at UNBC. Sophie Brooks, First Nations artist, had dated Declan until, rumour says, his dad put an end to it. Maybe she took it bad? Shawn Norse, ex-biker. It was Bronson Warner who beat Norse's wife into a coma for no reason. She died in hospital a few days later."

"We need to find out if there is a connection between the sons' deaths and Warner's."

Warner's face shows an empty expression. As a homicide investigator, I know why the faces of the dead hold no emotion; facial muscles go slack at death. Yet, it never fails to amaze me to see their blank expressions.

"Call in the coroner," I tell the closest investigator. "Constable Gregory will need to know time of death, etc., so we can get the remains to Kamloops as soon as possible; he's got an six-hour drive ahead of him. Tell them to bring the metal box. He can leave from here." I turn back Ryan. "What about the widow?"

"She was upstairs. Says this door was open when she came down. Didn't hear the shot or any other commotion, which could be why she's still alive."

"Or the shooter used a silencer and was satisfied with one target."

Ryan nods. "Mr. Norse is the husband of murder victim Jasmine Norse. Everybody knows how much he hated Warner. Considering Warner's son beat Mrs. Norse to death, he'd be our prime suspect, eh? He definitely has motive. Given his associates, getting his hands on a weapon wouldn't be a problem."

A monitor above the upright freezer catches my attention. "We'll use ViCLAS." I'm not convinced the analysis system can solve a murder, but we'll use whatever resources we have. "Collect all surveillance tapes and find out if there was a main recorder somewhere. Were visitors or home deliveries expected?"

"I'll find out."

"Is Mrs. Warner still in the living room?"

"Ident is with her. I took her statement."

"I'll question her further after we take her downtown, like everyone else."

Ryan shakes his head. "Apparently that ain't happening."

"Says who?"

"Superintendent Malden."

I clench my jaw, then relax. I'll deal with this break in protocol later. "They test for gunpowder residue yet?"

"She's clean."

"Skin and clothing?"

"Yeah."

"We'll need her clothes." I face Stan Carrigan, who immediately moves closer. "Have the team gather every bit of evidence they can find for criminal analysis." I say this out of habit. They can do their jobs blindfolded, but it's part of my responsibility to recite the same old spiel. "We'll need help searching this place."

"I'll make the call. And you're right, the bullet exited through the window. The glass shards are on the outside."

I look back at the window. Barely visible from this distance is the hole in the centre of the double pane. A sudden glare of morning sunlight shoots darts of pain behind my eyes. I squint, refocus. Warner's backyard is surrounded by a greenbelt of spruce and bare birch trees. A large calibre might have ricocheted off any number of trees before it lost projectile power.

"Stan, work backwards from the hole. Use infrared to see exactly where Warner stood, then do the same from the other side. Let's hope we find the bullet. John, you're sure it's one shot?"

Constable John Ryan glances over his right shoulder at the body. "Seems so."

"Assume nothing."

"Right."

"Have them check for biological trace so we can separate Warner from our shooter. Make sure they gather all the physical evidence on the fridge, counters, and floor. In other words: everywhere. I'll need a summary of his active court cases by day's end. See if Norse is connected to anything recent, not just what went on eighteen months ago. Concentrate on what might have set Norse off this morning, but don't wait for results. Before you head back to the detachment, let our file coordinator know you'll appoint a team of two to go through every file from the past six months at Mr. Warner's law firm. If nothing shows up, go back a year. Stan, I'd like you to supervise."

I don't wait to see Carrigan's reaction, but turn back to Ryan, who continues scribbling in his notes. "I want something for the National DNA data bank by the end of the day."

"Weather report says to expect snow tomorrow," Ryan volunteers. "We could lose evidence outside."

I frown. "What weather report?"

"Global news, BC. I watch it every morning before I leave home."

"Last night local news said no snow for the next three days." I hear the resistance in my voice.

Ryan shrugs. "I guess they changed their minds."

Snow, tomorrow? That's bad news for the investigation and my car. I haven't installed studded tires yet. Of course, until I came north, I didn't know I would need them. I'm still trying to remember which idiot told me all-seasons would be good enough in the north.

"Have them do a trace for tire tracks and footwear. Get a scale drawing for tomorrow in case we need to send a profile for behavioural analysis. Exactly how big is this place?"

"If I had to guess, I'd say about seven thousand square feet, but I'll find out."

I spot a vent cap near the floor. "Central vacuum system?"

"I'll find out."

"Have the filters checked. Get the blueprints. Now, I'll speak to the widow. Where's the living room?"

"Actually, it's called a gathering room. I'll show you." Ryan hesitates. "Uh, our first responder took some liberties."

"Constable Pincher?"

"Yeah."

"Explain."

"When he arrived, she was standing at the back door. Her purse was on the ground. He picked it up, looked in her purse, and recorded what he saw."

"Why? Never mind." I inhale a slow, shallow breath. "If she turns out to be our perp, he'll have to explain his mistake on the stand."

"No weapon." Ryan's face reddens fast. He shrugs. "Guess that's obvious, or I would have handed it over. Anyway, he made a list of the contents. I'll add a copy to my notes. As soon as he realized what he'd done, he asked if we had her permission to do several searches of her house pertaining to her husband's murder until we closed the case."

I shake my head. This just keeps getting better. "How long has he been out of Regina (RCMP Academy)?"

"Three weeks." Noting my surprise, he smiles. "I figured you'd want to know, so I asked."

"Follow up on anything he noted in her purse. Just in case."

"Gotcha."

I take off my coveralls and hand them to one of the Idents. "The gathering room?" In my culture, a gathering place is a place critical to strengthening traditions and community. I have a feeling Warner's gathering room is anything but.

Ryan leads the way down a long hallway to a large, high ceilinged room at the back of the house, directly across the courtyard from the kitchen. Two brown leather sofas face each other in front of the ceiling-high fireplace. The leather coffee table between them is four-feet square. I hadn't seen Mrs. Warner sitting on the sofa from the kitchen because it was out of view of where I'd been standing. A blind spot. Ryan returns to the kitchen while I pause at the entrance into the room.

Mrs. Sally Warner is dressed in an expensive two-tone linen pantsuit of dark brown, the jacket trimmed at collar, waist, and cuffs with satin stitch embroidery. Her matching slacks have the same trimming at the bottom of the legs. I don't normally care, but it's the type of suit Angie would have admired. She might even have carried it at the boutique shop she'd managed. She once asked me how much I thought a suit similar to this one would cost. I said, "Two hundred?"

She had smiled. "It retails for over two grand. Not too many men would have guessed correctly."

I'd seen enough shoes in Angie's shop to recognize Mrs. Warner's as Italian, probably costing fifteen hundred. Angie called them pumps. When I asked why, she shrugged. Their colour matches the suit.

Mrs. Warner is intent on her fingers being printed. She sits with her back straight and ankles crossed. Her complexion's softly wrinkled. This isn't a woman who indulges with Botox. Her skin is fair with no heavy makeup. Her light blonde hair is styled nicely, not in the usual granny-cut from the fifties. She looks like a proper politician's wife. Actually, she could pass for a politician herself. Composed, in control, privileged.

Sitting to her right is an Ident member. Pinscher, the first constable on the scene, stands at the front entrance to the room. He's watching me. Some of the colour has returned to his face. I cross the room towards him.

"When Mrs. Warner is ready, I want you to drive her to a hotel room downtown. Guard her door and make sure no one enters unless she recognizes them."

He nods.

"You'll make sure she's safe?"

He stands at attention. He probably hopes this gesture is seen as a sign of respect, a way of fixing his earlier mistake with her purse. "Yessir."

I cross the room towards the vic's widow. "Pardon me, Mrs. Warner. My name is Corporal Danny Killian."

The Ident member has a small fingerprint tablet open and is printing the fingers of Mrs. Warner's left hand. Mrs. Warner turns her gaze from what he's doing and looks up at me. She blinks infrequently, her gaze unfocused. Her right hand lies limp in her lap. No wedding rings. No earrings. No sweating around her hairline. Up close her complexion is grey, her breathing shallow.

All these years I still hate this part of my job. My step-dad raised me to be a gentleman, but even he had to admit human compassion didn't necessarily have a voice.

"On behalf of the RCMP, I'd like to express our deepest sympathy for your loss."

"Thank you, Corporal...Kil-li-an," she says, emphasizing the three syllables of my name while intent on my face. Is she surprised I'm not white? Killian is Irish. I wasn't born with the name. My real dad cut out when I was two. My step-dad is the only man I'll ever call *dad*.

"May I sit?"

"Of course." Her voice is soft, gentle.

"I know you've had a terrible shock." I sit across from her on the leather ottoman. "Are you able to answer a few questions?"

"Of course." Her gaze meets mine for the appropriate span of seconds before wandering towards the window to my left where she seems to gaze off at nothing.

The Ident officer cleans her left thumb.

"What time did you rise this morning, ma'am?"

"Six-forty-seven." She looks at me as she speaks, and her eyes sparkle. I think the question pleased her. "I woke yesterday morning at precisely the same time. And the morning before. I remember thinking how odd that was. How did you know?"

I didn't. But suddenly she thinks I'm more astute than I am. I'm going to use that to my advantage. "Was your husband awake?"

"Leland leaves his door open and likes to wait for sounds of me in the hallway before he sets down whatever novel he's currently reading and comes out of his room. I met him on the top landing about five to seven. We came down together."

I look at my notes while she studies me. "Then what happened?"

"I prepared breakfast, then went upstairs to ready myself for town. I came down at nine."

"You didn't hear or see anything?"

She shakes her head. "My bedroom is soundproofed."

"Soundproofed?"

"I suffer from insomnia. Leland hoped soundproofing my room would help."

"Before and after you returned upstairs, could you recall your routine, so we can set a time frame?"

"Yes, of course." She glances at the Ident member as he prints the fingers of her right hand. "Breakfast was prepared and ready by five after seven. It doesn't take much for bagels and jam. I cooked toast and an egg for Leland. I left him at half-past and returned to my room. I generally do that on those days when I have an appointment in the city. Otherwise, I would have stayed and shared the paper with him." Her eyes moisten. "When I have to go out, I take my time so I'm not rushed. At my age it doesn't take much to get my feathers rustled. I overheat." She pauses as if waiting for affirmation.

The Ident member closes his kit, cleans her fingertips, nods to me before leaving.

"Please continue, Mrs. Warner." My voice is gentle and kind.

"It took a while to decide what to wear. I laid out my clothes for the day; that may have brought the time to seven-forty. I located a good pair of walking boots, collected my toiletries, and prepared for my shower. That would have taken me another fifteen minutes or so, bringing the time to..."

"Quarter to eight."

"Yes." She smooths a hand down the buttons of her suit. "By the time I finished washing and rinsing my hair, it was probably quarter after eight. I dried my hair and styled it. Made one more trip to the restroom. Perhaps another fifteen minutes to sit and rest my legs, check my Facebook. I belong to various church groups. After that I dressed and came downstairs at nine o'clock."

A few moments ago, her eyes looked distant. Now they look feverish.

"This sounds like a lot of wasted time to you, Corporal Killian, but at my age it's actually hard work. Just holding my arms up to do my hair is a chore."

I nod. "You heard nothing unusual during the entire time?"

She shakes her head.

"Nothing at all?"

"My room is soundproofed," she repeats. "I came down at nine o'clock sharp because of the length of time it takes me to drive downtown. I detest being late. I was heading to the garage to warm my car when I saw Leland on the floor. I wasted valuable time just staring at him. I'm so sorry I didn't react faster. It was a few minutes before I could clear my mind and think straight. I—I think I was in shock."

I nod. "Had your husband been upset about anything at work? Any disgruntled clients?"

She sweeps a hand over her neck, temporarily wiping the wrinkles away. "Leland seldom brings his work home."

"Any problems with his finances?"

"No. My husband is quite good with money."

"He hadn't received any threatening phone calls or letters?"

"No, but you should ask his secretary. Since our sons' passing, Leland has—I mean, Leland tried hard to shelter me from...who knows what?"

"Did you sense anything out of the ordinary? Any problems while he was in Ottawa that might have followed him here?"

She shakes her head and lifts her chin to look at me squarely. "I'm sorry, Corporal. I'm not being helpful. I'm Leland's wife and I...I don't know what to say." Her eyes fill with tears.

"It's okay." I give her my best you-can-trust-me smile. "You were married a long time?"

"Thirty-seven years."

"Wow, that is a long time."

I jot down thirty-seven years, wondering what the seventh anniversary gift is supposed to be. Copper? I'm sure I wondered the exact thing last year, after the fact. The expression on Angie's face when I arrived home without a gift. I realized my mistake and suggested we go for dinner to a fancy restaurant; I can't remember which one. During dinner she didn't say much. Looking back at that evening now, I certainly don't blame her. She probably regretted having married such a selfish jerk.

I ignore the churning in my gut. "You had a good marriage?"

She hesitates. "We went through some difficult years. It took the death of our children to bring us close."

"I'm sorry. You've had more than your share of grief. I can't imagine how you've survived. You must be strong."

She wrings her hands.

"Do you own a gun, Mrs. Warner?"

She grimaces. "No."

"Is it true your husband had a collection?"

"He sold most of them."

"Did you clean up after breakfast? I noticed there are no dishes in the sink."

"Yes, I cleaned up before I went upstairs."

"The counters, stove, table?"

"Yes."

"When you came back down at nine, did you touch anything in the kitchen? Pick up something off the floor?"

Her eyelids droop. "No."

"Did you see any piece of metal, like the little casing for a bullet?"

"No."

"You didn't touch anything after you came downstairs?"

She hesitates. "No."

"You used the phone to call 911."

Her eyebrows rise. "Yes. I should have thought of that. I used Leland's cell phone."

"One more question, ma'am...for the record."

She steadies her hands and gives me her full attention.

"I need to ask you. Did you shoot your husband?"

Again, her eyebrows lift slightly. Then resignation replaces surprise, and she shakes her head. "No."

I hold her gaze and decide it's too soon to tell if she's lying. Her back stoops, as if the weight of her shoulders is too much. Her hands lay limp in her lap.

"Tonight, could you write down any names that come to mind, anyone who stands out as a possible threat? We can meet later and discuss them."

"Yes, of course."

"Could you jot down your husband's assistants' names and phone numbers here and in Ottawa?" I flip my notepad to a blank sheet, hand it to her, along with my pen. "One more thing. I'd like you to pack a bag and stay with a friend or family member for a few days. Constable Pinscher," I gesture to where he's standing, "will drive you down town as soon as you're ready. We'll need your clothes, Mrs. Warner. Later, Constable Pinscher will drive you to the detachment downtown where I'll take your statement." It's protocol; I don't care who she is.

"Again? I told the other young man everything I know."

"I wouldn't ask if it wasn't important."

"I'll do whatever I can to help, but must I leave my home? Is it necessary?" She hands back my pen and notepad.

"It'll only be for a few days." I stand.

"I want to change my clothes first. They sprayed something on my sleeves."

"One of my Ident people will give you a bag to put your clothes in. You understand we'll need them?"

"Oh, of course, yes."

"Someone from the RCMP Victim Services Unit will be here soon."

"Thank you."

"I'm sorry for your loss, ma'am."

She nods, then stands, and turning her attention towards the tall windows overlooking the yard, wraps her sweater tighter. "It's going to snow."

I look up at the cloudless blue sky. When did she find time to watch the news this morning? Or did the weatherman last night forecast snow for today? Remember to ask someone if there's a television in her room.

I repeat my sympathies before returning to the kitchen. I glance towards the window and the gathering room beyond, but again I can't see her from this angle. I crouch down beside the M.E., Carmie Webster, observe the hole in Warner's forehead again, and stand. My knees don't crack this time, but the pain's still intense. Later tonight, I'll apply the heat pad and orthopaedic pain cream. I've had this problem with my knees since flying down those cement stairs hanging onto *The Butcher*. Generally, I can manage the pain. Suppose I'll have to learn to live life without kneeling.

I face Ryan. "Make sure they do a swab. I want this whole house checked for evidence: toilets, laundry basin, showers, fireplaces. Don't forget the toilet handle."

Carmie looks up at me. "Good morning, Danny." She flings her wrist high, shields her eyes from the overhead lights, squints at me. "You weren't at the Christmas party last night." Her eyebrows furrow. "Is everything okay?"

"Morning, Carmie. What can you tell me?" Am I such a creature of habit that even co-workers can spot a change?

The ME gestures towards the window and the small hole. "The victim was shot and the bullet's outside somewhere." The corners of her mouth twitch.

I can almost hear her laughing on the inside. "Good to know."

"Yep, case solved. We can all go home." She glances at Warner, looks up at me, smiles.

This time I remember to return her smile. It's hard to do. Damn, do I look like I'm snarling? Am I betraying Angie by smiling?

The job. I'm here to do the job.

I visualize Warner facing the service door, seeing the gun, stepping back. Did he know his time was up? Even at the end, was there still hope?

I signal to Carrigan, my Senior Investigator, who's taking notes at the island. Carrigan comes closer. "Stan, stop what you're doing and take somebody outside with you while there is good light. Check the grounds, trees, and whatever's out back, then resume in here. Any word from the dog team?"

"No. Do you want the metal detector brought in if we can't find the bullet today?"

"Order it now to save time. On the chance this is a contract murder, check the roster at the airport, bus terminal, and train station. Match videos from their surveillance cameras to our criminal database. Notify Vancouver and any of the local airports. Find out if anyone chartered a flight during the past few days. Then check with all the hotels and motels. Have someone watch all the bank videos."

Carrigan leaves. I switch my attention back to Carmie. "Anything out of the ordinary?"

She inspects the inside of Warner's mouth. "Well, his facial muscles are beginning to stiffen, but his larger muscles haven't. The body's temperature has dropped two degrees."

I check my watch. "He died around eight o'clock?"

"Between seven and nine; you know that's the best I can do. From his position I'd say he faced the door when shot." She points to the pooled blood. "Notice all this blood? Death wasn't instantaneous. That's unusual, but not uncommon. And the shooter didn't fire at close range; there is no evidence of residue on the body. The pathologist in Kamloops will have more to say. Are you ready for me to take Mr. Warner back to the lab and prep him for transport? We've got a lock box outside ready." She ties paper bags around one hand then the other. "He'll be in Kamloops by tonight. They're generally prompt, so I should have the autopsy report for you by next Thursday."

"We're under time restraints. Can you prep him from here?"

"I suppose."

"Explain who he is and see if Monday is possible."

"Sure." She signals to one of the Ident members. "Let's bag him and get him into the box." She asks me, "Who's going with him to Kamloops?"

"Gregory is next on the list. He should be here any moment." I signal to another RCMP Major Crime investigator. "Check the perimeter out front, the yard, and the trees. Don't forget the garage and the garbage bins."

I glance towards the west side of the house and pull my notepad out as Ryan rushes in from the front foyer. He looks excited. "What?"

"During the door-to-door, they found a guy who fit the description a neighbour gave of a jogger he'd seen earlier. They've taken him in."

"How'd the dog react to him?"

"Kosher."

"Has he lawyered up?"

"No."

"Stick him in an interview room with a guard until I get there. Unless he starts yelling for his solicitor, tell them to ignore him. After I leave, post someone at both doors here."

Ryan presses his cell phone to his ear.

"I'm on my way." I step aside to make way for the long, silver metal box being carried in through the back door.

While the engine warms, I jot down my initial impressions of Mrs. Warner. My recall has been poor since Angie's death, so I don't want to rely on my memory.

Mrs. Warner: Wealthy, privileged, dazed, confused, possibly in shock, or Canadian Juno Candidate for Best Actress?

I leave out assumptions about guilt or innocence for when the scientific evidence comes in.

* * *

Back at the detachment, I set a file down on my assistant's desk with a Post-it note on top.

She looks up at me. Smiles. "Good morning."

"What? Oh, yeah, good morning." My voice sounds gruff. I don't mean to be cranky, but how else do I hint that I don't like her looking at me like I'm a potential boyfriend. I'm not.

"This is the number of Minister Warner's assistant while he was in Ottawa. The first name is Mr. Warner's law assistant here in town. Have them start the interviews now. I need a statement before day's end. Warner's doctor, his dentist, and anybody else connected to his overall physical condition need to be interviewed as soon as possible. Find out if Warner attended a gym. Have somebody interview Professor Brendell Meshango, her daughter Zoë Sheppard, and Sophie Brooks. The lawyers at his firm will need to be interviewed individually. Could you get me the newest suspect list?"

"Right away."

"Send two officers in a van to pick up the files at Mr. Warner's law office and home. We'll use one of the interview rooms for the time being. Give an update to the file coordinator."

"Right away."

"Where's our jogger?"

"Interview Room three." She lifts the small stack of papers off her desk, hands them along with a file folder to me, all the time trying to make eye contact. "Interview three's file, plus copies of the statements so far."

Sure her eyes are pretty, she's pretty, but I'll continue to avoid her eyes because I don't know what else to do. I'm a widower. I'm not dead. But no way am I ready for a relationship. I loved my wife. I can't...go there.

The job. I'm here to do the job.

"Warner's neighbours' statements?"

"Included."

"Somebody's observing from the viewing room?"

"Yes. They'll turn on the equipment as soon as you signal."

I hang my coat in my locker while preparing my mindset for the interview. If done correctly I may have my perp.

My entry into the interview room is met with a petulant glare from a young man in his early twenties, rolling a small, empty water bottle between his palms. He's dressed in a shabby red and white jogging suit, smelling like a dirty jock strap.

"It's about time, man."

Judging by the sound of his voice, I'd say his throat is full of phlegm. He's wearing worn, dirty high-back runners.

I take the chair opposite him, crack open the folder, and note the vital statistics: Wickstrom, Russell, age twenty-four...on probation for possession of a controlled substance for personal use: marijuana.

While I read the neighbour's statements, I keep a covert eye on the kid. Ignoring him will unnerve him further. It works most of the time.

He fidgets, shoves the water bottle aside, scratches both forearms through his sleeves, wipes his nose on his cuff, presses his palms flat on the table. His right foot taps the floor.

"Who are you?" he whines. "I've been sitting here for two hours, and nobody'll tell me nothing."

Seventy minutes is closer to the truth.

I pretend to read from the file. He's got the drawn, haggard face of a young man in an old man's body with signs of malnutrition and drug use. Is this kid capable of murder? With human nature being what it is, anyone is capable of taking a life if they're motivated enough. In the worse cases, the motivation has little to do with the victim.

I nod towards the camera mounted high up in the corner. "Today is December the third. My name is Homicide Investigator Corporal Killian from Major Crime. I'm speaking with Russell Wickstrom of Prince George, BC. The time is..." I glance at my watch and report the time for the video recorder, "10:32.

"How are you, Russ? Can I call you Russ? Would you like something? A bottle of water?"

He shakes his head, sets the bottle upright on the table.

"Maybe a chocolate bar?"

He looks tempted but shrugs. Although the room's temperature is a constant seventy degrees, tiny beads of sweat form on his upper lip. He's got a jaundiced complexion and dilated pupils. His shoe taps. This kid is nervous, possibly guilty-of-something.

He avoids looking at me. "I ain't done nothing. If somebody'd tell me what's wrong, I know I can explain."

"I need to ask you a few questions, but first I'd like to thank you for coming in. It's not everybody who cares to do their civic duty."

"Huh?"

"Russ, this interview is being audio and video recorded. You should also know you have the right to speak to an attorney privately at any time during our conversation."

"Why?"

"It's my job to inform you of your rights, Russ, even though this is simply an interview. Do you understand your rights?"

"Yeah."

"Do you know why you're here?"

"My aunt's neighbour died this morning. It happened while I was jogging. I don't know nothing. Did you say 'Killian'? Hey, you were on the news, right?"

I pretend I didn't hear that. "You're staying with your aunt and her husband?"

"Yeah." Another bead of sweat trickles from Wickstrom's upper lip to the corner of his mouth. He wipes it away. "I'm looking for work. I'm heading to Alberta after the weekend to see if things are better there. I heard they are."

"Good idea. Lots of jobs in Alberta." Anyone with half a brain knows that the economy in Alberta is in trouble. "Russ, what work experience do you have?"

"Construction. But I'd rather work for one of them big oil companies. I got no problem with heights."

"Check out the utility rigs. Good hazard pay."

"Yeah?"

I nod. "Do you have a letter from your probation officer, giving you permission to leave BC?"

"Huh? Oh, sure."

"Good. Try Grande Prairie first." They'll tell him straight up he's wasting his time.

Wickstrom slouches in his chair. "Yeah, I seen you on TV."

Here it comes.

"You looked different on the news. You're that Indian that caught The Butcher." The whites of his eyes are yellow. "Pretty psychic what The Butcher did to them hoes. Chopping them up in little pieces and selling the meat right there in his shop."

"How did that make you feel, Russ?"

His eyes narrow. "Made me gag, man. Really disgusting."

"You followed it on the news, did you?"

"No."

"No?"

"Couldn't help hearing. Every channel was about him. Still is." He sticks a dirty fingernail in his mouth and picks at something between his teeth. "They should bring back hanging." He presses his lips together, rubs his tongue over his teeth. He looks uncomfortable being watched and squirms in his chair.

I suddenly want to shower.

"Lucky for him, he'll probably do concurrent time for each hoe. Otherwise..." His eyes wander to the ceiling. "That'd be... eight hundred years. Wow." His gaze darts back to me, to the file, to around the room, never settling anywhere.

He wipes his tongue across his yellow teeth again. I try not to gag.

"You finished?" He looks at the file.

I skim the notes from my team. The Warners have lived next door to Wickstrom's aunt and uncle for less than a year. The husband said no attempt has been made on either's part to become neighbourly. "How long have you been staying with your aunt and uncle?"

"Since September."

"They've lived there a long time?"

"Since I was a kid."

"You meet their new neighbours?"

"Me? No. They're old, man."

"Your aunt and uncle get along with them?"

"I don't know."

"Did your aunt offer up any opinions?"

Wickstrom's eyes bug out. "Killian? Hey, your wife got murdered. Down on the coast, right? Stabbed a whole bunch of times. And you being a cop. And an Indian. Wow, that must have been shitty—not the being Indian part. Yeah, sorry about your woman, man. It wasn't that long ago, eh? Was she white? I don't have no problem with an Indian being with a white woman, but some guys do." Suddenly he presents his duh expression. "Hey man, is *Indian* like a bad word or something? Should I'd said Native?"

I present my best poker face, although, right about now I'd like to leap across this table and scalp his white man's head. "About your neighbour, Russ."

He groans. "I don't know the guy, man. My aunt never says nothing about them. I don't know why I'm here. I don't know nothing."

He knows something. And he's too stupid to hide it. I give him my of-course-I-believe-you look, followed by my everything's-going-to-be-fine smile. "You sure you wouldn't like a drink? I know you're tired of sitting on your butt, Russ, but you could really help me out."

His eyes widen. "How? I told them when they brought me in, I don't know nothing. It ain't good having cops show up at your door and taking you down town without saying why. Lucky my aunt and uncle weren't home. They would a freaked if they seen cops hauling my ass off." He scratches the top of his head, behind his ear. I imagine the globs of dead skin under his fingernails. His eyes dart from the file to me then back to the file.

"I thought you were asked to come in because of what had happened to the neighbour?"

"Well, shit—you're the cop."

I rest my chin in my palm. Gone are the days when we could beat the answer out of suspects. "I was told the constables said they needed your help. That's not what happened?"

"Man, that was like," he looks at his watch, "hours ago. I was going to shower and then go job hunting."

"I thought you were heading to Alberta next week?"

"If I don't find nothing by then." He gives me an incredulous look as if I'm the stupid one. "Ain't it police harassment making me sit so long?"

I shake my head as I eye his statement. "Sorry you feel that way, Russ. I got back a few moments ago. They know I prefer to question witnesses here instead of somewhere else where they might be distracted."

"Distracted? I'm trying to tell you—I ain't distracted cuz I didn't see nothing. I'm no witness."

I rest my forearms on the table. The kid's gaze keeps jumping everywhere. I'm actually waiting for his head to spin. "Without realizing it, you may have seen something. You could be the key witness to the biggest murder this city has ever seen. You could be Witness of the Year."

"Not likely," he says through a mouthful of spit. "Don't tell me there's a reward. I didn't see nothing." His Adam's apple bobs when he swallows.

I lower my eyes to the statement, giving him a chance to relax. "You always go jogging by yourself?"

"I keep saying—my aunt and her husband work. Their kids

are in middle school."

"You don't know anybody in the neighbourhood?"

"Nope." His pupils dilate.

"You don't know the Warners?"

"I already told you. They're old. I know who they are, but that's it."

"What do you mean by 'who they are'?"

"You know."

While keeping my chin low to appear less threatening, I shrug.

"Their sons had that shoot-out." Wickstrom scratches below his elbow.

"Your aunt and her husband tell you that?"

"No, I read about it. Or I saw it on the news."

"I just moved here, myself, but yes, I think I recall hearing something about it. So you saw the shootout on the news?"

"Well, fu—"

"Russ, language."

"I was going to say you should a heard about it cuz you're the cop. They were total psychics."

"Psychics?"

"You know...Insane. Crap, all you detachments need to get together and talk."

I almost smile at the first sensible thing the kid has said. "What time did you leave your aunt's place?"

What little blood Wickstrom has left in his cheeks sinks to his neck. His face continues to pale by the millisecond. "Eight."

"You're sure?"

"Yup." He pulls at the neck of his pullover as if it's strangling him.

"You jogged past the Warners' house going and coming?"

"How else would I get home?"

"And when did you get home?"

"Nine."

The coroner estimated that Warner died between seven and nine. At ten after nine, the ambulance was en route.

"I time my run." Wickstrom holds up his wrist and points to his dollar-store watch. "I run for thirty minutes, then I turn around."

I catch his eyes for a full second before he blinks. "I don't understand. The sound of a gunshot can echo a long way, but you didn't hear anything. How come?"

I watch his expression knowing that because none of the other neighbours heard anything, the shooter likely used a silencer. Is this kid desperate enough to kill in cold blood then lie like a pro?

31

"Maybe cuz I run so far I was out of range." His arms hang at his sides. "I told you, I was listening to my iPod. I had headphones on."

Lie like a pro? Yeah, right. "Maybe you figured it was a car backfiring."

"What? Yeah, maybe." Flustered, he shakes his head in a tight arc. "No. I mean...I don't know."

"Which is it?" I close the file, cross my arms, lean back in the chair. "You heard what you thought was a car backfiring? Or you knew it was a gun? Do you remember the time? Were you on your way back to your aunt's house? Or hadn't you turned around yet?"

"Look, I didn't mean to."

"Didn't mean to what?"

"I couldn't hear."

"You look like a good guy." I sit up straight. "I think you are. Help me out. Were you on your way back when you heard the shot? Did you see anyone pulling out of the Warners' driveway? Or maybe you ran through their yard? It's faster than going down your aunt's long driveway. Did you notice their door was open? Maybe you even saw old man Warner? You had words with him because he didn't appreciate you running through his—"

"I didn't know what else to do, man."

I hide my surprise, but I'm excited. Do I have my perp? "Tell me in your own words what happened. I'll do everything I can to help you."

His eyes fill with tears. He nods. "I run in the middle of the road cuz the whole fu–, I mean, neighbourhood's crawling with vicious dogs. And I play my MP3 player pretty loud. I didn't hear the car coming behind me until he honked. Scared the piss out of me, man. I jumped. Then I see the oncoming car. I cut right. This little dog come out of nowhere. The car behind me hit him. It's not my fault."

What dog? Is he talking about Mrs. Warren's dog? "What time was this?"

"Around, uh, maybe eight-ten." Wickstrom sniffs loudly and rubs his elbow.

"Did either driver stop?"

"I don't think the guy coming at us noticed. But the other guy, who run over the dog, stopped. I went to see if I could help. It was near the ditch. But man, it was in bad shape. Before I could ask the guy to help me, he says sorry and takes off. The dog's gurgling. Then blood starts pouring out of its mouth."

"The dog died?"

Wickstrom shrugs. "I got no car. How am I going to get it to the vets? I drugged him closer to the ditch, so nobody else could run over him."

Drugged him? Yeah, you're a real hero. "Any idea whose dog it was?"

"How would I know? Send a notice around the neighbourhood or something. It was one of them—I don't know—Terrier mixed with something. Small and scruffy-looking."

"Did you get the licence plate? We'll need to verify your statement."

"No. He was driving one of them '92 or 93' grey Sunbirds. And he was old. Fifty something. Kinda pudgy in the face. Three chins." Wickstrom waves his hand under his chin. "He had a sticker on his back bumper that said, 'Canucks rock'."

I grab the file. "I'll be right back, Russ." Constable Stan Carrigan is waiting in the hallway. "Give the kid half an hour alone. Make sure he's available for further interviews. Notify his probation officer. Tell him to revoke permission to leave B.C. until further notice. When we give them the okay, have his probation officer prepare a letter Wickstrom can show the closest detachment in Alberta. We can't cite him for being an idiot, but we don't need to make it easier for him either."

"You still want him tested?"

"I'd say do every examination you can without pushing the envelope, but it'd be a waste of time. Test for gunpowder residue, then send in somebody from the drug squad to question why a druggie is out jogging. Maybe he'll give up his dealer so the morning isn't a total waste. His aunt and uncle give you anything?"

"Warner gave the uncle free advice about a car accident he had. Saved him a lot of money."

"Anything about Warners' marriage?"

"The wife said they were good neighbours. She said Mr. Warner catered to Mrs. Warner. They were a loving couple. She saw them out walking several times and always holding hands."

"Okay, go ahead and take care of our witness. When Mrs. Warner comes in to make a statement, take care of her personally. Okay?"

Carrigan looks at me strangely. "You haven't heard?"

I blank out my expression. I'd forgotten that Mrs. Warner isn't required to come into the detachment like every other potential witness. "Slipped my mind. I'll question her at her location."

Carrigan nods, then turns to leave as Ryan flies around the corner and stops short of slamming into us. In his hands is a thick file. "You're not going to believe this."

"Try me?"

"Norse's neighbour reported his car stolen this morning."

"And?"

"They found the car. Norse stole it."

"Where?"

"Tagged him in Lejac. He says he *borrowed* his neighbour's car. Had a small suitcase in the backseat. Says Warner deserved to die for spawning the bastard who killed his wife, and they should give the killer the keys to the city. He says he took off because he knew he'd be our prime suspect."

"So far he is our prime out of a few possible suspects."

"Yeah, sure." Ryan smacks his palm on top of the files folder. "The detachment at Fort Fraser says to meet them at Vanderhoof's detachment because their back lot isn't secure. They're towing the car there. They did a preliminary search but didn't find anything."

"How's the investigation at the house?"

"They're still sweeping the backyard and canvassing the neighbourhood. Nothing so far. They pulled the hound."

"Have somebody check the ditches in the neighbourhood for a dog's remains." I point at the files folder. "Is that Norse's file?"

Ryan hands it over.

"Obtain a warrant from the judge and send two investigators over to his place. They can contact us on the road if they find something. Grab some plastic to cover the seats. We may need to tow the car back to our garage."

"We're running out of people."

"Borrow two from general duty."

While I gather files, notes, and replace the battery in my voice recorder, Ryan leaves, and returns with enough plastic for the seats in the vehicle Norse stole.

"You think Norse took the weapon and bloody clothes with him when he left?" Ryan sticks the wad of plastic under his arm.

"Maybe." I grab my parka and head for the door. "What's the forecast?"

"Partly cloudy. Sixty percent chance of snow."

"You drive, I'll read."

Outside, we cross the quiet street to the police parking lot. Small, light flakes of snow float to the ground and melt under the sun's heat. Something I had no idea could occur simultaneously.

Happy Anniversary, Angie.

The lump in my throat feels like it'll choke me.

The job—I'm here to do the damn job.

"This snow ain't going to last." Ryan looks up at the sky, then back to the road. "They didn't find anything during Norse's initial body search, but we might find something in his car. Oh, and guess what? He's cooperating." He slides into the car.

Ryan's comment doesn't make me feel hopeful. Nothing is ever that easy. Norse isn't Wickstrom. Norse is a retired member of the local bikers' group, with organized crime affiliations. He's also got enough street smarts to kill Warner and get rid of the evidence. The only way we'll catch him is if he brags to one of his biker buddies and that particular biker has reason to cooperate with us.

That would be a miracle.

Investigators dressed in white jumpsuits dab away in Leland's blood and brains. I see them through the French doors and across the courtyard of our upside-down U-shaped house. I'm not deliberately watching, it's just that they're in my line of sight. Shifting to the right, I face Leland's desk. It's covered in legal documents and the papers I've just signed. My lawyer slogs through the minuscule details of Leland's business assets. I try to show interest, but I can't. I couldn't care less about his estate. I'm trying to decide who I am without Leland. I understand in part, but I can't remember why I'm this way. Honestly, I vaguely remember who I was before Leland. And why are we going through Leland's affairs so soon? Wouldn't tomorrow be better? I don't feel well.

"Do you think they'll let me back in my kitchen today? Or will I be barred until the investigation is over?"

He glances towards the kitchen and shrugs. "We'll have an official reading of the will after the service. Shouldn't take long considering it is only you and a few charities. I want you to know that I am taking care of your affairs, Sally. You understand, don't you?"

I appreciate his concern but wish he would go. Not because I'm anxious to leave. A police car waits outside to take me to some cold hotel downtown. I have no family, and I'm certainly not imposing on my friends. I'll pay for the hotel myself if they won't let me stay here. Though I can't imagine why. The church ladies are meeting with the pastor's wife at the rectory. I should be there. They're taking care of the preparations for the service on Tuesday, five days hence. My lawyer decided I should have the service as soon as possible. When I told the deacon's wife, she said she'd get back to me. Twenty minutes later she called and said all the ladies had unanimously agreed that because so many things had to be done, they'd meet today and start the arrangements. When I suggested I be there, she adamantly refused my help, but I insisted. "I have to help." Perhaps hearing the panic in my voice made her agree. Though she was quick to add that nothing would be required of me. She didn't say it out loud, but I suspect they won't keep asking me, as my lawyer does, if I understand what's happening. Of course I understand what's happening. I'm not senile. And the women at church recognize that even in grief one is capable of carrying on.

The phone rings. The call display says Dr. Meshango. I pick up the phone and hang it up without speaking.

"Who was that?" my lawyer asks.

"Nobody."

"All the joint accounts will be closed before the end of the business day," my lawyer says, unconcerned. "Nothing will be left to chance. Do you understand, Sally?"

I see the uncertainty in his eyes and blink. Since I found Leland's body, not blinking has become a bad habit. I must remember to blink, because it shows I'm paying attention.

"Sally?"

Blink, Sally.

"I understand."

"And do not go to the detachment to fill out another statement. That won't be happening. If they want to talk to you, they come to you. Understand? The Prime Minister's office will back me up on that."

I'm disappointed. I always wanted to see the inside of our police station. Leland meant to show me, but life kept getting in the way.

"Sally?"

"Yes. I understand."

His expression softens. "I realize this is all happening fast. But Leland wasn't just anybody. We have to be prepared for the unexpected."

"I understand."

Seeming satisfied, my lawyer looks down at the signed documents and continues on the subject of Leland's estate. It's getting harder to concentrate on what he says, and my gaze travels from his face to the papers to the dull light seeping in from outside. My tearless eyes feel as if they're stuck open. I have eye drops somewhere. I could probably use a few.

My head turns in the direction of the kitchen. A young woman, dressed in a white jumpsuit, is on her hands and knees busy at the spot where Leland's body lay earlier this morning. Collecting more blood? I know from my CSI shows I watch that laboratory technicians require several samples for DNA and various other tests to determine physiological and biochemical states, such as disease, mineral presence, evidence of drug use, and organ function. They have to collect double the amount so the defence team can do their own tests.

I blink, and my gaze cuts back to my lawyer. Will my dry eyes close tonight and allow me sleep? Or will I begin to weep and never stop?

I wrap my sweater tight, cross my arms, and will myself to feel warm.

My lawyer's voice reverberates through the office. Soon he'll leave and silence will envelop me like a cocoon. Common sense says I should embrace the silence. I would, but it's painfully loud. The silence is a screech in my ears. Until today, the one diversion that drowned out the screeching was Leland's voice. Or Digger's yapping. Husband and dog talked incessantly. Both unintelligibly.

Without them...

Will I go mad?

* * *

We reach Vanderhoof detachment by half-past twelve. A lone Hyundai sits in the back lot guarded by a constable. "That's the neighbour's vehicle?"

Constable Ryan checks his notes. "Yes."

"Cover the seats with plastic. Do a prelim of the interior. I'll interview Norse."

Ryan pulls a pair of plastic gloves from his pocket.

Inside, I exchange the usual pleasantries at the counter. "Don't suppose Mr. Norse confessed while we were en route?"

The Corporal, with her arms folded across her chest, looks sympathetic. She's probably got better things to do than entertain my suspect. "He keeps informing whoever will listen of his rights. Knows his law as well as any lawyer. Strange that he hasn't asked to see his."

"Yeah, strange." I don't care because I'm anxious to begin. "They're searching his home as we speak. Can somebody interrupt us if they call? Or if Constable Ryan finds anything in the car?"

"Sure. And you'll want the interview taped?"

Strange question. Unless she too has heard the rumours that I threw The Butcher in Surrey down a flight of stairs and is worried I may assault a suspect in her cells. Sometimes there is no sense arguing with people; they'll believe what they want to believe.

"Yes."

She unfolds her arms and looks relieved.

Everything about this investigation has to be on the up and up. If I make a mistake and the killer goes free...that's another subject I'm not tackling today. "Any chance you can send me a copy today?"

"Sure. Nod when you're ready to have them turn on the machine. Signal if you want it turned off."

She buzzes me into the interview room. The door bangs into its locked position behind me, loud enough that it makes Norse jump. I smile, because there are so few pleasures in life these days.

"Mr. Norse?" I stand behind his left shoulder, my back to the door, a spot that doesn't interfere with the camera's view and forces Norse to crane his neck to see me. "My name's Killian. I appreciate you waiting."

Norse laughs, then twists around to give my street clothes and open parka the once over. "Hey, an Indian. Let me guess. The Indigenous community has overthrown Vanderhoof. Way to go, Tonto." He swipes a hand, middle finger extended, over his greasy, red hair.

"I'm with Major Crime." I imagine breaking his finger off at the palm.

"I've always wanted to know, when you were a kid, were you like the Indian or the cowboy?"

I slap Norse's file against my side and step to the left. "Today is December third. My name is Corporal Daniel Killian. I'm interviewing Mr. Norse of Prince George at the Vanderhoof Detachment. You understand, Mr. Norse, our conversation will be audio and video taped? At any time you may stop this interview and request a private conference with your attorney. Do you understand what I've said?"

Norse grins widely. "Sure. Hey, where's the famous Royal Canadian Mounted Police yellow stripe, constable?"

"It's Corporal."

Norse rolls his eyes. "Well, isn't that special. You must be an important fellow. Ain't too many corporals in these here parts, except for the cutie out there. But I imagine human rights people were screaming for more female bosses. How'd you crawl this far? You rescue the premier from a bunch of irate Indians?" He strains his neck to look up at me. "How's my old pal Sergeant Lacroix? He out there holding down the fort? Tell him to join us. We can all smoke a peace pipe."

"I'll be sure to give Staff Sergeant Lacroix your regards."

Norse scratches his chin, extending his middle finger. I imagine breaking it again, but this time I hear a loud snap.

"Speaks kindly of me, does he? Yep, we go way back. Bet he's no saint to work for. Give you a lot of flak?" His eyebrows shoot up. "Killian? Ah, you're the hero who nailed The Butcher. How's that working for you? That how a tyke from the Queen Charlotte Islands ends up in major crimes?"

"Actually, it's Haida Gwaii. Has been for some time."

"Oh, sure, I heard. But don't you want to know how I knew you were from there? No? How's your back?"

I tear my gaze away from Norse's snarl. The media went into overkill on the incident where The Butcher tried to kill me by throwing me down twenty-five cement stairs to the concrete basement floor. Rumours are it happened the other way round. Truth is, I'd grabbed his lapels at the last second and hung on. My knees smashed into the wall a few times on the way down, but I landed on top of him, which probably saved my life. It hadn't done my back, neck, or knees much good, though.

I consult Norse's file. On the trip out I didn't have time to read everything, but I'd gotten the gist. Norse was an active member of the local bikers' group until his wife died. He's been arrested for assault, two DUIs, drug possession, and resisting arrest. He'd beaten his deceased wife every other weekend. A real pillar of the community. Capable of murder? Most people are, if pushed hard enough. What set Norse off after two years?

"Do you understand why you're here?"

"Yes, Officer, I do."

"Would you like to consult with your attorney?"

"Hm. Would I?"

I sit down and close the file. Norse continues to sneer. I stare back. Two minutes pass. Two more. Norse's nostrils flare in and out. I plant my feet flat on the floor. The urge to kick him makes my leg twitch. My beloved Angie is dead, yet scumbags like Norse are alive to do as they please.

Finally, he swallows, sets his jaw, blinks twice. "You want to know why you don't scare me? I didn't kill him. And I'm not worried about you finding evidence, because unless you plant some, you won't. I wasn't anywhere near his crib this morning. I don't even know where they live."

"You knew he was dead."

"My fiancée is the head nurse in Emerg'. She's got a police scanner on her side of the bed. I heard the call this morning and I was gone."

"Your fiancée can verify your whereabouts?"

"Sunita left the house at six-thirty."

"Mr. Warner was shot between seven and nine this morning. That means you don't have an alibi, Mr. Norse. Even your next door neighbour said he didn't see you take his car."

Norse's left eye twitches. "Bet he told you I'd borrowed it before. That's how I knew the extra key was under the plate."

"He reported his car stolen."

His skin pales, and he gives me a tight-lipped smile. "So maybe I do need to see my lawyer."

"Your neighbour isn't pressing charges."

"Oops. Bet that made your day."

I don't react. "Where were you headed?"

"Away from you guys."

"What happened last night?"

"The Canucks slammed Pittsburgh. My neighbour watched the game with me because I got the 50-inch 3D screen."

"Who scored the winning goal?"

"Hank."

"Sedin?"

"Yup."

I jot a reminder to check if that's true. "When was the last time you spoke to Mr. Warner?"

"I wouldn't waste my time talking to that asshole." His lip curls, and he lifts his hand to admire his fingernails. "May he rest in peace." His hands are rough, but clean.

"Do you work, Mr. Norse?"

"Yes, I do, Officer." He shuts his eyes and aims his nose in my direction, then opens his eyes slowly. "And in answer to your next question, I operate a skidder for Murray Logging."

"Everything's good at work?" Is this my killer? I want it to be. Want it more than I care to admit.

"Yes, it is."

"Everything's good at home?" What do women see in pricks like this?

"Yep."

"If something has happened, it's better you tell me now. Better than me finding out later, because I will." Then I'll kick your ass all the way to Prince George. I'll be in court when they hand down the sentence. I'll wear our ceremonial clothing and do a happy-dance from the back of the room, accompanied by vocals—Asshole.

Norse smirks. "Ooh, okay, Officer. I mean Corporal. Hey—isn't Killian Irish? So what band you from? The MacIngins? Must've shook up the folks when their son became a white man's cop. Or did you grow up in one of them residential schools? No, let me guess. You got adopted by leprechauns badly in need of a mascot. Ah, that's nice."

I place my palm on the file. "You have some major infractions, but nothing as serious as murder. I'm trying to give you a break. If you killed Mr. Warner, I'd like to hear your side of it. It's no secret you blamed him because his son beat your wife into a coma and consequent death. Time has a way of eating away at a person. A jury will understand. Tell me the truth, and I'll do everything in my power to help."

Truth: Norse is a wife beater, and the jury will eat him alive.

"Well, ain't you a sweetheart. Only I didn't kill him. I would've killed his kid if I'd gotten to him first. The brother beat me to it."

Norse's snarl fades. He glances down at the thick file. "I know what I am."

He gives me a moment to digest that, then lowers his voice to what sounds like a staged whisper. "I know I was a lousy husband. If I hadn't slapped my wife around, I wouldn't have been in jail when she got beat up. She'd be alive. That's what I've been living with for almost two years. But now I got a new life with a good woman who, in honour of Jasmine, I'll protect the rest of my life.

"Do your tests. Examine my hands, my clothes, and search my house. Strip my neighbour's car. Stick your finger up my ass if you want, but it won't change the truth. I didn't kill him."

"I'd like to believe you."

His eyes aren't dilated, he isn't sweating, and his voice remains at a normal low pitch. All classic signs of someone telling the truth.

You're still a scumbag, paleface.

He gnaws at his moustache, contemplates my face for a moment. Shifting in the chair, he tugs at the cuff on his jacket, sits up straight. He is a hard man. Dangerous. But worse of all, at this precise moment, he looks sincere.

"I got nothing to gain by Warner's death. Think what you want about me, but I got a second chance with Sunita, and I'd be a dickhead to screw it up."

I pat his file. "Mr. Norse, this is a comprehensive record of your aggression, anger, rage, and disrespect for the residents of the City of Prince George and the district of Buckley-Nechako. There are photographs of your late wife's battered face. There is a list of verbal abuse towards police and authorities. There is—"

"I'm not that man anymore."

"As nice as it would be to believe people change, it's seldom the case. You beat your wife. If Zoë Sheppard hadn't shown up and phoned the police, who's to say whether you'd have killed Jasmine, instead of her dying from Bronson Warner's beating a few days later. Either way, she didn't stand a chance. Maybe

42

that's why you shot Warner? Repressed guilt."

Norse snarls. "I didn't kill Warner. And since you brought her up, why don't you talk to somebody with a real motive? Since Warner's sons are already dead, talk to that bitch Zoë and her old lady Meshango." He grins as if he'd figured out a secret. "Meshango may be some fancy University professor, but she's still one violent bitch. I got nothing against Indians, but she hates white men. Don't kid yourself, she's capable of murder. If her kid hadn't stopped her, I'd be dead. But was she charged with assault? No. Tell me why. I want to hear you say it."

What are you talking about?

I don't ask. I stare into his face with as much coldness and fury that I can muster.

Norse squints at me. "The day I was drunk and ended up in the hospital, the old lady took a bat to me. She never got charged because it was never written up."

What the hell is he talking about?

He gawks at my face. Laughs. "Ah, so you're not the wiz-cop CTV News made you out to be. What? If you're not in a butcher shop, you're out of your element? You don't know who she's shacked up with, do you?"

Is Meshango connected? Someone's protecting her? Who?

A tap at the door forces me to blink. I avoid Norse's smug expression and stand. When the door opens, I switch places with a general duty cop.

I find Ryan waiting in the hallway. "You found something?"

"We took the trunk apart, pulled out the backseat, removed the door panels—*kwanta*."

Frustrated, I stick my fists into my pockets, and swallow the bad taste in my mouth. "*Kwanta?*"

"It's Cree for 'nothing'."

"I'm Haida."

Ryan blushes. "The car's hoisted on the tow truck and ready for impound."

"What did they find at the house?"

"They're still looking, but nothing so far. Mrs. Warner's lawyer has been with her for the last hour."

"Doing what?"

"He's going over privileged legal matters with her in the study, which makes sense considering he's their lawyer."

"What did Norse's next door neighbour say?"

"Said Norse is the best neighbour they ever had. Nothing even remotely questionable happens on their street. He said he wouldn't have filed the stolen car report had he known Norse took it. He wants us to tell him that. Actually, he insisted we tell him that."

"What did he think about Norse as a husband?"

Ryan chews on his pencil while he checks his notes. "He told them he thought Sunita and Shawn were meant for each other. Real lovebirds. Apparently they're 'disgustingly attentive'. That's a direct quote. How you doing in there?"

"Do you know anything about Norse's altercation with Dr. Meshango the day he was arrested for beating his wife?"

While Ryan chews on his lip, I practice being patient.

"Dr. Meshango's daughter and Mrs. Norse were friends," Ryan says, "but I'm not aware of any altercation."

"Zoë Sheppard was the one who called it in?"

"Yeah."

"Nobody took a bat to Norse?"

Ryan shrugs and looks worried.

"Who's Meshango married to?"

"She's divorced." He rubs the nape of his neck. Looks bothered. "There's something else."

"What?" Damn, what now?

"Well." His eyes grow wide. "Norse was spotted by webcam heading west up Connaught Hill this morning."

"What?"

"I know—what're the odds. He shows up on the footage fifteen minutes after the 911 call came in. The camera is about seven minutes from his place. The neighbour said he noticed his car missing around nine-thirty. He's sure it was still there at nine."

This coincides with what Norse said about stealing the car after he heard the call on the police scanner. A pain cuts through my forehead, and I glance at my watch. Time's ticking away. "Have the techs look it over, so they can confirm one way or the other. And have someone question the neighbour again to see if he'd lie to protect Norse."

"We've got twenty-hours before we have to release him. We'll find the evidence." Ryan's tone is hopeful.

I shake my head. "Never make that mistake, John. Our job is to fit the crime to the perp, not the perp to the crime. If Norse is guilty, we'll get him. If he isn't, we keep looking."

If I came face to face with Angie's killer, could I show leniency? Or would it be easier to kill the piece of shit than worry about building a case?

An hour or so later, Ryan circles the parking lot of the Prince George Regional Hospital, so we can talk to Norse's fiancé during her shift. I read over my notes, finishing with my interview with Norse. Additional comments in the margins are kept to a minimum. My penmanship is poor under the best writing conditions—a desk on solid ground. Writing legibly in a moving vehicle is a recipe for disaster. I hope to close Warner's murder, but if left unsolved, I'll owe it to Cold Case to make notes they can decipher.

My scribble was a constant amusement to Angie, especially early in our marriage. I left scrawled notes on the kitchen table until the day she suggested I print in block capital letters so she could actually read what I'd written.

I feel myself grin, turn my head so Ryan won't notice. The kid is nosy enough without me giving him a reason. I don't want to trivialize what's going on today. Angie is with me. Her smile. She smiled a lot during the first years of our marriage. Even now the sound of her giggle resonates through me. If Disney had ever heard her, he would have hired her on the spot to play the female version of Dale the cartoon chipmunk. She had the perfect giggle.

Ryan makes a second pass around the parking lot, heads back towards the south side near the emergency entrance. I dial Carrigan's cell. A stickler for old habits, he never answers his phone or checks the Caller ID until the third ring. When I once asked him why, he said, "I like to be ready."

On the fourth ring, I spot an empty parking spot on the Lethbridge Street side, point at it for Ryan.

The phone rings again. Where in the hell is Carrigan?

"Yeah?" Carrigan's voice snaps.

"What's wrong?"

"What could be wrong? I'm stuck in an interview room with four unhappy campers checking Warner's case files. Oh, you mean because I took so long to answer. It's been one of those mornings. My phone was at my desk. Do you need me for something? Say yes."

45

"You're there for a reason. I thought you understood that."

After my first week on the job, I told him if he ever decided to change jobs, CSIS (Canadian Security Intelligence Service) would take him in a second. Nobody caught what Carrigan's eyes saw in a document search. He's proven it plenty of times.

"What do you need?" His voice holds no hint of an apology.

Ryan parks the vehicle, hangs the parking pass from the rear-view mirror.

"Norse's bank records." I switch the phone to my right ear so I can unbuckle my seatbelt with my left hand.

"Give me a sec. I'm heading to my computer."

As I wait for him to collect the records, I focus on the big question: *Why kill Warner today?*

I tap my pen on my notepad while I wait. Traffic zooms up and down Fifteenth Avenue. Across Lethbridge, fifty-foot tall birch trees line the front border of the Northern Health Unit. The trees stand motionless as a painting, branches bare except for a few patchy brown leaves. The entire scene holds an eerie stillness. No cars pull into the health unit's parking lot. In fact, nobody enters or exits the front entrance to the hospital. No birds flutter in the trees. No vehicles drive down Lethbridge Street. It's ironic given the sound of vehicles humming in the background reinforces the one constant in my life: *People you love die, and the world doesn't stop.*

High above the birch trees, the sky is the consistency of a thin, white haze; though with three pulp mills on the edge of town, it could be pollution. The air quality reminds me of early mornings in Surrey, except the air in Prince George isn't humid. Here it's cold and dry. Is this how it looks when it's about to snow? Is Mrs. Warner correct? More importantly, what does her prediction have to do with the case? Where is my focus? Did Carrigan's failure to answer his phone on time set a precedent for this dark hole I feel myself falling into? Or am I messed up today because it's my anniversary?

Does it stop being my anniversary now that Angie's dead?

"What do you need to know?" Carrigan's voice asks over the speakerphone.

I feel Ryan's eyes on me while I try to remember what I called Carrigan about. "Anything unusual."

"Describe unusual."

I flip down the visor to protect my eyes from the sun's sudden glare. "Any regular monthly withdrawals?"

"Two hundred dollars per month for the last...five months."

"Any large deposits unaccounted for?"

"No."

"Any rounded numbers that don't fit?"

"No."

"Nothing sends up an alert?"

"These could be my bank statements. They're that boring."

From the closest birch tree, a leaf spirals to the ground. Out of my peripheral vision I see Ryan turn away to watch a vehicle pull in. I wipe a lone tear that's slipped from my bottom eyelash. "Have you spoken with Warner's family doctor?"

"He's not cooperating."

"Okay, I'll deal with him." I jot myself a note. "What about Warner's assistant?"

"Somebody's over there right now."

"And Dr. Meshango?"

"Somebody took her statement."

"Sophie Brooks?"

"Being done."

"I'll need all these statements ASAP, plus blueprints of the house."

A rustle of paper comes from the speaker. "Anything else?"

"Were there any visitors or home deliveries expected?"

"No."

"Anything come of the interviews at Mr. Warner's law firm?"

"Not yet."

"I gather you haven't found anything suspicious in his files?"

"No." Again Carrigan's voice sounds unapologetic. "But we have a ways to go."

"Okay, thanks." I sign off, reach for the door handle, and catch the glimmer of my watch. The first forty-eight hours are crucial.

"Which ward are we going to?" Ryan asks.

"Emergency." I climb out of the car, look across the hood at him. "You start. I'll take over once I've heard enough."

"The usual routine. Sure." He smiles.

Was I ever that enthusiastic? I can't remember.

I follow Ryan into the side entrance. The space reeks strongly of pine detergent. Further along, antiseptic, then fruity urine. We walk swiftly down the hallway, make a sharp left turn, and follow the red stripe along the wall to the emergency ward. Up ahead, a nurse appears across our path and vanishes.

"Excuse me," Ryan calls.

We reach a spot where the hallways cross. She's gone. Ryan shrugs, points at something ahead. Out of the corner of my eye, I catch a flash of white speeding towards the north-end of

Emergency.

"Excuse me," Ryan says louder.

She stops and turns.

"Where can we find Sunita Singh?"

"She's here somewhere." She disappears into a curtained area on her left.

"Great." Ryan looks about.

I walk to the nurses' station, press the bell sitting on top of the counter. When nobody appears, I hold the button down. The screeching ricochets off walls and low ceiling.

"Can I help you?" An Indo-Canadian nurse rushes in from the doorway to the supply room four feet beyond the nurses' station. Her eyes are open wide. She presses her lips together. In her right hand are three syringes, in her left, a clear bottle of liquid.

"Miss Singh?" Ryan rubs his ear.

"Yes."

"My name is Constable Ryan, and this is Corporal Killian. We're RCMP Investigators from Major Crime."

I study her face. When she hears the words "RCMP Investigators," her expression and body language remain unchanged.

She smiles with eyes and mouth. "What can I do for you?"

"Do you have time for a few questions?" Ryan says.

She holds up the syringe. "Not really. Sorry."

"Do you know Mr. Norse of Quince Street?"

Her smile vanishes. "Yes."

"You share that address with him?"

"Yes."

The changes in her face are subtle. The worry lines around her eyes and mouth deepen. She lowers her arms slowly. Her shoulders hunch. I sense she's struggling with a fear I understand too well. Four cops stopped me in a parking lot in Burnaby and tried to block me from seeing Angie's body.

"Is Shawn all right?"

Ryan nods. "How would you describe your relationship?"

"He's my fiancé."

"Do you know where he was last night?"

"We spent the evening with friends at home."

Ryan pulls a notepad from his pocket and a newly sharpened pencil from his inside pocket. "What time did you and Mr. Norse go to bed last night? Do you sleep in the same room?" He looks at his notes. "Did you retire at different times?"

I switch from his flushed cheeks to Sunita's paling face.

"The lights were out thirty minutes after the hockey game ended. Eleven. What's this about?"

Ryan writes. "Do you know where Mr. Norse was this morning?"

Her hands, with the bottle and syringes, hang at her sides. "At home. It's his day off."

"How about between eight and nine o'clock this morning?"

"I told you." She shifts her gaze from Ryan to me. "Are you sure Shawn is all right?"

"He's fine," Ryan says. "Where was he between seven and nine?"

"You're sure he's all right?"

"Yes."

"Then why do you keep asking me where he is?"

Touché.

"He's fine," Ryan says. "We do know where he is. What we need to know is where he was between seven and nine o'clock this morning. Please answer the question."

"What's this about? Why don't you ask Shawn?" She sets the syringes and the bottle on the counter to her right, the first hint she's distressed. Her job will be in jeopardy if she walks away and leaves the pharmaceuticals out in the open. "Does this have something to do with Mr. Warner being shot this morning?"

Ryan doesn't answer. I bite my tongue to stop myself from coming to her defence. She looks from Ryan to me. The last of the colour has drained from her face, turning her skin an ashy grey. Damn, her response isn't supposed to bother me.

She shakes her head. "Shawn had nothing to do with that."

Ryan surveys the area. "Is there some place quiet we can talk?"

She points to a door across the hallway from the nurses' counter. I gesture towards the syringes. Her face flushes. She snatches up the bottle and needles and disappears into the storage room. I hear the click of a locked cabinet.

She reappears, leads us to a small broom-sized staff room, and leaves the door open. "I'm on duty. I have to keep an ear out, just in case."

"That's fine," Ryan says. "Please sit down? This won't take long. We just need to verify a few things."

Three dirty mugs in the sink. Despite a no-smoking policy, a clean ashtray is stuck in the corner under some napkins. The room stinks of cold coffee and the stale odour of sugar. The small fridge looks like it hasn't been wiped clean in days.

Sunita sits at the table against the wall and clasps her hands tightly. Her fingers are long and slender. There is an impressive diamond on her left hand. An expensive expression of love?

I wanted Angie's rings buried with her. When the funeral people handed me her rings, I handed them back. It never occurred to me to keep them. I bought them for Angie, not as a reminder of her life being snatched from me. The funeral director handed them back. "I'm sorry, Mr. Killian, it's not the home's policy to bury the deceased with rings. You'll have to take them."

I look at Sunita's rings. Are hers a warning for others to lay off?

Sunita sits as stiff as a board. "He said you're the corporal. Why is he asking the questions?"

I nod at Ryan, who poses his pen over his notebook. I take the seat opposite Sunita. "Are you familiar with the history between your fiancé and the Warners?"

"I know everything about Shawn's past. I know what happened to Jasmine and to Professor Meshango and her daughter Zoë."

"Then you understand we need to clear Shawn's name before we can dismiss him as a suspect?"

"He is not the man he was." She speaks her consonants slowly. "He has changed."

"Yes, that's what he says."

"You spoke to him? When? Is he all right?"

"Yes. In fact, he seemed calm and well rested."

"Really?"

"Yes."

"Thank you." Her face brightens. "What do you need to know? How can I convince you he is not the man you think he is?"

"How long have you and Mr. Norse known each other?"

"A year."

"And that makes you an expert on his character?"

"Yes," she says, eyes wide.

I detect a small lisp. "You're engaged. Have you set a date?"

"Shawn and I are to be married August sixteenth of next year."

"Is he a fair man, your Shawn?"

"Yes. And loyal. And...and generous."

"He handles the money?"

"No, I do."

"Why?"

She twists her diamond. "Shawn prefers it that way. He's not good with finances and is the first to admit it." Her tone is reminiscent of a proud parent. "I take care of the utilities, groceries, and daily expenses."

"He must have his own bills."

"I pay the bills from our combined income. Shawn receives a hundred dollar allowance twice a month."

"Only two hundred dollars?"

Ryan continues writing.

So life really has changed that much for Shawn Norse? He's found his place by relinquishing control to his woman?

As if reading my mind, Sunita adds, "It was Shawn's decision. It is all he requires. It covers his gas, lunches, and miscellaneous."

"And his beer?"

"Beer? Occasionally. Yes, but it's not what you think."

People like Norse don't change. "An ice-cold beer on a cold winter night. Or a few?"

She frowns. "I don't know what you mean."

"How much would you say Shawn drinks in a week?"

"A few beers on the weekend. If he does go out on a Friday night with the boys, he sleeps in our guest room when he returns home. I told you, he has it under control."

"So it's not true what they say about redheads?"

She frowns. "I don't understand."

"A temper to match. Has Shawn got a temper, Sunita? Has he ever frightened you?"

Big, brown, defiant eyes. Does the prick realize how lucky he is?

"Not even a little?" I ask.

She hesitates. "Once."

"When?"

"A long time ago."

"You did something?"

A deep blush rose in her cheeks. "I know what you're trying to do."

"Maybe you said something you didn't mean to say? Or forgot to—"

"One of his ex-biker friends said *that* word."

Am I supposed to automatically know what she means? "What word?"

"Raghead."

"In reference to your nationality?"

"I'm sure he meant no one in particular, just something about a raghead. Shawn lost it. I'd never seen him so angry. But the remark was a generalization, nothing aimed at me personally. Nothing I hadn't heard many times before. People often speak without thinking."

For a fleeting second, Angie's face flashes before my eyes. I swallow and wet my dry lips. "And sometimes we get used to the way people treat us, especially someone we love. Their methods become familiar, like a bad habit we can rely on. Does Shawn get angry a lot?"

"No."

"Has he lost his temper with you?"

"No."

"Threatened you?"

"No."

"Pushed you too hard? Or grabbed your arm a bit roughly? Or—"

"Shawn is the sweetest, gentlest man I know. He didn't kill Mr. Warner. He has never hit or bumped or pushed me. I know about Jasmine. He told me on our third date. I was born Canadian. I told him I would never stand for such behaviour from any man." She stands. "I have to go back to work. Unless there is something else?"

Ryan puts his notebook away.

I stand. "Thank you."

"Where is Shawn?" she asks.

I check my watch. "Probably at home." I squeeze by her and out the door.

"Corporal?"

I turn back.

"You're wrong about Shawn. You look at him and see his past. He is not that man any longer. If I need something or ask for his help, he doesn't stop to wonder what it'll do for him. He is there for me no matter what. You ask any woman and she'll tell you it is not the suit or the job that make a man. It is whether he is man enough to meet her needs. Shawn is." She brushes her hands as if to prove she's finished with us, makes a quick about-turn, and disappears inside the room behind the nurse's station.

Ryan smirks. "The sooner women realize there is no such thing as a perfect guy," he looks at me, "the sooner..."

"The sooner?" I say, clearing away the cobwebs from my thoughts.

"Are you okay?"

I observe the puzzled expression on his face and repeat his question in my mind. Am I okay? I head away from the emergency ward and towards Administration. "I'll meet you in the car."

I find the staff supervisor in her office. "Excuse me, ma'am."

A middle-aged woman looks up from her desk.

* * *

Ten minutes later, I climb into the unmarked police car and shut the door.

Ryan starts the engine. "This was a waste of time."

"Was it?" I buckle my seatbelt.

"Didn't tell us much."

"No?"

He backs out of the parking space, exits the hospital parking lot, and heads to the detachment. "She's the fiancée. We can't trust her judgement." He looks at me expectantly. "Don't tell me you believe her."

"Everything she said can be verified. You heard Stan. No withdrawals above two hundred in their bank accounts for five months. Her immediate supervisor says Sunita hasn't taken a sick day in a year. She's never shown up at work with a black eye or signs of bruising. This is a small town. We'll definitely check, but I don't think we'll break her story." I glance up from my notes and out the side window. "Head back to Warner's."

"So, I'm right. This was a waste of time."

Glimpsing at his side view, I can't help asking, "Let me guess. You're single." I already know he is. What I don't say is, "If you're lucky enough to love someone who loves you back with that kind of ferociousness, it should change you, if you're not a total a-hole."

"Yes, I'm single." Ryan looks puzzled but doesn't call me on it. "The evidence is at the house, right? We just have to find it."

"Yes." In truth, I have no idea if that's right or not.

After the meeting with the deacons' wives had ended, I finally took the sedative my doctor gave. I'm only now waking up. There is a strange hush, and it envelops me. Light drifts like butterflies across the semidarkness in front of my eyes. My blouse is stuck to my skin. I sit up, reach around, and struggle to untangle it. A moment passes before I remember where I am and why I'm here. Leland is dead. On a slab at the morgue. Alone. In the dark. Cold.

I shiver.

Should I be there?

And do what? Hold his hand?

My first pregnancy, I carried the baby five months. I lost her in the middle of a hot July night, and I woke screaming—the pain, excruciating, as if someone had reached a hand through my back and ripped her out of me. Leland carried me to the car. He cried with me later when the doctor tried to explain why. A beautifully formed, perfect baby girl. Dead. No reason.

"No one's fault," our doctor said. "These things happen."

I looked up through my tears. Leland stood over me. I thought he hated me. "Our sweet baby girl. It's not my fault, Leland. It isn't."

"Of course not—I know that."

Did he? I'm trying to remember what he looked like, what his eyes said.

I was beautiful when we met. He wooed me despite me making it clear that he wasn't my type. I planned to marry a doctor. I didn't say it outright, at least not to Leland; but my girlfriends knew. We were all looking for husbands among the medical students. A lawyer? No thanks.

He kept wooing me. And why not? I was young and full of life. Charming. And funny. Can't tell you how many times friends told me I should do stand-up comedy. Like Carol Burnett, only much prettier.

Their assumptions were sweet, although being prettier than Carol Burnett wouldn't take much. It doesn't matter, though, audiences terrify me. I discovered that when I tried out for the part of Maria in the West Side Story, and I clammed up on stage. Which was a shame because I was small, but I had range and volume. I surprised them at the University Theatre.

Leland promised me an exciting life. He knew he would be an important man one day. Maybe even Prime Minister. How could I resist such temptation?

He changed after we lost our baby girl. He was gentle, kind, and thoughtful during the difficult weeks that followed, but slowly the kindness ended. He turned distant. He stopped talking to me. Over time, I might have pushed him away with my nattering. Every chance I had I told him I wasn't to blame. Goodness, as if he would know whether it was my fault or not. Leland was no doctor.

He never accused me. Even when I lost three pregnancies after Bronson, he never accused me of being faulty or broken, or any of the other reasons I invented on my own. When Bronson and Declan died so violently, he never once insinuated or implied I was to blame for their deaths, either. Before they died, yes, he reminded me that my pathetic life was my own doing. After they died, he started talking again. He liked me again. This past year was the happiest time of my life. I'm just realizing that now. Is it any wonder I'm confused?

I slip out of bed and walk to the window. My legs feel rubbery. I pull back drab curtains to reveal a stark, grey scene surrounding the back parking lot of the hotel. Grey cement, grey skies, grey air. The sun has set, and it's the dim light of dusk. Grey.

I walk to the sitting room. The view from this window shows Connaught Hill and the beautiful blue spruce trees that look frozen in time.

A knock on the door.

"Yes?"

"Ma'am, you have company," Constable Pinscher says. "It's..." He whispers to someone. "Ma'am, it's your new pastor and his wife."

"Yes, dear Mrs. Warner, it's Pastor William and Tanya," Pastor Will hollers.

I look around, but there's no place to hide.

* * *

The first person I see when Ryan and I enter the Warner residence is our boss, Superintendent Malden. He gestures to me from the entrance to the receiving room and roars, "Good, just the man I want to see."

I cringe before I'm able to relax my facial muscles. "My report will be on your desk first thing in the morning, sir."

"A prelim report will suit me fine, Corporal."

Right. I squeeze through several tech members carrying files around me to the minivan outside. I know I have to update him on the evidence, I just didn't expect to see him so soon. But, of course, Warner's no ordinary citizen.

"This is a large home," Superintendent Malden says. "Has every room has been searched?"

"Yes, sir."

"How many rooms are there?"

"Seventeen. Three bedrooms upstairs. A guest suite with kitchen above the three-bay garage, a media room, and a library. Here on the main floor there is a dining room, gathering room, reception room, office, kitchen, and breakfast room. There are three washrooms down and three up."

"I'm assigning more men to assist you and your team. They're on loan."

"Thank you, sir. That's—"

"Your men are canvassing the neighbourhood?"

"Yes, sir. I—"

"Danny, I was observing the service entrance." Malden gestures towards the hallway and kitchen, indicating me to follow.

I dig my hands into my pockets, while Malden cases the room like a seasoned pro. I step forward to steer him away from the people working in the kitchen. Many of them are already loaners from the task force for the Highway of Tears. They'd be available for a few weeks, a month at most. Nobody thinks it'll take any longer to solve this case. You would think they'd know by now that nothing ever happens the way you plan.

Malden is so intent on studying the room, I start to wonder if I'm wrong. He may need an audience for his observations. He's been an investigator for more years than I can count. He could notice something no one else has. He has my respect. He deserves my patience.

At the far end of the kitchen, above the upright freezer, a surveillance monitor shows the covered porch outside the service door. Mrs. Warner said Mr. Warner liked to have his morning coffee at the breakfast table in the chair facing the monitor. Why? Made him feel safe? Was he watching for someone in particular or was he paranoid? Considering he's dead now, he had reason to be.

When the doorbell rang, Warner could look up and see who it was before crossing the room to answer the door. The killer could've known that and dressed accordingly. Disguised as a deliveryman, he'd appear harmless. Did they talk? Or did the shooter fire straightaway? Maybe he produced the gun when he realized they were alone in the kitchen. Or the plan had been to take out Mrs. Warner, too.

I'm not going to find the answers standing here. The way Malden observes the state-of-the-art kitchen, with quiet introspection, he might not notice if I slip away. He would have my report on his desk first thing tomorrow morning. Or by tonight if he lets me get back to work.

Don't be an idiot. This is not a man to piss off.

"You found the slug?" Malden asks.

Too late. "No, sir. We're still searching outside."

"What about the casing?"

"No casing."

"The shooter picked it up then. Has the ME in Kamloops identified the gauge?"

"She won't know until she cuts into him. She thinks it might be a 9mm."

"When's the autopsy?"

"Possibly Monday morning."

With three fatal accidents on the weekend and a stabbing in downtown Kamloops, Mr. Warner could be on ice for a few days. Like most MEs, the examiner in Kamloops isn't impressed by a victim's status when they were alive. Dead, they all get equal consideration.

I step forward and clear my throat. "There was no gunpowder residue on the body. The shooter stood approximately ten feet from Mr. Warner. He was close to the washroom door and the freezer just inside the kitchen. Both appliances had residue splatters."

"Yes," Malden injects. "I read Mrs. Warner's statement. She said she was upstairs in her room." He glances back at the hallway. "Somebody presumably knocks on the door. Warner opens it without checking the surveillance monitor above the freezer." He rubs his chin. "Or the shooter was dressed as a deliveryman and was able to step so far into the room. He waited for Warner to sign for whatever he supposedly delivered. Or he was someone Warner knew and trusted." He backs up to the space between the refrigerator and the island. He takes note of the residue left by the fingerprint techs and lowers his voice to a whisper, forcing me to lean closer.

"Pardon?"

"Does the missus have any familiarity with firearms?"

"No evidence to indicate she does."

Why are we whispering? Am I supposed to be worrying about her reputation or Warner's?

"Have you spoken to Mr. Warner's assistant yet?"

"It's being done as we speak."

"The missus didn't hear the shot?"

"Her room's soundproof." My team has already confirmed that.

Malden sticks his hands deep into his trouser pockets and fixes his attention on the service entrance. I fight hard not to groan.

"Any suspects on his client roster?"

"We're still scratching them off. So far we're not liking anyone."

"Keep scratching. The man had more enemies than an arms dealer. All the garbage cans inside and out were searched? And all the fireplaces? What about the toilets?"

"So far nothing of evidentiary value was found anywhere else but in this room, though we're still in the prelim stage."

"They're stripping her car and his?"

"Mr. Warner's vehicle is clean. We're working on hers."

"What about the collection of handguns he's said to own? Is it true he sold most of them after the night his boys died?"

"His Magnum was found upstairs in his bedside drawer. There was a small pistol in his tool chest in the garage. I'll be speaking to Mrs. Warner shortly, and I'll ask if she knows who Warner sold the rest to."

"That reminds me, Mrs. Warner isn't staying with friends. Dispatch knows what hotel she's at. Further interviews will take place there."

"I need to see her on camera. You know it's—"

"That won't happen, Danny. Interview her at the hotel."

I ignore the warning in my head to keep quiet. "May I enquire why?"

"Find out if Mr. Warner sold any of his guns."

I squint at our superintendent. It's difficult to imagine anyone intimidating him. The man is easy-going, but all of us who work with him know he's not the type to put up with any nonsense.

He glances over my shoulder towards the door. "Talk to whomever bought the guns. The shooter could be one of them. He or she had the good sense to pick up the casing. Could be an experienced gun collector, besides being an obvious adversary." He frowns. The skin above the ridge of his nose disappears into a rut. "There were no prints anywhere then?" He scratches his head as if he, too, is perplexed. "Death rooms often terrify people. Got to give the missus credit for deciding to have the wake here."

"What? When?"

He must see the expression on my face because he waves his hand as if the potential problem has already vanished. "If our investigation isn't done, she'll have to postpone or have it someplace else. I don't care who he was. Our tape won't be coming down until we're finished." He glances at the floor and back to the island behind us. "Has anyone thought to mention that she'll need to hire cleaners to get the brain splatter off?"

"I'll speak to her."

He switches his attention to a spot on the ceiling and studies it unblinkingly. Obviously, his attention has moved on.

I walk over to the tech at the sink. She has its drains taken apart and has filled several evidence baggies. "Find out which hotel Mrs. Warner is at, will you? Then call me on my cell."

She nods, pulls off her latex gloves, and leaves the room.

I turn back to my boss, who is facing the service entrance, staring at the monitor above the freezer.

"About these monitors, Danny. There is one in the kitchen, study, and his bedroom upstairs? Any more?"

"The garage."

"Why one in the kitchen? He didn't strike me as the type to spend much time in here. He wasn't an amateur chef, was he? Though perhaps it was more for Mrs. Warner's benefit?"

"Maybe."

"There are no video tapes?"

"No, sir."

"No command centre for these cameras?"

"No."

"Don't you find that strange?"

"The manufacturer says not all customers go that route."

"We're talking about the former Minister of Defence, Danny, a man born suspicious. Check it out."

"Yes, sir."

"No identifiable evidence on the jogger, or that Norse fellow?" He looks despondent. He's under as much pressure as I am to solve this murder. "Any possibility it was a hired hit?"

"It's not your standard hit, no, sir. As you know, a professional would have used a .22 up close and personal, between the eyes and the other through his heart."

I clear my throat. Time to broach the subject. "You were here when Warners' sons died. Do you think there could be a connection between their deaths and their father's? Anyone stand out in your mind? Dr. Brendell Meshango, for instance?"

Malden seems to reflect for a moment. "I don't believe the

public realizes that being an investigator these days requires more than your standard training. We're expected to be anthropologists and psychologists, not to mention criminologists. You've been a detective long enough, Danny. It was as you would expect. A distraught father and mother, a bloody crime scene, a hysterical young woman. A brave professor. Perfect movie of the week. In answer to your query, there are an unlimited number of potential connections. CIS will take the broader scope. Stick close to home. Meshango, Brooks, Mrs. Warner. The shooter could be any of them or any of their relatives. We best find out."

"Yes, sir."

"You requested the Investigative Analysis's crime scene reconstruction and any profiling they did on the unknown offender?"

"They offered some suggestions, but nothing we hadn't thought of. They're faxing a full report tomorrow."

"You have nothing new then?" His question sounds like an accusation.

"The phone lines remain busy. Three dozen or so calls have come in. My staff are doing their jobs, sir. As you can see." I sweep a hand across the area as if to prove it. "They're tagging and bagging the evidence, combing the area, particularly the backyard. We're still canvassing the neighbourhood. We're doing interviews, taking statements. Somebody will remember something. We've already done close to fifteen interviews. Mr. Warner's assistant in Ottawa is cooperating."

"Any possibility it was someone from back east?"

"The office of The Deputy Commissioner of Operations is looking into it."

"You checked all incoming flights then?"

"Yes. Ottawa is monitoring the high-profile Internet chat rooms. It may be too soon. Nobody's opted for credit."

"Too bad."

"I'm sure the investigators in Ottawa are doing a thorough job of interviewing government officials, all the VIPs in question."

"Of course they are. But keep in close contact with them, Danny. Meanwhile, keep a man outside Mrs. Warner's hotel room. Tomorrow we'll re-evaluate whether there is any threat to her."

"Sir, we can't let her back in here with the kitchen looking like this."

"No, I suppose not. She gave you full access to search the house at any time then?"

I smack my lips together and wonder how to answer that

question. My hesitation makes Malden's eyebrows rise. "Mrs. Warner was anxious to cooperate. We have her written permission to search the house and his office."

As I expect, he looks relieved. But we didn't have written permission to search her purse prior to doing so.

"There is one more thing, sir. It's rumoured Mr. Warner beat his boys."

"I've heard those rumours. What did their doctor say?"

"He's not cooperating."

Malden grunts. "Take care of him, Danny."

"Yes, sir.

"What did the missus say about any beatings?"

"I'm talking to her next. At her hotel room, of course." I flinch at the sarcasm in my voice.

"Do you believe, if it's true he beat those boys, it's a motive for his death?"

"I'm not sure, sir. The viable suspects are dead."

"How long before the DNA results come in then?"

"The usual three weeks."

"I'll call and put a rush on it for one week. Considering our victim is Prince George's most influential lawyer, it's the least we can do. Better we know for sure all the blood came from the victim." He pulls leather gloves from his pocket. "I know a few people in Ottawa and took the liberty of making a number of calls. Unofficially."

I give him my full attention.

"Our victim was considered an intelligent, shrewd politician. Powerful, influential, destined to run for and win the Conservative leadership race. His sons' deaths certainly guaranteed his seat. His not taking advantage of that shocked the political community."

"What kind of man was he before they died?"

"All of the above."

"Well-liked?"

"Not at all."

"A good husband?"

"Most thought no."

"Would he have made a good Prime Minister?"

"Yes."

"Anyone hate him enough to kill him?"

"That, I was unable to ascertain. Which could mean there were too many to count."

"Thank you, sir."

"You're forgetting something."

Right—there is still our number one suspect in these cases: the spouse. "Did anyone believe Mrs. Warner was capable of murder?"

"They did not." Malden stuffs his hands into his leather gloves. "So that's it then?" He glances at my face. "This case is high-profile, and you know how our leaders feel about that. They want it solved yesterday." He looks sympathetic, which worries me. "Nobody's forgetting it was your persistence that nailed that Vancouver serial killer. You found those women's belongings and had the good sense to suggest we set up that phoney illegal weapons charge. Not to mention you survived what might have been a deadly fall." He gives me a sudden look that probably means: *Now would be a good time to duplicate the miracle.*

"Find the motive, Danny." He lifts his collar, stuffs his gloved hands into his pockets, looks prepared to face anything the weather can throw at him. "Do everything you can to solve this case quickly." He heads towards the door, stops. I approach. "You should concentrate more on the missus—despite what everyone else thinks. And also Meshango."

When he exits the kitchen, I turn to one of our people. "Find out who we use for a cleaning crew and make sure they're on call."

"Yes, Corporal."

* * *

I say my goodbyes to my Pastor and his wife at the door. Constable Pinscher watches over us from the hallway. His eyes scan the right side of the corridor to the elevators, back to us, then the left side to the exit. If ever I have the good fortune of meeting his parents, I will praise them for a job well done. Pinscher is a good boy. Diligent.

Still, it is ridiculous to make him stand guard. I'm not important enough to kill. To warrant such emotion, a person would have to elicit a powerful and overwhelming reaction from someone. I'm not that person.

Pastor Will speaks of God's Mercy. Tanya nods her head. I wonder if she believes what he says. Or has she learned to play the obedient wife in social settings? When they reach home, does she share her thoughts and tell him he's full of hot air?

The idea makes me want to laugh. Until I remember Digger is gone. Neither of these God-fearing people expressed their sympathy over the loss of my best friend.

Finally, they move away, smiles plastered on their faces, interspersed by sad expressions. "Our deepest sympathies, Sally," Pastor Will says again before he and Tanya exit down the hallway, rushing to leave the building and get back to their lives.

Perhaps I'm surrounded by death and they're worried it's contagious?

Constable Pinscher looks at me as if he understands. I step into my room and close the door. I catch my reflection in the mirror on the sidewall. I see hints of my mother. Even after my brother was killed in Vietnam, and my father died from cancer, my sister Shirley and I never saw her weep, although red splotches stayed for days around her nose, and deeper-than-usual creases appeared on her eyelids. My face looks the same, only my sunken eyes seem more fearful than usual.

I walk to the chair next to the small table and sit. The hotel room is fine, but I long to be home. My bedroom is my sanctuary. Closing my eyes, I picture it as clearly as if I was there. The replica King Louis chair isn't comfortable, but I can cross my legs and lean back. My elbow nudges the phone, it's on the half-wall beside me. I had my own telephone line hooked up when Leland built his panic room. I dislike talking on the phone, but my privacy was all I had left.

I remind myself not to dwell on bad thoughts about my past. I exhale and relax. I expel thoughts of my mother and her dignity and, along with her death, my lost years: the doubt, shame, and guilt. I package them up as if they are returnable gifts. I throw the imaginary package into the light behind my eyelids. My concentration wanders, but I persist and focus on the bright, warm light...

Loud thumping on my door.

"Yes?"

The knocking continues, which means whoever it is can't hear me. I rise slowly, and my knees pop. If I believed in God, I'd ask Him to banish everyone from my house so I could go home.

"Who is it?"

I hear a buzzing noise. The door flies open, narrowly missing me. "Mrs. Warner, are you okay?" Constable Pinscher is pale and disturbed looking.

"Yes. I was sleeping. What—?" I'm not at home. How could I forget that?

Behind Pinscher stands beside the man I met earlier, the policeman investigating Leland's death. "Corporal Killian, hello."

"Mrs. Warner." He gestures to Constable Pinscher, who takes one more look around the room before he leaves and closes the door behind him.

Corporal Killian watches me closely.

I cannot read his expression. Friend or foe?

8

■ study Sally Warner's expression and body language, and I remember to show my cordial face. White people sometimes see what I think is my neutral expression as hostile. Looking at her, my initial thought is sad. Immediately followed by: suspect. Sad suspect...that's a first.

"How are you, Corporal Killian?"

"Well, ma'am. And you?"

She's wearing a blue flowery top, a small pattern, which flows around her when she moves and drops past her knees over white slacks. Her white-blonde hair still looks as nice as it did this morning, but her eyes look puffy. Has she been crying?

"I'm—I'm okay. Thank you." She gestures towards the sofa and chair. "I'd be happier at home, though I understand why I'm not allowed to be there. Please sit down."

Her hotel room is elegant, probably the best they have, the kind of room Angie would appreciate. Certainly not the room the RCMP would have paid for. I get a faint whiff of furniture polish. The Berber carpet is the colour of caramel chocolate. Next to the kitchenette there is a dark mahogany table and four chairs with a desk. At the far end of the room hang silk drapes the colour of harvested wheat. They're drawn to the sides of a large window covered in dark wood blinds with a view of the city visible between the slats. Two reproductions of evening sunsets hang on the wall above the tailored sofa. One photo looks like New York City, the other Paris. To the right is a closed door, probably leading to the hallway and the rest of the suite.

I know there is room service, but it never hurts to ask. "Are you okay here, ma'am? There are several stores nearby. Can I get you anything?"

She raises her eyebrows with an inquisitive look. "That's kind, but I was hoping I won't be here that long."

She sits in the chair near the end of the sofa, pulls her sweater tight across her chest, places both hands in her lap. I wonder if they taught her how to sit like that in finishing school. Though I doubt there was such a thing. It's something one of my buddies from the rez told me once when we were visiting Victoria. "Where do you think the white girls are?" "I don't know." "At them fancy finishing schools."

Mrs. Warner reminds me of my great step-aunt who used to visit the family on her way to Europe. My step-dad called it, "The Queen's annual visit to the commoners."

Andrew Killian rescued me from the residential school when I was ten. He and mum married secretly after they dated for five years. One of her conditions for accepting his proposal was he take her kids as his own. The day after they were engaged he came to the school and took me away. I don't know what was said, but the priest and nuns didn't look happy. The best part: I got his Irish surname. People stopped judging me by my student applications. My older siblings were in their twenties and didn't care much, but I jumped at the chance. Unlike them, I couldn't remember ever having a dad. Andrew Killian may have been white, but he was a god. I wonder if he knew how I watched his every move. He's the reason I became a cop. He taught me that every man is responsible for every other man no matter his creed. He taught me to approach every human being I met with compassion, though, his tolerance for his rich aunt's elitist worldview was stretched to the limit during her visits. It was the one time I ever remember him being stiff and unwelcoming. I can't say for sure that she looked down her nose because we were Haida, but I overheard dad telling her, "Money doesn't make a person worthy."

Would he react to Mrs. Warner the same way? Or would he see the pathetic soul I see now? I don't know whether she's a bigot, but rich or not, she's the saddest person I've ever met. I've interviewed street people who were more at peace than Sally Warner.

Another time I might have given her more space, but I set my briefcase on the coffee table and sit down on the end of the couch nearest her. I need to hear her breathing, feel her aura. "I'll get you home as quickly as possible."

She reaches across as if to touch my arm, pulls back. "Thank you, Corporal. I appreciate that."

She wears no wedding ring, no jewellery. She wasn't wearing any the last time we spoke, either. Does that mean Warner was stingy, or does she prefer no bling? I need to ask my people if they located any jewellery boxes or safes in the house.

Her fingernails aren't polished, and except for powder on her lightly freckled face, she's wearing no makeup—which could be personal preference, or could mean she no longer cares. Her skin is softly wrinkled around her eyes and mouth, and—Damn,

I'm staring.

I blink, glance down, turn my eyes gently to her. I need to maintain rapport between us, not frighten her away.

She tilts her head, looks quizzically at me. "Is something wrong?"

I open my briefcase, pull out a printout of names, hand it over. "Take a close look at this list of your husband's colleagues, and tell me if you have concerns about any of them."

She's staring through me. Did my question trigger something? Or is it me?

One night when Angie and I decided to check out a new pub, I ran into a known gang member. We exchanged a few words. When he took off, I caught Angie staring at me like Mrs. Warner is doing now. How could I explain that having Angie in the same room with a dangerous offender made me feel sick? She didn't get it. She said I was cold and uncaring. She said if she hadn't seen it with her own eyes, she never would have believed how hard I could be.

How could I explain that it came with the job?

I decide on a softer approach with Mrs. Warner. "It's been a terrible day for you. Is this a bad time?"

She pats her sweater pocket, looks suddenly paler than normal, blinks.

I wait.

She leans forward, squints at the paper while patting her pockets. She looks across the room. "I've misplaced my glasses."

I scan all the flat surfaces in the room: the coffee table, the side table with the lamp, the bureau. I look back at her, shrug.

Her face brightens.

Why does that seem weird?

"They're probably next to my bed. Would you excuse me a moment?" She walks to the next room.

I hear a drawer being opened, closed. Clicking sounds, as if objects are being shuffled together.

She returns with her glasses, sits, puts them on, glances at the list.

I can't put my finger on it, but something is not right.

Her eyes cut back at me. "Forgive my poor manners, Corporal Killian. Would you like a coffee or something to eat?" She reaches for the phone. "Room service can deliver anything you'd like."

"No, thanks."

"Are you sure? It's no problem. I imagine with your hours, it's difficult to eat regular meals. Your mother must worry about you constantly."

"My mother's passed." What made me share that?

"Corporal Killian, I'm sorry. No matter your age, a man should know the comfort of his mother. I'm sorry for your loss."

Her concern seems real enough. That's not what's wrong. She seems pitiful. This woman is more alone than she probably realizes. Regardless of her guilt or innocence, she deserves my sympathy. But is she guilty? If she didn't kill her husband, does she know who did? Is she covering for someone? A lover? Do sixty-year-old women have lovers?

Poker face. "Thank you."

"How long has she been gone?"

"My mother?" I'm losing control of the conversation. "When I was a kid." I gesture. "About the list."

"That must have been difficult for your father."

"Yes. The list."

She looks down at the sheet of paper. She seems to be reading, without hesitations, or retakes.

Too bad. Unless it means she's our shooter and the names are irrelevant.

"I'm sorry. Most of these people mean nothing to me. The ones that do couldn't possibly be your guilty party. They use their pens to cause grief, they don't need a gun." She tries to hand the paper back to me.

"Keep it for a few days and take a look periodically, in case you remember something."

"If you wish." With her gaze directed downwards, she folds the list, places it in her pocket.

"It's nice and peaceful here." I glance towards the windows and make no attempt to leave.

"Yes. But I long to be home."

I hear the plea and look back at her. "Has it occurred to you that being back at the house might be difficult?"

"Why? Oh, you mean because Leland died there. My grandfather lay on the dining room table for days after his passing while family and friends paid their respects, and life went on around him. My grandmother told me she and his sisters washed and dressed him themselves. Of course, that was long before I was born." Her eyebrows rise. "I see what you mean, though. At first, it will be difficult." With a hand supporting her elbow, she fusses with the top button of her sweater. "One day it might catch up with me. Right now, all I'm concerned with is my room. It would be comforting to be there."

Will I ever feel 'comforted'? Mall parking lots are a nightmare. I can't cross them without seeing Angie's lifeless body in the distance. I was running to her when members of the detachment caught up to me that afternoon. It took four of them to hold me back while my cries reached across the city and back. All I could do was yell, "Why?" Later, why turned to how. How could she die so violently in broad daylight without someone seeing or hearing something? Anything? If only I'd put her needs ahead of mine that day, then she'd still be alive.

Phlegm rises in my throat. I swallowed. "Did your husband have enemies?"

She tilts her head, laughs without sound. "You didn't know Leland."

That's funny? "It would help knowing more about him."

She leans her chin in her hand, seems to think better of that, grasps her hands together and sets them on her lap. Self-conscious? She knows I'm studying her?

"My husband wasn't always a people person. Leland was a born politician, though. Charming to a fault. Unfortunately, rather than step lightly to get something done, he stomped. Two years ago, before our sons died, he had his sights set on being Prime Minister. Afterwards, he changed so much that those once loyal to him gave up on him. His dreams died with our sons."

If what everyone says is true, Warner was about as well liked as Prime Minister Mulroney when he left office. "Your husband was well liked?"

"He was respected. He was feared. Not everyone liked him. He made a few enemies. And he could be cruel, so cruel." She pauses, showing a brooding face. "That was a terrible thing to say. I'm sorry. I shouldn't speak of my late husband in that manner. No matter what."

"No matter what?"

"Please don't judge me poorly, Corporal Killian."

"That's not what I'm here for, ma'am." Which is the truth. If what I've heard about Warner has merit, her life wasn't easy. "I'm trying to find out who killed your husband."

Her eyes glitter. On the verge of tears? Damn, I hope not. "Where did you meet Mr. Warner?"

"That was so many years ago." She smooths the lapels of her sweater and settles back against the sofa. "I volunteered at a women's shelter while I was at the University. Leland worked pro bono." She pats the side of her head as if in search of some uncontrolled strands of hairs. Two fingertips press to her forehead. "I tried not to love him."

Instead of opening that can of worms, I let her drift off for a moment. She has many secrets; it won't be easy to get her to tell me anything if I rush her.

I clear my throat. She looks at me. "Why didn't he run for the PM leadership?" I ask.

"Because the party withdrew their support."

I can almost hear her thoughts: *What does that have to do with his murder?*

This woman is too refined to speak her mind.

"Why did they withdraw their support?"

"Because he was no longer the tough politician they remembered. I'm guessing, of course. I don't really know." She rubs her eyelids with her right thumb and index finger. "Did you find anything helpful in his study?"

"We're still going through his files here and in Ottawa. They did find some interesting documents concerning the local First Nations artist Sophie Brooks. Do you know why your husband took an interest in her work?"

"Is she a suspect? The director from the Native Centre told me today that Sophie was at a powwow on Vancouver Island when Leland died."

And what brought that up, I wonder? "She's not a suspect at this time. I'm trying to understand your husband. It might help to figure out why he's dead." I take in her face. If she knows of improprieties between Warner and Brooks, I should spot it in her expression. "Your husband admired Sophie's work?"

She shakes her head as if the idea is preposterous. "Sophie dated our son Declan for a time."

"For a time?"

"It ended shortly before we went to Europe. Leland didn't approve of Sophie. On top of everything else he was stricter with Declan than with Bronson. He ordered Declan not to see Sophie again."

"Why?"

She doesn't answer.

"Mrs. Warner?"

"She's Native."

Which confirms what I've already learned about Warner. The man was a bigot. "So Declan obeyed and stopped seeing her?"

"His decision had nothing to do with obedience. I'm sure of that."

"Why?"

"Because after Leland ordered him to stop seeing her, they continued dating for several weeks. I think Declan stopped dating Sophie when it no longer annoyed Leland."

"So, afterwards, Mr. Warner and Sophie worked together?"

"A few days after Declan told her they couldn't see each other, Bronson got it into his head that Sophie had dumped Declan. He accosted her one evening at the Native Friendship Centre. Sophie's manager phoned the police."

Accosted wasn't the word I'd have chosen. The report said Bronson pushed and shoved Sophie. The constable who took her statement saw bruises on her. The girl's manager told the police Bronson had scared them.

"Did that lead to Sophie and your husband coming to a mutual business agreement?"

She grimaces. "That's a nice way to put it. That same evening, Sophie promised to forget what Bronson did and stop stalking Declan if Leland helped her career."

"She'd been stalking your son?"

"To know Sophie is to see a desperate young woman. I can't imagine how Leland's death would make things better for her."

"He continued to help her after your sons died." Some might call that blackmail. "How did you feel about that?"

Mrs. Warner rubs her hand over the chair's armrests, averts her eyes from me to the wool carpeting. "I'm sure you're competent at your job, but has it occurred to you that Leland's murder may have been political? As Minister, he had access to delicate information. Several times while he was in Ottawa he said the cabinet shuffle—after the money scandal—made several members nervous." She looks sideways at me, glances at my notepad.

As a show of respect, I jot it down, though what she's suggesting was unlikely to end in murder. Nothing out of Ottawa suggests Warner's death was political; otherwise he'd have been killed long before now. He was shot once, so it didn't appear to be personal either. In a fit of rage, a shooter generally can't stop squeezing the trigger; especially a 9mm with a short trigger pull. "Your husband stayed on after the Prime Minister retired?"

"Long enough to guarantee the programs he created were implemented."

"What programs?"

"New desert uniforms. The new helicopters. There are the rumours about the budget fiasco." She eyes my notepad again. "The previous minister evidently misappropriated funds, and it was hoped his resignation would thwart any repercussions."

"Really?" Old news. Personally, I didn't understand why Warner hadn't switched parties after the former PM resigned. He must have earned points with the opposition when he took over the Ministry the year before the new PM took office.

She looks straight at me. "What?"

Spooky lady. "Why didn't the Minister take advantage of his good works, switch parties, and pursue the leadership?"

She shrugs. "What does all this have to do with his murder?"

"Everything and anything about your husband is relevant at this stage."

Time might have renewed Warner's dreams if he'd given himself the chance. He could have made Canada a better place for a lot of Canadians, especially for kids on the street. He could have done something in memory of their sons and made a difference.

With thoughts of her own, Mrs. Warner's eyebrows lift and her eyes widen. Her crow's feet all but disappear. "What if he discovered something that put his life at risk?"

That sounded far too much like the ramblings of an old woman.

"What's to say Leland learned something while in office and that knowledge made him dangerous?" Her frown deepens, tripling the number of wrinkles around her eyes. I watch, captivated. "I'm just speculating. We never discussed his reasons in depth. All Leland said was he finally realized the futility of his actions."

She reaches across, pats the space above my hand sympathetically, careful not to touch me. "Please don't be sad. When you lose your children in one violent evening, you gain perspective on everything else. To understand Leland, you have to realize that."

The anguish in her expression is too much. I look down at my notes. "You can't think of anyone who wanted him dead?"

"Have you questioned my son's English professor?"

"Sorry?"

"That Meshango woman?"

"Dr. Meshango has an alibi." Is Mrs. Warner a bigot, too? I hope not. I'm beginning to like her even if she did murder her husband.

"What about her daughter?"

"Zoë Sheppard moved to Manitoba last year."

In spite of the horror Meshango and her daughter experienced at the hands of the Warner brothers the night they died, nothing in the files suggests either woman considered taking revenge on the boys' parents.

Mrs. Warner's gaze stays intent on my face. "What alibi did that woman have? Was it her boyfriend, one of the Mounties from your detachment? How do you know he's not lying for her sake?"

"Sorry?" One of my constables was dating Dr. Meshango?

I march their faces through my mind, and not one stands out as a possible boyfriend. The file says the doctor is fifty-two. Most of the cops I know are either too young or too married. I don't have time for gossip.

She puckers her chin. "You don't know, do you? No one from your office has bothered to tell you. Shame on them."

I try shrugging it off, but something doesn't feel right. Is somebody I work with withholding vital information?

"That woman has been dating Sergeant Lacroix since the night my sons died."

My jaw drops.

Lacroix?

"Leland told me they've been living together for almost a year." Mrs. Warner glances at my notepad.

Staff Sergeant Gabriel Lacroix?

"One of the lawyers in Leland's firm handled the Sergeant's new will."

My boss?

I close my mouth, grind my teeth, and almost laugh at my stupidity. The urge is so strong that I press my lips together. This information changes everything. Lacroix went to a lot of trouble to keep his relationship with Dr. Meshango a secret. Why? Reason enough for murder?

The possibility jabs a streak of pain between my shoulder blades.

Killian's troubled expression should disturb me, and it does, a little. He obviously didn't know Lacroix was living with Meshango. I wouldn't care, except I hate that woman. She turned Declan against his own brother. Why else would Declan kill Bronson, then himself? She tricked him somehow. Now I hate her with my whole being. She stole my sons from me, and no one bothered to punish her. Leland wouldn't. He had power as minister, but no—he was too busy trying to make a difference—too late.

What am I saying? She was lucky to get out alive.

My chest hurts. I'm close to weeping. I squeeze my eyes shut to stop the tears and concentrate on my shallow breathing. I hate Doctor Meshango because...Declan tried to save her instead of me.

I see her image in my head. Attractive even at fifty, slender build, dark hair, cut in a short funky style the last time I saw her. She's referred to as Métis, but she looks more Native to me. It could be the combination of being half Native and half white that makes her so alluring. Or it's her eyes. I remember staring at them at a parent-teacher conference at UNBC, knowing I'd seen her before. It's not that her eyes are particularly large, but they're dark and intense with a brilliant sparkle. Like black diamonds. I felt lost in them.

Meshango has a presence that I think most women would like to emulate. I know I would. If I could change places with her, I would in a heartbeat. She's striking even in jeans and a white T-shirt. I saw her dressed like that once at the garden store. I ducked behind the gazebos so she wouldn't see me and held my breath—as if that would help. But I couldn't face her, not the way she looked at me the last time we met, as if she understood what I was going through. The worst part was I believed her. She's the kind of woman who commands respect.

I hear movement and open my eyes. Killian stands. Because he's so respectful, I decide to make his job easier. I rise. He can't disguise how glad he is to leave. We're halfway to the door before he says, "Thank you."

Part of me wants to plead with him to stay. Talk to me as

though we've been friends forever. He's a nice young man, and there is an intensity to him that I admire. Let's face it, he's exquisite with that beautiful black hair, deep, dark eyes, and crooked grin.

On the way downstairs, along with Pinscher, we chitchat about Killian's transfer to Prince George and how much he likes the city. He hopes to remain here until he retires.

"Where did you grow up?" I'm curious as to whether he's accustomed to small town life.

"Sandpit on Haida Gwaii. It's—"

"Yes, I know. One of the largest ports in the Queen Charlottes. Whatever did your father do?"

I wonder if that's too forward a question, but he answers without hesitation. "He was a marine biologist. He retired to Sechelt after mom died."

My stomach churns. I glance at his wedding ring and change the subject. "Have you children?"

He looks away. "No."

"Prince George is a nice place to raise a family." I say this pleasantly, but inside my head I scream: If you have children, never allow anyone to take them away! Protect them.

I'm unruffled on the outside. As if my bad thoughts are thorny blackberry stems, I sweep them out of my way with imaginary gloved hands. The elevator doors open. I long to cross the lobby and peek my head outside. Pinscher stops me with a hand at my elbow. Killian takes the opportunity to leave. Will he confront Lacroix? That's unlikely. Men always stick together.

Constable Pinscher escorts me back upstairs to my room. Apparently it's unsafe for me to be out in the open. I thank him for allowing me a brief stroll, and then worry that I may have sounded sarcastic. I politely excuse myself and go to my room. Avoiding my image in the mirror, I slip into the en-suite and sit down on the vanity chair. There is no sense looking at my reflection, I keep seeing my mother in all her grace.

I am not my mother. She mourned my father's death with heart-breaking dignity. I squeeze my eyes shut while the pain in my heart grabs my breath. Thinking about her has renewed my memories of the morning after we buried our sons, when reality had sunk in.

I'd had a horrible nightmare the night before the funeral. In the dream, Declan shouted at me that it was my duty to put Bronson down, as if he were a rabid dog. "I am his mother," I cried. "Please don't make me do it because I won't!"

Then, Declan, beset with a placidity and strength I'd never

74

witnessed before, raised the gun and shot Bronson dead. I woke screaming. How could my son kill his brother? How?

Because he was trying to protect Dr. Meshango and her daughter.

What an incredulous statement. No wonder I'm insane.

My scalp hurts. I pat my head, remembering that on that particular morning my scalp also hurt. I'd wakened several times during the night to find myself yanking at my hair. Like a mad woman.

Have I started doing that again?

On that morning, the drapes were left open, and the first thing I saw above the news vans that had been parked outside for three days, were low hanging, black thunderclouds; a gloom on the edge of the new day, threatening rain. I dressed quickly.

I found Leland sitting in the kitchen, his breath smelling of whiskey. I asked, "What do you want for breakfast?" I had suggested food because I needed to do something.

"Coffee," he said in a doleful voice. He then looked at me long and hard as if on the verge of some profound revelation. One more secret added to his vault.

Not that I cared, but his tone reminded me how he hadn't scolded or snapped at me since the night the police came to our door. They came ten hours before he was due to fly back to his other life in Ottawa. Did he feel cheated? Their arrival meant he was forced to grieve in my presence, even if it was cerebral and dry-eyed.

We sat at the kitchen table and sipped coffee, our postures stiff, and the air thick with penance. No one called until late morning—some political VIP, a caller who lied and said he'd been unable to get through the first three days. Leland took the call in his den and spent the rest of the morning there, answering the phone, sorting through legal documents, and mumbling to himself.

At noon, for no other reason than to hear sound, I asked, "What are you doing?"

"Arranging things so you'll be taken care of if I go first."

His answer stunned me. After all, I was simply filling the silence. Despite his grief he had parliamentary duties to perform. I wondered if I should remind him of that, until I realized his response was the beginning of our new life together. The first step towards his redemption? Or was it self-pity I heard in his voice?

One week later with the yard still full of reporters, I joined Leland at the breakfast table, a routine that requires no thought, and was sipping decaffeinated coffee when he asked, "Would you consider moving to Ottawa?"

My mouth fell open. I accepted that we would exist in silent torment when we were together and relief when we were apart until one, or both of us, dropped dead from uselessness. Though I suppose he wasn't quite as useless as me.

I was about to ask him why the change in venue when I saw a flicker of remorse in his calm demeanour. Then, in front of my eyes, remorse turned to something pathetic. Leland—the stern man of my past, the man who, on more than one occasion, told me I disgusted him—began to sob.

I reached across the table to pat his hand, to console him, and then came to my senses. I was not his mother. I couldn't pat his hand and make everything better. He deserved his anguish. Our sons were dead.

Now Leland is, too.

Why has this happened?

A cold breeze sweeps across my chest, and I wrap my sweater tighter. I feel the walls closing in, and the air being sucked out of the room.

While I know I should get up and move, and try to find a reason to go on, I'm plagued by insolvable questions. Is Leland in heaven? Where are my sons now? I can't imagine God letting them into heaven. Does heaven exist? Could either of them ever find peace? Do they forgive me now? Am I worth saving?

Six kilometres up the hill from the police detachment, I see grey-bellied clouds hovering over the city of Prince George. They look like snow clouds ready to burst. I descend into the downtown core, close in on the first of several intersections, gear down, and swear. Hell if I knew a snow cloud from a rain cloud. Maybe the weatherman was right, no snow until after tomorrow when I get the new tires installed. I hope so. It rained during the night and the roads froze. Traffic creeps tentatively along on black ice.

At the bottom of the hill, I ease to a stop at the intersection of Victoria and Seventeenth. The roof of the detachment a few blocks away is now visible.

Mrs. Warner said Meshango and Lacroix are living together. How did I not know? Unless it isn't true?

It is. Sergeant Lacroix interjected himself on Doctor Meshango's behalf for a reason. But why? Because he thinks she killed Warner or because he knows she did? If no on both accounts, then why protect her?

Damn, what was he thinking? What was he thinking *with*?

I can't ask him outright, not without compromising my career.

I clutch the steering wheel. Enough with the stupid questions. I'm a cop, not a vigilante. What I need to do is not compromise the investigation by alerting Lacroix and Meshango to the fact they are now on our suspect list. I give my head a shake. Staff Sergeant Lacroix isn't stupid. Nor does he strike me as a willing accomplice to murder.

Before I left Warner's, I called dispatch from my car, spoke directly to a member of my team. Dr. Meshango wasn't questioned in person earlier. The constable, who had been instructed to interview her, had ran into Lacroix outside the detachment. When Lacroix asked him where he was headed and the constable told him, Lacroix said questioning Dr. Meshango wasn't necessary. Later, while I was with Norse in Vanderhoof, someone else caught the mistake, called Meshango, and interviewed her over the phone.

Bad policing.

Sure, Lacroix is our staff sergeant, sometimes intimidating, but he still knows better than to interfere in a murder investigation. He's not an idiot. Why stop the constable from interviewing Dr. Meshango? Why leave the report vague? He must know what kind of shit this will bring down on his head. All he succeeded in doing was make himself and Meshango look guilty. Dr. Meshango's alibi was written as solid in the report. When this gets out, those in a position to fire Lacroix's ass just might.

My fault. I should have followed up on it personally, not simply read the report and take it as verbatim. But I didn't, because, hell, he's still a good cop.

Can't fault him for trying to protect Meshango, though. Men do stupid things when they're in love.

The glare from the intersection's red light hurts my eyes. There is no excuse for murder, yet even I have to admit that if I had the chance to kill the sonofabitch who murdered Angie, I'd do it with my bare hands.

An explosion of snow hits the windshield and stuns me back to the moment. So much for trusting the weatherman. Weatherman...? Mrs. Warner is an amateur meteorologist? Does that mean something? Yes. Don't make the mistake of underestimating the woman. There is more to her than meets the eye.

The light turns green, I apply the gas gently. My vehicle slides sideways, I correct it, coast through the next intersection, get a red light at the intersection of Victoria and Fifth Avenue and, with the side street to the police detachment now in sight, relax. I turn left. Beyond the detachment, high-rise lights peek through the whiteness. Across the way the detachment's parking lot is barely visible.

The rhythmic thump of the wipers beats time with the edge of my nerves. I can't help wondering if I should question Meshango myself. It isn't my job to make a judgement call, but to follow the leads. I approach the turning lane to the RCMP parking lot on my left—make a snap decision—skid into the lot, make a U turn, slide sideways, and head back. I reach the intersection, continue down Victoria Street, proceed west on Fifteenth Avenue. I click the button on my steering wheel that activates my phone, say, "Carrigan" into the small mic on the visor.

Carrigan answers, gives me the full story on Meshango's interview (or lack thereof). Next, dispatch gives me her address on King Drive. A few minutes later, I pull to the curb in front of her house. Briefcase in hand, I'm at the door before I have time to second-guess my decision.

Two good leans on the doorbell and a husky, feminine voice says, "Just a moment." Locks turn.

When the door opens, I look down at her. One thought beats its way through my subconscious—Damn. If it's true and this is Staff Sergeant Lacroix's woman, whether she's guilty or not, I tell myself not to be a jerk. The man is still my boss.

"Dr. Meshango?"

Her allure is what I expected. Lacroix exudes the self-confidence that comes from having a pretty woman. I never pictured him having a personal life, but recognizing his interest in Meshango is easy. The sergeant has style, even if he is a bear of a man.

She wipes her hands on her apron, purses her lips, gives me the once over. It seems me being Native doesn't mean much. Damn.

I smile.

"Yes?"

I raise my RCMP credentials to chest level as I clear my throat. "Corporal Dan Killian." My voice sounds deeper than normal. I hope the heat in my face doesn't show like a neon sign.

She leans forward to squint at my ID. She smells good, like a home-cooked meal. There is a black satin shine to her hair. Despite sporting a short-cropped style—I prefer long straight hair like Angie's—she's...hot. Dark-brown eyes. I quickly lower my gaze. Small hips.

Damn.

"I'm investigating the Right Honourable Leland Warner's murder."

Her flashbulb eyes stare back at me. "Honourable?"

"Do you have time for a few questions?"

"No."

"Won't take long."

Judging by her narrowing eyes and pursed lips, she's not dazzled by the thought. "This is a bad time, Mr. Killian."

"Actually, it's Corporal." Now seems a good opportunity for some Irish charm. "Just a few questions and I'll be out of your hair. Scout's honour." Besides, it's too late to leave. The damage has already been done.

She studies my fixed gaze. "Scout's honour? Then by all means." She steps back, allowing me past. The door closes with a whish behind us.

Her small feet pad across the hardwood floor towards the kitchen. I follow. A photograph inside a large black frame on the wall catches my eye. The headshot of a stunning beauty, twenty-something, smiles back at me. Her hair's a long, shiny black, but it's her eyes that woo me. Surrounding the black pupils her eyes are a brilliant blue, outlined with a thin black line. The blue, the only colour in the photo, reminds me of the colour of my first car, a refurbished '66 Malibu. Tahitian blue, they called it. Next to her dark skin the entire effect is electric. Despite her blue eyes, I see similarities to the professor. She's Zoë, the daughter.

I catch up with Meshango in the kitchen. She stands at the stove, stirring a pot of rice with a wooden spoon. Whatever is in the larger pot smells great. Beef bouillon, onions, and is that Worcestershire? My stomach growls. "Sure smells good. Beef stew?"

"Moose stroganoff." She turns off the rice, sets the spoon on a small plate, chops onions on the breadboard. "Is it okay if I work?" She chops with confidence, working fast. She goes to the fridge, comes back with a tub of sour cream.

"Okay if I sit?"

"Suit yourself."

I set my briefcase on the floor, grab my notepad and pen from my pocket. Though she's a small woman, the muscles in her upper arms and shoulders are nicely buff. I imagine her trekking through the bush with a 30-06 slung over her arm. Provocative image. Bet Lacroix thinks so.

"Shoot the moose yourself, did you?"

"The meat was a gift from a student."

There goes my next question: If she could kill a moose, would killing a man be so hard?

"You used to be head of the English Department up at UNBC?"

"Yes, Mr. Killian."

"It's Corporal." I smile. I'm a sweet guy, eventually she'll notice. "You teach," I look at my notes, "Ojibwa and Cree?"

"Michif and Cree." She looks at me as if I'm the official dumb student. I bet she's gagging over the impulse to say, "Aren't you my brilliant boy."

"Michif?" I'm not up on Native tongues.

"It's a French-Cree creole." She looks back at what unfortunately is my duh face, adds, "Métis Creole uses French nouns, Cree verbs, and some vocabulary borrowed from Ojibwa and Dené. Why the interest? Are you thinking of taking one of my classes?" She flashes a mischievous smile before turning back to her vegetables.

I chuckle loud enough to let her know I, too, have a sense of humour.

"Do you speak Haida?"

My jaw drops open. Too late to pretend the question hasn't stumped me. "How did you—"

"Gabriel mentioned you were from Sandpit and that your mother was Haida. So say something and impress me."

"*Yank'ein guu dang súu?*" Are you telling the truth?

She smiles.

Had I grown in her eyes, proved I was more than another Indian without language skills. Does that make us equals? It never fails to amaze me how the toughest people to warm up to me are usually First Nations. It's as if because I'm an Indian I have to prove something.

"Don't keep me in suspense. What did you say?"

"I said I hoped your meal is as delicious as it smells."

She gives me that look again, the one that says, "*Yank'ein qwaa?*" Oh really?

I chew the end of my pen, letting my eyes drift away from Meshango towards the snow blowing in swirls past the window next to her. Annoyance boils below the surface. We should have talked this morning. I'd have witnessed her reaction to questions firsthand. I rifle through my notes, hoping to dispel my temper, then reprimand myself for not going to Lacroix first. It would be the courteous thing to do. For instance, right about now I should insist she sit so I can observe her face as she speaks. Dope. I should also insist that because I'm the man here, she show me due respect.

What a chump.

I switch from chewing my pen to chewing the cuticle on my index finger, a bad habit I picked up since quitting cigarettes five years ago. With a strong sense of foreboding, I announce, "We've a small problem, Dr. Meshango."

She stops chopping to glance at me over her shoulder. "We've just met, Mr. Killian. Isn't it a bit early for problems?"

You mean Corporal. I stifle a scowl and check my notes. "Warner died between seven and nine this morning. One of my constables was on his way to interview you when he ran into Staff Sergeant Lacroix in the parking lot, who told him not to bother interviewing you because your alibi was solid. My constable is the paranoid type. He thought he was doing the right thing and took Lacroix' request as an order."

"I spoke to your constable on the telephone a few hours ago."

"That was a different constable."

"I didn't know Gabriel spoke to anyone." She scrapes the

celery off the board and into the casserole. She grabs a green and a yellow pepper from the fridge. She must have decided on a different strategy because suddenly she stops, wipes her hands on her apron, sits across from me. There is a nice symmetry in her movements, the way she rests her chin on her dainty, entwined fingers. The mixture of suspicion and introspection in her dark eyes reminds me of my biology professor, the one who kept expecting more from me, demanding it in the same quiet, challenging way.

"I'm going to share something with you, because I want you to understand Gabriel. But don't abuse my good nature by sharing it with anyone. Understand?" Her eyes narrow in on me.

I don't doubt for a moment crossing Meshango could damage my career. "Okay. Fair enough."

"I have history with the RCMP, which goes back many years. Gabriel knows this. He also understands it took a lot for me to trust him, not without a great deal of effort on his part. Do I make myself clear? He didn't shield me from your questions because he thought I was guilty...he likes to protect me from myself. But he would never jeopardize his career to do so." She studies her clenched hands, and I bet she knows this is a lie. "As you already know, I teach at the Development Centre downtown. I was there at quarter to eight. I have eighteen students who will verify I never left the building until four in the afternoon."

"That'll help."

Dark eyes pull at me. I can guess what she's thinking. How could I betray my people and become a white man's cop? Well, I could say the same about her. At least I'm not sleeping with one.

"I can make a list if you'll share a piece of paper and your pen. I'm sure my students will find it amusing to know their teacher is a suspect in a murder investigation."

Not everyone will find that amusing.

I rip off a sheet, hand over my pen. "Thank you for explaining, Dr. Meshango. Despite being a noble guy, Staff Sergeant Lacroix made a mistake."

"You haven't spoken to him. You came to me first. What does this say about you, Mr. Killian?" She jots down a list of names.

I grit my teeth at the mister reference. How does she know I didn't go to Lacroix?

Even upside down, her handwriting is impressive. Classic, well proportioned. She looks up at me; her eyes sparkle.

I like this woman. "Did you ever have a problem with Warner?"

She shakes her head.

"Was he racist?"

"If you mean was he against Native land rights, I bet you already know the answer. Mr. Warner didn't want European ancestral blood mixing with Native blood. So, yes, he was racist. But not the first or last I'll ever meet."

"Ever have cause to run into him?"

"We ran in different circles." She adds one more name to the list then hands it and my pen back to me. "You'll have to find their phone numbers on your own." The stroganoff gurgles. She goes to the stove, gives it a quick two stirs, lowers the flame, and sits back at the table.

"Mrs. Warner says you've called the house a few times." I'm lying, but she doesn't know that.

"Twice."

"Twice?"

"A week after the boys died. I sympathized with her and wanted her to know she wasn't responsible. I called again this morning as soon as I heard. Both times she hung up on me. I haven't spoken to Mr. Warner since before his son kidnapped my daughter."

"How is your daughter?"

"She's fine."

"That night must have been frightening."

"She's fine."

I scribble Zoë Sheppard in my notepad.

"Gabriel told me about Mrs. Killian. I'm sorry for your loss."

The expression on her face surprises me. She's genuinely sorry. Yes, I like her. "Did the honourable Minister hold you responsible for his sons' deaths?"

"Not that I'm aware."

"Does Mrs. Warner?"

"Yes. But can you blame her? I was the last person to see her sons alive. At the inquest I tried to explain for the record how it happened. Nobody wanted to listen." She shakes her head in disgust. "They were more concerned with the gore, the blood, how many shots were fired, and where I was in proximity to the shooting. Did someone test the blood on my person? Stuff like that."

"Did anything happen that night to indicate Mr. Warner's life was in danger after the fact?"

She hesitates before speaking. "No."

"Is there something you didn't have a chance to mention at the inquiry? Because nobody was listening?"

Again she hesitates. "No."

"It could help if you mentioned it now."

The one hint of her emotional state—she blinks. "Warner's sons hated him."

"You didn't mention that at the inquiry because...you didn't want to upset Warner?"

"The Warners weren't present."

"You knew they'd have access to the transcripts."

"I felt sorry for Mrs. Warner. I didn't even consider him."

"That's because you never liked him. Like father like sons? They put you through hell. You must have resented him."

"It was heart-wrenching to witness her sorrow at their funeral. Mâtowak."

"Sorry?"

"It means woman who cries. One of the Elders at the service gave her the title. It was, and is, fitting. Sally Warner has suffered an unimaginable loss, Mr. Killian." She rests both elbows on the table, clasps her hands together, and again looks genuinely sympathetic. "Sally was a broken woman long before her husband was murdered. Now that he's dead I hope she finds peace. I hope his demons don't come back to haunt her."

"Did the brothers say anything about Warner beating on their mother?"

The look she gives me could match the frigid temperature outside.

"There is no evidence to prove they did, unless you know something." I give her a moment to compose herself and I add, "Have you discussed your suspicions with Sergeant Lacroix? He must have been surprised when you asked him to keep an eye on Mrs. Warner."

One eyebrow arches high. "You're putting words in my mouth, naughty boy." Nothing in her face makes me think she's amused.

"So you don't discuss personal stuff with him?"

"Gabriel is a dedicated police officer. If you doubt that, you should complain to your commanding officer. Or put in for a transfer."

"Forgive my insolence, ma'am. I'm just wondering why he never mentioned that you think Mrs. Warner killed her husband. Which I think you do. A motive would sure make my job easier. Looks like lots of people didn't like the former Minister. Trying to narrow it down is tough enough without interference from what's supposed to be my support system. Sergeant Lacroix shouldn't have interfered. Do I make *myself* clear? Ma'am."

This time both eyebrows lower; she glares at me. Then as quickly her face relaxes. "You are brainless if you think I could

84

sway Gabriel's opinion about an on-going case. He's known all along that Warner was a bad man. I think a lot of people wanted him dead. Mrs. Warner surely did." She smiles.

"That's interesting because she thinks the same about you." I smile back.

"I have an alibi."

Touché.

"Please don't misunderstand, Mr. Killian. Yes, I believe she might have killed her husband. I also believe if you charge her, she should hire the best defence attorney in the country. And if she can't afford one, I'll create a national committee: The Free Sally Warner Campaign."

"That's noble—"

"I'm serious."

"What I was going to say is, that's noble and gracious—considering Mrs. Warner believes you never got over what happened, so you killed her husband two years after the fact. Post-traumatic stress disorder. What makes you think she could have done it?"

"Asking the question proves you know nothing of their history together. If she killed him, it was because Warner molested their sons for years."

"Sorry?" I clamp my mouth shut and, try not to appear baffled. This information could change the direction of our investigation. Why am I hearing this for the first time?

The implications hit me. If this is true, it means our prime suspect is Mrs. Warner. I lean back in the chair and realize the news disturbs me.

I lean forward again. The good professor has offered up some conjecture. Gossip. Probably nothing worth worrying about. "Who told you that?"

"Declan Warner. The night he died."

I shut my notepad, slip it into my pocket, ease myself away from the kitchen table, and stand. Meshango watches me, eyes glistening, anxious to hear what I'll say next. Well then, hope I don't disappoint. "Why are you telling me this now? You know how the law works. I'm surprised you'd volunteer a motive knowing you could send the woman you claim to admire to prison."

"I know exactly what I'm doing. I'm repeating the assertions of a dead man. There is no one to substantiate what I've told you. No proof—unless you find some. Though I doubt you will."

"Why say anything?"

Dark glittering eyes lock on mine. "Because if what I've heard is true, justice means something much different to you."

She knows about Angie. Of course she does. She's living with Lacroix.

And as quickly as the compassion in her face appears, it vanishes. She points her finger over my shoulder towards the front room. "Meanwhile, I'm sure you can find your way out."

This time I can't help but grin. "Not so fast." I reach down, pick my briefcase off the floor, slap it on the table. Unfortunately, she doesn't jump. "I need you to fill out a statement so I can visit a judge downtown and get a warrant to arrest Mrs. Warner for the murder of her husband."

"What? Are you nuts?" she says with a fixed glare.

"You've just given me a motive for the killing. Warner sexually molested his boys, and when his wife discovered the truth, she killed him? When it comes to trial, you'll testify—"

"I'll do no such thing." She thumps back in her seat. "Silly me, I assumed you weren't a complete idiot."

"Careful, ma'am."

"Idiot is as idiot does."

"Maybe we should continue this discussion downtown, where you can explain to me why you didn't mention this at the inquiry."

"For Christ's sake, right out of a *Law & Order* script. So, now that we know how you spend your evenings. Now listen up. Molest: to harass, persecute, torment—"

"You said that Declan told you his father sexually molested him and his brother."

"I most certainly did not. Warner mentally abused his entire family. I never mentioned the word sexually."

"I got my notes right here." I scan several lines of my shorthand. I can't find the phrase.

"Do you conduct all your investigations this way, Mr. Killian?"

"It's Corporal." I glare down at her. She looks more amused than surprised. "You implied Declan told you his father sexually molested him and his brother. Don't try to deny it." I'm tired. I shouldn't be shouting at her like this.

"I said nothing of the kind."

"You let me think he sexually molested his boys."

"Now I'm capable of reading minds, am I?"

"You knew exactly what you were doing. You better tell me right now what the hell you're thinking, or I promise you'll be in handcuffs so fast your pantyhose will knot. Got it? What are you up to?"

"He molested—okay fine, abused those boys. He abused his

wife. What do you think I'm up to? And by the way, I don't wear pantyhose."

"You keep messing with me, and you're going to lose."

She stares at me.

Frustrated, I snap, "Hello?"

"Lose what?" Her voice is soft.

"What are you trying to do?"

"You men are incredibly naïve. Doesn't even matter what colour you are. It's a wonder any of you survive without a woman holding your hand. You know damn well what I'm trying to do. If she killed her husband, she has already paid. Now, goodbye."

She's right. She has no reason to fear me. Lacroix will have me transferred faster than I can say, "Here's some pantyhose."

"Don't leave town, Dr. Meshango."

She's laughing hard by the time I reach the front door.

Back in my car, my hands wind so tightly around the steering wheel that my knuckles turn white. I'm not supposed to be thinking about Angie. But even a dope can understand how the cop in me can't let it go. Revenge is sweet for a reason.

Is revenge what killed Warner? Meshango suggests that he died because he was a rotten husband and father.

Declan died seeking revenge. He killed his brother because Bronson was psychotic, destined to kill again as he killed Norse's wife. He killed himself to ruin his father's political career, and probably because he couldn't live with murdering his brother. Meshango may be right about one thing, if I want to nail Mrs. Warner for the murder, all I have to do is delve into her marriage.

Or I'm being a schmuck, and Meshango killed him. Her attitude seems to teeter between justice and revenge. Shouldn't I have seen the guilt in her eyes? Known immediately if she did it?

I didn't because my head is messed up. Since Angie's murder, my mind feels like a ploughed field after a war, a perfect landscape for an eternity of white crosses. Judge, and ye shall be judged. A lesson from bible class three decades ago. What made me think of that now?

The ice on the windshield evaporates from the metal-burning heat rattling up the defrost vents. Slowly, steadily, the view through the glass clears, like fog dissolving from my brain. No, I don't like what I see. No more than I like what I feel. I'm beginning to sympathize with Mrs. Warner.

I call Carrigan at the detachment. "Have you learned anything from Warner's cases?"

"Honestly, my head hurts reading this crap. It's all a bunch of bureaucratic bullshit. No wonder our penal system is in such shitty condition. Lawyers get their scumbag clients off on technicalities that should never have happened. It's disgusting."

"I was actually referring to our problem, Stan. Did you find anything that might explain his murder?"

"Not yet."

"Do you believe his death is related to one of his cases?"

"What's wrong, Danny? You're the one who says never speculate."

True. "Do you think Warner was an abusive father? Or an abusive husband?"

Carrigan hums and haws. I can tell he feels put upon by the question, but I need his opinion. Since the interview with Meshango, it feels as though my head is on backwards.

"You found something?" he asks.

"I spoke with Meshango and she confirms Declan killed himself in hopes it would destroy his father."

"Shit, that's heavy. I got a teenage monster living in my house, but...I'm pretty sure she's not that far gone. Yeah, I heard stories about Warner. His boys, especially Bronson, were on our radar a few times. But nothing serious, just stupid punk stuff. Every single time we picked one of them up Warner arrived to collect them, and the kid would look scared to death. I figure whatever we did to put the fear of God into them wouldn't compare to what the old man would do when he got them home. If he wasn't in Ottawa, he was here every time one of his boys got in trouble, bailing them out."

"It's a control thing," I say. "Anything from our database?"

"No. And guessing what your next question will be...there were no known shooters in this area at the time of Warner's death."

More bad news. "Thanks, Stan. If you need me, call my cell."

I click off, make a U-turn, head back to the Warner residence.

* * *

Bronson was three before he stopped having potty accidents.

One afternoon I was in town shopping; Leland was home babysitting. One minute I'm standing in the produce department in Overwaitea grocery store and the next moment I'm feeling near panic-stricken. I knew I needed to be home. I broke speed limits driving back. I kept praying I'd burst in to find the boys playing in the backyard, and Leland watching Saturday sports. That's not what I found. I ran through the house. The air was so thick with lemon aerosol deodorizer that its residue layered my tongue. Declan was hiding under his bed. He told me where Leland and Brandon were. I threw the main bathroom door open; it smashed against the wall. Leland had Bronson in a tight grip and was smearing a pair of dirty underwear into his tiny face. My baby could barely breathe, yet Leland kept yelling, "How do you like that? Eh? I warned you, you fifthly little bastard."

I screamed and beat him on his back until he let Bronson go.

Memories—go away!

The clock above the television shows ten minutes to six. I hang up after speaking with my sister. Her ceaseless questions leave me with a throbbing headache. She and her husband are coming up on Monday. She wants to help with Leland's memorial. "I'll be there for you, Sally," she said. I didn't question why. Though part of me still wonders. She was never there for me when I was young and helpless. She attended my sons' funeral alone and left the same night because she had to get home to her adult children and doctor-husband. To heck with her broken sister.

Why the sudden concern now?

Unable to locate plain tea bags in the small kitchenette, I order from room service, then sit and wait. Five minutes later, there is a light knock at the door and I rise slowly. The blood in the veins of my legs has thickened.

Pinscher smiles and hands me my tea.

I can't help but smile back. I hate this room, but I've just had a brilliant idea.

"Will there be anything else?" he asks, preparing to leave.

"Actually, could you please wait a moment."

He stands at attention by the door. Pinscher really is a fine young man.

I set the tea down, grab the phone, and dial my lawyer's number. My patience for waiting has worn thin over the years, and his secretary redirects my call immediately.

"Sally? What's wrong?" my lawyer says.

"Do you have the number for the Prime Minister's office?"

"Huh?"

"I don't have time to explain. Get me the number and call me back." I hang up. Pinscher looks surprised and impressed. I go to the closet, retrieve my coat, and slip it on.

"Mrs. Warner, I don't think it's a good idea to leave your room."

"Why? You're with me."

"That's true, but I have my orders."

I grab my purse and stare up at him. He's blocking the door. "You can drive me home now."

He shakes his head. "I'm sorry, Mrs. Warner."

"Don't be sorry, young man. In a few moments that phone will ring and my lawyer will give me the number I can use to speak directly with the Prime Minister of Canada. I'll tell him I want to go home. He'll hide his annoyance at being interrupted at this hour, but he'll assure me I'm free to go. I'll say there is a young constable stopping me, and he'll tell me to hand you the phone.

"I'd rather not submit you to that humiliation, Constable Pinscher. It's not my style to repay kindness in such a manner. Nor would I want your chances of advancement to be effected by a moment of poor judgement. Because when he's through talking to you, I suspect he'll call the Commissioner of the RCMP to complain."

"Mrs. Warner?"

I hear the frustration in his voice, but I'm not changing my mind. "Think of it this way. Would you rather deal with your immediate supervisor or the Commissioner?"

"I'll deal with either one of them, ma'am. It's my job."

I'm stumped. He's an honourable young man and not responding the way I'd hoped. But I'm not ready to give up. I step around him and open the door. "If I'm not mistaken, your duty is to protect me. I'm leaving with or without you."

Pinscher pauses for a moment, then reaches down and picks up my suitcase. I go with him, out the room, and into the elevator. I steal glances at his expression in hopes that I might read something there. Even though I am desperate to return home, I would hate to think I've lost a friend. Pinscher is good at his job. His face reminds me of Apollo; smooth and impervious.

On the way to the house, he's quiet. The silence makes me nervous. Perspiration has my blouse stuck to my sides. I sniff both shoulders, dreading that I may smell unclean, but it's too cold to tell. His brow is dry. Why shouldn't it be? It's minus fifteen outside. My stomach gurgles, bloats, and now my back aches. I feel uncomfortable in my skin; it's a sensation I haven't experienced for over a year. More accurately, since Declan's and Bronson's deaths, when I lost fifty pounds. I should have gone to the morgue to identify them. I should have insisted, but Leland had said no. He said I didn't need the sight of their dead bodies to haunt me for the rest of my life. But maybe I'd have closure now. I was there when they took their first breaths, I should have been there for their last.

I watch out the window, wipe away a stray tear, and try to think happy thoughts. The moon peeks through a hole in the clouds and casts a warm glow on frost-laden spruce trees waving at us from along the highway. It's a serene view, a naked view, but not powerful enough to lull the silence. I turn and choke out, "It's a lovely evening."

Pinscher doesn't seem to notice my cracking voice. He nods his head but keeps his attention on the road and the temporary whiteout caused by the logging truck ahead. I decide to appease him by saying nothing more. But I wish I had someone to talk to.

Mâtowak: Woman Who Cries

At the top of the hill, Pinscher gets a green light at the intersection and continues onward. The College Heights malls are full. The shops and restaurants are lit up and filled to capacity. The line-up at Tim Horton's drive-through is twelve cars deep. Art Knapps Garden store has three beautifully decorated, probably over seven-foot-tall, trees in their windows. Twenty shopping days until Christmas, yet already the crowds gather.

Christmas? I'd forgotten about Christmas.

My sad visions of what Christmas has in store for me vanish as we pull into my driveway. I'm shocked at what I see. As if for a party, all the indoor lights shine brightly through sparkling windows rimmed in snow, like a scene from a Christmas card. The crystal chandelier over the dining room table fires beams of lights in every direction. Blues, yellows, greens, reds. Snow covers every ledge, trough, and gable outside, transforming our Georgian house into white perfection. The chimney churns out fumes. Like the snow den of a polar bear, it promises warmth and comfort inside.

I squint. There are several police vehicles in my yard. A panel truck, a black SUV, and two patrol cars. We park behind one. Pinscher shuts off the engine, exits the vehicle, and comes round to open my door. He grips my elbow gently and assists me to the sidewalk. Figures move back and forth past the tall windows framing both sides of my eight-foot-high front doors. I hesitate; the constable's grip tightens. I'm not sure what to do now. I didn't expect they'd still be here. I wanted to come home to be alone. Why are they still here? I want them gone.

My larynx constricts as if wiry fingers have seized my throat. My head throbs. Blood pounds through my temples, and my eardrums feel ready to burst.

Something's wrong. I'm home, yet I feel like a prisoner sentenced to life.

My boots shuffle towards the door, making it sound as if I'm walking on cornstarch. I concentrate on slowing my rasped breathing. "Constable Pinscher, has something happened?"

He seems surprised by the question, and I worry whether I've said something I shouldn't.

"Ma'am, they may not let you stay."

"Why? Is something wrong?"

He glances at me with a frown as we head towards the front door. God, will my question ever be answered? Is there something wrong?

"You understand they have to search the house for clues as

to who might have killed your husband?"

"All day?" On the CSI shows I watch, the investigators are only at the crime scene for a few hours.

Through the windows next to the doors, a young woman in coveralls spots me, turns abruptly, and rushes out of view. Where is she going?

"Watch your step. It's icy," Pinscher says as my left foot slips on black ice, and he grabs my arm to stop me from falling.

I smile graciously. He's a good boy. "Thank you." I look back at the door in time to see Killian standing inside the foyer. My goodness, these people are like magicians.

He opens the door and, minus his usual smile, says, "Mrs. Warner? Constable? What are you doing here?"

I step inside and wipe my boots on the mat. Fortunately, I see no tracks of mud past the entrance. I'm still disturbed, though. I smell remnants of a faint, unfamiliar scent, like a powdery dust and chemical mixture. I'm unsure why, but I never realized strangers would search my house. I swallow my fear. "Don't blame him, Corporal Killian. I made him bring me home. This is where I belong."

My words seem lost to him as he hastens to answer his cell phone. "Yes...She just arrived...I haven't had time...I guess so." He shuts his phone with a serious expression. "Mrs. Warner, as I explained this morning, we need to contain the house until every bit of evidence is gathered."

"It's been nine hours. How much more time do you need?" I look into his eyes and wait for the answer. Am I a fool? Is he trying to trick me? I am a shattered woman. It feels as if my brain is floating around inside my head; and though I can't hear the sounds, I'm sure I'm screaming for help. Only he doesn't hear me.

"It's procedure for us to stay until every bit of evidence is collected. I don't need to tell you how important your husband was. There is protocol, and we have to ensure it's met."

"Why?"

His head tilts to the right. "Because every victim deserves justice."

"Justice won't bring Leland back."

Quite suddenly, he starts blinking. Blinking. Blinking. His Adam's apple bobs. His eyes water. Disturbed by his reaction, I wonder: *Am I falling apart or is he?*

Finally, he clears his throat, and glances at Pinscher. "Take Mrs. Warner into the gathering room. And ma'am, don't leave the room until we straighten this out."

I'm about to argue when something in his eyes stops me. He needs my assistance, and I mustn't disappoint him. I nod, take off my coat, gather it in my arms, and go off like the cooperative woman I have always been. I stop. An officer, carrying a small satchel and dressed in white coveralls with white booties, rushes down my staircase. She approaches Killian, who is still standing at the front door, and whispers something. Then she turns, and they both glance at me. I look past them through the front doors and see nothing but a heavy wall of snow falling. Pinscher nudges my elbow. I turn back and continue with him into the gathering room.

I switch on the gas fireplace, and drape my coat over the arm of the chesterfield. Why I didn't hang it up, I'm not sure. I'm not sure about so many things. They're making me feel like a stranger in my own house. I can't let them.

I hang my coat up like I'm performing an act of defiance then return to the room, sit, and face the courtyard and Leland's study just beyond. Pinscher stands next to the doors and glances over my head towards the breakfast room. I am interested in what he's looking at. I do know that the kitchen counter area doesn't show up from here. I study his expression, and once again note he is impossible to read. No frowning, no furled lip.

Sensing that now is not the time to make small talk, I let my mind and my gaze wander. Then I remember my tapes on living in the now and immediately concentrate on my centre, the spot three inches below my belly button. Breathing in gently, out slowly. In. Out. I feel the blood move through my legs, stomach, chest, and arms. Warm, flowing blood. Air. In. Out.

A sudden apparition appears at the end of the chesterfield. Startled, I twist my head in that direction. Thank God I didn't jump. It's Killian. He looks down at me.

What? Am I required to stand? "Your people searched my home all day; they're still here. How many searches do they need to make?"

He looks sympathetically and unwraps the wool scarf from around his neck. I don't remember seeing his scarf before. Actually, I'm sure he wasn't wearing it moments ago. Did he leave and then come back? Did I drift off again?

"It's important and necessary. It's a colossal house, and we'll need access to more searches for possibly up to three months."

Three months? "Should I call our attorney?"

He looks down at me as if I've said something peculiar. How do I know they aren't here to take advantage of me?

Three months?

With furrowed brow, he glances in the direction of the breakfast room, and says, "No need to, ma'am. He'll be here in twenty minutes."

What?

Why?

A chill targets my spine, and my eyelids feel as if they're stuck open. I wrap my sweater tightly around myself, and fold my arms across my chest.

Blink, Sally.

Through the French doors and across the way to my husband's study, an officer rummages through Leland's desk and filing cabinet. How many are upstairs going through, well, who knows what? How many are in the kitchen and the garage?

Bad images cloud my judgment. Why is Corporal Killian disrupting my life? I trusted him. I thought he liked me.

Blink, Sally.

Does he sense my fear?

I focus on comforting visions. Images of blackberry bushes rise in front of me. My gloved hands sweep the stems aside. I concentrate on relaxing by slowing my breathing. Out of my peripheral vision, on the fringe of the room, I see someone hunting through the wet bar and the cupboards beneath. He knocks about on the shelves with only his shoulders and head visible. The small refrigerator door swooshes open, and he looks in. Another officer says something to him and he shuts the door.

What are they after? What have they been doing since I left this morning? I should never have left. I should have stayed and—and—and...

I pull a tissue from my pocket and face the fireplace. Next to it are the French doors leading out back. I dab at the moisture on my upper lip. A gust of wind swirls the white flakes outside, throwing them to and fro. I feel like the snow, my thoughts blowing in many directions.

I twist to the left away from Pinscher's and Killian's scrutiny and, through the other French doors, see a man pass from the breakfast room to the kitchen. He disappears. The upright freezer door opens. The door and adjacent wall block my view, but I imagine him unwrapping each package, then rewrapping sloppily and tossing them aside. He does this until he's opened every package. He returns them to the freezer. I see all this in my mind. After they leave, I'll have to rewrap everything. A voice

96

inside of me says you're being absurd. Of course they wouldn't go through my food. The door closes. Now I sense him going through the pantry...

Fifteen minutes have passed according to the grandfather clock near the entrance wall. I'm grateful I'm sitting in my gathering room and not in my bedroom. The idea that a stranger would go through my lingerie drawer is too much to bear. I feel violated. My skin crawls.

Killian speaks to someone. I turn in time to see Lacroix. I recognize him immediately, though I haven't seen him since my sons died. He's coming this way. I look to Killian for support. He's too busy eyeing his boss. Lacroix sits across from me, but something distracts him near the room's entrance. I drop my hands to my lap and, remembering my *Law & Order* TV shows, try hard not to appear frightened.

I control my breathing, when, quite suddenly, my lawyer appears. Anger and confusion meld together in his expression. Punctuating his voice with wild hand movements, he snaps at Lacroix. Lacroix stands up, takes him by the elbow, and guides him to a doorway clear across the room. In their low voices, I hear phrases like zone search, grid search, integrity of evidence, and something about problematic charter issues. What in blazes are they talking about?

"This is her home," my lawyer barks.

Lacroix speaks too low for me to hear a response.

My lawyer seems more agitated than normal. A few moments later he shouts, "The Commissioner sees no problem!"

Killian gets up from his seat and joins them. He speaks softly. He seems in his element. His expression, calm and controlled, is a quality I have always admired. He is the kind of person who is not frazzled by poor manners or difficult situations. I wonder if there is a dark side to him as there was with Leland, who would fly off the handle at any minor thing the boys did or said, yet in court, remained as calm as a monk. It was a trait that irritated the Crown prosecutors he argued against.

When did he change?

What prompted him to despise me? When did it start?

Why do I bother trying to remember?

* * *

One-year-old Bronson, sitting in his highchair, and Declan in his booster seat. Leland reading the morning paper with his suit jacket draped over the back of the chair so the boys spilling anything on it. Bronson was at the age where he liked to spit out his milk. Leland only had three suits back then. I joined them at the table, moistened a napkin with my tongue, and then dabbed at the food on the corner of Bronson's mouth. He fought, twisting his tiny face right and left.

"I forgot to tell you. I went to the college yesterday afternoon and signed up for more courses."

Leland replied, "What the hell for?"

"Well," I glanced at the boys as if the answer were obvious, "it's time. I was thinking about going back to school and getting my degree in business. Or, you know, a degree in education. I should put all those English courses to use."

"That is not going to happen."

"Pardon me?"

"Don't be stupid, Sally. Your place is with our sons, not trying for some trivial degree."

"Trivial?"

I'm sure I was gaping at him because he lowered the newspaper and smirked. "Our sons are more important than your silly attempt to polish your ego. Besides," he raised the paper, "you should leave the heavy thinking to people with more qualified brains."

"Darling," I remember saying to Leland with a light tone. "I'll have you know, I received good marks in college. I'm quite capable of thinking, thank you very much." I laughed to prove that what he said hadn't burned a hole in my heart.

He lowered his chin and stared at me from under thick, bushy eyebrows.

It was the poet Louis Dudek who wrote, "As language... Silence is also a language."

In that moment, I knew Leland truly did realize how capable I was. Perhaps that's why what happened next came as such a shock. He picked up his glass of orange juice and, with a flick of his wrist, threw the full contents into my face. The juice burned my eyes and went up my nose. I coughed. The boys gawked. Bronson started screaming. By then my vision was blurry, and I couldn't see what Declan was doing beside me. He was as quiet as a mouse.

* * *

My lawyer's loud demands disrupt my disjointed memories. He flings his arms up as if to wash his hands of whatever they've told him. His lips curl back in a comic snarl exposing an expensive set of dentures. Lacroix looks agitated. Killian looks as if he's dealing with children.

My lawyer dismisses Lacroix with a wave of his hand. Lacroix says something to Killian then storms out. The floor under his feet vibrates. Killian and my lawyer close in. I'm trying to remember what happened after Leland threw the juice in my face. All I recall is that I quit drinking orange juice after that.

"I have to leave, Sally, but I'll drop in tomorrow," my lawyer says, buttoning his overcoat. "Don't let these gentlemen intimidate you. This is your house and you have every right to stay." He pulls on his expensive, leather gloves. "Don't get up. I'll see myself to the door."

My head hurts. Squinting, I stare after him until he disappears. I strain to listen and faintly hear the front door close. When I face forward I see Killian and Pinscher watching me.

"You've had an awful day," Killian says. When I don't respond, he turns to Pinscher. "You'll be relieved at midnight. Be back here at eight a.m."

Pinscher nods and then heads towards the kitchen.

"Are you okay, Mrs. Warner?" Killian looks at my hands.

I glance down to see that I've ripped the tissue apart. I still my fingers. "Headache."

"Can I get you something?"

"No. Thank you."

"My people will be finished in a few minutes."

I want to close my eyes.

"We may have to come back tomorrow or the next."

The blue, green and purple flames in the gas fireplace dance.

"Until then, you need to stay out of the kitchen. You have a coffee maker in your room. The cleaning crew will be here first thing in the morning."

I look at him. "Cleaning crew?" He doesn't have to say anything because suddenly I remember the blood, Leland lying on the floor, something dark and mucky spattered on the island's countertop. "Yes, of course."

"It's for your sake."

"I understand."

"Don't be concerned if in the next few days you don't always understand what's happening. It's normal for anyone suffering from shock to be confused."

My head hurts. "Yes, of course."

"After the cleaning crew finish you're free to go into the kitchen and return to some sense of normalcy. Whatever normal means to you."

He means, "Get back on the horse." The analogy makes me want to laugh.

Or does he mean women belong in the kitchen?

"Would you like me to call someone?"

"Who?"

"A friend."

I have no one. "My sister is flying up from the coast on Monday."

"Is there someone closer you'd like me to call?"

"No."

"There will be an officer in the house with you all night. You won't be alone."

"What happened tonight? Why was my lawyer here?"

"After you called and asked him for the Prime Minister's number, he called you back and the hotel reception told him you'd checked out. He was worried and called Staff Sergeant Lacroix, who called me."

"Did I get you in trouble?"

"No."

I believe him. No one can lie with that much sincerity on their face. Besides, I think I saw the beginnings of a smile.

My head hurts, yet I need to ask, "Have you spoken to Professor Meshango?"

"Yes."

"Can you tell me what she said?"

"No. But I can tell you she's concerned for your wellbeing. She asked if you were all right."

Meshango was dealt a terrible blow by my sons. Her compassion doesn't surprise me, though I loathe her. "Do you think she shot Leland?"

"I can't discuss the case."

"I don't think she did. I don't know for sure, but..." His gaze meets my eyes, deep and penetrating. I try to shake the cobwebs away. "I don't know why I said that. I don't know her. I don't know what she's capable of, but I can tell you she's never deliberately done me harm. I thought when Sergeant Lacroix showed up so agitated that something bad happened to her. It's generally love that sends people into such a frenzy."

He smiles briefly.

"Is there anything you need to ask me? Anything Professor Meshango said that needs clarifying?"

Despite his quiet manner and his gentlemanliness, Killian is alert. You can see his life force behind his eyes. There is a depth there that I haven't witnessed in a long time. This is not a happy or contented man. His expression is so thought provoking that I can't tell whether he's setting a trap and I'm falling willingly into it, or if he is the closest thing to a friend I have at the moment.

"Mrs. Warner?"

"Yes."

His eyes sparkle. "It may surprise you to know that Meshango is on your side."

"Corporal, are you laughing at me?"

"No, ma'am." He looks dead serious.

But what does that mean? On my side? No one is ever on my side. "Who is Meshango, really? Do you know?" Why is she more worthy than I?

"Someone who was also caught up in circumstances she had no control over."

I nod. "She survived."

"Yes."

"Is that because of who she is?"

"I don't know. Some people are too plain stubborn not to survive."

Am I too stubborn?

"Do you think she can be trusted?"

His momentary silence interests me. Is it the way I formed the question that has him hesitating?

"I don't know, ma'am."

I frown. "She evokes a strange emotion from me. It has nothing to do with her being a Native."

"I never thought it did."

"It's because Declan chose her as his confidant, and I'll never understand why."

"Will knowing help?"

"Perhaps not." I'm getting tired and suddenly wish he would leave.

"Your husband was a strict father."

The image of a teenage Bronson in his chair flying backwards to the kitchen floor, and the loud crack that followed. How many times did Leland backhand him like that? "Yes."

"Some would even say he was abusive."

I bite my tongue to stop from screaming, *It's true. I didn't protect them.*

Killian's expression is full of pity. I fight to think of what I should say. Then without warning, my body suffers a hot flush, and I'm forced to inhale deeply. My breathing is ragged and grating. I feel dizzy. Agitated.

"He could be cruel," Killian states matter-of-factly.

I pull my sweater away from my throat. Please, don't let me pass out.

Breathe, Sally. Breathe.

How does he know Leland could be cruel? Does the whole

world know? I'm sure I never told anyone.

Did Declan tell Meshango?

Killian keeps his gaze intent on my face. Does he believe what Meshango said? As they believed her that day at the inquiry? I could feel the eyes of the media on me outside the courthouse, like his eyes now. Does he suspect I was a bad mother? Does he think I allowed Leland to break my sons? I watched Oprah for years. I know the mother is usually blamed.

"I tried to stop him." A bolt of ice-cold fear washes over me at the memories. Immediately sweat saturates my blouse, sticking to me like a second skin. Killian continues to stare. I wish I could force him to tell me what she said. Why is he torturing me like this? I thought he liked me. "I tried to protect them. I screamed. I beat his back, his head. I pulled his hair. I threatened to ruin his career. The saving grace was he was absent for most of their childhood. When he got out of control, I—I made him stop. When they reached their teens, I was too weak. I..."

In my mind's eye I hear Leland shouting obscenities. Globs of spit stick to the corners of his mouth. The whites of his eyes are etched with bolts of broken blood vessels; they match his clown-shaped nose. Before I'd reach for another drink, I'd stare at him and wonder where my soothing fantasies had gone. Why didn't I know who he would turn into?

I stuff the shreds of tissue into my left pocket, produce a fresh tissue from my right and dab my upper lip. Did I say too much? Killian watches me as if he's witnessing my mental demise. I press the tissue to my lip, and our eyes lock. What is he thinking? It's difficult to tell.

It's not me he's frowning at, it's something behind me. I turn in time to see Pinscher with a group of investigators all dressed in white coveralls. Pinscher is still wearing his coat, but has his hat off in my house and is holding it with both hands. Pinscher is a good boy.

"Excuse me, Mrs. Warner." Killian leaves his seat and joins his people near the entrance to the receiving hall. They whisper. I face the window and watch snow blanket the terrace. In the glass I see reflections of men and women grouped together on the fringe of the room. I strain to listen but hear only indecipherable murmurs. Finally, Killian says, "Good night," and they disperse, leaving my house by the front door. A weak breeze grabs my ankles and sends shivers up my legs.

He returns. His coat is still unbuttoned. He sits across from me. "Can I get you anything before I leave?"

An inextricable thought struggles to release itself from my

mind. I feel on the verge of knowledge momentarily unobtainable, yet willing to spare me great confusion if only I try harder. My visible world comes in colours of red and blue in the gas fireplace; browns, crèmes, greys in this room; and white, perfect white outside. Everything around me is a model for the normal, yet I'm stunned at how abnormal my world feels as if I'm a displaced visitor. I have brief memories of peace—recently. Leland and I comfortable in our language of silence. His breathing a form of recognisable security. We exhaled in unison. For a time.

"I'll have Constable Pinscher bring a pot of tea up to your room."

I have a sudden compulsion to reach out and grasp his arm, beg him to stay, and plead that he be my steadfast friend.

"May I walk you to your room, Mrs. Warner?"

"A cup of tea sounds nice." I lean my chin on my icy-cold fingers.

He looks at me strangely. "You must be tired. Would you like to go up to your room?"

I'm sinking into the leather-soft chesterfield. Leland gave up telling me when to retire for the night years ago when I began spending more time in my room than out. No reason to venture into the rest of the house. My needs were met, and I felt safe. No confrontations, no danger, no explosive outbursts.

No threat of that now.

"Will you be okay tonight?" Killian asks.

His thick black eyelashes lower for a split second before his gaze into my eyes becomes hypnotic. He sees my depression. I nod. Then burst into tears. I don't want to need his protection, but how can I not?

Mrs. Warner sobs big round tears. Her grey-yellow face twists into a moment of ugliness. Her shoulders shake. I remember the name the Elders gave her: Mâtowak. They were right; it fits. But does it tell the whole story of the woman who cries?

I tug at my collar, hoping to ease the blood pounding in my neck. Pressure builds. My jaw aches. Her words are caught in my throat. *Justice won't bring him back.* I came close to letting my emotions overtake me when, for an instant, I saw a glimpse of my life after Angie's murderer is caught and convicted. A life empty and fragmented.

I should ask her if she killed her husband. She's vulnerable. I could study her expression and determine whether she's telling me the truth. With any other case, that's exactly what I would do. So, why don't I ask?

I shudder. I've been moving through the investigation like someone suffering from PTSD.

I leave her, locate the washroom near the kitchen, grab some tissues from the box, return, hand them to her. She wipes her eyes, cheeks, blows her nose.

I sit down. "For your sake, tell me."

She looks questioningly at me. Her eyes spill over with tears.

"Did you kill him?" I ask.

Wet eyes, half-shut. She looks as if shock had sucked blood from her face.

"If you did, I promise I'll do whatever I can to help you. I'll speak to the Crown. I'll go to the Supreme Court of Canada if that's what it takes. There are lots of people who want to help. Your husband's assistants. Dr. Meshango. Your lawyer. Your friends at church. The attorneys at your husband's firm." I pause. "Did you kill him?"

"He was all I had left. I'm alone now." She hangs her head. "How will I bear it?"

"Did you kill him?"

"Why would I do such a thing?"

All the victims I've interviewed over the years who know this pain are here now. I see the faces of parents, grandparents, sisters, brothers. Life beats you down. Being strong or weak has little to do with surviving. This much they taught me. It's a game. Some lose. Some skate through. For some the loss is inevitable. For others...no rhyme nor reason explains it. No fault can be assigned.

She sinks lower in the sofa, a woman rotting away from guilt. Her sons are dead because she stood by and watched her husband break them. She stood by and did nothing. I understand her anguish. How many times during our last week together did I promise Angie I'd be on time for our appointment? At one point I got annoyed that she kept reminding me. Yes, I'd pick her up at the shop, and we'd drive over to the realtor's together on her lunch break. She only had an hour. I was forty minutes late. Now purgatorial fires can't extinguish my shame. Sure, on an intellectual level I know I'm not to blame–I didn't stab her. Most days I run on empty, in a perpetual fog. If I wasn't at fault, who was? The killer? Or the husband who didn't show up on time because he was at work, brown-nosing? And Angie, tired of waiting, walked to her car. There her life ended. Someone decided she had to die while I was at work, concerned more for my career than my marriage.

Asshole.

What else do you call a man who betrays his wife, and then can't solve her murder? Go ahead guilt—chomp away.

Through the tall windows snowflakes float, spiral back onto themselves, controlled by a wind they can't fight. They sneak between the frameworks of the pergola, land on the powdery ground. It's a tranquil scene devoid of violence—yet, in my life violence and anger are never far away. Seeing Mrs. Warner like this, I recognize her thoughts. Why embrace life if it's this painful?

Is the answer to accept a drugged version of reality? Or accept whatever else drifts by and call it destiny.

"Don't let me down," Angie said the morning she died. "I can't go on like this, Danny. Please, be there."

I'm cold from the voices that haunt my mind, accusing me, reminding me Angie would be alive if not for my selfishness, my lack of duty as husband. My disloyalty. I sense Mrs. Warner understands what it means to be possessed like this. She's driving herself crazy, too.

"Are you going to be okay?"

She wipes her eyes, blows her nose again, nods.

"Are you sure? Can I call someone? Do you want me to get Pinscher?"

She shakes her head. "I want to sit here by the fire." She wraps her sweater tighter. Her gaze stays fixed on the flames.

I watch her a moment. Is there something more I should do?

Idiot, you've said enough already.

I jerk free of thoughts that make me feel like her accomplice. I button up, wrap my scarf around my neck. Hat in hand, I say goodnight. Haunted by Mrs. Warner's nightmares, I leave through the front door.

Bronson liked to brutalize anyone who crossed his path, but Declan terrorized one person: Meshango. Did they learn cruelty from their father?

I glance back at the house and know in my gut that it's possible Mrs. Warner had killed him. She had the means and the years of abuse to justify murder. There isn't another person I can link to the crime—not Meshango, not Norse. At least not yet.

Maybe Mrs. Warner reacted so emotionally just now because she regrets murdering him? Like she says, she's alone now. Better to be with an abusive husband than with no one?

But she'd said Warner changed. He wasn't the same man after their boys died. Then what brought him down today? Or is she lying about that, too?

And what in the hell is Meshango up to? I can find that out, at least. I'll also find out what kind of man Warner was. I'll need proof of the man's abusive nature if we find enough evidence to arrest Mrs. Warner. Dates, facts.

If she told me the truth and she didn't kill him? No harm done. As far as the brass is concerned, we don't have a suspect. We're still actively investigating the crime.

I shake my head at the justice system, a bureaucratic wasteland. I wonder how many murderers get away with their crimes, and how many don't but should have. A sharp pain stabs me between the shoulder blades, and my breath catches. Inhale. This glitch in the investigation could have been resolved if I'd interviewed Meshango this morning, and not at the end of a long day when fatigue had me jumping through hoops.

Besides, we work as a team. The day I have to do everyone else's jobs, will be the day I quit. Okay, so the investigation started off badly. So be it. Meshango is still our prime suspect. At least until we verify her eighteen alibis. And I don't give a flying rat's ass who she's living with.

At the south end of the property, a lone birch tree towers above the row of dense blue spruce. The moon looks to be caught among its branches. I stare at the moon, will myself to move. Another sharp pain between my shoulder blades, and

I concede that Meshango is as innocent as Norse. They both had the opportunity to kill Warner long before today, but for whatever reasons, reasons I don't care about, chose not to.

This morning Warner stood straight and confident, challenged by little more than the complexities of minor cases piling up in his office. At the end of the day, he lay on a slab in the morgue. Bringing us to the all-important question: What happened today to contribute to or facilitate his murder?

It is this simple: Find out what was different about today and we have his killer.

I try imagining Mrs. Warner pushed to the edge, willing to do the unthinkable, kill the abusive husband turned nice guy. That would make it a crime of passion. But where's the evidence? A single shot doesn't imply passion. A clean crime scene doesn't imply passion. A suspect void of gun powder residue, blood splatter, trace residue, doesn't imply passion.

Angie's murder wasn't this clean, yet her murderer still walks. Spasms of pain shoot into my neck. I clench and unclench my fists, surprised by my reaction. It's been six months. I rub the back of my neck. Is it the cold or thoughts of Angie that bring tears to my eyes, a lump in my throat? I have a right to be angry. She's dead and she did nothing to deserve it. She wasn't like Warner. Her life was simple. Guiltless and innocent.

On days when the sky is clear, and my head doesn't feel all messed up, the idea that somebody will solve her murder—the killer behind bars doing twenty-five years in maximum security—leaves me feeling hopeful. As if life might become bearable and I'd be left...satisfied. Except I can't imagine anything replacing the pain I feel every day of my life since her death.

Mrs. Warner nailed it: *Justice won't bring him back.*

Solving Angie's murder won't place her next to me, her hand in mine, her breath against my throat. If it's like I think and God doesn't exist, then ceasing to be means nothing. You die. Your flesh rots. You no longer are. People forget about you. When the last person who knows you dies, it's as if you never existed.

After I'm dead and gone, when her family is dead and gone, will anyone remember Angie Killian? Will the killer's thoughts be the one thing linking her to this world? Will appeals for a lighter sentence be the link keeping her memory alive? Wouldn't it be better for everyone if that asshole was dead, too?

I aim the remote, press the necessary buttons to start my car. The engine roars to life, sending exhaust fumes billowing towards me. I wipe my hands down my face, shiver at the coldness, and curse myself. I'm not here to judge. Damn, how many times do I need to remind myself of that? I'm supposed to gather evidence and make an arrest. It's the court's responsibility to render justice.

In a perfect world, I'd hunt down and kill the man who took Angie from me because I live to see the bastard gagging on his own blood, suffering the way he made her suffer.

I hesitate on the edge of the sidewalk. A snowplough speeds past the driveway. Snow and sand spray the ditches, leaving the road left behind as clean as an airport tarmac. What would I do if I came face to face with Angie's killer? Would I be capable of doing my job? Or would I become the criminal?

I squeeze my eyes close, shout inside my head: *Stop thinking about her. Job. Job. Job. Think about the damn job.*

My cell phone rings. I answer without looking at the view window. "Killian."

"Hey, Dan," one of the lawyers from the Crown's office says cheerfully. "How's it going, buddy?"

Of course. They'll come out of the floorboards and hustle to get this case. High profile, sure to have benefits attached.

"Don't have a suspect yet."

"Damn, eh? I was just checking."

"Why?"

"Oh, well, there is a rumour..."

"What rumour?"

"You may have a suspect."

The muscles in my neck cramp. "Who told you that?"

"Obviously you don't have a suspect."

"I'll hand the file over when and if we do." I hang up. Not exactly a cordial approach if I want a friend at the Crown's office. Except at this precise moment, I don't give a damn.

The phone rings—The Crown again.

"Killian," I say.

"Sorry about that, man."

"You're apologizing when I'm the one who hung up on you?"

"No. I'm apologizing because you've got a bitch of an investigation. And me calling prematurely ain't helping. Sorry, man."

I close my eyes. Is Warner worth this bullshit? "I shouldn't have hung up on you. You're right, the case is a bitch."

"Of course it is. Take it easy."

I say, "Yeah, you too," and then sign off.

Rubbing the back of my neck, I sense someone watching me from the house, but don't look. First thing tomorrow I'll question the family physician, get the coroner's report, have my people interview anyone who might suspect Warner was a tyrant to his family. We'll talk to his assistants here and in Ottawa, all the lawyers who have ever worked for him, and as many of the prominent mourners at his funeral we can reach. All under the guise of searching for a murderer. If even one person asks why the personal questions about the vic's family life, my team will supply a pat answer, a statement with a measure of truth to it: *Knowing the victim often leads to the killer.*

I step off the sidewalk and shuffle towards my car. The snow slows my movements. The exhaust fumes from the vehicle increases my headache. The list of things I have to do first thing in the morning rests heavily on my mind. I pull my cell phone out, whip off my gloves, and call the coroner's personal cell phone.

"Do you remember the autopsy report on Warner's sons?" I ask when Carmie answers.

"Good evening, Danny. How are you?"

Her comment feels like a sentry in my head. I smile. Right. Remember your manners, buddy. "I'm good, Doc. How are you?"

"Tickedy boo. Give me a sec and I'll pull the files."

I step into a slushy pile of snow, open the driver's door, climb in. My soaked pant legs send chills up my legs.

"What did you want to know?" she finally says.

"Declan and Bronson were in their twenties at the time of their deaths?"

"Yes. Bronson was twenty-three and...Declan was twenty-eight."

"By chance, were there any old bruises? Scar tissue or anything consistent with abuse?"

Dead noise echoes back at me. I flick up the heat and fan, watch as the small mound of fog dissipates on the inside of the windshield.

"The usual scars you'd expect, but nothing indicating abuse. A few hockey injuries. Sorry, Danny."

"Thanks, Carmie."

"They're doing the autopsy in Kamloops first thing tomorrow."

"Great."

I click off my phone, grab the scraper, and climb out. I clear off the hood, windshield, back window while my wet pants smack against my legs.

Listen to what your evidence is telling you.

The hell with this. I don't care what time of day it is.

I jump back into my car, turn the defrost on full blast, dial Meshango's number. The phone rings twice.

"Straight answers," I say, once I recognize her voice. The thought that Lacroix might be there flashes through my mind.

"You mean rather than my usual crooked ones?"

"Is it possible that Declan was lying to you about his dad?"

"Oh sure, he killed himself as a joke."

"What if it was all about you? He was playing you?"

"No."

"Then tell me something, anything."

I hear a deep sigh. "Declan felt responsible for leaving his little brother behind when he left home. He thought he should have stayed to protect Bronson. He decided to destroy his father as a last act of revenge."

"It worked. Within a year of their deaths, Warner retires from politics, giving up any hope of ever becoming Prime Minister. Any school records that might prove Warner abused his sons?"

"No. Why? Are you trying to find...?" I hear a softening in her tone.

"Is there anything at all I can use to prove what kind of husband and father he'd been?"

"If you talk to the right people." The hardness in her voice is back. "Their friends, doctor, school nurse, pastor. Please don't tell me I have to do your job for you." She hangs up.

I can't help it—I laugh.

My laughter sounds like a horse neighing. I shut my mouth, put my phone away, slam the shift stick into drive. None of this is funny. And I'm tired. Trying to understand a woman, particularly Meshango, without a decent night's sleep is stupid. Why can't people just say what they think without all the games?

I stay inside the minivan's earlier tracks, drive out onto the road, paying special attention to the patches of what the weatherman reports as black ice. On the coast I remember wondering what the hell they meant. Ice isn't black. Now I know. Half a block later the car's rear end hits a black spot, slides sideways. I right the vehicle. Adrenaline rush.

No more delays—I'll have the shop install studded tires in the morning.

Conscious of the faint ache in the back of my neck, I park, enter the detachment. It's late. I can't bring myself to go home. The house in Fort George is just a house. Without Angie no place is home.

The ache in my neck worsens. I've a couple of choices. Either visit a chiropractor or a sweat lodge. Or the third, suck it up.

Focus on the job.

My stomach growls.

The vending machine holds two of my favourite chocolate bars. Three painkillers later, accompanied by a mouthful of coffee and one of the bars, I roll up my sleeves, read over the crime reconstruction report from Surrey.

Gauthier, the investigator on the case, someone I've worked with in the past, left a voice message saying he'd call me after his interview with Warner's assistant in Ottawa. Though Warner hadn't worked with her for almost a year, Gauthier thinks she'll have insight into the man nobody else can give us.

GIS Security at House of Commons writes down the additional questions I have for Warner's assistant and promises they'll pass them along. After ample assurances that I'll hear back from Ottawa ASAP, I hang up. It's amazing how cooperative everyone is when the victim's an ex-minister. Normally, I'd have to wait until morning to get anywhere.

Mâtowak: Woman Who Cries

I finish the last chocolate bar, switch on the computer. The analysis program used to profile cases doesn't give much. Once again I key in the particulars. Immediately it comes back flashing Mrs. Warner's name. Probability strong.

"Where's the evidence?"

No gunpowder residue was detected on her person or her clothing. No weapon. The shell casing is missing. There were no tire tracks or footprints on the property. So far, no records or files hint at political improprieties; none of the nasty e-mails most politicians live with daily. No revenge-seeking stalkers. No hint of a jilted lover.

I chew the cuticles on my right hand as I visualize Mrs. Warner squeezing the trigger. Anybody is capable of murder if the right buttons are pushed.

We took swabs of the skin on her arms, hands, and face. We found no bleach or any chemical able to cover up gunpowder on her skin. Nothing was found in the toilets, her bedroom or closet, the laundry, shower, drains, or vacuum filters.

She wore long rubber gloves?

Up to her armpits?

Where are those gloves now? Where are the clothes she wore? Nothing was found in the garbage. The lab found nothing suspicious in any of the six fireplaces. The grounds weren't disturbed in her garden. Nothing was discovered in the bushes or trees bordering the circumference of her property. Nothing outside the kitchen window. How did she dispose of the gun? She had an hour at best.

I fidget with my pencil, scribble "motive" on the pad in front of me. She's Warner's beneficiary, but she seems helpless without him. There are no large cash withdrawals from any of her accounts. If she didn't kill him herself, how did she pay for a hit? If guilty, why is she so distraught?

Am I looking for something that isn't there? Am I wasting my energy on the wrong suspect?

I jot down a note to check Sophie Brooks' and Brendell Meshango's bank accounts. In a joint effort, they could've hired someone.

The first forty-eight hours of a case are vital. The clock's ticking in my head. I should go home, and let tomorrow sort itself out. Some of the reports might be completed by tomorrow.

"Listen to what your evidence is telling you."

Hard to do if you have no reports to analyze. I flip through the few reports I do have, check transcripts from Ottawa again. As Carrigan reported, GIS confirmed there are no known hired guns in the Prince George area. The organized crime units, who specifically target biker activity, can account for every suspected gangland shooter from Vancouver to Halifax. No one is known to be in this area. Besides, nothing links Warner to organized crime.

I make a note to have as many political bank accounts checked as possible. But I know a judge will never permit it without evidence of suspicion. It's not common to investigate a murder and obtain little evidence from the scene. Though, in cases where the body is dumped, there is often little evidence available. We ran into that same problem with remains found off Highway 16. But Warner died at the scene, and we should have been swamped with evidence.

I wipe a hand over my face. Whoever killed Warner knew how to commit a clean crime. Somebody with basic knowledge of crime scene forensics. Mrs. Warner? No. Or is that me saying I don't want her to be guilty?

I crack the file open to her written statement.

"Thursday, December 3, I woke at 6:47 precisely. The exact same time for two previous mornings. Five minutes later I met Leland at the landing leading down to the receiving hall. He retrieved the newspaper from the slot outside the front door and joined me in the kitchen. He sat down at the breakfast table and read the paper front to back. This was something he did every morning. I poured two coffees. I prepared and served breakfast. I toasted two extra English muffins, since it was a particularly cold morning, and placed them with an assortments of homemade jams on the table. Leland handed me the Arts and Entertainment section while he continued reading the Sports section."

At this point she asked Constable Ryan if this was too much information. He said no, so she continued.

"Leland fed Digger the last of his muffin as I returned upstairs to my room."

Officers later found the appropriate dirty dishes in the sink.

"I volunteer a few times a week. I used to volunteer four days a week, but my feet won't let me. I'm down to two days, except for the four days a month I volunteer at the cancer clinic. Wednesdays, I work four hours at the United Way office on Brunswick Street. When I came down at nine, I found Leland. I knew from all of the CSI shows I watch not to touch him. I called 911. I waited by the front entrance for the police and ambulance to arrive."

Maybe watching CSI was the teaching ground for committing the perfect crime? Her handwriting didn't deteriorate even slightly, not even when she reached the part of finding the body.

She ended the report by apologizing for going on too long: *I ramble when I'm upset.*

Angie had the same habit. A Newfoundlander born and bred, when she was nervous she could talk so fast only another Newfie could understand her. I smile at the sound of her accented voice running through my mind—flip to the police report. Pinscher, the first officer on the scene, general duty constable, found the service door ajar, Mrs. Warner hysterical. Her initial response, repeated several times was, "What will happen to me now?" That's a common thought among survivors. Generally, their first thought is concern for themselves.

I yawn while rubbing the fatigue from my forehead and eyes. My headache is gone, but not the pain in my neck. I should quit for the night and go home. But I can't. I have to figure out why Warner is dead. What does his death accomplish? Or what hadn't his life provided? I knead my fingers into the muscles in my neck. Peace of mind for Declan Warner? Declan is dead. Political enemies, disgruntled client? The victim received no threats. Sally Warner out for revenge? Her own form of justice two years after their sons died.

The clock on the wall shows nine twenty-five. I search through the file, locate the cell phone number for the Warner family doctor, dial. I get the answering service, so I leave a message. I read the interviews my team recorded during their canvass of the neighbourhood. Drum my fingers on the desk...

My phone rings. It's the doctor. I introduce myself.

"It's late. One of my patients is in the case room as we speak. Can't this wait until tomorrow?"

"Why didn't you mention possible child abuse when the constable interviewed you this morning?" My gruffness surprises me, but I'm fed up with people concealing information.

"Child abuse? What are you talking about?"

"Allegations have been made that Mr. Warner abused his boys."

"Who said that? Leland went overboard disciplining them. That's all."

"That's all? What exactly is your interpretation of child abuse, doctor? Why didn't you report him?"

He clears his throat. "Corporal...Killian, is it? Those boys were a handful. Especially Bronson. Leland did what he thought best. Sometimes force was called for. It's unfortunate, but—"

"So he broke a few bones?"

"Nothing that serious. The man occasionally lost control. The youngest boy, Bronson, was belligerent. Declan was clinically depressed. I tried to intervene on the boys' behalf. I set up appointments with a family counsellor. Leland refused to go."

Belligerent? The kid was a psychopath. "What about Mrs. Warner? Couldn't she reason with Warner?"

"You're joking, right? Sally was a fixture, nothing more."

"She ever come in with bruises or broken bones?"

"I'm not comfortable answering that question without her consent."

"Did you like the man, Doctor?"

"Not especially."

"Did he beat her or didn't he? Simple question."

"Let's just say...he didn't have to."

I set the soles of my shoes firmly on the floor.

"After the boys died," he adds, "Leland changed. But before that, long before that, he broke her. That's all I can tell you. Don't try a subpoena, I know nothing more. If I did, it's privileged. Goodnight."

I replace the handset and lean back in the chair. Once again, I imagine Mrs. Warner shooting her husband. It's a clear and sad image, one without evidence. Except for one important clue: Leland Warner was a lousy husband to a broken woman and an abusive father to two destructive boys. Did she reach her limit? What was the final straw? Did Warner say or do something to set her off? It would have had to be big. Or maybe not.

I check the stats on both boys. Neither one was born on December third.

"Listen to what your evidence is saying." I yawn, rub the whiskers on my chin, flip the report back to page one.

* * *

After Killian and the others left, I remained in front of the fireplace until my legs felt as if they are full of mercury. Outside the bedroom window, snowflakes the size of loonies fight against the wind to reach earth. I watch and feel glued to my chair. Now I sit at my bedroom window beyond exhaustion.

My mind is closing down, faking its hold on reality.

I look behind me. Strangers with sticky fingertips have touched my things. I dread going into my closet. I imagine the disarray, my clothes and personal articles tossed about, the contents of my drawers disturbed. Tomorrow I'll see for myself what they did. When the investigation is over, what I can't sell, I'll give away. I'll start over. With enough to make do.

I pull my sweater tightly across my chest. My vision takes in the greenbelt protecting our property from the road. Closer to the house is our snow-covered circular driveway and the front gardens, so lovely in spring and summer with a display of foliage and shrubbery. I exhale, expecting my breath to expel as steam.

In the east, creeping moonlight scars the edge of midnight. I shiver. As if on command, the furnace cuts in, blowing warm air from the floor vents into the room. It tickles my skin. The small refrigerator on the sidewall hums a deep mechanical exhale. Silence being underrated, I reconfirm my decision. When this is finished and the nightmares have ended, I'll start over.

"Simple as that."

I rise slowly, put weight on my numb feet, and shuffle off to bed. As I slip beneath my duvet, imaginary blackberry bushes sweep aside. Their thorns are harmless. I settled in, tuck the duvet beneath my chin, and curl into a foetal position. Fatigue pulls my thoughts into glassblower streams of semi-molten crystal. Drifting, floating. The existence of a damaged woman. Darkness, numbness descends upon the second worse day of my life.

I don't believe I can withstand a third.

I pull into the RCMP shop first thing the next morning, set my keys on the counter, ask for studs to be put on.

"Sorry, Corporal, no can do..." the service manager points to the calendar on the wall behind him, "until tomorrow. Ouch, that'd be Saturday—so more likely Monday."

"Okay. I'll take a courtesy car."

"I think you've mistaken us for a dealership."

I retrieve my keys off the counter. "I'm supposed to do what exactly?"

The head mechanic, overhearing the conversation, wipes grease from his hands with a dirty rag, looks from the service manager to me to the service manager. They share a glance that makes me squirm.

Finally, the service manager gives me a sympathetic shrug, points towards the bay doors to the flurries outside. "If you drive like you got no brakes, you should make it."

"You're joking?"

The mechanic laughs.

"Funny."

"You got me," the service manager says. "Leave your vehicle and take one of the patrol cars."

I know it's stupid, but I haven't driven a patrol car since Angie died. It's not something I can explain, except to say that I'm Haida. We're a superstitious bunch. I shake my head.

"Okay, so, leave your car here. We'll get to it when we can. Have somebody pick you up."

I think about it.

"You're driving on summer treads. You got a death wish? You better take one of the patrol cars. You got to be a damn good driver to travel on these highways without studs."

Everyone knows I'm from the coast. The theory is nobody south of Cache Creek can drive on snow. I wait for them to laugh, not sure I'll say something pleasant in return. What I see looking back at me are straight faces, not exactly concerned, more like fascinated.

A layman talking to a professional, I open my mouth, and

say, "I'm not driving on summer tires. They're all seasons."

The head mechanic chomps down on his upper lip. His eyes sparkle.

The service manager shakes his head. "Whoever told you that must have been dumb and blind. They're not just summer treads, they're worn summer treads."

"Yeah, well, guess I'll leave the car here." I drop my keys, face away from them, pull the cell phone from my pocket. Ryan's line is busy.

Carrigan's line is busy.

I try both constables again.

Still busy.

After the third attempt, I swear, and swing around.

The service manager holds my keys out to me. "Stay off the side roads."

I'm not stupid, so I nod. Then I remember my manners. "Thanks. I'll see you tomorrow."

He shakes his head. "Monday."

The head mechanic raises his chin to look down the rim of his nose. "Good luck."

Funny.

On the way to work I turn into the entrance to Tim Horton's Donuts and slide four feet before coming to a stop—two feet from the fender of the car in front of me. Okay, so the service manager has a point. Although, last week one of the guys said he drove all winter on all seasons. He said, "It's all about experience, Danny, my boy."

I'm guessing now he was pulling my leg. Jackass.

I shift into low, deciding to place my order at the drive-thru.

With my special blended coffee and six-pack of old-fashioned donuts in hand—it used to kill Angie to see me eat this way and never gain a pound—I exit the drive-thru. On the way to the detachment I keep my foot off the brake and gear down, narrowly miss a patrol car.

I park.

Walking across the road requires more skill than I expected. A skater I'm not. I watch my footing on the sidewalk and reconsider driving a patrol car.

The detachment smells like burnt coffee and oiled leather, two of my favourite scents.

During several telephone calls, I consciously make an effort not to glance at my watch. At one point I feel someone looking down at me. I glance up to see Lacroix and his oh-so-friendly scowl.

"Rumour has it you're still driving on summer treads."

"I've got an appointment Monday to have new studs put on."
I give him my confident I-know-the-score face.

"Good. Before somebody tickets your ass." He walks away.

I'm dying to see him with Meshango. Can't imagine him talking to her with that look on his face and getting away with it. "Okay, woman, bend over." Yeah, right.

I attend the morning meeting, verify what the file coordinator shows on the wall monitor, and then return to my desk to settle down to work. Reports have come in overnight. When I get up to refill my coffee, I check the new reports on the Highway 16 missing cases. I was taken off those cases but that hasn't stopped me from tracking their progress.

Missing persons has a new entry. The DNA from the body found in Haines Junction didn't match the DNA of the young woman gone missing in early February or the tree planter missing since May of last year. Both were last seen on Highway 16, one near Mud River, the other on the outskirts of Moricetown. Both remains were found near Mackenzie.

Now there is a third missing person.

I fill my coffee, return to my desk. I understand the families' need for closure. Life won't resemble anything normal until Angie's killer is brought to justice.

My phone rings.

"Killian."

"*Comment ça va?* Danny? It's me, An're."

I sit up straight, glance at my watch. "Andre. Thanks for getting back to me so fast. What did you learn?"

"I know you get static on this one, *mon ami*, so I visit on my way this morning the assistant. I fax her statement when I think you like to hear what she say." Paper rustles. "First thing is how come it take so long to ask about the other womens." Gauthier clears his throat. "She say her boss return from Prince George after the boys' funeral a changed man. She say he's no gift to secretarial pool before. Not to mean he turn nice either, just too sad to care."

"She confirmed the rumours about girlfriends, for sure?"

"She say to me, Monsieur Warner poke pretty well all womens in 5-kilometer of his office. I get three name you check there in Prince George. But remember all that change when his boys die. He new minister and take many more thing serious."

"Did she have any theories on who might have killed him?"

"No. She say to me his murder terrible. She don't understand why somebody want him dead. We talk political rivals. She think

119

he step on people but nothing monumental. She don't say, but I think she think he not important enough to kill."

"Yesterday she had good stuff to say about Mrs. Warner. Anything change?"

"No. She say to me Madame Warner not always treated wit' respect. Just like assistant, I think. The assistant say to me nobody deserve what Madame endure. She free to go home at night. The wife not free—"

"Did she suspect Mrs. Warner capable of murder?"

"Oh, she say Madame sooner choke to death than hurt a moose. *Excusez-moi*, I mean la souris...a mouse." Gauthier shuffles more papers. "I say to myself this woman *préjudice*."

"If he made such positive changes in the government, how come he retired? Somebody scare him off?"

"After the boys die, his heart no longer in politic."

Which is what Mrs. Warner told me. "Why did he accept the posting as Minister of National Defence? Because he never planned on serving long-term?"

"*Oui*."

"So there is no connection between his death and the party not planning to approach him about running for leadership?"

"They seem pretty happy wit' Monsieur Turnbridge. Back then, anyway." Gauthier laughs at his own joke. The House of Commons had voted a non-confidence motion last week.

"There is nothing to lead us to Ottawa?"

"No."

I hesitate. Chide myself. I'm supposed to be an instrument of facts, but there aren't any. "About the accusation?"

Gauthier is quiet for a full two seconds. "Oh, you mean abuse? I give two hint before she say Monsieur Warner's personal business none of hers no matter the many rumour of abuse. So, I ask for her confidence and help. She say he a lot of thing, a real bugger, and *oui*, he beat his boys. I say did she see him beat his boys. She say no, she did not see he beat his boys. But she know. She say a mother know these things. That may be true, but no help in court, eh? Also, she say check wit' doctor. Warner like women too much, *il aime trop les femmes*."

"Gonorrhoea?"

"Three time."

Interestingly, the doctor failed to mention that. "Did they keep in contact?"

"No. She say he busy wit' new law firm, and she wit' new MP."

"She wouldn't know whether he had a problem with a disgruntled client?"

"She know nothing. But this morning I learn this news. Warner have GIS investigate the *professeur*."

"Meshango? We investigated her?"

"*Oui*."

"On his authority?"

"*Oui*."

"Under what pretence?"

"She may be threat to Madame. Of course, that not reason he say, but because of her horrible ordeal with sons. Nobody have balls to argue."

"Do you have the report?"

"I am this second to courier to you."

"Anything interesting?"

"No. I read her statement she make at the boys' inquiry. Sad. Not just for *professeur*."

"What did Warner find out about her?"

"She was abuse as child. Had bad mother. Drunk father. Many of her siblings dead. Two suicide. Two, three drug addict. One of them Child Protective Services rescue. Madame Meshango fight her way up. Go to University, meet husband. He lawyer there in Prince George. They divorce but friends. She solid citizen, lot of volunteer work for native community."

"Nothing in her file to suggest she might have sought revenge on Warner?"

"No. This lady take bad situation and build good."

Is that Meshango's game? She's tricking me into helping Mrs. Warner instead of hanging her? Why bother?

The knot between my shoulder blades returns. I scrunch the muscles together. "Did his assistant think of anything else?" I don't care how pathetic I sound. "Andre, right now I'll take any size bone. Hell, I'll take scraps."

"No, but you maybe find this interesting. She say to me, 'What come of her love affair with cop?'"

Love affair? Sergeant Lacroix and Meshango? So it's true that Warner told Mrs. Warner about Meshango and Lacroix living together. "What did you say?"

"I say nothing cuz I don't know what she mean. Maybe you do?"

"Right." I cross off one more motive.

Warner, for whatever reason, chose not to make Meshango's life difficult. So, it's true? He tried to be a better human being.

"*Merci*, Andre. Thanks for your help." I hang up, rub the back of my neck.

Footsteps behind me. "Danny?" someone says.

121

"Superintendent would like to see you in the conference room."

I've been expecting this. I grab my files and join Malden, Lacroix, and the file coordinator. I take the seat across from Lacroix.

"Corporal Killian," Lacroix says without raising his head and looking up. Asshole. "The forensic pathologist in Kamloops is expecting your call in ten minutes. So get to it."

Normally, I'd be angry at being dismissed, but I'm anxious to talk to the coroner, so I rush back to my desk. Lab reports don't generally come in this fast. Without dwelling on it, I know it's because of who Warner was. Not some First Nations woman missing off Highway 16.

The autopsy gives us nothing. Warner was in good health until he was shot dead, one bullet to the brain, weapon undetermined. The pathologist believes it was a nine gauge because of the path, the exit wound, internal damage. As for the rest of her report, there are no signs of cancer or any organ deterioration or health issues. Nothing interesting came of the tox reports. There were no poison or drug use prior to Warner's death.

That's too bad because discovering where the poison or drugs came from might have led to the perp. Answers to these questions would have opened up new avenues to the investigation.

When I exit the detachment, I'm surprised by the black clouds hanging over Prince George, making it feel more like four in the afternoon than noon. On the way to my vehicle the soft wind on my face stops suddenly. Three steps further—stinging rain.

For the rest of the day it rains hard. The icy roads thaw, dry, making driving easier.

Any evidence we might have discovered in Warner's backyard is washed away.

Saturday, the sun shines all day. With Mrs. Warner watching us from the gathering room, we walk at arm's length across the perimeter of Warner's yard. No new evidence is unearthed. The bullet may have hit enough trees that it resembles a stone instead of a slug. The metal detector will be in on Monday.

We continue interviews Saturday and Sunday, and finish canvassing the neighbourhood. Monday morning, we still can't find the bullet. Almost all the reports we need have come in, but nothing points towards a possible suspect for interrogation. None of the surveillance cameras at the airports, bus station, or train station spot anyone interesting, either.

Like every other murder since Angie's, failing to find the killer eats at me. It's a vicious cycle.

A telemarketer called this morning. She wanted to know what products I favour. I said I didn't know and tried telling her that my husband had just died, but she interrupted and spouted a list. "How many children do you have, ma'am?" I'm wondering what this has to do with advertising when she says, "Do you know millions of parents in South Africa have seven children and they're all dead before the age of five?" Instantly, a bottomless wail sprang from my mouth. It shocked me as much as it must have shocked her. I didn't hear what she said next, just the sound of the dial tone after she hung up. More than five minutes passed before I grew quiet. I set the phone back in its charger, and then plopped down at the breakfast table. I've been here since.

How many children do I have? After Declan and Bronson died, I practiced saying, "None" until I no longer choked over the word.

"None."

The one good thing about being in the public eye is everyone had heard of our tragedy long before we returned to Ottawa to finish Leland's term. I practiced saying "It's just Leland and I," but it was an exercise in vain. No one until this morning has asked.

My chest hurts. So do my eyes. The microwave clock is blurry. Nine-forty already?

I press my hands to the table and slide the chair back as I rise. I've begun a bad habit of staying in my housecoat far too long into the day. I must stop. I shuffle from the breakfast room through the house and towards the stairs. There are things to be done for tomorrow's memorial service, but after that? I know from watching all those educational programs on the health network, and from my volunteer work at the hospital and the United Way, that an effort must be made to fill my day. My relationship with God is iffy, some days I believe in Him, some days I don't, but regardless I'll stay in contact with the ladies from church. I could have a few over for tea and cookies next week. No, I'm not ready for small talk right now. Maybe in a few weeks. I'll go through my jewellery first. The ladies deserve at least something of value from me.

Flash of movement on my right—my hand flies to rest against my heart, which now pounds through my palm. I inch closer to the window next to my front door. He appears inside my porch. I move towards the door. He smiles. Leland?

I catch my breath. Smile. "Good morning," I say once the door is unlocked and opened, and I can see it is Killian. The winter air rushing in behind him is refreshing but chilly. It bites at my ankles. I shiver and glance down at my housecoat and slippers. "You've caught me at a disadvantage." I pull my robe's belt tighter.

He stomps the snow off his boots, and then does a strange thing, he slips off his boots and stands in his stocking feet. My eyes drift from his toes to his face. He sees my bewilderment and blushes. "Sorry, ma'am. Guess I left my manners next to the snow blower this morning. May I come in?"

I smile my reply, but I'm sure he guesses what I'm thinking. Do I have a choice? "If you don't mind, Corporal, I'd like to dress first. It's not my custom to greet visitors in my housecoat."

"Sure." An innocent smile. "I'll wait in the Minister's den."

I nod and go up to my room.

When I return, he's standing twelve inches from our Bateman Dozing Lynx glicee with his hands deep in his trouser pockets, and his heavy jacket unzipped. He's so intent on the fine strokes of the cat's face that I'm almost sorry to interrupt him.

"If you like the glicee, it's yours."

He twists around and looks at me wide-eyed. "Glicee?"

"The colour is sprayed or squirted on."

"Oh."

"It's yours."

"What?—Oh, no, thanks. I've just never seen an original up close. I've seen a lynx, but not a Bateman. It's a real nice picture, but no thank you."

Because he's a policeman? Would they consider it a bribe? I wonder about this, but say, "I plan to sell the painting anyway. You can buy it for a reasonable price." I can tell by his expression he's interested. "You'd be doing me a favour. What do you say to...one hundred dollars? Does that sound fair?"

"Five thousand is probably more like it."

"All right. Let's compromise and say two—"

He shakes his head.

"Fifty." I reach out, grab his hand and shake it. The skin on his palm is smooth. Warm. Nice.

He's surprised by my action, but manages to compose himself. "Ma'am—"

"Good. Two hundred and fifty dollars it is. I'll have it delivered after the investigation is closed. You can write me a cheque then. I'd much rather you have it than a stranger."

He shakes his head one too many times, and glances towards the leather chairs in the corner. "Can we sit?"

"Would you like tea or coffee?"

"No, thanks."

It's a second before I realize he's saying no to a beverage. I close my mouth and hope I haven't been gawking at him. He stands next to the chair, and I realize he's waiting for me to sit. Is this how it feels to have your brain freeze-dried, a term Bronson often used to describe me? Why can't I be like other women? I hate feeling as if I'm missing something.

Satisfied there is no way I can delay the inevitable, I take my seat. My outburst on Friday still bothers me, but I'm inclined to believe I shouldn't apologize. What's the point? My emotions are all over the place.

"I can't imagine what you and your husband must have gone through after your sons died, Mrs. Warner. I'm sorry I keep bringing it up."

The way his eyebrows slightly bow, and his eyelids droop makes me believe his sincerity is genuine.

"Do you think their deaths have something to do with Leland's murder?"

He pulls his notepad from his pocket, searches his other pocket and pulls out a pencil. "It's possible."

"Then it must be linked to that woman—that professor. Or possibly Mr. Norse's in-laws. Or they all conspired together?"

Bronson, for reasons I will never understand, abducted Mr. Norse's wife, Jasmine. She was Meshango's daughter's best friend. Mr. Norse was in jail for assaulting Jasmine when Bronson kept Jasmine captive in her own home for two days and subsequently beat her mercilessly. She died in the hospital a few days later. The memories make me cringe. What she must have gone through.

"It's possible Mrs. Norse's family had someone kill your husband in retaliation, but there is no evidence to prove it."

I have nothing to offer in defence, so I shrug.

"Did you have a chance to look again at the list I gave you?"

"Oh, no. I'm sorry. I'll look at it later, if you think it's important."

"Thank you." Killian looks at his notes. "It's important."

I tuck my legs beneath me, a feat I was never able to do until after my sons died. Grieving caused me to lose over fifty pounds. It's difficult to think of food when you're either throwing up or sobbing your eyes out. And to think I once believed being thin would solve all my problems.

Does Killian dismiss my theories because I'm still alive? If Mrs. Norse's family intended to retaliate, they would have killed me, too. "What about that Meshango woman? Why did she try to slander Leland's good name by suggesting Declan died to destroy his father?"

His eyebrows rise then, lower quickly. Is it because I said 'Leland's good name'? It was a slip of the tongue. It's not a good name. That's why Leland quit politics. That's why I hate being called 'Mrs. Leland Warner'.

"She believed what Declan wanted her to believe," he replies as if I hadn't said anything stupid. "There is no proof his last wish was to make certain your husband suffered, but it fits. Can you explain why there might have been that much animosity between father and son?"

His dark eyes sparkle. Now I remember who he reminds me of. That Native actor Bronson liked. He starred on North of Sixty. He was from Manitoba, and more recently starred on one of the *Law & Order* shows. His name is...Adam Beach. Except Killian's older. He's better looking, too. The point is they say everyone has a twin. I should tell him he has one, somebody famous.

I wonder where my twin is. I could trade places with her.

Killian seems intent on what my possible response might be. He leans forward as if in fear he'll miss something. I have to think for a moment until I remember what his question was.

Why did Leland detest our sons, and why did they hate him?

How can I describe a lifetime of misunderstanding and resentment? I'm not even sure when it began, the dissent that kept them close to blows since before Declan turned sixteen. The saddest part of all was I neglected Declan to prove to Leland I did not favour son over father. I did the same thing with Bronson to prove I loved him as much as I loved Declan. No wonder they didn't survive.

Blink, Sally, blink.

"After they died, I tried to dwell on happier memories. Like the many times Bronson and Leland wrestled together when Bronson was little. Bronson would scream with delight. I'd have to cover my ears." I rub the skin under my chin and feel consumed by the horribleness of it all. A lump forms in my throat. I swallow hard and try to massage it away. "After Bronson turned ten they stopped horsing around." My voice is hoarse. Please God, don't let me cry. I lay my hands in my lap, resigning to the fact that my past is full of sorrow and that will never change. "Once he was a teenager they argued constantly. I thought it was another awkward stage: father expecting son to be a man but treating him as a child; son expecting father to respect him as a man but responding as a child. The whole experience was ridiculous. They were at odds with each other. I had hoped it would pass."

"And Declan?"

"Leland thought Declan was strange because he didn't like rough play. He never entertained his father with tall tales, and he preferred to be alone in his room. In other words, he was his father's opposite. They despised each other early on. This, too, I had hoped would pass. Though I must admit, whenever Declan stood up to him I was always amazed."

And terrified. The beatings were severe. Leland had an abusive personality. After a time, clawing at Leland and screaming at him didn't work. Like the time he accused me of raising a gay son. I slapped him. He slapped me back and kept slapping me until I passed out.

"But, Corporal Killian, you're a man. You must understand better than I what it means to be a son. Wasn't your relationship with your father different than your relationship with your mother?"

"My mum died when I was eleven."

"You told me that. I wasn't thinking. Please forgive me."

"It's okay. It was a long time ago." He makes an effort to glance at his notes, but I can tell he's still grieving. "I only knew her as a kid."

"It must have been traumatic. To lose a mother at such a young age. It shouldn't happen to any child." Unless their mother is no good.

"It was harder on my dad," Killian says. "He was a single father. I have older sisters and brothers, but they were on their own by then and gone a lot. Yeah, my dad had a rough time."

"Was it cancer? Cancer took my mother and my father."

He nods. His eyes cloud over, and I'm sure he's remembering painful events. I wonder whether I should shut up or ask more questions. Possibly he needs to talk about his mother. He leans his head on his hand and lets out a deep breath; his small notepad dangles in his other hand.

My senses are aware of the intoxicating leather smell of the Tibeca chairs we're sitting on. You would assume leather would be cold to the touch, but Leland's chair maintains that worn cloth feel. I wonder whether the comfort of the chairs clashes with Killian's memories or amplifies them.

"My dad was a great guy," he finally says. "He took a leave of absence from his job to spend time with me. We went fishing almost every day. Hiking. He was a marine biologist."

He smiles. I assume not all memories are bad.

"He was a wonderful dad. We were close. He passed away a few years ago. It's too bad because he would have liked living here in Prince George, having the convenience of a city and the wilderness so close by. He lived with us for three years before he died." He rubs his face and eyes. "I miss him."

I nod because I understand. Because of a demanding father, I was an obedient daughter, a silent daughter. "There is no doubt in my mind, Corporal, that you were a good son."

His dark eyes brighten. "I hope so."

"I don't doubt it for a moment."

"It's not easy...without him." His voice wavers. He looks at me intently. "My dad made me want to be a better man."

I don't smile, but I wonder how long it will take before he realizes I've gained control over the conversation. It's not nice of me, I know. Killian wants to understand Leland better through his relationship with our sons, so he can find Leland's killer. Though I'm not quite sure how the two relate. I decide to make his job easier. "I wasn't a good mother."

My statement surprises him. Is it my honesty? He looks at my face with such compassion that I blink back tears.

"I don't believe that, ma'am." His voice is tender. "I bet you tried real hard. I think you were outmanoeuvred by an intense, abusive, and larger-than-life man."

Yes, that's true. I was never equipped to countervail Leland. Still, I should have tried harder. I don't say this to Killian.

"He was hard on your sons. That must have been difficult for you."

A fleeting image of fists flying.

"Leland might have been a better father if we'd had daughters. It's probably wrong of me to say this, but he would not have expected as much from girls. As it was, he expected more than Declan could give—not that he wasn't a bright, sensitive boy. He was. Whereas Bronson showed a cruel side, Declan was gentle. You're going to think this is awful for a mother to say..." I can't form the words.

"Even though you loved them both, you related better to Declan," Killian offers.

I smile. Killian is far more astute than I've given him credit. I think he knows I meant to say I loved Bronson but I didn't like him. He was a stranger to me. I kept yearning for that bond, the intuition that can come with motherhood, like the way it overpowered me when Declan was born.

"How did Mr. Warner cope after your sons died?"

I clasp my hands together, and take a deep calming breath. I know what he's thinking. Every man wants sons. To lose them... the horror of it. How did Leland survive?

He just did.

I feel I owe it to Killian to speak honestly, and not sit in judgment of Leland's sins. Besides, his eyes are so intent on my face I feel I should say something relevant. Something helpful.

"Thirty years ago the Premier of Quebec, while intoxicated, hit a pedestrian, and then fled the scene. The victim survived. Two broken legs, I believe. The whole thing was scandalous, yet the Premier retained his seat in parliament. Had he been American it's doubtful his career would have survived.

"Leland said our lack of interest in the private lives of our elected politicians was due to the fact that none of them were worth our efforts. He thought he could change that.

"During his last year in parliament, the horror of how Mrs. Norse died began to sink in. How do you cope with the knowledge that your son is a psychopath? I still can't fully answer that. Except you feel responsible. And Leland did feel responsible. For Mrs. Norse's death, and for the deaths of our sons. He tried to make up for both.

"That's why he felt so strongly about improving conditions for our soldiers. He worked closely with the National Defence committee to rally the public behind the purchase of new desert uniforms and tanks and helicopters. And you know how Canadians feel about taxes. But he felt obliged to the parents of our soldiers to make sure they came home alive. Regardless of race. Because as you know, Mrs. Norse was East Indian, and Leland had a lifelong prejudice against them and others. He came to regret those prejudices."

I'm taking too long to answer his question. "Leland coped with our sons' deaths by concentrating on making life better for others."

I sense I should shut up.

"Someone hated him enough to kill him, though."

"True."

"Did he receive any strange calls in the last—I don't know— five months? Maybe longer?"

"I don't believe so." He's asked me these questions before.

129

"I know it's exhausting for you, ma'am, but could you tell me again what happened?"

"Do you mean the morning Leland died?"

He nods.

As quickly as possible, I repeat the morning's events. "We had breakfast. I went upstairs. When I came down, Leland was...I found him...the blood...he was..." I fold my arms, hiding my sweaty palms from view.

"He didn't give you any reason to suspect his life was in danger?"

"None."

"He never mentioned any problems with any of his clients?"

"No."

"He hadn't been unusually quiet or worried?"

"No."

"Or nervous?"

"No."

"Did you see any strangers in your neighbourhood the day before?"

"No."

"What happened to your dog?"

The question stuns me momentarily. I expected him to ask, but I assumed he'd warm up to it. "Digger was run over by a car." Again, an uncomfortable lump forms in my throat.

"When?"

"Thursday."

"The day your husband died?"

Talking has become difficult. I rock forward to indicate a nod.

"What happened?"

A moment ago I had possessed a composure I've so often admired in other women. Where is it now? I lay my folded hands in my lap, and clear my throat. "Digger got out."

"Before or after your husband was shot?"

"I went outside to wait for the police. I forgot about the door being open. Digger saw his chance."

Killian looks at me strangely with his eyebrows furrowed. "I'm sorry, Mrs. Warner."

I nod. Then I'm blubbering like an old fool.

* * *

As my car's engine warms, and the defroster clears my window, I call my assistant. "Contact CSIS and ask them to send you everything they have on Mrs. Warner. Remind them you need it ASAP. In fact, call every morning until you get results. And make sure they understand to address it to me personally."

"You mean use some tact and don't forget to be courteous?"

I can visualize her smile on the other end. Does this girl ever have an off day? "No, I mean hound their ass until they send you that report."

Tuesday, one-thirty in the afternoon, I watch as Warner's foyer fills with mourners. Outside, Carrigan sits in a white unmarked van with darkened windows, photographing everyone entering and existing. I down two finger sandwiches without tasting them, and hear Angie inside my head.

Sorry, babe.

Four days have passed since the murder. I study the room, feeling the mounting pressure down the chain-of-command. The sandwiches do little to replace the anxiety centring inside my chest. My shrink said indigestion is my body's way of telling me to ease up. That made me laugh. Easing up isn't part of my job description.

"Finding your wife's killer isn't going to make your problems go away," the shrink had said.

"Ah," I snapped back. "You have a lot of patients who are victims of crime, do you?"

"Yes, actually, I do."

From hidden speakers throughout the house, the Celtic Woman singers sing "You Raise Me Up". The music softens my mood and helps me refocus. I search for anyone or anything out of the ordinary. An inappropriate stare, a suspicious stance, perspiration, or an unlikely flushing in the cheeks. I make eye contact with those who don't avoid my gaze and wait for nervous tics. There are over four hundred faces to study in the house, over seventy in the foyer alone. I'll study their photographs repeatedly before the investigation is over.

Liking no one in this specific area, I stuff my hands into my jacket pockets. Looking up at the high ceilings and crown moulding, it occurs to me that if the roof caves in a lot of important people will die.

Including me.

Behind me, a man chuckles.

Life goes on. You bet your ass it does. Annoyed by the thought, I continue to observe the surrounding elegance. How did maintaining this house impact Warner's life? The fancy horseshoe-shaped staircase takes up half the receiving hall and would make the staircase in *Gone with the Wind* look like a fire escape. The fifteen-foot high fireplace in the gathering room seems too clean to have been used. Heating the place probably costs a small fortune. Maintaining the whole house and all that involves was probably a bitch for the old man, despite his lucrative law practice.

The front living room resembles a high-end florist shop. A strong aroma of pinecones mingles with scents of gladiolas and gardenias. The music stops. A second later, out of the speakers comes Celtic Woman's rendition of "Let It Snow."

Mourners warming themselves in front of the fireplace remind me of the Norman Rockwell puzzles stocked on the shelf at the grocery store. There was a time when I fell for that stuff.

The conversation centres on somebody's kid being recruited to Prince George's Junior A hockey team.

"You must be so proud," one woman says to another.

Feeling my mood deteriorate further, I keep moving. "Life goes on," I whisper to no one.

Does Mrs. Warner believe that? Or does she, too, think the Great Spirit is a snob who never intended for everybody to be happy? He's probably up there somewhere laughing at His cosmic joke.

I square my shoulders. If I think I have problems, they are not comparable to people like the Warner's. Or any of the surviving family members I've had to face. Money can buy crap like this fancy house, and for what? So, you dwell in luxury for the rest of your life by yourself? No thanks.

I continue south to the rear of the Georgian home.

In Mr. Warner's study, the scent of roses dominates. I study the men grouped around the mahogany desk next to the glass doors. Recessed lights in the square mahogany panels on the walls cast shadows on their features. I gauge their expensive suits, wonder if any of them would risk murder to further their careers. People are capable of doing unspeakable things for any number of reasons. It's one of the first things they teach us at Homicide. While the public, more often than not, associates murderers with lowlifes or stupid people, the truth is most killings are done in a moment of passion–thoughts of getting away with it don't come until reality sets in. Usually too late.

Warner's death is too sterile for spontaneity. Whoever killed him knew what they were doing. The scene was void of any useful evidence and left clean. That calculation doesn't fit Mrs. Warner's character; it sounds like a professional. Except, there were no known professionals in the area. And Meshango?

Could she shoot Warner dead, then go home to prepare moose stroganoff?

Like blades of steel, the last of the day's light cuts through the hedge of twenty-foot blue spruce fencing the five-square-acre boundary. The way the house was built, the Warners could sit in the kitchen, great room, or study and be screened from nosy neighbours. I manoeuvre around the room for different views, careful not to disturb the Lieutenant Governor who occupies Warner's chair. I stand two feet behind the man, working the angles. From his desk Warner could look through the glass door and across the yard to the gathering room. He could've designed the house for that purpose. He didn't need to leave his study to see what Mrs. Warner was doing across the way.

How did she feel about that? Was it reason enough to hate him? Hatred turned to murder? I know better than to grasp at straws, but what if it's that simple? Warner said or did something to set her off. She goes upstairs, grabs a gun, comes down, shoots him dead, hides the gun, the casing, her clothes? Then calls the police? And when they arrived, knows enough to be the hysterical widow?

I stop to inhale the aroma of huge arrangements of lilies of the valley, Angie's favourite, then admire the eclectic mix of decanters on an antique chair in the corner.

Angie would have loved this room.

I stop at the limited edition print Mrs. Warner offered me yesterday for a ridiculously low price. My stomach growls. I grab another finger sandwich off a server's plate as she floats past. Then I accept a cup of tea from a lady carrying a full tray. I lean against the double doorjamb leading into the great gathering room, sip my tea, watch the server move through the room like a skilled caterer; nobody gives her a glance. That's the thing about waiters and waitresses. They're invisible. Should I grab a tray?

"Your Honour, who'd they say was in charge of the investigation?" the MLA, member of the Legislative Assembly for the Bulkley-Nechako, says to the Lieutenant Governor.

"Major Crimes here in Prince George."

"You mean they're letting the locals handle this?" He shakes his head. "Guess we can all look forward to the same treatment if we happen to be retired by D-day."

The MLA for the Prince George riding sits on the edge of Warner's desk with his back to me. He chuckles. "Speak for yourself. I don't plan to get my head blown off in my own kitchen. I'm going the old-fashioned way; in bed with a twenty-year-old."

"Male or female?" someone asks, and guffaws erupt.

The LG spins Warner's chair to the right to face my direction. I glimpse his stony expression before turning away.

"The locals are handling the case, because as far as Ottawa is concerned Warner was a civilian." He clears his throat. "The Deputy Commissioner realizes the implications of his death, and I'm sure she'll keep us abreast of the situation. I've been informed that the lead on this case is responsible for catching The Butcher down south. It's believed over twenty women were murdered. A little respect, gentlemen."

LG coming to my defence? If I ever need a favour, I now know who to call.

"Besides, E-Division promises to keep a close watch," a lawyer from the Federal offices in Victoria says.

Does that mean babysitters will be coming out of the woodwork?

"Got any ideas who you think could have done it?" somebody asks.

"No, and that's not something we'll be discussing here," the LG announces.

"I'm surprised the old man didn't show."

Are they referring to our retired prime minister? Does that mean Mr. Branford and Mr. Warner were friends, not just colleagues? Lovely.

"I hear he's not fit to travel. Especially in a plane," some suit says. His gold cufflink sparkles in the dim lighting.

"Nah, he's never liked this kind of fanfare. Didn't attend the Queen Mother's funeral. He was at Trudeau's only because they were long-time friends, and he couldn't get out of it."

"Like you would even know," one of them remarks. "He's still recovering from a recent ear infection."

"Somebody from Ottawa should have attended. It's disgraceful. Poor Sally."

"Yeah, especially considering what a fine fellow our beloved former minister was." More laughter.

"The PM's man arrived ten minutes ago," the LG reports. Immediately the others cease grinning.

I sip my tea. I saw the Minister shaking hands with his subjects in the front foyer when he arrived. Rumour from Ottawa has it that Warner was a nasty fellow who beat his sons and got away with it because nobody dared intervene. Maybe I should ask the Minister what he knows.

"How long does one have to remain at these functions? The Canucks are playing on home ice in less than an hour."

Not a hockey fan, I leave the room. Time to question Mrs.

Warner again.

I enter the gathering room.

The front entry is decorated in woodwork, while the gathering room has slate flooring and recess lights over the built-in wet bar. Lots of windows show a view of the backyard and pool. A framed, covered outdoor kitchen takes up the corner on the left side outside the glass doors to the breakfast room.

My eyes run along the ceiling from the front to back, which I estimate is seventy feet. The sheer magnitude of the place makes me think: maintenance costs. Before now I was too absorbed in collecting evidence to notice the home's grandeur. Today I've counted three fireplaces on the main floor alone. One of my people mentioned there were three upstairs in Warner's bedroom, Mrs. Warner's, and the library. Carrigan said something about there being a media room. Was our primary search, and the two that followed, thorough enough?

I catch sight of my boss who gestures at me like I'm the kid sent to the principal's office. I shrug before I can stop myself, then square my shoulders.

I approach the nearest server. "Could you please tell Mrs. Warner that Corporal Killian would like to speak to her?"

"Yeah, okay." The woman smiles as if her call to duty is what she's been waiting for all morning.

Cut the bullshit, Killian.

I get sarcastic when I'm frustrated. Rubbing my eyes as if that'll dissolve my sarcasm, I smile. "Thank you."

"Hello, Danny," Superintendent Malden says when I reach him in the middle of the gathering room.

We shake hands. Malden's fingers are ice cold and he is still wearing his outer coat. It's buttoned to the neck; his leather gloves peek out from each pocket. Maybe he won't be staying long? Good. Time for discussions can come later when we actually have something to discuss.

"How are you, sir?" Adding anything else seems premature since this is our first encounter in a social setting since I transferred. Generally, I avoid social situations where I will run into people from work, but this is different, this is work.

Malden spent the weekend at E-Division in Vancouver. I can only imagine how quickly the conversation switched to the detachment's obligation to find Warner's killer fast. That would lead to conversations about the points of the case, the evidence, and whether I'm the man for the job. All of which will eventually lead Malden to ask me how close we are to making an arrest. I hate this part of my job, the justifying when I don't have enough evidence yet.

"How was your trip, sir?"

"I took a copy of your report along. Everyone agrees you're doing everything necessary to find the shooter."

But? "Thank you, sir."

"They're loaning us more people. They'll be here tomorrow."

I stuff my hands in my pockets, and bite the skin on the inside of my lip to stop my response. Better that I don't say anything. Better if I don't ask whether it has anything to do with Warner being a public figure and not one of the hundreds of ordinary Canadians who deserve the same consideration.

"You don't look surprised," Malden says.

"I know how important it is that we close this case, sir."

He nods. "I know you don't smoke, but join me while I go outside. There is something more I'd like to discuss."

Of course there is. "My coat's in the kitchen closet."

"Let's grab it and head outside then."

I retrieve my coat, follow him back through the gathering

room. When Malden stops at the huge picture window and gazes out at the snow falling, I wonder if he has bad news, if that's the reason he's hesitating. Or I'm paranoid and all he's waiting for is the cluster of smokers to disband.

"Actually, Danny, the extra people aren't for the Warner case. The task force for Highway 16 needs them."

My jaw drops. Good thing I didn't say the first thing that came to mind.

He gestures towards the patio doors and the terrace. "Let's go outside."

I reach the door while bracing myself for the inevitable cold, then we step out onto the snow-dusted terrace. The cold wind bites at my cheeks. The air smells fresh, frosty, invigorating. Yeah, right. My frozen earlobes are about to drop off. I look up at the framework over the outdoor kitchen, and wonder why they didn't put up a full roof like they do in Mexico. At least there'd be no snow to shovel.

"You don't look convinced about the merit of more people," Malden says.

I zip my coat. I'm surprised by his observation because it's the opposite of how I feel. "I'm surprised, but not disappointed."

He nods, reaches into his coat, pulls out his cigarettes. He lights one and shrugs. "Dirty habit. Good for you for not smoking."

I lift up the collar of my coat and have the sudden urge to ask for one.

"Bureaucrats." He expels a lungful of smoke. "Unfortunately, it's all about diplomacy these days. Yes, we should have had a task force set up three years ago. Five years ago. But we don't look a gift horse in the mouth. Agreed?"

I nod.

"Cancel all leave. When it's deemed necessary, I'll okay overtime. But for now—"

The patio door opens. Three couples sidle past, give their greetings, proceed down the sidewalk and through the outdoor kitchen behind me. I get a strong whiff of flowery perfume that burns my nostrils before the wind carries it away.

I wipe my nose with the back of my hand. "I apologize for the bad timing, but I'd like to be considered for a transfer to the task force, sir."

The truth is I'm still angry I was transferred to MCU. I owe those families something. What exactly, I don't know. But I picked Prince George because of them, not to work major crimes. I came here to make a difference. If that's naïve, so be it.

"Unfortunately, your timing is not good," Malden says.

"But, sir, constables Carrigan and—"

"As soon as you close Warner's murder, I'll consider it."

He's pacifying me. Unless there is an opening for a corporal I'm shit out of luck.

"We haven't talked since Friday. Do you have any leads?"

"No, sir."

"Suspects?"

"No."

"But you suspect someone?"

"There is no prime suspect, sir. He left his wife a substantial life insurance policy, but the crime doesn't fit with financial gain. The scene was too impersonal."

"What about Dr. Meshango?"

"There is certainly no proof to suggest she's the shooter." Even with Lacroix's involvement.

"The partners at his firm?"

I cup my ice-cold ear lobes, hoping to warm them. "Their alibis check out. So did those of every member of parliament Warner ever dealt with. We're still verifying his client roster."

I can tell by the look on Malden's face this isn't what he wants to hear. He stares out over the Warner's massive back yard so intently that I can't help wondering if not finding the shooter will come crashing down on my head. My job might be at risk.

Why am I here? Because I questioned a witness, sensed something wrong, returned with that mind-set to then be thrown down a flight of stairs that should have killed me? I cover both ears again, wonder how long I have to freeze my ass off before I can get back to work.

Malden smiles at me. "You'll get used to the cold."

I give him a half-hearted grin. A gust of wind shoots through my coat. I fold my arms across my chest. How in the hell can the sun shine so brightly while it's freezing out?

Malden's expression turns serious, and he puffs at his cigarette. "If the media get wind that we're investigating a grief-stricken, pathetic woman who's had more tragedy than most people experience in a lifetime..."

So, he knows I'm investigating her. "I understand, sir." Of course he does. He's the boss—he knows everything—I erase the grin from my face.

"Is there any possibility she may have done it?" he asks.

"Anything's possible."

"Danny, the time for specifics is now."

"There is no evidence."

"That's not what I asked."

I curl my toes in my boots to try to ease away their frozen numbness. "I can't see how she could commit the crime without leaving us something. Honestly, I don't know that she's capable of murder. I do believe she's hiding something."

"What?"

I shrug.

"Find out."

A white veil covers the sidewalks where twenty minutes ago there had only been wet footsteps. Since I arrived, five inches of snow has fallen. Which reminds me I still need to get studs. Even if the snow melts, worn tires won't cut it in this town. I forgot to stop at the shop yesterday.

Suddenly a burst of sunlight hits my face. To escape the sharp pain behind my eyes, I turn to the spot beyond the kitchen window, see the blue spruce standing tall. It's unlikely the bullet hit the tree because the spruce stands off centre. The window's location was specifically placed to allow Mrs. Warner a clear view of the wildlife wandering past while she worked at the kitchen sink. We checked the tree regardless. There are a few small shrubs and perennials crowding around its trunk. To be as thorough as possible, we dug through the dirt. My eyes drift to the soil sheltered from the snow by thick branches. We left the ground flat. Now, it isn't. In the top right corner there is a mound.

"What's wrong?" Superintendent Malden asks.

"The ground's been disturbed."

He moves to the edge of the patio, crouches down. I crouch beside him, sift my fingers through the dirt. Whatever is buried is too deep to be dug out by hand. I stand while brushing the dirt from my numb hands. Without waiting for Malden to decide what to do next, I announce, "I'll be right back."

In the garden shed off the greenhouse, I grab a handle, looks like it might be for an extra broom, pick up a hammer, and rejoin Malden outside. Looking to see that no one's around, I jab the pole into the ground, push as far down as it will go, then tap the end with the hammer. It sinks slowly, two feet, three feet. Hits something. Footsteps approach from behind. I let go of the stick, press the hammer to my side.

"Rock or box?" Malden says.

Two couples stroll past, chatting amicably. They disappear around the west corner of the house.

"I'm not sure. If it's a box, the timing couldn't be worse. Guess I better make some calls..." My voice drifts off.

Malden flicks his cigarette, smiles.

I've done it again. I roll my eyes at how dense I am, chomp down on my bottom lip. A little too hard...I taste blood. There is an unspoken protocol to follow. I should have waited for Malden to make the first move.

He pulls out his phone. "Were there any shovels in the garage?"

"They're in the garden shed."

Surely to God he isn't thinking now's the time to dig a hole? Not with the house full of VIPs and the front street packed with news vans. Solving Warner's murder shouldn't require humiliating the widow further, for Pete's sake. "Sir, Mrs. Warner's dog was run over by a car."

"What?" Malden says.

"Her dog died Thursday. The dirt wasn't disturbed yesterday. Where were his remains for the past five days?"

He speaks into his phone. "Have the GPR brought back from loan ASAP." He listens then adds, "I want it on hand in case it's needed. No explanation required...Good, then." He clicks off.

"We are going to wait, right?" I ask.

He holds up his hand, presses a number, places his phone to his ear again. "We've discovered disturbed dirt in her backyard...I know...yes, I agree...Good then." He returns his phone to his pocket, studies the ground.

"Sir?"

"Danny," he looks at me, "have somebody check it out later tonight. Dig it up. We should use the GPR as well."

I relax. Of course it isn't the time. "Yes, sir."

"Post two of our plainclothes members. Change them up every hour until this wake is over. Then we'll bring in the shovels."

"Yes, sir."

"Meanwhile, there is something else I want to discuss." His voice sounds off.

"Sir?"

"They're questioning someone in regards to your wife's murder."

I swallow the lump in my throat. "What?"

"He's a person of interest. They'll know more in a few days. Meanwhile, you have a job to do. They'll keep me posted, and I'll keep you posted. Understood? No contact with any of their investigators."

I try to hide the disgust on my face, but judging by the way Malden's looking at me, I fail miserably. I feel like saying, "What would you have me do, sir?" But I know better.

141

Malden pulls on his gloves, gestures towards the house. "No contact whatsoever, do we understand each other?"

I nod.

"Say you understand, Danny."

"I get it," I say, choking over the words. "I understand. Sir."

Wishing I could kick someone, I follow him back into the kitchen and into the hallway leading to the service door. At the door he looks at me squarely. I see pity in his eyes and look down.

"I know you feel as if your hands are tied, Danny."

You have no idea how I feel.

"But you have to be patient. You know the investigators as well as anybody, they're doing all they can to solve her murder."

Her name was *Angie.*

"I'm not implying Warner is worth the extra precaution. You have me to deal with, and I have my own boss to deal with. As soon as this wake is over we'll check the disturbed ground."

Agitated beyond common sense, I show my poker face.

He pulls a scarf from inside his coat, lifts his collar, wraps the scarf around his neck. "Talk to the missus and ask her what is buried there. At least you'll know whether you can trust her answers based on what we find. I'll see you in my office for a briefing tomorrow."

When I forget to respond, he looks at me with patience. "I better talk to the reporters before they get antsy and start making up things. Meanwhile, Danny, do everything you can to solve this case." He clears his throat, then says in a lower voice, "I think you should concentrate more on Dr. Meshango."

He hesitates for a brief uninterrupted moment, and in that instant, I recognize a mixture of sympathy and suspicion in his grey eyes. This man isn't my enemy, but he's not sure if he can trust me not to become a problem now that I know a suspect had been found for Angie's murder.

Without another word, he disappears outside. From the door's window, I watch him cross the circular driveway towards the media along the border of the property. As soon as one reporter recognizes him, they all rush forward like chickens in a feeding frenzy.

I'm too numb to move. I try to visualize Angie's killer slouched over the table in one of the interrogation rooms at the Vancouver detachment. I know the investigators. They're good at what they do. They'll pound the questions at him.

The stabbing pain in my neck worsens. Wincing, I return to the kitchen. All around me the aromas of poultry, minced pies, cabbage rolls, and chilli remind me that two finger sandwiches aren't a decent meal. I skim the platters of ham and cheeses on the counter next to the freezer while reminiscing about one of the last meals Angie and I prepared together. Chef salad with pickles, chunks of cheddar cheese, and Angie's favourite: chopped roasted almonds.

I take another look around the room. She would have loved this kitchen. I imagine her happy here.

Are they really close to an arrest? Or is this one more dead-end? Three times I've rushed down to Vancouver in time for them to report false alarm.

"How are you, Corporal Killian?"

I hear the familiar voice and turn to see Mrs. Warner standing near the marble island. Yes, the job. Focus on the job.

She's wearing a sleeveless black dress. Unsure why, but half-expecting to see blood on her shoes, I glance at her black cotton slippers. I blink away the image of blood from my mind. My eyes jump to her face. She looks sad.

"Hello."

For the first time since we met, she's wearing eye shadow, mascara, and lipstick. Her hair's styled in a straight feathered look with bangs and blonde streaks that make her look younger than her sixty years. She still wears no jewellery, yet one of my men said she has a jewellery box full of the stuff, some of it expensive.

"How are you, Mrs. Warner?"

"Fine." She glances over her shoulder and sighs. "At least I will be once this day is over. By the way, thank you for coming." Instantly, her wan expression changes to something between confusion and despair. "You have news?"

"I have more questions. I know this is a bad time and I'm sorry about that."

"It's all right. I understand you're under pressure."

I appreciate the sentiment. "Could we discuss the list I left with you?"

She gives me a complacent nod, and I can't help wondering how I'd have felt if someone had questioned me during Angie's wake. I can't remember much of that day, so it probably wouldn't have mattered. The difference between Mrs. Warner and me is that I was never a suspect. Questioning her during one of the toughest days of her life is another way of determining her guilt or innocence.

She gestures towards the crowded countertop. Nearest to us a golden roasted turkey fills a huge silver platter. "The ladies from my church have been wonderful. And they're terrific cooks. I'll grab a plate for you."

Again with the food? Is my stomach growling, and I'm not aware of it? At least she isn't trying to ply me with alcohol. Damn. Give her a break. This woman has had enough. "I don't need anything, ma'am. Thanks."

"All right then." She heads out of the room. I follow.

The crowds draw aside as we enter the dining room. Her composure is admirable. Without stopping, she speaks softly to those nearest. "John, thank you for coming...Don and Louise, so nice to see you...Mr. and Mrs. Stanfield, thank you for being here...Blanche, yes, I'll call you."

"I'm so sorry, Sally," one man says.

"Please call if you need anything. It doesn't matter what," says another.

An expensively dressed woman of about fifty says, "Sally, you're in our prayers."

"Thank you," she replies, and keeps walking.

We climb the stairs to the second floor, those around us look as if they want to reach out and touch her. Even these powerful men greet her with genuine compassion. Behind them the hum of conversation stills for three more steps, then resumes at a lower octave. At the top landing I wait while she slips into her room. I notice Warner's bedroom door and wonder briefly what it would be like if Angie had ever decided to move out of our bedroom.

Dumbass. That's exactly what happened.

The sudden loneliness chokes me. I swallow, survey the crowd of mourners below. Indistinct voices waft up to me. Conversing in their little groups, no one person stands out as a cold-blooded killer, though most of them are certainly intelligent enough. The killer picked the perfect day and the perfect time.

Mrs. Warner exits her bedroom with a black, cashmere sweater draped over her shoulders. She shows me to the media room at the back of the house, unlocks the door, gestures towards one of the red leather chairs, then sits next to me. A theatre-size screen takes up the entire wall thirty feet ahead. Thick velvet curtains hang on each side of the screen. The possibility of watching football, particularly my favourite team, the BC Lions, makes me feel like a kid again, back when life was simpler. I catch a whiff of popcorn, glance behind me at the bar and all its paraphernalia, including an empty popcorn maker.

"An opulent room, don't you think?" She hands me the folded piece of paper.

"You're asking the wrong person, ma'am." My back melds into the chair. "I spent most of my teens at the Odeon Theatre in Sechelt. It didn't smell this good, but it looked a lot like this."

"Let me guess? Steve McQueen was your favourite actor."

"Worse. Sylvester Stallone." I make a face, whine in low voice, "Adri-aaaan."

Mrs. Warner fakes a cringe, covers her mouth and laughs. "Yes, I remember the film. *Rocky.*"

They don't make movies like that anymore.

Sitting erect, she settles her hands in her lap. "During Parliamentary recess Leland would spend one day doing nothing but watching his old favourites. He preferred European films from France and England. I'd warn dinner guests not to get him started on today's films. If encouraged, he could go on for hours about the Americans being either too violent or too corny, and the Canadians too dull or morbid. Although he was particularly fond of Leslie Nielsen."

"What were his three favourite movies?" I pull my pad and pencil from my pocket, noting the expression on her face. She thinks I'm going to write down her answers. "Knowing more about him helps," I lie. It's her I'm trying to understand.

She relaxes against the seat. "Well, his least favourite was *Panic Room.* As for his favourites?" She thinks for a moment. "He must have seen *Bridge Over the River Kwai* a dozen times. Oh, yes, he loved the series *Horatio Hornblower.* He made certain he saw it every year. And third? Let me think. Possibly *Monty Python.* "

"Are they your favourites, too?"

She shakes her head, looks surprised by the question. "Oh no. I watch television in my room. I like *CSI* and *Law & Order* and the Discovery Channel."

I skim the list. None of the names have been checked.

I must be frowning at her because she says, "I'm sorry. I don't know half those people. The ones I do know are harmless."

"There was no one who might have scared you or made you nervous?"

"No."

"What about Dr. Meshango?"

"You think she killed my husband?"

"No, ma'am. I mean did she, or does she, make you nervous?"

She squints at me. Then her face relaxes. She leans back. "No."

"What about Sophie Brooks?"

"Yes." She leans forward. "Sophie has always made me

nervous. However..."

"Sorry?"

"Nothing."

"Please, ma'am."

"I'd rather not say anything bad against her."

"Fair enough. Would you classify their relationship as civil?"

"Leland wasn't always patient, but he tried with Sophie. Sometimes when they were on the phone together he'd roll his eyes and take the phone away from his ear and stare at it, then place it back to his ear. If we made eye contact, he'd smile as if to say, 'Yes, I know. Be nice.'"

A pleasant expression crosses her face; I see glimpses of the pretty woman she once was.

"He was a fearless man?"

Her eyes widen. "For a long time he was exactly that, fearless."

"Until?"

She frowns. "Grief changes a person."

It always goes back to losing their sons.

"I was so involved with my own grief that I never stopped to wonder how Leland coped."

"Have you figured it out?"

She shrugs. "As I said before, he made conditions better for our soldiers in Afghanistan. His life wasn't in vain."

He also had Meshango investigated to see if she was a danger to what was left of his family. When he realized she wasn't, he let her be. Is that what nice guys do? "He became more compassionate," I say.

The statement provokes a thought, and she nods as if realizing something. "It wasn't that he made sense of our sons' deaths, just that he was able to justify their lives. I think he thought Declan and Bronson were *born* to die, so that he could change and make life better for so many people." She shakes her head. "That's insane."

"If you believe the church, everyone is born for a reason. And when they fulfil that destiny, they die. I guess it depends on if you believe the old saying: There is a purpose—"

"Under heaven, yes."

"They died. He coped by making life better for a lot of people."

Her eyebrows shoot up. "Why else would God allow someone's children to die, if not for their death to make us change?"

You've got it wrong. It's how we conduct ourselves while they're alive that matters. "Your husband did make a significant difference."

Her frown returns. "Did Leland die because of what happened

to Declan and Bronson?"

"Do you think he did?"

"I don't know. Grief can make you see things differently, in ways you never thought possible."

"Do you think that describes your husband?"

"Yes."

"I know when my mum died, my grandfather turned into a nicer guy."

"Same with daddy after my brother died," she says.

"What was he like before?"

"Oh, you know," she says, "demanding."

I fold the list, stick it in my pocket. "The dirt under your kitchen window has been disturbed."

Her attention stays fixed on the screen.

"Ma'am?"

She whispers, "My neighbour buried my dog."

"Digger is buried under your kitchen window?"

"Yes. A neighbour down the road found him in the ditch in front of his place. He was run over by a car." She blinks, as if to reacquaint herself with reality. "You already know that."

"What took so long to bury him?"

"Digger was cremated." She looks back at the blank screen. "Does it matter?"

Yes, it does. "I'm sorry for your loss, Mrs. Warner." Should I tell her now that we have to dig him up? One more insult to injury.

No.

Corporal Killian excuses himself, and I walk downstairs with him. He goes out the front door without looking back. I watch until he disappears, wrap my sweater tight, and avoid making eye contact with anyone. It's bad enough I feel their eyes upon me. Too many of them are wearing outlandish aftershave and perfume. I turn, hoping I can make it to the kitchen before someone asks me something. No such luck. Cold fingers touch my arm. I stop and look at a woman's face. I watch her lips move. The man next to her adds something. Out of my peripheral vision my sister Shirley moves in my direction from across the room. She thinks because she and her husband are doctors, and Leland was a politician and I was a nobody that they were better than us.

I'm so tired of her condescending ways that I excuse myself from this couple expressing their shock and dismay. Not soon enough. Too many guests circling. Closer. Tighter. Condolences come from all sides. I glance back at Shirley. She looks as if she's lost her best friend. She's the only family I have left and since she appears healthy enough I wonder if I really care what's happened to upset her. She never once cared about what happened to me.

Yes, I am a callous hag. *No wonder no one but Digger loved you.*

Is that Leland speaking inside my head?

But why couldn't Shirley, just once, say she was sorry for deserting me?

I escape into the guest washroom to splash cold water on my face. I pat my face dry, sit down on the toilet lid, and imagine Digger with me now. He adored me so. It was wonderful being loved that much. I imagine patting him and feeling his soft fur under my fingers.

Someone knocks loudly on the bathroom door.

"Sally, when are you coming out?" Shirley says.

"Give me a few minutes, would you?" I place cold hands over my eyes. I don't want to let go of my memories yet. They're so comforting.

More knocking on the door. I'm too numb to answer. I try to go back to the place where Digger's face is alive in my memory, alive and happy and such a comfort to witness.

Again, someone knocks. The impulse to get up and smash the door in their face is strong. I picture throwing it open to see whomever it is pressing a hand to a bloody nose, shouting at them to leave me alone.

My chest tightens. "Just a moment, please." I hear nothing in return.

A minute passes, I get up and exit the room. I would like to yell for them all to leave my house, but of course I won't. I cannot soil my mother's memory. Actually, yes I could. She was never there for me.

Nattily dressed politicians and their Pilates-sculpted wives smile at me. I smile back. They speak of things my brain is too lazy to retain until I concentrate and hear someone say, "If you need anything...?"

Someone agrees, and adds, "We're a phone call away."

"Yes, of course. I'll call." I manoeuvre my way through the hallway to the kitchen where I hope I can be of use.

"Can I help?"

One of the ladies from church gazes at my face as if at a loss for words. Worse, she is attempting to find the right words to console me. I don't want consoling. Luckily, good manners keep me from saying that.

After an awkward moment, her eyes moisten and she touches my arm lightly. "Yes, I'm sure we can find something for you to do." She smiles a genuine smile, and I long to embrace her, but that would be out of the question.

I'm refilling platters of goodies when Shirley reaches me.

"Sally, honey," she says. Her voice loving, so loving, in fact, I expect syrup to ooze from her mouth. My sister is a phoney. So is her husband. And so are their three do-gooder adult children. "You should have told me."

"You'll have to be specific. My days as a psychic are over."

She lapses into a momentarily stunned silence. Finally, she sighs deeply. My sister never deals well with my sarcasm, though I suspect that is because my witty remarks are rare.

"I've been asking around about Digger. I was hoping one of your neighbours might have taken him in."

I stop adding food to the tray and stare at her. Stupidity must run in the family.

"Why didn't you tell me he was run over by a car?" She glances at one of the church ladies gathering dirty dishes and leans towards me. "The least you could have done is tell me. You know, Sally, you make things much worse with your secrets. Your neighbours looked at me as if I'd gone mad. How do you think that made me feel? The man said Digger died Thursday morning, and he buried him in your garden this morning. Please don't tell me you had him on ice for four days."

At that moment I hate my sister. Who else but a cruel bitch would remind me of what I've really lost? Digger. I've lost Digger.

* * *

I see the last of my guests to the door and notice the CBC, Global, CKPG, and other news vans are gone. A single police car has replaced them.

"Thank you for coming," I say, hopefully for the last time.

I close the door and lock it. Concerned faces glance back at me through the glass. I smile and wave. I mouth, "I'll be fine," then turn abruptly and start for the kitchen. My footsteps resonate through my home, and I decide "quiet" is my new favourite word.

I reach the kitchen grateful for its wonderful smells: cinnamon, nutmeg, and poultry seasoning. They're the smells of my youth, happier times for the most part. At the kitchen window above the sink, I check to make sure Digger's grave hasn't been stomped on. Snow covers the small mound. When I find a new home, I'll dig up his ashes and take them with me.

The clock on the microwave shows ten after four. It has been a long, long day. My sister and her husband should be halfway to Maple Ridge by now. I must remember to send a thank-you note to the deacon's son for driving them to the airport. My rich brother-in-law is too cheap to rent a car. The drive will give him and my sister a chance to pump the young man for information.

The kitchen is sparkly clean. The ladies from the church are a blessing, but it's nice to be on my own.

With thoughts of solitude, I switch on the burner and fill the kettle from the wall spout on the back of my stove. I drop a fresh bag of blackberry tea into my ceramic teapot. The sterling silver tea set we inherited from Leland's mother has been rinsed and returned to the china cabinet in the dining room. Its opulence is fine for guests, but tea doesn't taste like tea unless it has steeped in my old, brown ceramic pot.

To whom do I pass Mother Warner's teapot? Some stranger? I'll drop it off at a thrift shop.

Damn. The string and tag slip inside the pot. Now they're wet from the leftover water. If I can't retrieve the bag, my tea will steep too long. I hate strong tea. My stubby, arthritic fingers squeeze through the teapot's small opening, but the tag slips through my fingertips. Damn. My eyes tear. My jaw cracks. Goodness, it's a stupid tea bag. Deep breath. The odour of blackberry stings my nose. Retrieve the tag. Exhale. All is right with my little world. Calm now.

Goodness gracious, I certainly overreact.

Platters of food line my countertops because my refrigerator is already full. I make a mental note to call the soup kitchen and have them pick up the leftovers. Good food should never be wasted. I must also remember to call the hospital and have these flower arrangements picked up.

It hurts my eyes to look out the French doors to the back yard. I think I see someone out by my spruce tree. I blink. It is no one, just my foggy cataracts. The sunlight is dull, and the sky is white. I close my eyes. I hear something. Music. Inside of me. The tune of "Down by the Sally Gardens" escapes my lips. The words come next, a bittersweet song about dreams, lost love, and new beginnings.

"Down by the sally gardens my love and I did meet;
"She passed the sally gardens with little snow-white feet.
"She bid me take love easy, as the leaves grow on the tree;
"But I being young and foolish with her did not agree.
"In a field by the river my love and I did stand,
"And on my leaning shoulder she laid her snow-white hand.
"She bid me take life easy, as the grass grows on the weirs;
"But I was young and foolish, and now am full of tears."

"Down by the Sally Gardens" was big during and after WWII, and I wonder what brought it to mind until I remember my grandmother used to hum it while she braided my hair. Sometimes tears would roll down her cheeks. Then she would tell me to pray that my father went to hell.

Spotlights from beneath the eaves of my house shine down on the terrace. Sitting at the table in the breakfast room, I sip my tea and watch snow float from heaven. In no time, another inch covers the ground beyond the pergola. The new moon is round and bright in the south sky.

I love snow and its perfection, but only if it stays untouched. Once footsteps and tire tracks mar the surface, it's not the same. Human and animal contact ruins it. Dogs leave dark-yellow pee marks. Graders push piles to the side of the road where sand trucks turn it brown. In spring, the sun melts the snow into slushy mud.

My tea cools.

The house is still. Bigger snowflakes fall. In my mind I see the snow surrounding my house...a giant white wall growing grey until I'm completely enclosed. A prisoner.

What silly thoughts. Think of something else.

I pour more tea.

I think of my parents. I'm glad they're dead.

Somewhere it has been advised that a widow should stay put and not make any big decisions for the first year. I decide to make one. Pack up and move. As soon as the investigation is over, I'll put the house up for sale. A downtown condominium would serve my needs better. Who will shovel the snow or work the snow blower? Leland hired a man to do that. I can't remember his name. I'll be trapped. What if the garage doors won't open? What if I get stuck in my driveway and freeze to death? What if the furnace quits and I die from exposure? What if no one ever comes to check up on me? What if—

My pulse races. I place both hands flat on the breakfast table. Plant both my feet flat on the floor. Deep, deep breaths.

Wild snow, the kind wind creates, dances somersaults across the terrace. Snowdrifts push up against the French doors off the gathering room. I continue to breathe deeply. All bad thoughts disappear as I concentrate on the sound and the feel of my lungs as they expand and contract. One day at a time is my new motto. I'll be okay. I'll get organized. The ladies at church won't desert me. My pastor will help; that's his job. In the Bible it says the most important thing is love. What good does it do to wonder why I'm still alive after such tragedies? There are no answers to satisfy me. Therefore, I refuse to feel sorry for myself. I'll do what God put me here to do: live the best possible life I can live and serve others. There is so much I can do, the soup kitchen, the crisis centre, the hospice house.

I miss Digger. If he were here now I'd hold him. I'd calm down while he snuggled his cold nose under my elbow. Should I get another dog?

The question shocks me. On the verge of more tears, I know I could never soil Digger's memory by replacing him. Not my precious friend.

The door chimes ring—I jump.

I am quick to stop myself from getting flustered. Or worse crying. If my new life is to begin, I must change.

Guests are welcome in my home, so I slide my teacup aside, rise, and enter the kitchen. The monitor above the freezer shows several men standing inside my porch. Their shoulders are laden with snow. They're talking amongst themselves. One man removes his fur hat and, facing outwards, shakes it vigorously. Another man holds a shovel. It's Corporal Killian. He hands the shovel to a police officer, and the men with him head towards my garage.

I don't understand. I rush into the hallway and throw open the service door. "What is it?"

Killian brushes the snow off his shoulders and arms and steps into my house. "Mrs. Warner, I'm sorry to bother you." He grips my elbow gently and leads me back into the kitchen.

I try to look around him to see where the others went. "What is going on?"

"My men need to dig up the spot in your backyard."

Acid rises into my throat. I cough it down. "What—what are you saying?"

"We need to dig up the grave."

"No."

He doesn't speak for a full second, and now I understand why he is here. "You want to disturb Digger?"

He nods, as if not speaking will lessen the blow. It doesn't. The vision is too much. I can't speak. The misery I feel chokes me.

"Is there someone I can call?"

I manage to shake my head, and then gather myself, swallow hard, and say, "Is this necessary? Please tell me it isn't. How can I help? Talk to me and let's leave poor Digger alone."

Killian looks tormented. How can he look one way and act another? "It's important to the investigation. Otherwise I wouldn't."

"What has digging up his grave to do with Leland's murder? Can you explain that?"

"Stay calm, ma'am."

With a hand pressed to my heart, I rush to the kitchen window. The backyard lights up. Officers dig up the small box holding Digger's ashes. I swing around, facing Killian. He is right, I have to stay calm. I can't fall apart now. Not after everything that has happened. But, oh dear, I'm crying again. Big gulps of noise escape from my mouth. Suddenly I'm cold. My ears register the agony erupting from deep inside. I can't stop.

He puts an arm around my shoulder and leads me out of the kitchen. I follow because I have no energy to fight him. The next thing I know we're in the breakfast room. He disappears and then reappears with a glass of water. He holds the glass to my lips, and I take two sloppy sips. The front of my blouse is now wet. My hands fly up. Enough.

"Do you remember I promised I'd do everything I could to find your husband's killer? We have to make certain there is nothing else buried with Digger. As soon as my men are finished they'll place his ashes back in the grave and cover it up. I promise." He hands me a tissue.

Dear Lord, who is this man? My guardian angel? My Nemesis?

* * *

I tear my eyes from Mrs. Warner to see Carrigan gesturing to me from the terrace. I get up, grab a tissue for her from the desk in the corner and, unable to stop myself, pat her back. I hand her the tissue.

At the kitchen patio entrance, I unlock the door. Snow melted during the day and turned to ice, blocking the bottom edge. It takes the combined force of Stan and me to slide the door open.

I whisper, "What did you find?"

He glances over my shoulder to Mrs. Warner sitting with her back to us in the next room. "The ashes are there." He removes his gloves and blows into his cupped hands. "We used the GPR in case there was something buried deeper. Nothing. Do you want the ashes shipped back to the lab?"

I shake my head. "Take a sample. Rebury him. Make it look as it had. Get everybody out of here as quickly as you can. I'll meet you back at the office."

Carrigan nods and leaves.

I return to Mrs. Warner sitting at the kitchen table. She's staring straight ahead through the adjacent glass doors into the gathering room on the other side of the house.

"Can I fix you a cup of tea?"

"Oh dear." She blinks. "I'm so sorry. I should have offered you something." She makes an attempt to stand. "I'll fix—"

I lay my hand on her shoulder. "Would you like something stronger?"

"No. But thank you. You're a nice man." She unfolds her crumpled tissue, blows her nose.

I retrieve the box of tissues from the desktop, set it in front of her, sit down.

"Thank you." She grabs a fresh tissue. "I've made a fool of myself in front of you. Again. I've been crying my entire life, and I'm sick of it." She wipes her eyes. "I'm so embarrassed."

"Don't be."

She dabs her nose before slipping both tissues into the inside cuff of her sweater. "You promised you'd do everything possible to solve Leland's murder. You had to check the grave to make certain no one had hidden any discriminating evidence there. I understand that now. I never faulted you. I'm just...bleak."

She looks at me straight on, and in that instant I witness more grief than most people experience in a lifetime. I understand how she feels. Life is a bitch, yet what I've learned from her is a worse lesson. Experiencing one horrible tragedy doesn't exempt you from more.

She reaches out, touches my hand. Her eyes fill with tears. "May I ask you something?"

"Sure," I say, knowing I'll lie if I have to.

"Do you understand grief?"

"Yes."

She nods as if it confirms what she already suspected. "Then you understand what isn't easily understandable." She pulls the tissue from her cuff and dabs her eyes. "Remember we talked about Leland being fearless?"

"Yes."

"After we talked, I tried to recall one single thing he was afraid of. There must have been something, don't you think?"

I shrug.

"Do you suppose he was frightened of death at the end?" She dabs at a big, round tear rolling down her cheek. "Did he know he was about to die? I keep imagining the horror of the moment."

The degree of my sympathy surprises me. I hardened after Angie's death. Yet here I sit, suffering at the sight of Mrs. Warner's tears.

Light from outside glazes her iridescent skin. "I should have been there," she said softly.

I thought the same thing after Angie died. "Then you'd be dead, too, Mrs. Warner."

She nods, as if being dead might possibly be a good thing.

Seven o'clock in the morning, my screams wake me. I see Leland shooting both our boys dead while Meshango holds Digger in her arms, squeezing the life from him. I'm tied to the chair opposite Bronson and Declan. I can't twist free. Blood sprays in my eyes.

Fully awake now, I sob and rub my eyes. A moment passes before I can see clearly. It's another moment before I catch my breath. Afraid to succumb once again to sleep, and to the chance of returning to this horrible nightmare, I wipe my face with my hands. I roll over on my back and try to focus on happy thoughts. All I can think of is Declan and how badly I failed him.

The first time Leland broke his spirit Declan was three. A heat wave had swept through the Interior and left forest fires roaring. I was pregnant with ankles double their size. Every fan in the house ran at full tilt, but there was no relief. Declan was playing outside in the sandbox under the afternoon shade of our birch trees. Through the screen door I heard his imitation of miniature dump trucks and imagined him manoeuvring them over the make-believe hills and valleys of sand. The sound of his sweet voice reminded me of an ad for the Disney "Jungle Book" movie. I hear him now, a happy little boy with no hint of the young man who would one day kill his brother, and then himself.

Dear God.

I wipe my wet face with the bed sheet.

It was the July long weekend. In those days, besides running his own law firm, Leland was on the city council.

Being under a lot of pressure was no excuse.

I sit up in bed, pull the duvet to my chest, and wrap my arms around my knees. With my eyes tightly closed, I can picture that day as if it were yesterday.

Due to the intense heat, I had prepared a second pitcher of lemonade for Leland. I planned on sitting outside on the veranda where there was a slight breeze. Being heavy with child made my response time slow. Declan wanted a drink and banged on the screen door for my attention. The door had one of those

156

awkward latches. I hollered, "I'm coming."

Possibly he didn't hear me or grew impatient. I had the pitcher in my hands, resting it on my stomach. My intent was to carry it to the table so Leland could have his drink, and then let Declan in. He was three and impatient. He banged again, loudly. Leland looked at the door. I tried to hurry. I set the pitcher on the table. Declan kicked the door. Leland was out of his seat, sweeping past me. He hurled the door opened, reached down, yanked Declan up by one arm until he was level with Leland's shoulder, and then struck Declan across his backside. Declan screamed. I screamed.

"Leland—stop!"

He wouldn't.

I rushed towards them and grabbed his arm. "Stop it. Put him down. You're hurting him."

Leland wouldn't stop, and so I did the one thing I could do. Leland had removed his shirt to air it out and was wearing a T-shirt. I raked my nails down his arm and left big red welts. Leland dropped Declan. I scooped my son off the floor. I checked to see if any of his bones were broken, and shouted at Leland my biggest lie to date, "You ever touch my son again—I'll kill you."

The hatred in Leland's eyes terrified me. Sobbing, Declan clung to my neck and glanced up at his father from under my chin. I can still feel the fear. The air was saturated with it. I hugged Declan to me and waited to die, praying that he wouldn't hurt my son. Five long seconds. The hatred in Leland's eyes...

Please God, leave me in peace. I don't want to remember.

With an old woman's effort, I stretch out my legs. My knees crack. Through the window, the morning's light is whiter than normal. White enough that I feel calmer. Six days have passed since Leland died. If today is Wednesday, it's my day to volunteer at United Way. I shift my body and lay supine. Should I call? Would they even expect me to show up?

I slide my legs over the edge of the bed. I'll go. One look at my pathetic face and they'll send me home, surely?

I flop back onto the bed. Do I want their pity? Is this what my life has become?

No, I'll go because it's the right thing to do.

In less than twenty minutes I'm dressed and in my car. At my age what's there to do but apply a little rouge to my lips and cheeks and make certain there are no holes in the back of my hair. It's an added blessing that my blouse is buttoned correctly, and toilet paper isn't trailing out the back of my pantyhose.

One of my neighbours has kindly ploughed my driveway.

While my car warms, I open the garage door and easily wheel both the tall garbage carts to the road. I return to my vehicle and drive away. I'm proud that this time I remembered to close the garage door.

At the United Way, I am fortunate to find a parking space out front. Everyone is surprised to see me. The hugging is the worst part. My body stiffens under their touch, like a mannequin with no moveable parts. My supervisor raises her eyes to heaven as if only God can explain my behaviour.

Feeling suddenly guilty, I stutter, "I...I wa-wanted to th-thank you f-for th-the flo-flowers and th-the food." I sound horrible. It's been years since I stuttered, and it takes a second before I remember what to do: Concentrate on my words and speak slower. "You have all...been...so kind. Calling didn't...seem enough."

The women say it was their pleasure to help me. They smile sadly. They become teary. There is more hugging. I make excuses, slide out from their embraces, and head for the door.

"Sally, take as long as you need," our supervisor says.

I nod and disappear outside. I can't get to my car fast enough. Coming downtown was a mistake. The air is so thin that breathing is difficult. I start the engine, open my window, and take deep breaths. Cars zoom down Ospika Boulevard past my window. I jerk each time as if they're about to sideswipe my car. They are that close. I lean away from the window. Brisk winter air nips at my cheeks. I shiver, close my window, and pull away from the curb. Perhaps the trip has done some good. I feel strong enough to drive over to the hospital to thank the auxiliary supervisor there. I turn onto Fifteenth, cross Highway 97, and head downtown. The city is alive with ploughs and graders.

A quick walk through the main entrance to the Gift Shop. No need to fear emotional intimacy here. Hospital volunteers are different. They deal with death and decay on a daily basis. Hugging is not a prerequisite.

Within minutes, I'm back outside and on my way to my vehicle feeling comforted. I focus on my car across the parking lot, satisfied I have done my duty and can now return to the safety of my home. The closer I get to my car, the better I feel.

"Mrs. Warner?" a squeaky voice calls.

Without thinking, I turn. It's that artist, the one who dated Declan and blackmailed Leland because Bronson assaulted her. She is rushing towards me. She's about to hug me. I panic. My breathing quickens. My heart pounds in my chest. Before I can speak Sophie Brooks has her arms around me. She grips my shoulders so her beady eyes can look directly into mine.

"Mrs. Warner, you poor thing. How ya doing?"

It sounds condescending the way she says that, and my anger erupts. She doesn't care about me. She certainly didn't care about Declan.

"What do you want?" I unwrap her hands from my forearms. She looks wounded.

"Are you okay, sweetie?" she asks in a singsong voice. She's wearing expensive Mukluks, high-heels, no less. I've seen them in the Native art stores in town. They start at four hundred dollars. Hers are probably eight hundred. They have more beadwork than usual, full fur, with beaded trim. I suspect her coat is deerskin; it has full beadwork front and back.

My eyes rise to her face. Her smile looks more like a snarl.

"If you'll excuse me, I have to go." I try to rush past. She is at my heels. Her wedge-heel boots smack behind me.

"But really, how can I help you?"

"I have to go."

"Let me help you."

"I have need of nothing."

"Hell's bells, course you don't. Warner left you taken care of good, I bet. But, like, do you need someone to talk to? I could give you my shoulder to cry on. It's not big, but it's strong."

"Your shoulder? No."

"Mrs. Warner, I'm just trying to be nice."

"Why? Are you going to blackmail me now that Leland's gone?"

"No. Geez." She grabs my arm, and I'm forced to look at her. "I don't understand why your family always treated me so bad. What'd I ever do to you guys? I loved Declan." Her face puckers up as if she's about to cry.

"When people tire of your copied art imitations, you should take up acting. You could be a star." I yank my arm free.

"Look who's acting, now, Miss Sally-homefaker." The expression on her face turns ugly. "You were a terrible mum and a crummy wife. Declan told me hundreds of times how embarrassed you made him. Leland used to complain about what a cold fish you were. Even Bronson called you a fat cow behind your back." She rests her hands on her hips. "Guess they had good reason, eh?"

"Ah, now your true colours come out."

She thinks she's so smart. Bronson called me a fat cow to my face.

I turn to walk to my car. She roughly grabs my arm from

behind. I swing around to protect myself, but something in her smile startles me.

"I know secrets about your family, you old cow." Her eyes narrow and disappear inside her round face. "If you don't watch your step, I'll make your life hell. How would you like that? I bet you killed your pig of a husband, too. Hell, I used to vomit after he did his thing. He'd grunt and groan for the count of three, and then collapse on top of me. Yeah—I let him hump me cuz I felt sorry for him. He'd huff and puff and tell me what a fat slob you were. Guess you've lost some weight. Bet your boobs hang down to your waist, huh? Bet when you get naked all that loose skin drops to your ankles, eh?" She laughs and looks at my feet as if she can picture the folds of skin.

"That is quite original, Sophie," a woman to my right says. "If you had spent more time in class, you'd have a larger vocabulary by now. Leave Mrs. Warner alone and run along."

I don't turn to look at *that woman* because I won't take my eyes from Sophie. I want her to see I'm not afraid of her or her threats. Part of me can't believe Leland ever slept with her; he was too prejudiced against Indians. Another part of me sees and hears him saying exactly what she said. I wonder if he told her about his secret room. If he did, he was stupider than I thought.

"Move it," *that woman* says.

Sophie flaps her arms against her sides. "Professor, you don't understand. She insulted me. I want to hurt her like her whole family hurt me. They were backstabbers. All cuz I'm Indian. Like I never was good enough. If anybody should know how crazy her family is, you should."

She leans towards *that woman*. "Look what her sicko sons did to you and Zoë. It freaks me out just imagining what you guys must have gone through. You got to know it's only cuz these white people think we're no good."

"Sophie, I once hoped you'd grow out of being a conniving schemer. Your problems have little to do with being Native. Now, get."

Sophie hesitates. Her eyes dart back and forth between us. She looks as if she's going to say something nasty, but I suspect she's afraid of Meshango. Sophie gives me one last snotty sneer, hops around on her heels, and, almost airborne, struts into the hospital like a plucked chicken.

Without speaking, I rush towards my car. Meshango follows. "Go away and leave me alone," I snap.

I pull the keys from my pocket and aim the remote at my car. Nothing happens. I pray I'll be behind the wheel and approaching the exit before she can stop me. I press one instead of two buttons, but as usual it doesn't work. Damn, I'll have to manually unlock the door again.

"Sally, please don't let Sophie upset you. What happened between her and Mr. Warner has nothing to do with you. And don't believe that part about them sleeping together. Sophie speaks, therefore Sophie lies. Please Sally, can we talk? I was pulling into the Health Centre across the road when I spotted you. I had a feeling she was bothering you. My appointment shouldn't take longer than thirty minutes. Could we meet for coffee afterwards? What happened to your sons had nothing to do with you. I want you to know that."

I twirl on the slick pavement, slip, and aright myself quickly. "Leave me alone." Then I realize something and add, "And the name is Mrs. Warner."

It's doubly irritating to see her dressed in a stylish long black coat with tailored pockets and lapels. The material is one hundred percent man-made, not real animal fur. There is dark faux fur around the collar. Her short silky hair matches the colour. For a moment I think of the first time we spoke; it was at a poetry reading at the university. Declan preceded her that night. I remember thinking that she was an attractive woman. Not like the Native women one sees in the seedy parts of most Canadian cities. Meshango looks as I have always wanted to look and feel; radiantly worthy of breathing.

"I'm so sorry for your loss, Sally—Mrs. Warner," she says in that soft, husky voice. "I can't imagine the pain you're going through. It was not your fault, and I never blamed you."

"Blamed me?" Less than ten feet from my car I stop and glare back at her. My body trembles. People walking past look at us. "It's you who are to blame. I don't know what you did—but I have no children. And you spread vicious rumours that Leland abused our sons while I did nothing to protect them. Shame on you."

She shakes her head in a tight arc. "By the time I realized what Declan had planned, it was too late. I tried to save him. Please believe me, I truly did. He berated his father. He said he was cruel and abusive. If it's a lie, I'm sorry. I never meant to hurt you."

"I don't believe anything you say." Damn, my voice cracks. "Go away...leave me alone." I advance towards my car, point the remote, press first one button and then the next. Obviously, I've pressed the wrong sequel. The taillights should flash and the engine should start. They don't. My chest hurts. I'm exerting myself beyond reason. I turn around to refute her further, but she's backed off. She looks hurt. I want to yell, "I'm the one who's hurt." But I'm not going to lose it here. I unlock the door, climb into my car, start the engine, and drive away. Her image disappears in my rear-view mirror.

When I'm able, I pull to the side of the road and call my lawyer from Leland's cell phone; I've yet to figure out how to use the hands-free system. His secretary puts me on hold while she hunts him down. I'm furious by the time he reaches the phone. "Why do you insist on keeping me waiting? I can always go somewhere else if you're too busy for my business." Traffic shrieks past my window.

"Calm down, Sally. What's wrong? I got a call early this morning. The police dismissed the allegations about there being something buried with Digger. What's happened?"

"Sophie Brooks threatened me in the hospital parking lot, and Meshango decided she was my protector. I want a restraining order against Meshango."

"Sally, think about what you're saying. That doesn't make sense. You have no provocation. Listen to me. She's not part of your life. Her experience was unpleasant, but it has nothing to do with you. If she needs closure, she'll have to find it on her own. Meanwhile, stay away from her, and I'm sure she'll stay away from you. Posting a restraining order against her isn't the answer. It'll bring unwanted attention you don't need. Let's talk about this later. I'll stop by."

I switch off and throw the phone onto the passenger seat. It's bounces and lands with a crack on the floor. I shift into drive. My tires spit up salt rocks as I gun the engine and swerve onto the road.

Of course I won't speak to Meshango. Never. I'd sooner sleep with a dead squirrel.

* * *

I'm crying as I arrive home. I miss Digger. He used to greet me at the door and jump nearly level with my face. It would scare me because I feared he'd hurt himself. I would set my groceries or parcels on the floor of the garage door and pat him until he calmed down. He'd make low throaty sounds I interpreted as adoration. Then I'd let him into the garage to do his business on the paper, whereupon he'd rush back inside and patiently wait for more pats.

He loved me despite everything. I didn't have to look a certain way or speak fluently about important issues. He was a sweet dog who loved me more than any other living being.

I reach my bedroom sniffling like an old fool. My life seems so tedious. There is nothing left to do but lie down and give up. I don't even make the bed first. I straighten the duvet and crawl inside. Life is too damn depressing. I think of Meshango and wipe my nose on my sleeve. I whip the duvet over my head and squeeze my eyes shut. As I wait to die, I will my bed to transport me somewhere else. Anywhere.

When Bronson was fourteen he put a dead squirrel in our bed. I never told Leland. He was away in Ottawa. I struggled for months to raise the boys myself. Leland was such a disciplinarian I was constantly bombarded with problems when he went away. Declan spent every waking moment in his room when he wasn't in school. Getting him to do his chores was nearly impossible. He was supposed to take turns helping me with the dishes. I'd end up doing them myself.

Bronson said dishes were a girl's job.

"What do you suppose families with no mum do?" I asked him once.

"Pay somebody," he said.

He was right. I had to hire a boy down the street to shovel the driveway because neither Declan nor Bronson could find the time. I never told Leland. I threatened to, but after a time, the boys knew I wouldn't. They were whipped enough without help from me. When Leland finally bought a snow blower, I never let on I knew Bronson took money from the younger kids in the neighbourhood for the privilege of snow blowing our driveway when he was already receiving an allowance for the chore.

Were they bad boys through and through? Or did we make them that way?

I've asked myself this many times. What could I have done to change their fate?

Once he hit puberty, Bronson frightened me. I never saw love, compassion, or respect in his eyes. At sixteen, he stopped looking fearful when his father reprimanded him. It occurred to me that he hadn't been afraid of Leland for some time. He hated both of us. Placing a dead squirrel in our—my—bed was one of the many ways he chose to tell me that.

I can't remember precisely why he put the squirrel in my bed. Possibly, I'd finally said "No" to some demand. As soon as I entered my bedroom for the night, I smelled something bad. It was worse than rotten eggs or burnt tires. I checked under the bed, on the floor, and in every corner. Finding nothing, I opened a window and climbed into bed. Fresh air didn't help and, wondering whether the cat had killed a bird outside my window,

I got up and closed it. I climbed back into bed and rolled over onto a matted lump. The sensation was appalling. I threw the covers back, exposing a headless squirrel. I screamed bloody murder. Bronson had decapitated this helpless little creature. Why? I continued screaming until Declan came running. Bronson lurked in the hallway. Declan lifted the squirrel into a paper bag and carried it out to the garbage bin. I heard him tell Bronson on the way back to his room, "You're an idiot. Isn't it bad enough around here without you making it worse? Don't do it again."

Bronson said, "Can't a guy have any fun in this stinking morgue?"

But he never did anything like that again. Declan was the only one who could control him.

At noon, the buzzer at my front door blasts. I'd forgotten my lawyer said he would stop by. Damn, I'd hoped to stay in bed for the rest of my life.

I flip the duvet aside and struggle to my feet. I straighten my clothes as I'm descending the stairs, and answer the door with as much bravado as I can muster. I'm embarrassed to be caught napping at this time of day.

"Sally, are you okay?"

I shrug as though the question doesn't warrant an answer, and lead him into the kitchen. He sits at the island and watches while I grind enough coffee beans for two cups. He continues muttering concern about my welfare. When the coffees are ready, I set the mugs on the breakfast table and suggest we sit there. The sun is shining through the French doors, and because I know it's temporary, I'm anxious for its warmth.

He takes a seat opposite me.

"Victim Services said it would take me a few weeks to function properly. I'll be fine." Without looking at him, I grip my mug and hope its heat will warm me.

"I talked to Lacroix an hour ago. He say Meshango ran into you by accident, but she's hoping the two of you can meet."

I close my eyes. I can just imagine what *that woman* said. I tried to help her, but all I got for my trouble was abuse. It's ridiculous that Lacroix went running to my lawyer like a sissy.

"Lacroix agrees with me. Speaking with Professor Meshango is certain to do more harm than good. Of course, his concern is for her; but trust me, it won't bring you peace."

I sip my coffee, determined to control my temper. It occurs to me I've been doing that my entire life. Time to change. Before my mind disintegrates completely, I give him my best rendition of

Leland's scowl, the one that says, "Do I look like I give a damn?"

Apparently, it doesn't work because he says, "Lacroix assures me that Meshango doesn't possess any damaging information. Sally, don't look at me like that. If you're ever going to have a decent life on your own, you need to put this behind you."

"For pity's sake, my husband just died."

"I know there was no love lost between you two. You'll be fine without him."

"I thought you were his friend."

"I was Leland's lawyer. I'm *your* friend."

I'm touched. I have always sensed he liked me, but I never let the thoughts linger. And I won't now. "I have no intention of meeting with her."

"Good. Forget about her. That will bring you the peace you need." His lips thin, and he frowns. "Did you tell the police about Leland's hidden room?"

I shake my head. The man changes topics like he changes ties. He never wears the same one twice. The one he's wearing now is blue with a thin yellow swirl running through it at a right angle.

"Should I have?" The sun hides behind a black cloud, and I wish I had my sweater on. My coffee mug is cooling fast.

"It's not relevant."

"Then why bring it up?"

He hesitates before giving me his lawyer face. The you-need-to-trust-me-because-I-know-best look.

I turn my gaze to the window and find my mind wandering. I think of nothing in particular. Blackberry bushes. Thorns that can rip your arms to shreds.

He sets his coffee down. "Listen to me, Sally. Don't volunteer anything. Some things are better left alone."

The sun breaks through the clouds and shines brightly across my snow-blanketed terrace. The grounds look crusty and hard. The perfect texture for Digger, so he could walk without sinking up to his neck.

"I'm right about this, Sally. Leland could have anything locked away in that room."

I sip my coffee. I don't need to look at my lawyer to know he's waiting for my reply. I don't respond, because for the first time in a while, I agree. Some things are best left alone. I concentrate on the view through the French doors. Outside, across my backyard, tiny crystals of snow glitter under the harsh sun. Inside...my thoughts break apart like pieces of semi-molten glass.

The local weatherwoman thinks a Chinook is on its way Friday afternoon that will raise temperatures from a bone-chilling minus fifteen degrees Celsius to a small reprieve of three degrees above zero. The chill in Lacroix's office is equal to the cold outside, but I doubt warm winds will improve the trouble between us. He and I have been avoiding each other since I spoke with Meshango without his consent. For the last five minutes, I've been weighing my options. I estimate that I've got three. Either I can ignore Lacroix, kiss his ass, or tell him to go screw himself.

The idea of kissing his ass isn't an option, so that takes care of number two. Option three isn't looking much better. More than likely it'll end with me sorting paperclips in Tuktoyaktuk. Nobody in authority has ever verified this, but I figure a guy like Lacroix could make unpleasant things happen, especially if you piss him off.

That leaves option one.

I fold my arms across my chest, wonder how I feel about being posted somewhere else. Part of me isn't sure I feel anything. There are no guarantees I'd be transferred closer to the investigation into Angie's death. A transfer back east would be torture.

It's all about the unknown, I realize, while the afternoon wastes away, and freezing in an unproductive staff meeting wears on my nerves.

This unscheduled meeting is about what exactly?

I force my thoughts away from Lacroix's possible revenge to the staff meeting. More specifically, the report one of the task force members outlines to those present.

"The liaison says the skeletal remains discovered at a gravel pit near McKenzie last month may prove to be the tree planter from Moricetown who had gone missing off Highway 16, and maybe the girl missing from Prince George," the constable says.

I spoke with the lead investigator last night. Because of natural decay and seasonal effects, everything's been boxed up and sent to Vancouver. Scientists there will reconstruct the skulls in hopes of identifying the deceased.

"We weren't able to identify either of them through dental records?" Lacroix asks.

"The killer smashed in the upper and lower jaws on both post-mortem so, no, there is no hope of identification that way. The one verification the coroner here in Prince George could make was that the pelvic bones were those of a female, along with possibly another female or child."

"Is that three found from the same area?"

"Yes, three out of the four missing since the summer," the constable says.

If all the hitchhikers who'd gone missing over the past ten years were added to the list, the total was closer to twenty. I glimpse the look on Lacroix's face. He is as disturbed by these deaths as we all are. The sooner we catch whoever's responsible, the better.

As if reading my thoughts, Lacroix looks at me. Even in that split second there is no mistaking what he's thinking: *Solve Warner's murder so we can all get back to what's important.*

I'm trying.

Cursing myself, I rub my eyes. Communicating telepathically with the man is a long way from ignoring him.

My neck's killing me. I feel like kicking someone. The worst part is I've been a homicide detective long enough to know not to let one case get to me like this. Yet here I am ready for a fight. Those three kids had bright futures. Warner, on the other hand, was an abusive husband and destructive father who'd used up his families' futures.

I wet my dry lips; aware that I've broken my first rule. No sitting in judgment. My job is to bring closure. I owe it to the victim and their families to bring their killers to justice. That simple.

Truth be known, I'm in a bad mood because I've been ordered not to contact the investigators working Angie's case. The first day or so I was okay with that because I had figured they'd contact me. It'd be the courteous thing to do.

Nobody called. And I'm left stewing.

Is it true? Do they have a suspect? Or another dead end?

One more thing I have to let go.

Lacroix listens intently to the constable's report. There is a small nervous tic in the corner of his left eye. His face shows a mixture of fatigue and frustration, along with a tic on his left eye that generally means...?

He's been reprimanded for trying to protect Dr. Meshango. His interference didn't cost us the case, but it could have. I'm guessing somebody let him know his actions were unacceptable.

How? A slap on the wrist? For someone like Lacroix, that would put him in a foul mood.

He looks at me and back to the constable. His left eyelid continues to twitch.

I didn't go to the brass, so who did? I glance around the room, angry that one of them may have. What Lacroix tried to do was crap, but having a rat in my unit is worse.

He looks my way again. He thinks it was me.

"Okay, that's it for today," he says. "Let's close these cases. Killian, stay behind."

I adjust my wristwatch, rest my elbows on the arms of the chair, entwine my fingers together. Lacroix gestures to the last constable leaving to close the door. As it shuts and clicks into place, he narrows his eyes on me. The hard stare is meant to unnerve me. I don't flinch. Being able to read him is like entering the ring against Mike Tyson to find George Chuvalo, Muhammad Ali, and Rocky Balboa in my corner.

"You want to say something?" He does that thing with his eyebrows again. Maybe to a street punk he looks menacing.

I feel a strange sensation. I wish I could swallow my pride, and tell him I'm not a threat. In fact, I'm sorry I spoke to Meshango without speaking to him first. Just because he didn't do the right thing doesn't mean I shouldn't.

He looks anything but impressed. He can't come right out and accuse me, but he wants to.

His left eye twitches again. "You said Mrs. Warner had no formal weapons training?"

"That's right." I think of adding that apparently Dr. Meshango does. That might be pushing things. No sense rubbing the man's face in it.

"On the list of things in her purse that morning it mentions a library card. Where did that lead?"

Carrigan never got back to me. Worse, I didn't followed up. It's not too late.

"Did you check to see what books she'd borrowed in the previous twelve months?"

He does that thing with his eyebrows again. I don't blink, but I feel the heat rush to my cheeks. "My mistake. I'll call today."

"Better yet, check with the library personally before you do anything else. Next time, try not to be so sloppy."

Right. I stand and walk to the door. Option number one it is.

"One more thing."

Now what?

"Next time you don't like the way I handle a situation, speak up. Don't go behind my back."

Hesitating, I grip the door knob. "Option one or option three?"

"Pardon me?" Lacroix asks. Though his voice is calm, I hear the agitation. "Did you say something?"

I can't help but smile. "She seems like a nice lady, Dr. Meshango. The consummate teacher, but a nice lady. And I didn't say anything." I don't look back to see Lacroix's expression. Enough said.

I reach my desk, locate the library's number in the book, call. As far as I'm concerned, Lacroix and I have resolved the problem. I won't bring it up again. Unless he does. I will find out who talked and straighten them out, though. No way that bullshit will be tolerated on my watch.

My call goes through. I ask to speak with the librarian, give my name and rank. Rubbing my neck, I listen to the local radio station while she's got me on hold.

The music stops. "Good morning, ma'am. My name is Corporal Killian. I'm investigating the murder of retired Minister of National Defence Leland Warner. I understand Mrs. Warner has a library card. I'll need a complete list of everything she's borrowed in the past year."

"I'm afraid it's not library policy to give out that information."

"This is a murder investigation, ma'am. Beg your pardon if it sounded like a request."

"Privacy rights exist. I'm following—"

"I'll bring a requisition form."

"It will take a few moments to access the information."

"No problem. Leave it at the front counter. I'll be right over."

"We close in ten minutes. Winter hours."

"I'll be there in less than five." I hang up.

The library is across the street. I fill out a requisition form, print it out, grab my parka and fur cap on my way out. Chinook? Not a chance. I check for a break in traffic and run across the street. As I do, I recall a case that had taken place a few years ago about Private Investigator Aidan Roth who was shot by a relative in that exact spot. I glance over both shoulders to the rooftops. The skin along my hairline tweaks. It's been a weird day.

I bypass the elevator and head up the thirty cement steps to the front entrance. Behind me, the sun sets for the day. Already the temperature feels as if it's dropped ten degrees. Freezing. The weatherman is nuts if he thinks there is a Chinook on its way.

At the main counter I give my name. The clerk smiles and hands me a printout. Two columns add up to fifty-three numbered entries. Mostly Romance and Historical novels. Several craft books, a few ethnic cookbooks, several self-help books geared to spiritual enlightenment. Nothing too exciting. I'm feeling a big relief when—the third to last entry, three months prior to Warner's death, Mrs. Warner had borrowed a book and kept it the full thirty days.

Rolling my neck, I hear a crack. Pocketing the list, I head towards the exit with the book's title burning in my brain: The Canadian Oxford Guide to Handguns.

I box up the Bateman. Tears dry on my face. Why was I crying? It's beautiful, yet I hate everything about it. Leland bought the limited edition the day after he'd spent the entire weekend with one of his floozies. Not that I cared who he slept with, but the idea he bought something for me then decided to place it in his study still stings.

I stood at the door after dinner, watching him unbox it. The process was quite involved. He had to take care not to damage the frame while carefully separating the boards along each corner and then at the back. I'd offered to help, but he said he could do it by himself. Besides, it was a surprise. Something special he'd seen that he knew I would love.

Balancing it against the back of his chair, so the picture was faced away from me, he took down the heavy mirror from the mantel and set it on the far wall where it was sure to lean without sliding.

"I think this will look better in the foyer, and this will be perfect right there." He gestured towards the spot above the fireplace. Then he lifted the painting, set it in place, and said, "Isn't it magnificent?"

"Yes. Are you supposed to place valuable paintings above fireplaces? Won't the heat ruin it?"

He rolled his eyes and laughed, as if what he said next was meant as teasing. "Sally, it's probably better if you don't think too hard. It can't be good for you."

I hated the print from that moment on.

Under the terrace lights, snow falls so heavily that a wall of whiteness separates me from the dark world outside. The ground-hugging fog looks frozen in place. Though the air around me smells like lilacs, lilies, and pasta spices, I know breathing deeply outside would be painful.

There is a strange hush as my false teeth masticate the last of my dinner. No, I'm wrong—the refrigerator has cut in, and its hum is thunderous inside my head. A wrenching, ugly noise comes from my throat. Tears fill my eyes, and I search the room as if somewhere in this space there is a reason to hang on. I'm a fighter, aren't I?

I want to be.

My tired eyes close. I survived my children's deaths, I can survive this desolation.

My chest heaves. Death is preferable to being pathetic.

A faint bleep interrupts my thoughts. I open my eyes. I look over my left shoulder and squint up at the surveillance monitor. A figure stands under the light inside the entrance to my front door. He looks up at the camera. It's Killian.

My shoulders feel heavy. I wonder what he could want.

The sound of the doorbell blasts through the kitchen. My hands cover my ears. If I ignore him, possibly he'll go away.

Three more blasts.

I draw myself up from the table; my legs feel as if they're full of water. Splish, splash. I grab the plastic microwave dish and drop it in the garbage bin as I shuffle past. No sense presenting evidence that I'm too uninspired to prepare a real meal.

I smooth down my blouse, recheck my buttons, straighten my cardigan, and practice my smile so it will appear natural.

I unlock the front door and invite Killian in. "It's nice to see you again, Corporal Killian. Please don't worry about your boots. These floors couldn't care less."

Killian looks uncomfortable. I suspect his news isn't good. He takes off his Balaclava and shakes it. Snowflakes spatter. A fine spray lands on me. I shiver.

"Is everything okay?" I wrap my sweater tight.

"Sorry to bother you during the dinner hour." He runs his hand through his short, dark hair. It spikes up. "It couldn't wait. I called earlier, but you weren't home."

"I had a doctor's appointment."

"I hope everything's okay."

"I'm fine." I gesture towards Leland's study, because Killian had appreciated that room during his last visit. I also want him to see that I've boxed up the Bateman for him. "Please come in. Have a seat."

He looks at the space where the picture had hung, walks over to the Tribeca chair on the right, and waits beside it. He's waiting for me to sit first?

I sit on the chair to the left—then stand halfway. Where are my manners? "Would you like a coffee or a cup of tea?"

"No, thank you." He reaches into his breast pocket and pulls out a small notepad before sitting. He flips through several pages, scans something, and looks at me intently. It feels as if he is struggling over the right approach.

The silence is comforting. It gives me a chance to marshal my thoughts.

"Mrs. Warn—"

"Yes, Corporal?"

A fleeting smile crosses his face. "Could you tell me again what happened the morning your husband died?"

Outside the French doors and beyond the lights the night is black and endless. I repeat my version of what happened while trying to focus through to the far side of the house where I know my gardens lie. I imagine Digger's ashes.

"Is there anything you remember that you forgot to mention the last time we spoke?"

It's not like him to ask such stupid questions. Is something wrong? Maybe it has nothing to do with Leland's murder, after all. "Unfortunately, my memory is terrible. It's better if you ask me something specific."

He glances at his notes. "You borrowed the Canadian Oxford Guide to Handguns from the library. Can you tell me why?"

"A guide to handguns? Leland asked me to borrow it for him." I'm not sure what the expression on Killian's face means.

"Why that particular book?"

I shrug, and catching his look of disappointment, decide to try harder to come up with a plausible answer. "It was last September, or possibly October." I shake my head. "It may even have been earlier. I was going downtown. Leland told me the book would be waiting at the counter on the second floor." I tap my fingertips to my chin. I'm making most of this up to appear helpful. "I can't remember the clerk, though. Does it matter?"

Killian is intent on studying my face. He is pleasant and respectful always, and I wonder if I should tell him his mother would be proud if she were alive today. No, he might see that as false flattery. Expressing my feelings always leaves me feeling awkward anyway; hence I don't always appear genuine. I want to, though.

Back to what he's saying.

Ah yes.

At my age, because every day feels identical to the next, most days are forgettable. I try harder to remember that day. At best, it is blurry. Then bad memories surface, and immediately I imagine blackberry bushes.

"Leland seldom asked me for a favour. I'm sure I was happy to borrow the book for him. I doubt I asked him why. I remember glancing at him through the gathering room's French doors a few hours later and seeing him sitting here at his desk. He had one of his guns apart. It was fascinating to watch him.

"The pieces were spread on an old white tablecloth on his desk. If I watched him long enough, I could sometimes gauge whether it was okay to interrupt him. He didn't like the idea of an intercom system. He planned the house so we could see across one corner of the back yard from the gathering room here into his study on one side, and the kitchen on the other. That worked best for Leland."

I tap my chin again. "I'm sorry, what did you want to know about the book?"

"He didn't say why he wanted it at that particular time? I got the impression Mr. Warner was already knowledgeable about guns." Killian's expression softens, but I'm quickly learning there is far more to him than meets the eye.

"Yes, he started collecting when he was twenty-two. Possibly there was something in the book he needed to research. Does it list current prices?"

"No."

I shake my head and shrug. I want to help, but I can't think of a reason that will suffice. It's now that I notice Killian's nails have been chewed to the quick. I force my eyes away. "Periodically, he liked to take one or two of his guns apart. Possibly he needed the book so he could recalibrate one of them."

I smile to myself because I have no idea what that means, though I like the sound of it. I also decide that calling my lawyer is no longer necessary. I look over at Killian, his notepad, and then back to his eyes.

"Leland said guns didn't kill people, people did. He was referring to our sons." I blink back a tear. Goodness, I can't mention them without tearing up. It's been eighteen months. When will it stop? "Leland patiently tried to teach me to use a gun."

"How did that go?"

"Not well. I was terrified. He promised they wouldn't go off, but I was so sure I'd do something wrong."

"Did he insist?"

"At first, but when I confessed guns made me think of our boys and..." I'm teary again.

He nods and folds his notepad back into his pocket. The serious look on his face makes me sad. I wonder if his fingertips hurt. Chewing them is a sign of a greater problem.

How can I help you, Corporal Killian? Tell me.

His raw fingertips remind me of my brother. Davey chewed his fingernails to the quick whenever something frightened him.

He'd scrunch his eyebrows together, pop a fingernail in his mouth, and chew away. I could see the fear behind his eyes. Problem solving was difficult for him. Davey's lot in life was to try to do the right thing. When he couldn't, he escaped to Vietnam to die fighting a war. Poor Davey.

"Would knowing why he needed the book help to find the person responsible?"

"Probably not," Killian says woefully. "But I hate loose ends."

"Considering your job, that makes sense." I refrain from reaching over and patting his hand. Touching him feels inappropriate, although I remember touching his arm one day and it was okay. "Why do you suppose people kill each other?"

"Usually it's over money or sex."

That answer surprises me. "What about revenge?"

"That, too." His eyes are intent on mine while the rest of his face appears relaxed. There is no mistaking what he's thinking—I'm his prime suspect.

"Did you always want to be a policeman?"

Again his expression softens. "It was my third choice. Medical school proved to be a bitch—sorry. I mean...it was over my head. I switched majors to Education. Didn't take long to realize teaching wasn't for me either. I wasn't cut out for anything but hunting bad guys, I guess." A grin appears briefly. "My mum wanted me to be a biologist. And in her memory, I tried."

"She's proud of you, Corporal Killian. I'm sure of that. Being a policeman is a noble profession. You bring closure to families." I pause, not sure if I should ask the next question.

"What, Mrs. Warner?"

"Forgive me if this sounds ignorant. But has being Native made it difficult for you? I assume our Native populations have a reason to distrust policemen."

"It's never been a problem." A light blush appears in his face.

I rise from my seat, because I assume our time together has ended. "I wrapped up your Bateman print, so you can take that with you tonight."

"Mrs. Warner, you shouldn't have done that. I told you before I can't take the picture."

I don't recall him saying any such thing. "Why not? It's collecting dust here."

"It would be inappropriate of me, ma'am. I can't buy it now or in the future. It's a...bad...idea." He says this slowly as if he's speaking to a deaf person.

"And why is that? It's not doing me any good hanging onto it. I plan on selling everything, so you'd be doing me a favour."

"Do you mind me asking? Are you having financial difficulties?" Being a policeman, he surely knows the answer.

"No. I simply don't need all these things. As soon as you find Leland's killer, I'm going to sell everything and move into an apartment or condominium in town."

"That's probably a good idea. But I can't buy your painting."

I'm shocked to hear this and quickly cover up my irritation. I want to say, "But you said you would." However, I know it could make matters worse.

"Why don't you have an auction?"

"An auction?"

"There is a company in town. They'll come in, estimate everything, take care of the advertisements, and do the auction here."

"Wonderful." I smile, though I'm thinking that in my day, once you accepted a gift, you didn't renege. I turn away, pretending not to notice that he's watching me intently.

* * *

After breakfast I stay seated at the table, perplexed by a nagging question. Why did I marry Leland?

Because I thought he'd take care of me. I thought if I outlived him, I wouldn't end up in a home like my grandmother. Though, come to think of it, she refused to live with us. She knew before we did that we were unworthy.

I shake my head, try to dispel such attitudes, and instantly my emotions are fed by memories of Leland's face when he was disgusted by something I'd said or done. It got so I expected that look, that voice, that tone that said I was worthless, and how could he have ever thought I would be the ultimate life partner when it's so clear to him what a wasted piece of brain tissue I've turned out to be.

I hate him for those memories. More so since our sons died.

I waited.

It was only a matter of time before he reverted back to the old Leland.

I waited.

Now I sit here at the breakfast table, in the dawn of a new and equally depressing winter morning, wondering if I would have eventually seen the old Leland.

Snowflakes fall. Snowflakes thickened by whatever it is that is going on inside those clouds slowly drift to the ground, adding to the already heavy accumulation. The same terrace that beckons me in the spring now represents the minefield of my future. I know I'm supposed to see the beauty surrounding me; God's easel of brilliant designs and patterns and textures. I know that. Yet, all I see is grey.

I called my lawyer last night after Killian left. He pleaded with me to stick to the rules. No explaining to the nice policeman that Leland had a secret room built off his bedroom upstairs. No confiding that I had a miserable marriage and a dysfunctional home life while my sons were alive. (Too late) No hint I believed my husband responsible for their deaths, the death of Mrs. Norris, and the terrorizing of Zoë and her mother, *that woman*.

My lawyer insists I must stay away from Meshango, yet, my pastor says I need to speak with her. He wants to mediate, of course. He's worried about me. He says I need to hear what she has to say. He says I can set the terms. I can instruct her on what she can and cannot mention, and then I all I have to do it sit back and listen. My lawyer says not to listen to my pastor because he's an idiot.

My lawyer has a point. I can see it now: Meshango vomits a bunch of technical terms in that kind voice. But I know she's being snide and blames me for the horror everyone put her and her Barbie-doll daughter through.

Why is my pastor so convinced I need to do that? Because I can't carry on with my life until I put my past behind me? Stupid me for saying anything to his big-mouth wife.

Meshango has nothing to say that I want to hear.

The morning she was scheduled to testify at the inquiry into Bronson and Declan's deaths, I was searching for my light spring jacket when Leland came out of the kitchen. I searched through the cloak closet near the front door for my suede mid-length jacket, instead. I glanced over my shoulder, pondered briefly why he was shaking his head, but I never expected he meant I couldn't go. Of course I was going to be there to hear what she had to say.

"We're not going." His tone was low and strangely gentle.

"I'll wear my autumn jacket. I can always take it off if it's too warm inside the courtroom." I checked my pockets. Sometimes I found money, but most often it was old tissue; my allergies always give me problems in the spring.

"We're not going." His voice went up an octave, but still I could tell he wasn't angry.

"What are you talking about? We have to be there. We have to hear what she says about our children. Our dead—"

"No, we don't."

At that point I was so agitated that I glared at him. I was never one to argue, but I was on the verge. "Don't do this to me,

Leland. I have to be there." I slipped into my jacket.

Suddenly, he was beside me, sliding the jacket off my shoulders, hanging it back on the hanger, closing the closet door, and steering me towards the living room. "Our lawyer will be there. We'll have access to the transcript. We don't need to attend."

I tried to twist away from him, but he kept propelling me forward. "I have to be there." I started crying.

"Trust me about this, Sally. We don't need to see all those people hanging on every word she says. The news reporters will hound us. There are still three news vans outside. We aren't going. You don't need to be put through that, and neither do I."

It was the only time I had ever defied him. But that day I was determined. I broke free, retrieved my coat, and rushed for the door. He was close behind, calling for me to stop. As I reached the car, reporters started shouting questions at me from the road. Leland gestured for me to move, he would drive. I climbed over into the passenger's seat. All the way there he instructed me on how he would like me to act. We arrived at the courthouse in less than six minutes.

I never entered the building.

Before I knew what happened, our lawyer was there, spouting something about a recess and Meshango already testifying. Then the reporters saw us. They rushed forward so fast I jumped back, fearing they would trample me. The look, the accusations in their questions and their expressions—I began to cry. Leland shouted for them to step back. I can't remember what else he told them, but the next thing I knew we were back in my car, and then finally back at home. Leland coaxed me out of the car while the media snapped pictures of us from the sidewalk.

The accusations I'd seen in their eyes haunted me for weeks. They blamed me. After all, I was their mother.

I never heard the whole truth. I never read the transcripts. I never saw any newspapers. Leland muted the sound on our television if our names were mentioned. When I finally watched TV on my own again, we were old news. Friends and family never asked me questions. They assumed I knew what she'd said. What I learned was mostly second-hand and garbled.

The truth is: I didn't want to know.

What good would it do? How would it help to know I'd ruined my sons' lives by being a hollow body of fear who turned them into killers?

Besides, I didn't want to hear the awful things they did.

I still don't.

Can't I be left alone to remember them as my children? My sons?

"No."

Pardon?

I glance behind me. There is no one. I look towards the monitor, but no one's standing at the door either. My backyard is deserted. Does that mean I've gone insane? Then there is one thing left to do, tell whoever's speaking inside my head to, "Get out!"

"It's possible she's telling the truth about the book. What did the librarian say?" Lacroix asks, after our regular morning meeting has ended and we're alone.

"Nobody remembers her borrowing the book. The surveillance footage isn't clear enough to show the book's cover."

"Even if she read it, it doesn't prove she killed him. It was over three months ago. Why did she wait?"

I rub my eyes. "I don't know."

"But you think she shot him?"

"We've gone back six months through his cases. Not one red herring. We're now going back a year. Like you said, why would someone wait that long?"

"We need evidence, something to present to the Crown so they can present it to the jury. That's how the penal system works. We find the bad guys—"

"Give me a break."

"Pardon me?" Lacroix looks calm.

I need my head examined. "Look. I'm sorry about Dr. Meshango. But that's your fault. I didn't ask you to interfere in a murder investigation to protect her."

"Be careful what comes out of your mouth next."

I shake my head. I don't have a clue what I hope to gain by sprouting off. Except I'm tired of not speaking because I'm afraid I'll lose my job.

When all is said and done, not much matters any longer except my job. Sally Warner probably killed her husband, because he deserved it. I don't care. I just need this asshole off my back. Anyone who expects people to sit in this piece of junk he calls a chair doesn't deserve their respect.

"Fine, call me a dumb shit. But my people and I have been working this case night and day for a week and we have nothing. Nada. Zilch." I lift my hands, palm out, and then drop them to my lap. "Help me out here. You've read the report. Why do you believe Sophie Brooks, Sally Warner, and Dr. Meshango are innocent?"

Lacroix glares at me. "Dr. Meshango has an alibi. Apparently, so does Miss Brooks. If Mrs. Warner is your killer, where is the evidence? What happened to the weapon? Where are her bloody clothes? Your gut instincts aren't going to cut it with the Crown Counsel."

I lean forward, rest my forearms on my knees, clasp my hands together. "Ain't that the truth."

"Is she guilty?"

"I think so."

Lacroix's eyebrow shot up. "But there is no proof."

"No."

"Where was Warner's lawyer at the time of the killing?"

"At the courthouse preparing for a nine o'clock bail hearing."

"Due diligence," Lacroix says. "We go over everything again because the answer is there. Go back to the house. Go through his personal papers. Pay attention to his business correspondence. Ask somebody from the Crown to recheck his legal papers. Have an expert look over his portfolio, not just his summary. Re-interview his broker. There has to be something we missed. I'll contact Ottawa and have them re-interview his former staff. They'll bring in his personal assistant, his administrative assistant, and anybody else who might have had a motive—until something comes up. We'll do the same here. This time we'll pay closer attention, and try to make a connection to his wife."

"And if we don't find anything?"

"I know what you want me to say. It ain't going to happen. Look at their marriage. Talk to their doctor, friends, colleagues. Talk to Declan's and Bronson's friends. Somebody knows something."

I clench my jaw. The victim was once an important member of parliament. A respected attorney. He had connections. He had influence. Why in the hell shouldn't GIS in Surrey be handing the case so we can get back to more important police business like the missing and murdered off Highway 16?

Any other time Surrey's Special Crime Unit would jump at the chance to work this case. What is the bloody hell wrong with these people?

One of the constables from the task force pops his head in, says to Lacroix, "One of the IDs for the remains found near McKenzie came in."

"That was fast," Lacroix says.

The constable checks his notes. "District's liaison is in with the superintendent. Turns out she was a local teen from Moricetown."

"Moricetown is a long way from McKenzie," I speak up. "What

about the second skull?"

"They're still working on the ID."

"Tell them thanks, and to let us know the history after they talk to the Littlemans," Lacroix says.

"He's talking to them now," the constable says, and then steps out and shuts the door.

I face Lacroix. "I've got cases up the yin-yang that deserve my attention more than an ex-minister. I can turn this over to Surrey SCU."

"That's not for you to decide."

"I know that. It's a suggestion."

"The task force will handle it."

"Where do I sign up?"

"Get back to work, Danny."

I stand. I'm now in a foul mood. Until recently, I never considered begrudging Warner his day of justice. If Sally Warner killed her husband, she's no danger to anyone. Why put a broken old lady in prison?

There goes the rule breaking again.

Lacroix's phone rings. He fixes his eyes on me as he answers. "Sergeant Lacroix."

I make an attempt to leave. He stabs a finger at the chair I'd been sitting in. I wonder if I should bark like an obedient dog.

"Why?" Lacroix says into the receiver. "When...? What are you going to do...?" He turns his back on me. "Do you think it's a good idea...?"

I sit, examine my fingernails, note there are no nails left to chew, then observe the scuffmarks on my shoes. I wonder who Lacroix is talking to. It doesn't sound like Ottawa or E-Division because his tone isn't kiss-ass. It might be personal.

"Can I call you back in five minutes?" He hangs up and studies me.

I wonder what I've done now.

"That was Dr. Meshango," Lacroix finally says.

A strange way to describe the woman you're sleeping with. I gnaw on my thumb cuticle, decide it might not be so strange. Lacroix probably refers to his father as mister and his mother as ma'am.

"Sally Warner agreed to speak with her," he says.

"Why?"

"You tell me."

I wait. He continues to stare. "I'll look over my notes. She hasn't said outright that she means the doctor harm."

"She said she'd walk out if anyone else showed up. Namely

182

you."

"Me?"

"Are you losing her confidence?"

"No."

"Then why doesn't she want you there?"

"I don't know. Maybe because she's guilty."

"But you can't prove it."

"Maybe Surrey can."

"Not going to happen."

"Would Dr. Meshango consider wearing a wire?"

This time Lacroix gapes at me as if I'm the stupidest cop in the west. "You obviously don't know her."

I shut my mouth lest I say something else equally stupid.

"How's Mrs. Warner's state of mind?"

"I'm no shrink, but I'd say she's fragile."

"Either prove she killed her husband or go find who did. Conjecture isn't going to close this case. Hoping Surrey will take it off your hands isn't going to happen, either. Stop looking for an out. You keep treating this as if you're above it. Every case has merit. Every murder victim deserves justice. You have fifteen years of experience, so I shouldn't have to remind you of this. If you plan to spend the rest of your life hunting your wife's killer, quit the force." Lacroix narrows his eyes, looks up from beneath the bush of hair he calls eyebrows with an expression more than likely means: *Don't be an asshole*, and says, "Understood?"

"Yep." I stand.

"Forget you don't like the guy. Forget you sympathize with his widow. When the time comes, the case will be passed to Cold Case Files, but until then, the investigators in this detachment will exercise due diligence beyond their duty. Or I'll transfer their sorry asses. Clear?"

"Clear." I reach for the doorknob.

"Mary, Jesus, and Joseph," Lacroix says. I turn. He shakes his head yet again, frowns. He obviously isn't finished his speech. "Danny, pull up your socks. Stop acting like one of the cherries Regina sends us every year. If you believe she killed him, then the evidence is still in the house. Get a copy of the blueprints."

"We're still waiting."

"Make it happen. Get the GPS over there and search the entire yard. If she killed him, trust that her lawyer will plead it out, and she'll get a slap on the wrist."

I gag, choke, thump my chest to help dislodge whatever is stuck in my throat. More than likely it's my foot.

"Are you okay?" Lacroix sounds alarmed.

Despite possibly choking to death, I nod. My throat clears. Gasping, I straighten up, gasp.

"Then stop choking and get back to work."

The fact he won't give me any slack because of Angie should mean something. It does. Who'd have thought the good sergeant was a decent sort. He doesn't like the idea of nailing Mrs. Warner any more than I do.

I exit his office, cross the room, glance towards the only window in the detachment. What little sky I can see is clear of snow clouds. But what about what I can't see? If I got special treatment because my wife was murdered, serving here in Prince George would become unbearable. Snow or no snow.

Damn. Lacroix' little pep talk actually helped.

Halfway to my desk, I speak to a member of my team. "Track down Warner's broker." I instruct the next constable at the next desk, "Grab volunteers from the Crown's office to finish sorting through the boxes of Warner's files in the conference room." She gives me a why-me face. I try Lacroix's trick and scowl at her.

I turn to the next constable. "Go back over the autopsy report one word at a time. Before you do that, post a memo saying no more than thirty-minute lunch breaks and over-time until this case is resolved."

I sit down at my desk, open Warner's file to page one, lean over it. I'll read through it repeatedly. All day if I have to. I'll read until something pops. A clue. Something we missed. Lacroix is right. I'm good at my job. It's because of me the worst serial killer in Canada's history, The Butcher, is under lock and key. I've got the brains, the instincts, the patience. I'll find Warner's killer because that is what I do.

I chew on my thumbnail; my optimism fades in the blink of an eye. Facts speak for themselves. Vancouver has become the world's largest market for heroin and cocaine, and the battle ground for the gang wars. I took the post in Prince George for two reasons. Because it was 500 kilometres from Vancouver, an hour's flight from any progress in Angie's murder, and because they told me I had to go somewhere.

If only I listened to Angie, and moved before...

My neck throbs. I rub hard. Worry: Does destiny, which seems to screw up on a regular basis, not exist at all? Is fate sheer chance with no reason? Or hope?

Damn, that is too heavy even for me.

The liaison from the task force exits the communication room and heads towards me. His face is pale, drawn. I imagine he's just gotten off the phone with the Littlemans, a part of the job that never gets easier.

"Did you learn anything new?"

He nods, clears his throat, looks down at his notes. "TJ—stands for Therese-Jolie Bernalda Littleman, eighteen years old, went missing two summers ago. Her dad said she'd been working for Forestry for three weeks when she and some friends got a weekend off. During an unscheduled party down at the river, TJ, who wasn't an experienced drinker, wandered off. Her friends thought she'd gone on a pee-break and didn't go looking for her until a couple of hours later." He looks up from his notepad.

"How long before a search was organized?"

"Daybreak. Elders from the band called in local trackers. They followed her tracks all the way up to the highway. Whoever stopped and picked her up knew enough not to pull to the side of the road. The trackers found no tire marks. Just dead-end shoeprints. But why take the body all the way to McKenzie?"

"Do they know who the second body belongs to?"

"No. But the question caused quite a stir. Seems a lot of people have gone missing off this highway."

My point exactly. "Did Vancouver give you cause of death?"

"Blunt force trauma to the head. And they're pretty sure she was strangled. Post-mortem."

"Time of death?"

"Most likely within hours of her disappearance. She's been missing for two years."

"Could her dad supply any possible suspects?"

"No. He said TJ did well in school. Hadn't caused them a minute of trouble. No gangs, no run-ins with police. No boyfriend. Not an aggressive or assertive type. Other than working occasionally for the band, Forestry was her first job. I haven't talked to any of her teachers yet, but her dad said she excelled in math and science. She'd been accepted to UBC and hoped to work for Forestry's research department after she graduated."

"An all-round good kid." Nothing like Warner or his two sons.

"Yes." He looks towards the exit doors. "I better get back to District and let them know."

The phone rings. "Yeah." I pick up the phone, mumble my usual, "Corporal Killian, how can I help you?"

"Laurier from Victoria here. Got some news I thought you'd need to know. Turns out the Native artist, Miss Sophie Brooks, wasn't at the powwow like she claimed."

"You've got witnesses who will testify?" Many eyewitnesses weren't always quick to help law enforcement.

"Two Elders and three organizers."

I think but don't ask, "How did they slip past your investigators?" Questioning Victoria's methods won't encourage cooperation in the future. "Can you fax me the statements?"

"They're on their way."

"Thanks." I hang up.

My assistant sets a large Manila folder on my desk. It's marked *Killian, Confidential.* I recognize CSIS's insignia. She smiles down at me. "How are you doing?"

"What?" I shake my head. I haven't got time for small talk. "The file on Mrs. Warner?"

Still smiling, she nods. "See what a little manners can accomplish? It only took a week."

The phone rings. The call display shows Dr. Meshango. I let the phone ring three times before reaching for it. The thought of irritating her fills me with glee. Sometimes it's difficult being a good Christian. "Hello."

"Mrs. Warner, it's Brendell. How are you?"

"The same as I was two hours ago."

"You haven't changed your mind."

"Why would I change my mind? Oh, you must think I'm one of those flighty, hysterical types."

There is a pause on the other end of the line. The fine professor seems to be at a loss for words. Finally, she says, "Do you still want to do this?"

"I said I would." I hear a thump in the background and wonder if I've caused her to drop something. I don't like who I am right now, but I can't seem to stop myself. This woman was the last person to see my sons alive. I need to hear what she has to say.

"Where would you like to meet?"

"Up on the hill."

"The University?"

I'm a little surprised myself. Because Declan liked it up there? "Yes."

"Okay."

"Unless, of course, you've changed your mind. I wouldn't want to force *you*." The sarcasm in my voice is thick, and I have to admit to myself that I'm shocked at my sharp tongue. I sound like Bronson. "Aren't you going to ask me when?"

The expected pause. "When?"

I glance at my wristwatch. It's fifteen after ten. I don't want to put this off now that I've made up my mind. I don't want to appear anxious, either. "One o'clock in the recital area near the circular fireplace."

"I'll be there."

"Yes, I'm sure you will be." I hang up.

My palms are wet. I wash my hands at the kitchen sink. Dry them. Now they're shaking. Instead of sitting or going to my room to rest, I stand there. I'm plagued by a weird thought. Did

Declan choose this woman because he loved her? Or hated her?

I can't remember the moment when I stopped loving Leland. Or when I started hating him. Maybe my love died over time and not in one precise instant.

One morning, I looked at him while he read the newspaper at the kitchen table, the boys ate breakfast—wolfing it down—and I felt like a stranger in my own home.

They were discussing the Canucks' win the night before in the series against Calgary. Leland said something about the Vancouver Canucks being bums, and Declan retaliated by insisting their new line-up was as good as they come. They were short on defence. To which Bronson remarked that they were a bunch of cocksuckers, and New York was going to wipe their asses all over the ice.

I stopped sipping my tea and glared across the table at my husband, who still had his head in the paper. I waited for him to scold his son for speaking in such a vulgar manner in front of me.

Leland didn't look up. "The Rangers are going to kick their butts."

Bronson laughed.

I'm trying to remember how old they were.

Declan was...fifteen. He stopped laughing shortly after that. I don't know why. Though, considering how his life ended, I should have tried to find out.

That particular morning, I looked across at Leland and saw a man I knew I couldn't trust. I don't mean faithfully; I knew he'd been sleeping around for years. I couldn't trust him to protect me, to defend me, or to think enough of me to recognize my virtue. I felt betrayed. Yet, not surprised. I looked at him as one might look at a co-worker who has no respect for what you bring to the job. That was a revelation; I equated my participation in this family as a job. Worse, as I studied Bronson—subtly, because I'd learned to heed his temper—I had a harder fact to acknowledge. I didn't like him.

What kind of mother doesn't like her twelve-year-old?

I drove Bronson further away because I was convinced I had to make myself like him. Hence, I doted on him, hung on his every word. I was at his disposal.

I cringe now at the memory of the confusion—no—the pain in Declan's face. What must he have thought of me? I was his mother, but I betrayed him.

In time, the pain in his eyes turned to indifference. That is the saddest part. Just as Leland had betrayed me, I betrayed

188

Declan. I became the fool who treated the child I didn't like better than the one I did. I thought Declan would forgive me. Wrong.

* * *

The parking lot at the University is crowded. I circle several times before locating a space along the far edge. I lock my doors, button up my coat, and retrieve my gloves from my pockets. Trudging through the snow towards the entrance proves difficult. The tip of my nose is frozen by the time I enter the University. I feel sick. Meshango is waiting for me on the chesterfield near the fireplace. She is dressed in a black pantsuit with a long, light brown overcoat. Her calves are crossed. She has on high heel boots. Her hair is styled in messy spikes. I hate her because she looks so competent and self-assured. Her bone structure is perfect, though she is in her early fifties. Dark brown eyes, tight auburn skin over high cheekbones, perfectly arched eyebrows; she is everything I wish I was.

Why does God hate me? That is not correct. Hate implies acknowledgement of one's existence, and God forgot about me a long time ago.

Meshango waves. A faint smile crosses her face until she recognizes the expression in my eyes; she nods her acknowledgement instead. I want to pick up something lethal and smash in her face.

I sit down beside her at a safe distance. I don't glance her way. I study the area. I can smell popcorn. Or is it stinky socks?

I look up. Meshango and I are the focus of attention. Student, professors, even the cleaning staff watch us. And why wouldn't they? She was once the head of their English Department. Me? I was married to the Minister of National Defence. No, that is not what they remember. They remember I am Declan's and Bronson's mother, and they tried to kill Meshango.

I say to myself, *Mrs. Leland Warner, mother of killers,* and choke up.

The many eyes overwhelm me. Their expressions are a mixture of curiosity and the assumption of my guilt. Oh, yes, and pity. I smooth the skin on my throat. I glance at the floor, at Meshango's shiny pointed boots, back at their faces. I struggle to my feet. "I can't do this."

She stands. "Let's go."

For once, I agree with her. We head towards the doors. From behind me, Meshango whispers in my ear to smile. I do. I smile and imagine myself brushing blackberry branches out of my way.

Outside, winter slaps me in the face and steals my breath. I tighten my collar and lay gloved hands over my covered throat. This is pneumonia weather. The smart thing to do is to take shallow breaths. What little air I do inhale stings.

Meshango's firm hand touches my arm. "We can sit in my vehicle." She points to an SUV parked a short distance away.

The perks of being a scholar: a parking space for life.

She pulls a remote from her pocket and presses some buttons. I have a similar remote for my car, but no one ever took the time to show me how all the buttons work. And I was too stubborn to ask. The whole thing seems so silly now.

Her SUV's engine fires up, and the doors unlock. I climb into the passenger seat while she holds the door open, and then closes it for me. The inside still has that new vehicle smell. The leather seats are comfy and soft to the touch. She walks around the front of her vehicle to the driver's side. It occurs to me that I could lean over and open her door, but I don't. I'm not here to be courteous. If I were, I would ask about mileage and whether this thing feels as if it will tip on corners. I hate that sensation. I once travelled to Vancouver with my brother-in-law who owned a 2000 Tahoe at the time. I was so sure we would end up toppling to the canyon floor below. Worse, I never once asked him to slow down. What kind of a fool experiences such horror and says nothing?

The answer is easy.

A willing victim.

"It will be warm as toast in here in a few moments," Meshango says.

I'm no longer cold, so it doesn't matter.

She adjusts one of the knobs on her dash, which is lit up with fancy blue and green lights, like an airplane's cockpit. Instantly the fan slows from a loud hum to a soft murmur.

"At least now we can hear ourselves think."

Small talk, who would have guessed she'd be so poor at it.

"Do you want to ask me anything?" She shifts in her chair with her back half leaning on the door.

I glance at her face, and it occurs to me that she's uncomfortable. It also occurs to me I am not. "Why aren't you in class? I thought you were teaching Cree or Mich-something?"

"Cree and Michif. I'm thinking I'll teach an Ojibwa class, too. This semester Tuesdays and Thursdays are my days off."

She's wearing a pretty emerald pendant on a gold chain around her neck. It's shaped like a teardrop. Her earrings match. Her gold wristwatch is two sizes too large and fits like a bracelet. She has no markings, no tattoos, or scars that I can see. I envy her. After my sons died, there was much speculation about Meshango's past and why she was chosen as a confidant by Declan. Rumours have it that she was abused as a child. I wonder if Declan knew that. I'm sure he did. Why else was he so obsessed with her? She was twenty-three years older than him, yet he romanticized his plight as hers and hers as his. Comrades in their bitterness?

"Did my sons suffer?" My words shock me.

"No." Her eyes are wide.

"Was he afraid?"

"Declan?" She looks directly at me. Something in her eyes change. "He hesitated. Yes, I think he was."

Good, she's not going to lie. "What about Bronson? Did he know?"

"That he was about to die? No. He had no idea."

Across the way is a cluster of silver birch trees. Normally, I wouldn't know the difference between balsam, cottonwoods or birch, but Declan took the time to explain the differences one day. I'd taken the boys up to Connaught Hill. Bronson was off chasing squirrels with a plastic baseball bat while Declan had his pencil crayons out and was recreating the park's magnificent autumn scene. Imagine the greenest grass, white picnic tables, and trees with orange, red and gold leaves.

While I kept my eye on Bronson, I asked Declan why he'd painted some of the tree trunks white, some light grey, but most silver. "To show which are which," he told me. His favourites were the silver birch. In his painting, the birch leaves were sparkling diamond shapes.

"Bronson didn't know what was coming," she says. "Moments before Declan shot him, they'd been laughing together. I didn't know it then, but Declan was helping Bronson to relax. Bronson had no time to react. I was sitting next to him...when..."

She stares over her left shoulder at something. I glance around her to the University's doors to see what she's looking at but see no one. Perhaps it's what she sees in her mind that has her attention. She mumbles something.

"Professor, you'll have to speak up. I can't hear you."

She leans her head back against the rest, and clears her throat. "It was harder for Declan. He wanted to die, but he had hoped..."

I turn my gaze from Meshango to the silver birch. Her silence is a reminder of my many nightmares. I take a deep breath and glimpse her out of the corner of my eye. She is staring straight ahead.

191

All this time, I'd thought I couldn't hear what she had to say because it would be too painful. Now I see that to say what she knows is also painful.

I feel suddenly cold, and I shiver. My hatred for this woman has kept me warm for months. I dreamed about making her pay for allowing my sons to die. I wanted, needed her to suffer. Now I sit here in silence when there are too many questions I should be asking. "He was hoping for what?"

"He wanted me to do it. After he killed Bronson, he wanted me to pick up Bronson's gun and shoot him."

Declan wished to die in a shootout. Why doesn't that shock me?

"I wouldn't, and it was the only time I ever saw him lose his temper."

I understand her surprise because I can't remember the last time he lost control either. "Did he say why he wanted to die?"

"No."

"He told you his father had molested them?"

"He implied it."

"Which do you suppose is worse, Professor Meshango, mental or physical abuse?"

By the pain on her face, I'm guessing the good doctor came away from the experience scathed. A small wrinkle forms between her eyebrows. She looks as if she's about to cry. Now I understand why I didn't want to speak with her. Instinctively I knew I'd feel apathy. Shame on me.

I never thought about the impact my sons' deaths had on her. Or did I? She knew a young man who, faced with an uncertain future, chose to die rather than fight.

My son.

Before I began ignoring him, I should have taught him how to be a fighter.

"I begged him not to do it," she says so softly I barely hear her.

Still, there is no denying the pain in her voice. She failed him, and I want to ask her how she sleeps at night.

The underbellies of the clouds low to the west are blackening. They're moving this way. I've seen enough of the northern skies to know I have less than ten minutes before those bellies burst. I reach for the door handle. I need to get away from this woman as quickly as possible and go home to Digger. "Go home, Professor. There is a blizzard coming."

She looks up through the window above her head. I'm a little annoyed I never noticed the moon roof before. As an afterthought,

I glance into the backseat. I'm not sure what I expected to see, but it's empty. I open the door. There's nothing more I can say, because I'm also empty. Her answers won't fill the hole in my life. I step from her vehicle, pull my collar up, and look back at her. Her expression is intense. Her eyes fill with tears. She mumbles.

"What was that?" I ask.

"Mâtowak."

"Mâ-to-what?"

"Mâ-to wak is the name the Elders have given you."

Though I have no idea what she's talking about, I close the door and walk away as fast as I am able. I don't want to know anything else.

Two o'clock in the afternoon, Carrigan stops at my desk. "They picked up Sophie Brooks, like you asked, and she's in interview room four."

"Thanks."

I grab the files for Declan and Bronson Warner, a writing pad, and tuck a pencil behind my ear. Carrigan disappears inside the observation room. I give him a few seconds to turn on the recorder.

I enter the room. Without looking at her, I sit opposite, set down the files, pull the pencil from my ear. I extract my writing pad, set it to one side, and repeat the usual spiel: date, name, location, etc. I look into the frightened face staring back at me. "You have the right at any time to stop this interview and request a private conference with your lawyer. Do you understand?"

She pulls her fingernail from her mouth. "Are you a real cop?"

"Do you wish to speak with your lawyer?"

"I didn't know Indians could be cops."

"Do you wish to speak with your lawyer?"

"Are you going to arrest me?"

"Did you do something wrong?"

"No."

"Then all I'm going to do is ask you a few questions."

"Maybe I better call my lawyer."

"Do you have something to hide?"

"No."

I shrug. "Then you probably don't need to speak to your lawyer. Just answer my questions as honestly as you can."

She nods.

"Is your name Sophie Brooks?"

"I don't understand why I'm here. I didn't do nothing. The cops came to my house and questioned me already. They wrote everything down. I want to go home."

I stare closed-mouth at her.

"Yes...I'm Sophie Brooks."

"Can I call you Sophie?"

She twists her fingers together, then yanks on her sleeve

194

cuffs. "I guess."

"Would you like something to eat? I can send out for a sandwich, or whatever you'd like."

"No. I just want to go home."

"A few questions first, okay?"

She nods while hugging herself.

I set the blank pad to my left, open Bronson's file to her statement. "Sophie, you told the police you were at a powwow on Vancouver Island when Mr. Warner was shot."

"Yeah. I—I—"

"You weren't, Sophie. You lied."

"I did not."

"Yes, you did. I have statements." I pat the files, though neither one of them contain the Elders' statements. They haven't arrived yet. "Several Elders have already agreed to swear in front of a judge you did not attend the powwow."

"Huh? They said that?"

"Yes."

"Why would they do that?"

"Because it's the truth."

"I had to lie. The cops always blame me. I mean us."

"I'm not blaming you, Sophie. I'm just curious why you lied. Do you lie a lot?"

"Huh? No."

"Did you lie the night you accused Bronson Warner of assaulting you?" I scan her statement. "Or were you lying when you withdrew your statement? Which is it, Sophie? Did Bronson hurt you or didn't he?"

"I had to lie."

I read the first paragraph of her statement, dated over two years previous. "It says here you told the first officer on the scene that Bronson hurt you. He grabbed your arm and twisted it until you cried out, then punched you. Your manager phoned the police. When Mr. Warner arrived a few moments after the police did, he took you to one side, whispered something, and suddenly you apologized to the officer, saying you regretted the police involvement because nothing had happened. Your manager overreacted. You said you were sorry for lying and it wouldn't happen again. Does that sound about right, Sophie?"

She leans forward, trying to read her statement. "I don't know what you mean."

"You implied that you lie when it suits your purpose."

"I didn't say that. You're mixing me up."

"How am I doing that?"

"Huh?"

"How am I mixing you up, Sophie? Tell me, and I'll help you understand. Did Bronson assault you at the Friendship Centre, or not? No lying this time, Sophie. Did he?"

"Yes."

"Why did you lie?"

"Shit, you know why. Mr. Warner said he'd help my career if I didn't press charges. He'd get me assignments."

"Did he?"

"Yes."

"Did you kill him?"

"No." Her eyes tear up. "I swear. I wouldn't hurt anybody. Ask my mum."

"I want to believe you, but you lie so much it's hard to know when you're telling the truth."

"I swear. I never killed him. Ask my mum. She'll tell you I'm not that kind of person. I couldn't hurt anybody ever."

"Maybe I should ask your dad. He doesn't seem quite as anxious to lie for you as your mother might. He says you're a handful."

"What? He said that?"

She's just a dumb kid trying to fit in. This isn't our perp.

I lean my chin in my hand, tap the pencil on the table.

Teary brown eyes stare back at me.

"Of course, Mr. Warner could have been more helpful with your career. If he had, you wouldn't have blackmailed him, you wouldn't have been forced to shoot him. In fact, you could be the one behind Declan and Bronson's strange behaviour, because your dad was never there for you. Were you in charge, Sophie? Was it your idea to beat Mrs. Norse to death, then have Declan kill Bronson, then himself? Did you mastermind the whole thing?" I'm suddenly tired of witnesses lying to me. "Maybe you plan on taking Mrs. Warner out next. Especially since you did such an effective job killing Mr. Warner."

Sophie's response isn't what I expect. Her small eyes grow large, her mouth drops open. She flings herself forward, striking her forehead hard on the table—*crack*. Then cries—LOUD. So loud my ears hurt. In fact, if I didn't know better, I'd say she was trying to exorcise my demons.

I exit the room fast.

Out in the hallway, I almost collide with Lacroix and Superintendent Malden. Sophie's wails blast at us from the interview room.

Lacroix glares at me. "What in hell's name is going on?"

As if she can hear him, Sophie's screams quiet to muffled sobs.

I try wiping the exhaustion from my eyes. "Unstable witness comes to mind."

"Can you fit her to the crime?" Malden asks.

"I'll know more once we get a psych-evaluation." I shake my head. "Never mind. It would be a waste of time. While she's mental unstable, she's not our perp."

"Her lawyer's here. He wants her out now," Lacroix says.

"Can you give me five minutes?"

He glares at me before marching off.

I ask the constable at the door, "Grab me a bottle of water, will you?"

After he tosses me one, I step back inside the interview room, set the bottle on the table. "Are you okay?"

She unscrews the cap, gulps a mouthful, wipes her mouth.

"I'm sorry about your dad, but I need your help." I sit.

Wet, suspicious eyes scrutinize me.

"I know you didn't kill Mr. Warner. But I think you know something. You may not even know what it is, but together we can figure it out."

"I don't know anything."

"Why did Declan hate his dad so much?"

"Because he was a shithead."

"Did he hate his mum, too?"

"No. He felt sorry for her."

"Why?"

"She's damaged goods."

"He said that?"

"Yeah. He said his grandfather broke his mum, and his dad just finished the job."

A tap on the door, it opens. Lacroix says, "Time's up."

* * *

I can hear the phone ringing as I approach the garage door leading into my kitchen. The first few days after Leland's death, colleagues throughout the province called. But how many times can they say, "We're so sorry"?

Now, because my phone so seldom rings, I rush to answer. Possibly it's my sister. Except she only calls Sunday mornings after church. Someone else's voice might wait for me on the other end of the line. My expectations urge me on. "Hello."

"Sally," my lawyer hollers as if surprised to find me home. "Why aren't you using Leland's cell phone?"

I switch hands and rub my ear. "I don't like cell phones."

"How did your meeting go? Did she talk? Or better still, tell me you changed your mind and decided not to share anything personal with her."

"How did you know about our meeting?"

"One of my colleagues saw you together at the University. He said you walked in, and then both of you walked out. So, what happened?"

"Nothing. She said her peace, and now I'm home."

"Are you okay?"

"I'm hungry and tired." I stuff my gloves into my pockets and undo my buttons with one hand. "There is something. What does Mâtowak mean?"

"Sounds Native."

"Who would know?"

"Dr. Meshango. Or the director at the Native Friendship Centre."

"Yes," I say, making a mental note to call the director. I could have simplified things by asking Meshango, but that would have been too easy.

"You won't be seeing her again, I hope."

"It's doubtful." Part of me hopes I will. Too many questions left unanswered.

"Are you sure you're all right. Do you need me to come over?"

That seems a strange question until I remember he thought meeting with Meshango would send me into a frenzy.

"What did you two talk about?"

I press the volume control and hear a soft beep. "I have another call. I'll get back to you."

He's stuttering as I set the receiver back in its cradle.

I hang my coat in the closet, set my boots on the rubber mat, and half expect Digger to come running until I remind myself he's dead, too. I shake off the sadness and head to the kitchen to switch on the kettle. When it's ready I pull out my favourite china and while the tea steeps, carry it into Leland's study. I turn on the gas fireplace, sit on the chair closest to the west window, and concentrate on the warmth of the tea permeating my throat and chest.

The phone rings.

I reach the desk. "Hello."

"Mrs. Warner?" a girl sobs. "It's me...Sophie. Sophie Brooks."

My eyes close, and I grimace. "What do you want?"

She blows her nose loudly, sounding like a trumpeter swan. I switch the cordless phone to my other hand. This is getting ridiculous. I rub my sore ear.

"Mrs. Warner, I'm real sorry about the other day. I was a total bitch. I don't blame you if you don't ever want to talk to me again."

"Good, then I'm about to hang up." My nerves feel frayed.

"I need your help. I don't know what to do. They're messing with my parents. They keep calling them. They as much as called my dad a bad father. He's real ticked at me. You got to help. He says if I'm involved, he's disowning me."

"What are you talking about? Why would he disown you, and who keeps calling?"

"The cops. They found out I wasn't at no powwow. But I swear—I had nothing to do with your husband's murder. I wouldn't kill him. Shit, I got no career without him."

"You shouldn't have lied." I sit at the desk. Leland's leather chair is cold against my back. I lean forward.

"I'm Native, Mrs. Warner. I had to lie. I knew they'd come after me if I didn't. The Indian is always blamed. It's like we're the perfect scapegoat. White people assume we're all losers."

I have no idea if that is true, but it wouldn't surprise me if it were. I, myself, once assumed all Indians were on welfare. People are people. Some are worse than others. "What do you expect me to do?"

"Can't you tell them I'm innocent?"

"I don't know that you are."

"But why would I kill him? He was getting me jobs."

"You were lovers," I say with such sincerity I come close to gagging. I rise and walk out of his study.

"No. Oh shit, Mrs. Warner, I lied. We never had no sex. I'm sorry to say this, but he wasn't exactly good-looking. Not even a little bit. Anyway, you know how he felt about me. I said that stuff cuz you were mean to me—I mean cuz I was hurt, and sometimes I say stupid stuff. But I'm sorry."

"You seem to lie a lot, Sophie. You should start telling the truth."

"I know...I know. And I will. As soon as you fix everything and tell them there is no way I killed your husband."

I walk to the front foyer and gather up the mail on the floor. "You're asking a lot considering your actions in the past. Besides, there is an investigation. I won't interfere with them trying to find Leland's killer." I sort through the mail as I return to Leland's study.

"Oh, please, Mrs. Warner. Nobody's listening to me. My dad won't listen to me. The cops aren't listening to me."

I set the hydro bill and a handful of sympathy cards on the

desk and sit down. "You're a successful artist. Why wouldn't they listen?" I swing Leland's chair around to look out the south window. It's snowing again. Big, heavy snowflakes fill the space.

"You and me both know my art ain't nothing spectacular. It's good, but I'm just one of lots of good native artists. If somebody important like you tells them I'm innocent then they got to listen." She sucks in a deep breath and sighs. "You don't believe I did it, do you?"

I look up. The snow is so thick I can't see its start.

There is no need to dwell on Sophie's question. I know she didn't kill Leland. Some people are users. She's right, though. Killing him would have done nothing for her career.

"You'll need to work out your problems with your father. I'll tell the police I can see no way that Mr. Warner's death would have helped you. But that is all I will do."

"Oh, thank you, Mrs. Warner. I'll make it up to you. Name it and it's done. I'll do whatever you say. If you ever need anything—"

"There is something."

"Yeah, sure."

"When you and Declan were dating, did he ever mention me?"

"He didn't like the way his dad treated you. That's all he ever said."

"He talked about his father?"

"Yeah. Declan hated him."

I lean back in the chair and close my eyes. I knew that; so, why didn't I leave and take my boys someplace safe?

Because I'm a coward.

"Did you know Declan planned to kidnap Dr. Meshango?"

"God—no."

"Did you know about Bronson hurting Mrs. Norris?"

"I didn't know nothing about it. Honest. If I had, I'd have told somebody."

Without seeing her face, it's difficult to know whether she's telling the truth, though I suspect she is. "Did you know Declan was considering suicide? I want the truth, Sophie."

"Honest to God, Mrs. Warner, I didn't have no idea. I really, really liked Declan. I never lied about that. But he didn't tell me much. I knew he had secrets, and I tried to get him to talk to me. After everything happened, I did wonder about that accident he had in the garage. You know, the one where he just about hung himself. He said he was trying to link the ropes so they could hoist his motor out of his car. Like, it made perfect sense, right? But after he died, I started wondering if he was trying back then to kill himself. The thing is, Mrs. Warner, some people are just born sad."

Sad? It was the perfect word to describe my son.

I have to hold my breath for a moment to gain control. "Was he ever happy? Did you two laugh together? He must have...was his entire life a lie?" I choke up. I can't believe I'm asking this girl such private things.

"He liked driving. Sometimes we'd go out to Lejac and back. He'd play the music loud and keep the windows down so the wind whipped through his hair. He was so beautiful on those trips. So beautiful...."

I swallow the lump in my throat. "Tell me what Mâtowak means."

Sophie stutters. "It's...uh...what the Elders called you after Declan and Bronson died."

"All the Elders?"

"It's not a bad word. It's a title of respect. I think."

My frayed nerves are getting hot again. "What does it mean?"

"Mean...? Mrs. Warner, the word's Cree, I'm Carrier. I don't know any Cree."

"Think, Sophie."

"Oh, okay. Uh, I think it's something like a name for people who have lots of horrible bad stuff happen in their life. It's like a badge women use to honour each other for surviving. The more you suffer, the more God gets a grand palace ready for you when you die. I think for people who suffer real bad, they don't have to stick around inside animals."

"You're making this up, aren't you?"

"I know I'm not smart, Mrs. Warner. But it is true that dead people don't always go on to heaven right away. Sometimes their spirit hangs out inside wolverines and eagles. Bears. Rabbits, for sure. And—"

I'm no longer listening to Sophie. "The Elders call me Mâtowak?" I can't imagine why.

"One of the Elders gave you the name the day of Declan's funeral. I think it's something to do with tears. Mrs. Warner, asking me about Cree would be like me asking you about Italian."

I think about Meshango and her tears. Then I remember my tears. "Thank you, Sophie."

"No, Mrs. Warner. I don't deserve any thanks."

"Don't say that, Sophie. Everyone deserves to be appreciated."

I hang up from Sophie's call and look Mâtowak up on the Internet. I finally locate it through the Cree Dictionary at the University of Saskatchewan, where it gives the meaning as *a weeper. One who cries.* I can't help but laugh.

It's time to stop crying.

I grab my coat, keys, purse, and head for my car.

I know Sophie's been terrible in the past, but she needs me. If there is a God, wouldn't He want me to help? Regardless of whether she's a bitch or not?

"Bitch."

Ohmigosh, that felt good.

I'm laughing as I pull out of my garage. I stop laughing the moment my tires hit the first of many jagged ruts. I'm no sooner out of one when in the next instance, my back tires spin sideways on black ice.

I reach the detachment, park, and uncoil my fingers from the steering wheel. If Corporal Killian isn't in, I'll plant myself in the nearest chair and wait for him. All night if that is what it takes. Better yet, I'll insist on his home address. If I'm crazy enough to help Sophie and drive on black ice, I might as well act the part.

The young woman behind the glass knows who I am. I can tell by her stunned expression. She rushes to the nearest policeman, who in return disappears down the hallway. I'm wondering if I should ask for a tour. Leland promised, but never had time.

A few moments later, Killian approaches. His face is difficult to read. Though he's smiling, I'm not sure if he's pleased to see me. His eyelids look heavy; perhaps he's beleaguered by the investigation into Leland's murder.

"How are you, ma'am?"

"I'm fine." I wave aside any additional attempts at small talk. "I spoke to Sophie. She was hysterical. I know it was wrong of her to lie about her whereabouts. She was home alone the morning Leland died."

"Lying, for whatever reason, is a no-no." He shakes his head as if he remembers something. "Ma'am, I'm sorry. I can't discuss the case."

What kind of serious talk is no-no?

An officer in plainclothes, with a holster under his windbreaker, enters and approaches the receptionist. I lower my voice. "She didn't kill Leland."

"That may be, but she can't verify her whereabouts. I feel bad for you, ma'am. If she's a friend, this must be hard."

"Sophie's not a friend. She relied on Leland's influence. With him gone, her career is in trouble."

"Sorry?"

"Leland was able to help Sophie by locating commissions. He spoke to people on her behalf. It wasn't as you might think. She meant something to Declan once."

"Yes, I heard about that."

"I wouldn't be bothering you, but Sophie is as much a victim in this as the men in my life."

"She's a lot healthier than they are."

"Pardon me?"

His eyes are intent on my face, and I know he's trying to read my mind. I think he also realizes I'm aware of this.

He clears his throat. "Victim or not, I can't talk to you about anything connected to this case. I'm sorry. I'd like to help, but I can't." He hesitates, looks over his shoulder, then back at me; and I wonder if he's annoyed at me. For what? I'm the one who should be annoyed.

I summon my pathetic voice. "Sorry to have bothered you."

"You're not bothering me."

If I'm reading the expression on his face correctly, he appears concerned for my wellbeing, yet his constant scrutiny of my face is disconcerting.

"If Miss Brooks isn't a friend, why do you care?"

That is easy. Because it's time I worry about someone other than myself. "You don't know Sophie. She's quite pathetic. Somebody has to help her."

He's quiet for an uncomfortable moment with his eyes downcast. I fret about what he thinks, even though my small voice says his opinion means nothing.

I'm concentrating on his thick black eyelashes and wondering why men always seem to luck out in the curly-lash department when he finally looks up and smiles. When he speaks, his voice is filled with sincerity, but his eyes are saying something different. "Good for you, ma'am." He says that, but I imagine he thinks Sophie isn't the only one who's pathetic.

I turn abruptly and leave the building.

When I arrive home, I sit at my breakfast table and question what I should do next. The answer doesn't come. I feel numb. Dazed. Surrounded and enshrouded by nothingness. The ringing in my ears clang loudly.

I wake from my reverie uncertain how much time has passed. The day's light is fading. The sun disappeared while I was about the business of saving Sophie Brooks, artist-extraordin-not, and it occurs to me that I can do something. I'm no politician, but I have contacts. I know important people all across this country. I could help Sophie.

That small voice inside me asks, "Why bother?"

Because Killian is correct; I'm more pathetic than she is. Maybe helping her will help me.

"She's trouble. She was trouble in the past, and she's trouble now."

I shake my head and set out to make a nutritious dinner. The fridge is full, so I take stock of what I might use for homemade soup. After dinner I'll make some calls. I'm through feeling rueful and having conversations with voices in my head; it's time to pick up the pieces of my life and carry on. No more Mâtowak. No more cry baby.

Five hours later, I close my address book and lean back in the leather chair in Leland's study. I suppose it's my study now. I feel confident that what I have done for Sophie's career matches anything Leland had accomplished. The difference is I want to help her whereas Leland had an agenda. I pause over that thought. Leland had tried to save his soul. Isn't that what I'm doing? I flip through my call display, see the number, and press the dial button.

"Sophie, it's Mrs. Warner."

She begins to cry. Perhaps I'll give her the Mâtowak title now that I'm done with it. I give her a second and then interject. "Enough. If you want your life back, you had better start being accountable. Dry up those tears, right now, young lady."

She blows her nose. "I just spoke to my mum. My dad won't talk to me."

"Seems to me that has been the case since you were a teenager. You can't change the man's mind, but at least you tried to mend the problems between you."

"Yeah, I did."

"Let it go, Sophie."

"Really?"

"Yes. You've done what you can. It's your father who should ask for your forgiveness."

"Yeah." She sniffles.

"That is not why I called. I've decided to take over where Leland left off."

"Huh?"

"Listen to me carefully, Sophie. I've arranged for you to travel to Kitwanga. You'll have to take a bus, I'm afraid. The school board doesn't have the money to send a car, and at this time of year it would be a mistake to drive. I'll give you some spending money; consider it a donation. One thing though, I don't want your manager calling me. This is not a business arrangement."

"I don't get it."

"You will in a second. I spoke to a friend of mine with the Provincial School Board. Kitwanga is looking for an artist to help the high school seniors create murals on their recreational centre inside and out. Obviously, the outside can't be tackled until summer. However, what this does mean is you'll be delegating instructions. Can you do that?"

"I don't know what that means, Mrs. Warner?"

"From what I ascertained, they will explain everything to you when you arrive. For now, all I'm sure of is they need an artist to help coordinate a huge project. The young people want to turn their drab recreational centre into something wonderful. Funds are being procured for the paint and supplies. Apparently, they have some exceptionally gifted high school artists. What they need is an experienced artist who can take on a project of this size, someone who can be billeted in someone's home. I suggested you. I also reminded them you did the mural in the parliament buildings in Victoria."

"Yeah, I did," she announces in a higher-than-necessary voice.

"And you did a beautiful display for the Olympics, if I do say so myself." I smile at how easy it is to compliment her when I'm being honest. "You're expected in Kitwanga on Monday for interviews, though I'm positive you have the job. They'll break for Christmas and then resume in the New Year. Here's the number: 555-2543. You have to decide quickly and call her first thing in the morning. Any questions?"

"I don't know what to say, Mrs. Warner. Except...why?"

"Why what?"

"I said some bad things to you. Why are you helping me? What about the police?"

"Forget the police. I spoke to the investigating officer. He can't dismiss you as a suspect at this point. But don't worry. I doubt he believes you murdered Leland. If he did, you'd be brought in for questioning."

"They did bring me in. This afternoon."

"But they let you go."

"Yeah, that's true." She's quiet for a moment. "If they change their minds, I promise I won't tell them nothing."

What does she mean? Tell them what?

"Me not deserving your help reminded me of something Mr. Warner said a few weeks ago. In the beginning, he got mad every time I tried to thank him. He'd call me a liar. So I got used to not saying much when he'd call with a job. Except for the last time. I didn't mean to—it just come out. Right away I knew I'd done something wrong, and he was going to chew my head off. Only he didn't. Instead of snapping at me, he said, "Don't say that. I'm the reason my boys are dead.""

I don't care about that. "What do you mean, you won't tell the police? Tell them what?"

"You know. About how he treated you. About how mean he was."

"Tell them the truth, Sophie. Don't hold anything back on my account. You're in enough trouble. Understand?"

"Okay. Thank you, Mrs. Warner. I don't get why you're doing this, but I appreciate it. I wish I could thank you."

"Do me proud, Sophie. Do Declan's memory proud. Paint from the heart."

I hear her quiet sobs and, rather than say more, set the phone back in its cradle.

A light snack of apple and orange wedges takes less than five minutes to prepare. I've decided to watch the late show tonight. I haven't watched TV or read a book in bed since before Leland died.

I love my bed and its soft fluffy duvet. I nestle into my pillows with my plate of fruit on the bedside table, my remote handy, and the room smelling apple fresh. I change to the CBC channel. Darn, the hockey game is still playing. The schedule says it should be *Cirque du Soleil's Solstrom*, but the Calgary Flames are playing. Third period has just begun.

I sink against my pillows, aim the remote, and try to find a substitute. How can there be all these channels, yet nothing worth watching? How can that be?

I'm no longer hungry. Or comfortable.

Calgary is on home ice. Just as they'd been the night before Leland and the boys sat at the breakfast table and discussed the Canucks' place in the Western Division series. The morning Bronson used the bad word. And Leland didn't flinch. He sat across from me with his head in the paper. It was as if he'd found it normal for a twelve-year-old to speak such vulgarity in front of his mother.

The memory leaves a bad taste in my mouth. Like a morning after too many Tom Collins.

What had I expected from him that morning?

A word?

Some form of disciplinary action?

I think not. I wanted him to say, "Don't you dare speak like that in front of your mother."

Instead, I watched Bronson gulp down his cereal and thought, *you disgusting little pig. I should slap your face.*

As I thought that, Declan said something. I can't remember what, but it was funny. Funny enough that when Bronson laughed, he spit out the cereal and milk in his mouth—and Leland, without looking up from his paper, backhanded him across the back of his head. The sound made me jump. The shockwave sent Bronson's chair teetering. Before I could reach out and stop it, the chair fell backwards. Bronson with it. His head hit the floor with a crack. It must have hurt. Except for a flush to his cheeks he didn't show any signs of trauma. He stood, righted his chair, and then sat down and finished his breakfast. No one said a word. I went to the washroom and threw up.

Funny how it never occurred to me then that we'd all be better off if Leland were dead.

At the end of a long shift, when all but two of my major crime unit team members have gone home, their meals probably waiting for them in the warming oven, I approach constables Ryan and Carrigan. "Care to join me at Tim Horton's?"

They exchange glances, nod. "Sure," they say in unison.

I sympathize. At this stage in their careers they probably think they have no choice.

"The wife expects I'll be late every night until this case is solved," Carrigan says, after meeting up with us in the parking lot across the street. "Oh, I had to promise it wouldn't be McDonalds."

Ryan laughs. "You old guys crack me up."

"Sure, go ahead, enjoy yourself," Carrigan says. "The day my high cholesterol results came in was the end of life as I knew it. And I wasn't forty yet."

In sympathy, Ryan pats Carrigan's back. "Old man, you're breaking my heart."

Still uneasy with their camaraderie, I pull out my keys. "I'll meet you guys there."

Ryan clears his throat. "Yeah, sure. You know you're tires need replacing, huh?"

Rather than comment, I smile and head for my car.

I take my time driving to the restaurant. The roads have been ploughed, sanded, and salted, but any place where vehicles idle for more than a moment, like intersections and stops signs, the asphalt is layered in ice. Studs would help. Damn it. I pull into Tim Horton's behind Carrigan, careful not to get too close.

Ryan waits at the entrance for us. As Carrigan and I reach him, he throws open the door, says something to Carrigan about "Age before beauty, old man."

I reply, "Are you talking to me, constable."

"Uh? No. Course not."

Both of us laugh at Ryan's scarlet complexion. The atmosphere lightens.

As soon as it's our turn at the counter, I order my usual soup, sandwich, maple donut. I grab the hot water and tea bag, ask the cashier to add the other two meals to my tab. I find an empty table near the window, take the seat facing my vehicle, then watch, amused, as Ryan silently contemplates who should sit beside me and who's left to sit with his back to the door. Carrigan inches by Ryan, makes the decision for him, sits next to me. Ryan lets out a grunt, takes the seat opposite.

Starving, I take a huge bite of my sandwich, filling my cheeks.

"Do you think Mrs. Warner killed her husband?" Carrigan asks straight out.

Ryan raises his eyebrows. By the expression on his face, either he's anxious to hear my reply or surprised Carrigan had enough nerve to ask.

I glance sideways at Carrigan. "Yes."

They stare at me.

"What?" I chew a full mouth. "You don't agree?"

Ryan reacts first. "The murder was too calculated. She sounds undone on the 911 tape. Pinscher says she was hysterical when he arrived. But calm enough to get rid of the weapon and dispose of the spent shell? How? And anyways, there wasn't enough time. Nope, I think, in the end, we'll find out it had something to do with one of his cases."

I wipe my mouth with a serviette. "You think?"

"Yeah or the death of their sons," Carrigan says, taking several bites of his chicken wrap.

Ryan shakes his head. "Too late for it to be connected to them."

"Unfortunately, there is no time limit on revenge," I say.

Ryan brushes the crumbs from his mouth, looks at me. "You think she killed him. Wow."

"I'm a little surprised you think she did it," Carrigan says.

"You mean because there is no evidence. You asked me, I told you."

Carrigan shrugs, dips his wrap into the sauce provided. "I thought you liked her."

"Our job is to collect evidence and present it to the Crown. It's their job to prosecute. It's the judge's job to render punishment. Standard policing procedure we all learn at homicide. Nowhere does it say we're required to judge." Shit, I'm starting to sound like Lacroix.

Ryan sets his sandwich aside, scratches the icing off the cinnamon with his fingernail, then sticks his finger in his mouth. He squints at me.

Carrigan, busy devouring the rest of his wrap, grabs his donut. One big bite, then he smears his tongue over his teeth, licks the icing from the corner of his mouth. He refrains from looking at either of us.

"Too pat an answer?" I ask, not sure why I feel the need to defend myself. "Whether you agree or not, as investigators, our reactions or feelings should never be part of the equation. If we can't keep our prejudices to ourselves, we're in the wrong profession. It's the evidence that directs us."

"Fair enough. But what evidence?" Ryan asks.

"Ryan's right, Danny," Carrigan says. "I think you're wrong."

"Won't be the first time." I look at their expressions. "It's a gut feeling. Nothing more."

"Interesting," Carrigan says between mouthfuls.

I sip my warm tea.

"She could have left him any time. She's got a good lawyer. He'd have made sure she got more than half," Carrigan adds.

"My girlfriend can't believe a woman could do that without there being another woman. She's a big believer in the old saying, a woman scorned," Ryan says.

"Your girl may have a point." I wipe my mouth again. It's sticky.

"If she was going to do me in, she said she'd make it look like an accident." Ryan reacts to Carrigan's stunned expression. "She's an amateur sleuth. She likes to—"

"She has no access to files. Correct?" Carrigan says.

Flustered, Ryan starts stuttering, "Yes. Of course. Right, no access to files—ever."

"When my daughter was a kid, she wanted to be a cop," Carrigan says. "That was before she turned into a teenage monster. My little guy wants to be a truck driver," he adds in a solemn voice.

"At least he doesn't want to be a lawyer," Ryan says.

"Hypothetically speaking," I ask Carrigan, "what if your daughter killed her abusive boyfriend and was smart enough to leave no clues, except you knew she did it? Could you prosecutor her to the full extent of the law?"

"Unfair question. I'm personally involved, so I wouldn't be on the case."

"I didn't say you were on the case. I asked if you would do your job."

Carrigan folds his arms, rests them on the table, smiles. "I'm not answering on the grounds it may incriminate me."

"*Touché.*"

"You think Mrs. Warner is guilty, but you don't want her to be," he says. "If he'd been shot four or five times or if the killer used a full clip, I'd say yes, it was most likely his wife or a close family member. Since there is no one left but his wife, we could also look for a girlfriend or a jilted lover."

"Yeah," Ryan says.

"If he'd been shot in the chest, then the head, I'd say a professional hit. But consider the crime scene and everything we've learned so far, ask yourselves what kind of person killed him."

Both Carrigan and Ryan seem to contemplate this.

All the discussions in the world won't prove one way or the other. Whether they agree with me or not, it doesn't matter. Nothing good ever comes from speculating. Besides, these men have families to get home to. Time to change the subject.

After a brief silence, I ask Carrigan, "How many kids have you got?"

"Four."

I'm about to respond to that when Ryan injects, "What's the real reason you got transferred?"

Carrigan gawks at him. "John!"

Ryan shrugs. "I want to know."

"It's none of your damn business," Carrigan retorts.

"What's going on?" I look from one to the other. "John?"

"There is a rumour that you were a suspect in your wife's murder, so after you caught The Butcher, they used that as an excuse to get rid of you. Is that true?"

"Holy Damn," Carrigan says.

"It's okay. It's a valid question." I face Ryan. "I was at HQ when her body was found. I was never a suspect."

Ryan looks relieved. Carrigan's still annoyed with him.

"Why come up here if you didn't have to?" Ryan asks.

"I wanted to work the highway missing. And there was an opening for a corporal."

"You don't need to explain anything to us," Carrigan says.

"Your assistant's got the hots for you," Ryan says, and smiles.

I glare at him. Carrigan's mouth drops open.

"I've seen the way she looks at you. She's hot," Ryan says.

Carrigan gapes at him. "Holy Damn, Ryan, she's a nice girl."

"I didn't say she wasn't."

I can't stop glaring at Ryan.

He pales. "I'm an idiot."

I nod.

Carrigan laughs.

Ryan looks at his watch. "Hey, it's already 10:30." He stands, then puts his coat on. "I got to go. I may be single, but I still have someone to answer to."

I stand.

"You're breaking my heart." Carrigan reaches around the back of his chair for his parka. "But yeah, I should get home, too. I hate missing out on saying goodnight to my little guy. The older ones, not so much. Thanks for dinner."

"Yeah, thanks," Ryan says. "And sorry about—"

"F'get about it," I say in my best Italian mobster voice. I walk in the direction of the head. "See you both bright and early."

They're gone when I step out into the night. The sky is heavy and low. But even with a cushion of clouds holding in part of the day's heat, the temperature is bitingly cold. I pull up the collar on my coat, notice the man approaching from the left.

He is a large Native man with drooping shoulders and a slight limp. A BC Olympic balaclava covers most of his head. The lights along the edge of the building overshadow his features. Five foot ten, possibly two hundred and twenty pounds. Heavy construction boots. Hands stuffed deep into his coat pockets.

I know instinctively he intends on approaching me. I unclip the safety and face him full on.

When he's ten feet away, I ask, "Can I help you?"

He looks surprised, glances over his shoulder as if expecting to see who I'm talking to. He looks back at me. "You Killian?"

He's within four feet. I glance at his hands still stuck deep inside his pockets. "Take your hands out of your pockets."

Again, he looks surprised. He pulls out his gloved hands, smacks them together. "You Killian or not?"

"I am."

He's younger than I thought. Forty-something, with striking shoulder-length dark hair, deep black eyes visible below his balaclava. His face muscles relax, and I see that his frown is what makes him appear older. What could be taken for a smile softens the laugh lines, reveals youthfulness in his face.

"What's your name?"

"All Indians from the coast this suspicious?" He steps closer. I see the lack of a gleam in his eyes. Flat dull orbs. "I'm TJ Littleman's dad. They just found her body a few days ago."

"Mr. Littleman." I snap to, extend my hand. "I'm sorry for your loss, sir."

He looks back at the direction he'd come as if unconvinced by my sincerity and thinking I'm talking to someone else. He looks back at my face, then at my outstretched hand.

Is my demeanour that unfriendly?

That's the bad part about being a cop. I see a big, imposing man and think: threat. *The Butcher* had come at me in a friendly manner. Look where that got me.

"I'm Danny Killian, sir."

We shake hands as well as can be done wearing thick winter gloves.

"Can I help you with something, Mr. Littleman?"

There are moments in life when conversation is pointless and inconsequential, and saying how sorry you feel is an empty gesture. I feel that way now.

"I saw your name on some of them statements about the investigation into finding my girl. Then I heard you was Indian. They told me at the detachment you might still be here. It was your signature on them statement, right?"

"Yessir. However—"

"You going to find the person who killed my little girl?"

I stand still. "We're doing everything we can."

"You got a suspect?"

"No."

"How come?" Mr. Littleman presses his arms tightly against his sides and shifts from foot to foot.

"A lot of time has passed, Mr. Littleman, as you know. We're not likely to find any evidence, but perpetrators often get careless. Either they brag to a friend or slip up and get caught in a lie."

"Like that case on the news? That guy that's up for parole after serving twenty-five years for killing the family down south?"

"Yes, that's exactly right. We got him because he needed badly to be credited for their deaths. He was looking for notoriety. We…"

I'm spewing crap. The same crap they gave me after Angie died.

"We'll do everything we can, Mr. Littleman. But all we can hope for is either a witness comes forward, or the perpetrator makes a mistake."

He stares straight through me. When he finally speaks, I feel as if he's directing his conversation at someone beyond the perimeter.

"I'm taking my little girl home tomorrow. I'd like to tell her mum and her grandma I believe you people care. Her mum and her grandma don't think so. They think you care little for some kid from the Rez. They think she's just another Indian to you policemen. They think you're more concerned with finding out who killed the important white minister. They think you being Indian don't mean much."

"We've set up a task force, sir. TJ's murder is a priority. We'll pull out all the stops to find who killed her."

He hides his gloved hands under his armpits and continues shifting his weight from foot to foot. I find his rocking motion soothing, and wonder if he does, too.

He gives me the once over, brings a gloved hand to his cheek, wipes his chin, hides it back under his armpit. "You from Haida Qwaii, eh?"

"Yes, sir."

He nods, as if that sums up everything. "Should go, let you get on your way."

I think of shaking his hand again, but decide to cut it short. I nod my respects, then turn to leave.

"Is it true you couldn't find your wife's murderer?"

Stunned by the question, I hesitate before turning back. Words fail me.

"Sorry. Shouldn't speak so quick."

I look up at a sky dotted with stars. I want more than anything to believe Angie's one of them, twinkling down on me because she's so damn happy. Happier than I could ever make her.

"They have a suspect. That's all I know."

I observe the anguish of a father without hope and know I have to tell him something. Like what I wanted to hear after Angie died; that it was all a huge mistake. After reality sank in, I wanted to hear that Angie's death mattered.

I look back at the sky, because suddenly I can see her incredible smile.

When she was passionate about something, the blue in her eyes looked as if streaks of white ran through them. And her smile—it could melt the hardest of hearts. Most days just looking at her made me weak at the knees. Even when I needed to stay angry.

Clearing the bullshit from my mind, I study him.

"Mr. Littleman, please tell TJ's mother and grandmother that from what I heard about TJ, she was a good person. She lived a short life, but she made a difference. Even after we solve her murder, we'll never forget TJ, Mr. Littleman. Please tell them that. We never forget any of them."

Losing Angie was the worst kind of horror ever. And more than anything I want to kill the sonofabitch who'd killed her. Make him pay so his screams will break glass.

I swallow the lump in my throat, blink away the moisture in my eyes. "I know hurting whoever hurt your daughter would feel good. But...it won't bring TJ back. Please tell them not to dwell on the why or the who, but to think about her smile, her laughter, how, for a little while, the world was a whole lot better with her in it."

I blink fast. Mr. Littleman studies me. His face is an expression of strength I wish I could own. This father understands better than me the finality of death.

Feeling the tremor moving up my arms, I want to ask him if he could teach me the truth, teach me how to live without Angie. The sting of a tear dries up my voice, though. I hand him one of my cards then watch him walk to his truck and drive away. It's when my toes turn numb that I climb into my car and drive home to my empty house.

From my living room window, my eyes follow the mini-blizzard underway outside. Six-foot snow-tornados twirl down the street until the division between asphalt, sidewalks, and lawns disappear. Across the way, my neighbours gather in their living room. Two figures on a sofa, two children racing back and forth past the huge window. Lights from the TV flash into the room, softening the muted shadows on the walls.

I draw the blinds tight, lower the thermostat to eighteen. Determined work is what I need, I return to my computer on the desk in the corner of the kitchen, sit down, click on the Warner investigation.

When I open the top drawer of my desk, spot the mickey of whiskey, I don't stop to question, but pour two ounces in the empty glass left over from the night before. I take a sip, feel it burn on its way down, then explode into my stomach. The space around me smells stale. I jot down a reminder to crack the windows before I leave for work tomorrow, front and back, to air the place out. If I'm ever going to invite people over, I better make the place presentable.

Inviting? My therapist says inviting people into my personal space might fill the hole in my heart, mend the scars. I take another sip, curl my bare toes into the carpet, and wonder if it's true.

Taking a deep breath, I look at the files. I can't rub the stiffness out of my neck, or stop my concentration from wavering between thoughts of the highway missing and the suspect they might or might not have in Angie's death. I glance at my watch. Fifteen minutes, gone. How do I do that? Kill time without experiencing gratitude?

I find the number for the task force leader and make a courtesy call. No apologizes for calling so late. Nor does he ask me what I want or why I'm calling. It's no secret I have a stake in both cases. Maybe they even feel weird that they'd taken over the job I worked hard on for so many days, because like most of the families with missing persons, I'm First Nations.

"I talk to the families of the missing on a regular basis. In fact, I spoke to Mr. Littleman earlier tonight. I'd like to be able to tell them something."

The detective is silent for a moment. "We're doing everything we can to find the killers."

Killers? "You think there is more than one perp?"

"Possibly. I don't know what else you can tell them. Officially, the Littleman girl is now considered part of the investigation. Nobody wants to hear that. We know she wasn't a sex worker and we will make that clear to the media. She was an eighteen-year-old tree planter from Moricetown. Both victims were Indigenous, young, and under five-two. Manageable. Whether they were friends is not certain. They may not have even known each other." He pauses. I don't know why. "The others, the ones who were connected to the sex trade, their cases are as important to us as these two new ones."

Sure, I'll tell them that. Guaranteed to make them feel better. "I didn't ask Mr. Littleman, but was his daughter found with any jewellery?"

"No."

"Did the family say if she was wearing earrings or a ring?"

"Yes, they did. But no jewellery was found with either girl."

Which could mean the perp collected souvenirs, and they'll be able to connect him to the murders because of it.

"We've already added descriptions of their personal belongings to their files."

"Of course. That is how we'll get him," I say, hopeful. "Because we *will* get him."

"Yes, that's the attitude," the detective says, then clears his throat, and adds, "We think there are three killers, one definitely a serial killer, but it's nothing concrete, and I would rather you didn't mention it. Tell them we got the best profilers in the business working this project. We're doing everything we can."

Too many dead.

"At least you were able to give these two kids back their names."

"Yeah, that is right. Never thought of it that way. Hey, you'll be back on the case as soon as you and your team solve Warner's murder, right?"

"Right."

"How's it going?"

I take a deep breath. "Slow."

His laugh sounds forced. "Well, I hope your luck changes."

"Thanks. So you know who the other girl was?"

"Yes. A young Native woman from a First Nation community

near Battleford, Saskatchewan, last seen hitchhiking near Blackwater Road. She'd been tree planting in the Williston Lake forest district. Went missing seven months after TJ. We're waiting on tox screen reports, but the fact they were killed at different times and found together means something. This will prove to be important eventually. She also suffered a blow to the head. There were no other fractures or evidence of wounds on either body. None of the bones show ligature marks. Both bodies were still intact, so we'll continue doing tests for the next ten hours, then they'll be released to their families. Again, the fact they were found together is encouraging."

Sure, from an investigator's point of view, but from the family's point of view? "Any idea what she was doing near Blackwater?"

"Not yet."

"I'd like to call North Battleford detachment in the morning and let them know. If that is okay?"

"Thanks," he says. "I'll fax you over what we've got. If you've got a pen, I'll give you her name."

At ten o'clock I stretch the kink out of my neck, shoulders, close Warner's file. I pour myself another drink. In the living room, I glance at the DVD player, wonder if I should give my brain a rest. Generally. I'm good for ten minutes before falling asleep. Luckily, my couch is firm.

I hit the reject button to see if there was a DVD already inside, and something strange happens. Suddenly, I'm outside myself looking in. Channelling Warner's tactics. I race back to my office, set my drink on the desk, grab the phone. Carrigan answers on the fourth ring.

"Sorry for the late call."

"Not a problem." He sounds half asleep.

"Did you speak to the security company who installed Warner's surveillance cameras and equipment?"

"A company in Vancouver bought them out. The company president assured me a recorder or command centre would have been set up at the time they installed the equipment. They had no paperwork pertaining to Warner's system, though. I talked to him again today, and they still couldn't find anything."

"Is that normal?"

"No. In fact, he was embarrassed they couldn't find anything tracing back to Warner's job. Apparently, his people arc trying to track down why. He's convinced the particular unit Warner had installed came with a remote for each camera and one receiver. He said one receiver was quite capable of handling the complete system. I let them know at the house and they double checked, but found no command centre."

"Okay, thanks." I hang up.

I find my cell phone in the living room; locate Warner's attorney's number. When the man comes on the line I say, "Was Warner paranoid or was he somebody you'd say was in complete control of his faculties?"

"Corporal Killian, I'm tired. It's been another long day, and I don't have time for this. You can reach me at my office tomorrow after eleven. I'll be in court in the morning."

Whatever happened to cooperation and a little courtesy? "You know it doesn't work like that, sir. A murder investigation isn't nine to five."

"Fine." He sighs loudly. "Why do you want to know if he was paranoid?"

"He had the means and the foresight to install sophisticated surveillance equipment in almost every room of that house. Why?"

"Gee, I don't know." No mistaking his sarcasm. "Because he could."

"The camera inside the front entrance is activated by a motion sensor mounted on the outside of the covered porch. All the outside cameras are connected to the wireless monitor sitting on top of the standing freezer in the kitchen, to the monitor over his desk in his study, to the monitor in the garage."

He takes an exaggerated breath. "Is there a question in there somewhere?"

"Mr. Warner went to all the trouble of installing cameras and monitors so he could see if anyone was on the grounds while he was inside his house. What about when he was away? Wouldn't a man who went to that much trouble have a command post set up somewhere in the house that would house a time lapse recorder unit, something with a slot for a video tape?"

"If you say so."

"That way when the motion detector kicks in, a time lapse recorder automatically starts recording. Otherwise he'd have no way of knowing who's been trespassing on their property when he's gone. There'd be no record for court proceedings."

"Where are you going with this?"

"You have the same system?"

"No."

"No?"

He snorts what sounds like a mumbled obscenity. "We have an alarm system. Please don't tell me I need to explain what that encompasses to a member of the RCMP?"

"Mr. Warner needed something more sophisticated?"

"Of course. Leland never did anything half-heartedly. I'm surprised you don't know that about him by now."

"Do you have contact information on who installed the surveillance equipment for him?"

"It was a small company here in Prince George that, I believe, was bought out by a larger company down south. You're sure there is no recorder? That seems strange. Leland was thorough. The walls in his house were constructed with two by tens and his floors were three quarter inch plywood. The man wouldn't skimp on security."

"Then it doesn't make sense to you that there is no command centre or video tapes?" I ask.

"No, it doesn't."

The surveillance company had said they were almost positive there would have been several remotes. So where were they?

"Thanks." I hang up.

The phone rings.

"The company was sold a year ago," Carrigan says, "but the new owner swears it's the store's policy to include a recorder with all the units in that product class."

"So, where are they?"

"I don't know. It's definitely a puzzle. I stopped by at noon and took the serial number off the monitor in the kitchen. When I asked where the remotes and receiver were, Mrs. Warner said her husband lost them and never got around to getting replacements."

"I'll go back tomorrow and look." I decide to change the subject. "They identified the remains found with TJ Littleman. The girl went missing seven months after TJ and died from blunt force to the head."

"Did they think strangulation, too?"

"Post mortem showed no signs of ligature strangulation or markings anywhere else on the remains that suggest stabbing or torture. Nor do they believe either victim died where their remains were discovered."

"Is it true one of the victims had a hair caught in her fingernail?"

"I don't know." I feel sick to my stomach. "The media will be told that TJ never worked the sex trade. And they don't believe there was any sexual assault."

When I don't reply, he says, "I know what you're thinking. It shouldn't matter if they were connected to the sex trade. And it doesn't. It's hard enough for a parent to accept their child is dead, but to know they were tortured or raped and brutalized... it..."

"I got to go." I hang up.

I reach for the CSIS report on Mrs. Warner. This will be my third read-through.

As the meteorologist predicted, a Chinook blew in from the ocean, seven hundred kilometres away. By morning the roads are dry, the trees bare. As the horizon lightens to a paling cerulean in the east, I leave the dark skies of the west behind, descend the hill into a city soaked in bright lamplights. I inhale two maple donuts from Tim Horton's, arrive at the detachment at twenty to seven. I call North Battleford to speak to their Staff Sergeant.

Though I'm addressing another cop, I inform him as reverently as I can that the remains found in a gravel pit near Mackenzie, B.C. were positively identified as a young woman from his area. I repeat her name and listen to dead air.

"She died from blunt force trauma to the head," I say, wondering if the connection's been broken. No dial tone, though.

"Was death instantaneous?" he finally asks, his voice a sorrowful tone I wasn't expecting. "The killer didn't...?"

"No."

"Good."

"They'll send you the autopsy report ASAP."

"Even after seven months the family never gave up hope of finding Briana."

"You knew her?"

"No, but I've gotten to know her family pretty well. They're from Little Pine First Nation."

"I'm sorry."

"Briana's dad speaks the old language and is known as a pauwau. You and I would say powwow. It means he travels a lot, going from village to village, sharing with other speakers, making sure the language lives on."

"A gather. Yes, I know what it means."

"After Briana disappeared, he did everything he could to find her. Whenever there was a sighting or a body found, he'd go. He went as far as the Maritimes and even down to Montana."

I understand then that the Staff Sergeant is digesting the news and isn't speaking to me, but to the part of himself trying to comprehend her death. This is unusual for a veteran cop.

"Even if it was rumours or something mentioned briefly on the news, he'd stop in and we'd talk. His wife teaches at the school, so she had responsibilities and couldn't leave whenever he did. They have five other kids younger than Briana. Thank God I never made them any promises."

"Knowing them personally is going to make this tough for you."

"They're the kind of people who would want to know. Sure would be nice if I could tell them there is an arrest pending."

"You have no idea how much I wish you could."

"Any possible motive? I need to tell these people something."

"As soon as I know anything, you'll be the first—" I stop, embarrassed I'd say something so stupid. I'm not dealing with a civilian. This man knows the drill. "There are others."

"Dead or missing?"

"Both."

"The Highway of Tears? Highway 16?"

"Yes."

"I heard it's bad."

"Yes."

"Dear God, I don't envy you."

It seems stupid to add anything else. Besides, it's not me who has to call the family and explain how their child died for nothing at the hands of a madman.

"That's why the task force is taken over?"

"Yes." I doodle rolls of crosses on my notepad.

"Maybe *The Butcher* taught us something after all?"

I know exactly what he means. *The Butcher* taught us that every life is precious, regardless of what the victim did for a living. The bad part is it takes a lot of funds to catch a killer. Because of higher crime numbers in urban areas, the monies and manpower necessary are being allotted to Vancouver, Toronto, and other large cities across Canada. It's nobody's fault, and everybody's fault.

"A lot of families out here were impressed it was an Indigenous policeman who caught him," he says.

Yeah, I'd pat myself on the back if I could. Big hero.

"Sure a lot of news coverage on your ex-minister Leland Warner, though."

Rather than argue against the truth, I don't respond. Besides, he knows the drill.

The silence grows uncomfortable.

He mumbles something, and then in a clear amicable tone says, "Thank you for calling so quickly, Corporal Killian. Hope to hear from you soon."

"Goodbye."

I dig into work, trying not to think about the girl's family.

Ten minutes to eight, Carrigan arrives, goes directly to his desk without so much as a glance my way. He keeps his head low.

Finally, I whistle softly. When he looks up, I mouth, "Everything okay?"

He nods, then lowers his head.

At 8:45, Malden comes out of his office with the announcement that Ottawa has scheduled a news conference for later in the day. Before I can utter objections, he adds that they've decided to offer a substantial reward for information leading to an arrest into the murder of retired Minister Warner, courtesy of the taxpayers.

Everybody groans. A reward means hundreds of calls to sift through, wasted man-hours following leads that will probably go nowhere.

At nine o'clock, I join my team in the conference room. What we hear from the file coordinator isn't good. There was no appropriation of funds from any of the accounts Warner had access to. In fact, there was nothing strange or suspicious. No leads to any suspects or any political scandals. Nothing peculiar in Warner's portfolio. His will was standard for a man of his means. Within his law firm, it had been business as usual. The DNA tests gave nothing that would point to a perpetrator. No fingerprints, hair, or fibres except from the Warners. In similar investigations with little or no evidence, what often broke the case was the perp's inability to keep his mouth shut. Bragging is frequently an investigator's best friend.

"This feels hopeless," one of my people say. "I've tried to imagine the killer approaching the house without anyone in the neighbourhood noticing. Seems farfetched in this day and age when everybody knows everybody else's business."

Nobody argues.

They begin to stir, gathering their files together so they can get back to work.

I say, "Besides the monitor in the kitchen, garage, study, did any of you see a surveillance receiver or a fourth monitor in the Warner's residence?"

"Yes, in Mr. Warner's bedroom."

"How many cameras outside?" I'd seen five.

"Six," someone says. "One at the service entrance, the front door, the side of the garage, and three out back. One was in the trees, pointing towards the house. The other two were up high on each edge of the house facing inward."

"Notice a receiver or any remotes?"

Everyone shakes their head.

"That's what I thought." I stand.

Blank faces look back at me, until one-by-one, they gather their paperwork, head back to their desks.

I tell my assistant, "I'll be out in the field for the next few hours. If you find anything, contact me on my cell. It's going to be off for the next forty minutes or so."

"Are you okay?"

"What? Yeah, why?"

Shuffling the papers on her desk, she lowers her gaze. "No reason."

Looking down at the top of her blonde head, I wonder if my reply is convincing enough, and consider shouting that I'm fine.

Thirty-seven minutes later, after a brief appointment with the shrink, though I'm in a bad mood, I welcome the fresh air, which, for a change, doesn't burn on its way to a healing heart. Yeah, I know, corny. Healing heart; it's what my shrink said. The session was cut short after I explained the urgency of my current workload. But before I left I shared something painful, something I'd been hiding for too long.

"The hardest part has been knowing that because of me, because of my selfishness, Angie's last few months were unhappy."

"Can you forgive yourself?"

"I don't know." No.

"Do you believe you have the power to influence others people's behaviours?"

"No." Sure, if I show them my gun.

"Yet, you said you influenced Angie's behaviour. Some would say that's a god-like frame of mind. Do you think you exhibit that sort of power? I can tell by your expression you don't."

"I made her life harder. You can twist the words any way you want, but that's what I did."

"It's about a healing heart, Danny. Either you forgive yourself and move on with your life, or you don't."

I left then, not convinced I deserved to be forgiven.

The warm weather does little to improve my mood. While the interior of the car warms, my seat softens, I stare through the window to the hospital across the street, realize I miss the time spent scraping ice and snow off my windshield.

My therapist also mentioned I needed to reawaken my

passion for life. When I asked how, he said, "Register what you see, smell, hear, and feel. In other words, pay attention, Danny. The passion will return."

I didn't tell him I couldn't do both: see the passion in life and process murder scenes.

Murder and passion?

Passion and murder?

The crime scene at Warner's is void of passion. Should I ask my shrink what that means?

As for the reward posted, either it'll help or it won't. I refuse to worry about the end result. If I don't find Warner's killer, they'll be happy to transfer me back to District, I'm sure.

I hope.

The last morning of Angie's life, she said to me, "You haven't been listening."

"Yes, I have."

"Okay, repeat what I just said."

"You want me to pick you up at noon, we'll go to the realtor's office, see how much they think we might get for the house."

She'd placed her fingers to her temple, as if my hollow words gave her a headache. I was ready to repeat her favourite phrase: *I can't read your mind.* Thank God I kept my mouth shut and didn't say anything stupid. No, not me. Instead, in my best self-righteous imitation I spewed, "I don't know what else you want me to say, Angie."

"Don't say anything, just be there."

Be there...

I swallow hard.

Maybe the shrink's right. I have to let it go. Focus on the job. The job. The job. The damn job.

Meshango has the only solid alibi. If she hired somebody, how'd she pay them? What about Brooks? She lied about attending the powwow. How many more lies has she told?

The coroner estimates Warner was dead an hour before my team got there. Time of death isn't an exact science so that means fifty to seventy minutes. Which fit with Mrs. Warner's statement about her being upstairs. It also gives her ample time to commit the crime, hide the evidence.

I rest my chin in my palm. Did she have time to dump the gun and bloody clothes in the icy river? If so, why couldn't we find trace evidence in either vehicle?

The coroner, along with the re-enactment stats, say the path the bullet took through the body then through the kitchen window estimates the shooter to be one to three inches shorter than Warner. This depends on how she held the gun, how familiar she is with weapons. Warner was five-eleven. Mrs. Warner is five-six and a half. Meshango is five-five. Sophie Brooks is five-three.

I slip in behind the wheel of my car. As soon as I start the engine, a gust of cold air from the vents hits me square in the face. I catch my breath, turn down the heater's fan, secure my seatbelt. Mediocre tasks.

Though all three women are too short, high-heel boots would have made a difference. Maybe he threatened to ruin Brooks' career. Maybe Meshango decided to punish him for what his boys did to her. Or Mrs. Warner reached her limit and finally lost it.

Or some unknown assailant—for no apparent reason— knocks on the door, knowing Mrs. Warner is upstairs and won't interrupt. How unlikely is that? Warner answers, sees the gun, back-steps into the kitchen. Maybe they had words, or they didn't. The end result: Warner's dead and there are no evidentiary clues pointing to the shooter.

Another important question: if Mrs. Warner is our shooter, why would she come in the service door entrance?

All this time the proof could be hanging over the freezer in Warner's kitchen. The damn surveillance equipment.

I attach the earpiece for my cell phone to call my assistant.

"Danny, how's it going?"

"Re-interview all the students in Dr. Meshango's class. Find out if she stepped away for any reason. Also, find out if Meshango's daughter Zoë Sheppard has any physiological problems since her abduction and whether she's ever been under a psychiatrist's care.

"Trace Sophie Brooks' whereabouts during the critical hours of Warner's death, re-interview her whole neighbourhood if you have to, then compare Mrs. Warner's prints to all the guns we retrieved from the Warner's residence. I want to know if she lied about handling even one of them."

My assistant clears her throat.

"What?" I snap, and then realize my poor mood has set precedence for the day.

"You know Surrey's CUI already checked all this out?"

"We're not Surrey. Let's rely on our own evidentiary procedures. One of the three women may have killed Warner. Unless the evidence says otherwise, we're sticking to them like glue—without making a public issue of it. Mrs. Warner's the widow to our retired member of parliament; let's not forget that."

"Yes," she says with more oomph than necessary.

"Put me through to Ryan."

"Ryan here," he says in short order.

I slow towards the intersection at Highway 16 and West Lake Road. "Did you hear back from the architectural firm in Vancouver? We need blueprints of the house." A car pulls across the intersection in front of me. Before I realize what I'm doing, I recite the licence plate number in my head.

"E-Division said they'd send somebody from the Attorney General's office to talk to the CEO of the company."

The light turns red. Snowflakes the size of quarters hit my windshield. So much for the Chinook. "Call them back and tell them we need those blueprints ASAP. If they give you any flak, call me." The SUV to my right has brand new winter tires. "After that I'll be at the shop getting studs put on." My cell keeps cutting out. "Do you understand what I'm saying, John? I want you to do whatever it takes to get me those prints."

"Oh—I get it. You think the prints will show any fancy wiring needed for the surveillance equipment. Couldn't we just ask the surveillance guys?"

The light turns green. Large, dry snowflakes flow across my windshield. "The surveillance company has disbanded. We need to know how the house was constructed." Sensing his next question: *How come?* I say, "Got that?"

"Okay. Gotcha."

"Is it snowing there?"

"No."

My cell beeps. "Get it done."

"Yep."

I end our call to answer the next one. "Corporal Killian."

"Thought you should know we're making an arrest in Angie's case."

I gulp a mouthful of air, and cough. "When?"

"We're on our way there now."

"Right now?"

"Yep, just wanted to give you a head's up. I'll call later—" He's gone.

Ten minutes behind me the sky above the city's bowl area is clear. In College Heights, thick dry snow blankets my windshield outside the wiper's reach. The traffic whizzing past sweeps the snow off the roads, but already the pavement's slippery. It should concern me, but I'm having trouble focussing. At this moment, they're arresting the killer responsible for Angie's murder.

Is their evidence solid? Will the wrong lawyer get the case and plead out?

A pickup truck with a plough attached is clearing snow from Mrs. Warner's driveway when I arrive. Half the job is complete, but already an inch of snow covers where he's cleared.

Careful not to park too close to the soft shoulder on the street, I lock the car, manoeuvre around a mountain of snow big enough to fill a dump truck. Crisp air stings my lungs. I trudge across the driveway with my pants already rock-hard halfway to my knees. Having failed to anticipate the change in weather, I left my snow boots back at the detachment. My feet cramp with cold. Swirls of flakes obscure my vision. I pull up my collar, trying to protect my face. The man in the truck waves. I wave. Nearing the front door, I decide to walk to the service entrance. The Georgian home stands solemn and quiet as I pass. I look up at the camera. It looks like it has shifted some since my last visit, though we already determined it is securely fixed under the porch's roof and can't swivel. I keep walking, expecting the camera to move. Are my eyes playing tricks on me? I reach the backdoor, let out a short, "Humph." Too damn cold. I cup my hands together and blow into them.

Two hits to the doorbell button later, Mrs. Warner appears. She's wearing an apron of rainbow colours over casual clothes, blue slacks, white blouse, is holding a spatula like a baton. The brief second as our eyes meet I see something in her face that I can't describe.

I remind myself to pay heed to everything that happens. She has a habit of switching topics during our interviews. Today I'll pay attention to when and why she does that.

"You're in time for cinnamon buns fresh out of the oven." Her voice is without the baritone notes of most women her age.

"I had breakfast, thanks." If the two donuts three hours ago could be classified as breakfast.

I brush the snow off my head and shoulders, step into the entrance, and immediately smell the delectable aroma of cinnamon and raisins. My stomach growls.

"One cinnamon bun won't hurt," she says, without enthusiasm. "I've got salt-free butter."

I slip off my shoes. Standing in my wet stocking feet, I relinquish my parka. She hands me her spatula, puts my coat in the closet, takes back her spatula, as if we've done this a dozen times.

In the kitchen, a rack of cinnamon buns cools next to a plate of buns she's already topped with frosting.

"There is a stool for you. Would you like a cup of tea?"

"Sure. Thanks."

One bite and it melts on my tongue. Just the right amount of sweetness. The raisins are soft, plump, juicy. They're like the ones my older sister used to bake when dad was away and she wanted me to keep it a secret that she'd had her boyfriend stay overnight.

I inhale another bite, no longer caring that my pant legs are thawing and will soon be wet, or that my calves are still cold.

"Delicious," I mumble after my last bite. I glimpse the monitor mounted above the freezer.

She hands me a wet napkin, turns her back on me, peeks inside the oven.

"That was delicious. Thanks." I wipe my face, hands. "Mrs. Warner?"

She closes the oven door. "Yes?"

"Could you take a moment?" I glimpse the monitor. Outside, the scene is a wall of thick flakes.

Her pale face looks from me up to the corner behind her. "Of course."

"It's nothing. Please sit down. I need to talk to you." I pull out the stool adjacent to me.

She swipes sugar dust off with her cloth before taking the seat. Her hands, clasped together on top of the marbled island, tremble. The skin around her eyes is grey. The crease between her eyebrows deepens. Her upper lip looks moist.

I blink. I've done it again; stared too long. Damn. I've got to stop doing that.

"I'm embarrassed to admit something." I give her the same look that used to work wonders on my dad.

First a frown, and then a smile. "No need for that."

I shake my head. "I'm ashamed to admit that I've been treating this case differently. Honestly, Mrs. Warner, your husband being so important spooked me. And I'm sorry about that. I should have been more professional."

She reaches over as if to touch me, pats the air above my hand. "Don't be silly. You've been professional."

I nod my thanks, dab at the loose icing on the plate with my thumb, pop it into my mouth.

"Do you have other cases besides ours?"

I nod.

"I don't suppose you can talk about them?"

I shake my head.

She rests her chin on folded hands.

"You're doing okay?"

She nods. "I'm appreciating my home. I didn't always. It's so big." She glances towards the courtyard to the other wing of the house. "I'm trying to make sense of things, doing what I always do, baking and cleaning. Keeping busy."

I study her.

"I hope that doesn't sound odd?"

"Your husband travelled a lot. You must be used to being on your own?" I note her furled expression.

"It's actually taking some getting used to, admitting that he won't be back. I'm sure I'll be fine. Especially after I move into a smaller place. Of course, it's only been eight days. Somebody told me once that you shouldn't make any drastic changes after a loss. Do you agree?"

"Makes sense."

"This house was too big for two people."

"You got good surveillance equipment? Everything's working?"

"I suppose."

"You don't have a serviceman who updates your equipment?"

A small shrug. "Leland took care of all that. I know nothing about the system. What does it have to do with moving?"

I get up, walk to the freezer. "It could take a while to sell the place. Being alone may be something you're used to, but you still need to be safe. I should take a look at it."

"No, no. Don't bother. I lock my doors at night. The motion sensors work. If anyone approaches the house, the yard lights go on. If they try one of the doors or windows, besides going off here, the alarm at the police detachment sounds. I can see whomever it might be in the monitor."

"What if you're upstairs? Do you have a monitor in your

room?" I watch her jaw muscles and the muscles around her eyes.

"No. If the alarm goes off, I'm to lock my bedroom door and stay put until the police arrive."

"Without a monitor, how do you know when they've arrived?"

"There is an intercom locked inside the alarm panel."

I strain my neck. The monitor sits on top of the freezer. Above the freezer is an eight-inch high cupboard and above that a camera mounted on the ceiling. There is no visible VCR or DVD. Unless it's sitting inside the cupboard. There's enough room, but my team assured me it didn't exist.

"How's this work? Is it a multiplexer system, built in or wireless?"

She stands next to me. "Beg your pardon?"

I reach up and fiddle with the monitor's buttons. The picture brightens and then darkens. "If this is set to record when someone triggers the sensors, should I check and make sure it's working okay?"

"What do you mean? You can only see what's happening outside in real time."

I rub my finger over the sensor window. "Where's the remote?"

"Why?"

"This monitor has channels that change with a remote."

"I don't know what you mean."

"Mrs. Warner, there are multiple cameras outside your home. This monitor gives you a view from every camera. You need a remote."

"But there is no remote. Leland stepped on it a while back and never got around to having it fixed. He meant to. He just—" She shrugs and returns to her bowl of frosting.

I grab the stool; test to see if it'll hold my full weight.

"What are you doing?"

I position the stool, climb up, open the cupboard. Shit. "Where's the recorder? Where's the VCR?"

"You mean the one in the gathering room?" She shakes her head. "It's not a VCR. It plays CDs."

"You mean a DVD? Is it connected to this camera?"

"No," Mrs. Warner scolds. "It's for movies." The buzzer on the stove rings. She grabs the mitts from the counter, pulls a fresh batch of buns from the oven. A steam of hot cinnamon rises up to tempt me.

"I should probably let these cool a bit. Would you like one of the warm ones?"

"No. Thank you. I'm good for now." I climb down from the

stool. She either doesn't get it, or knows perfectly well there has to be a multiplexer system for all these cameras. "Ma'am," I'm already aware of the answer, "how many cameras are outside?"

She sets the scraped bowl next to the sink, then starts filling the basin with hot soapy water. "Six, I believe. Inside we have one in the receiving hall, gathering room, kitchen, dining room, Leland's bedroom, the media room, and the library. That is a total of," she uses her fingers, "twelve."

"How many monitors?"

"This one, but you already know that," she says over her shoulder. "One in the garage, Leland's bedroom, and his study."

"Why the garage?"

"Before entering the house he could make certain no one was inside. You're free to check it out, if you like. It's in the cupboard on the far side of the garage. There is a folding stepladder on the wall. Watch out for the door leading into the garage, it locks automatically."

I enter the hallway and unlock the garage door. "Do you have the manual for your surveillance recorder?"

"It's probably with Leland's files. The RCMP took them all after he died."

"Right. Thanks." I stop. "If Mr. Warner had spotted somebody inside the house, what would he have done?"

With her back still to me, she shrugs without pausing from doing the dishes. "He never did."

The red twenty-one drawer tool cabinet and chest is impressive. In fact, the whole garage is. Every conceivable tool hangs in its proper place. The old man had a 14.4V cordless drill, not to mention the compressor I've always wanted. Nice router with every bit a guy could dream up. A small, unfinished wooden jewellery box sits on the workbench. The mouldings are well-crafted. An unfinished gift for Mrs. Warner?

I'm convinced there's a remote. The monitor is too high to switch channels manually. I bend down, cup my hand on the window, then look inside Mrs. Warner's vehicle. The driver's door is locked. I pull down the ladder, unfold it below the cupboard, climb up, switch on the monitor. A clear image of the front foyer appears.

There is no recorder.

I shift the monitor forward so I can see behind it. Several wires disappear inside the wall. I check all four corners. It's disappointing not to find a channel changer, but I'll get an electrician to check it out.

After relocking the garage door, I return to the kitchen. Mrs.

Warner is icing the remainder of her cooled cinnamon buns. The whole ordeal of me being here shows in her stance. The skill with which she'd worked earlier is gone. Her shoulders are stooped. Her movements are slow.

"What happened to the remote for the monitor in the garage?"

"The security company supplied Leland with three remotes. A few months later, I noticed he only had two, one here in the kitchen and one in the garage. He kept that one in the cupboard under the monitor, or he'd have it in his car. The one from here he'd take upstairs every night. He would never admit it, but I think he accidentally threw the first one out with the garbage. His wastebasket is right next to his bedside table. I can't tell you how many times I retrieved his eyeglasses. He'd reach over to set his glasses on the table and end up dropping them in the basket. Probably the same thing happened to the remote. He drove over the second one, and I suspect he left the driveway with the third one on top of his vehicle, because one minute it was there and the next he was gone and so was the remote."

"But how did he check the house?"

"Leland had a case before the Supreme Court of Canada in Ottawa last month and planned to have the one he drove over fixed once he returned. I never used the surveillance cameras, so having no remote wasn't an issue for me."

"When your husband came home, he was okay with not being able to change the channels on any of his monitors?"

"Every so often I'd hear him cursing. One day he did mention he would need to purchase a replacement."

"But he didn't. Suddenly the remote, the cameras, your security system weren't important?"

"I know it's difficult to understand, but when you suffer a great loss, every other problem seems minor in comparison."

Yes. "I'm going to recheck the entertainment centres in your home. That means your gathering room, your home theatre upstairs, plus any others I find. I'll need the key to Mr. Warner's bedroom."

"Of course. Do whatever you need to." She takes it out of her sweater pocket, hands it over.

The layout of the top floor of the house is pretty simple. Mr. Warner's bedroom takes up the south side of the house. Mrs. Warner's bedroom takes up half of the north side, enabling them both to have a view of the front yard from their bedroom windows. The large landing in the centre area is open to the receiving hall below. The back centre is the library with accessibility from inside Warner's bedroom and from the landing. Next to the library at the back of the house is the media room, which shares the north side of the house with Mrs. Warner's rooms. Warner definitely got the larger room.

At the top landing I glance over the rail, curious if she's there. She's not.

I turn and enter the media room first.

The remote is in clear view on the counter next to the pop machine. After turning the huge LCD screen off and on, changing channels, pressing every other conceivable sequence of buttons, I switch it off, enter the backroom behind the screen. Using my fingers to inch along every wire, I double-check which wire goes where. I can account for them all. Not one comes in from an outside source. Which doesn't prove anything. The recorder could be wireless.

Only, where is it?

I check each cupboard, find snack foods, paper plates, glasses, canned soft drinks.

I cross her bedroom and enter the bathroom; it's the size of our bedroom down south. I shake my head at the extravagance, re-enter the bedroom. A large oak entertainment centre houses the TV and DVD. I check the cabinets. Mostly photo albums, craft books, rubber tubs full of birthday and Christmas wrapping paper, ribbons and bows. On top of the long bureau adjacent to her bed is a grouping of seven framed pictures. Family photographs. Only two are of their sons. I pick one up. A boy about nine-years-old has a smaller boy in a headlock. Both look to be laughing. They're standing outside on a summer day with clusters of trees in the background, wearing matching short sleeved T-shirts and cut-off jeans.

I set the picture back, pick up the one behind it. In this framed picture they're about sixteen and thirteen, leaning against a beat-up red mustang. Bronson has a large smirk on his face with one arm around his older brother's shoulder. Declan sits on the bumper with a far-off look in his eye. Bronson's eyes look dead. I set the picture back.

After checking all the drawers and cupboards, I enter Mr. Warner's room using the key, locate two remotes, one that operates the 42-inch LCD screen that pops out of a built-in chest at the foot of the bed. There is no multiplexer recorder. I pick up the second remote, push some buttons while pointing at the TV, then the security camera. Nothing happens. I set the remote down.

I pull out my cell phone, step out onto the landing, look over the railing. Sure she's not lurking, I return to Warner's bedroom, key in Corporal Callaway's number at Surrey SCU.

"Is it true they can waste our time in court over access to the blueprints?" I ask once he comes on the line.

"We're looking at years of legal haggling."

"Don't they get it that we're trying to find the man's killer? What if we get Mrs. Warner to sign an affidavit giving her permission?"

"The man was a lawyer. Who better to know what to put in the fine print? Our legal adviser says to find another way. There is something in there about her consent not being legal. You got to try another way."

"There is no other way."

"What about the electrical company, the plumbers?" Callaway asks.

"They all signed the same waiver."

"I don't know what to tell you."

I make a slow 360 degree turn, sensing something odd. "Any idea why he went to so much trouble?"

"The CEO said Warner was a cautious man who, after losing his sons in such a violent way, was hounded by the press and finally had to have all his home numbers changed. Seems every nutcase in the country crawled out of the baseboards to harass him. When he had his new place built, he wanted the best surveillance money could buy."

"Anything come of the nutcases. Any viable threats?"

"No. Sorry, Danny."

"Any chance it was a bogus excuse? There were no nutcases?"

"I didn't know the man, but those who knew him say he was tough, smart, and ruthless."

"But why make everybody sign waivers? Doesn't that sound like he had something to hide?"

"I don't know. Maybe he was paranoid. Oh yeah," Callaway pauses. "I heard about the arrest this morning in your wife's case. I hope they nail the bastard."

Something catches in my throat. I cough, then choke.

"You okay?" Callaway asks.

"Do you know any particulars about the arrest?" My voice comes out like a squeak.

"The guy's got plenty of priors. In and out of the psyche ward. They'll do their job, Danny. No doubt about that. And I'm sure they'll get back to you after the arraignment tomorrow."

"Tomorrow?"

"Yeah, well, I heard his lawyer is screaming bloody murder about police harassment. The Crown worked their magic, I guess."

"Any idea how many times he was brought in for questioning?"

"Three, I think. Look, let those guys do their job and don't worry."

"Yeah, sure." I thank him and click off.

I dial the local surveillance company's number, identify myself, and ask to speak to the owner. When he comes on line, I give the model number, brand of the monitors and cameras, explain the situation, then ask if we can brainstorm.

"Sure. What do you want to know?"

"I've got a home residence with twelve stationary cameras equipped with sensors. There are four monitors. What's the chance there is no multiplexer system to record anything that sets the sensors off?"

"Nil. What would be the point otherwise? If you spend that kind of money on the best equipment available, you'd be stupid not to include a control centre. One monitor, or more, would house a recorder or multiple recorders that would simultaneously record from more than one camera. Beginning with the sensor at the end of the driveway. This means—"

"If perps come at your house from all directions, every camera would automatically send a recording to the control centre."

"That's right."

"Where's the best place to house the control centre?"

"Depends on personal preference. I usually advise my clients to install it in their bedroom because—"

"Most break-ins occur during the late hours of the night."

"Right again."

I thank him and hang up. I make another 360 degree turn, move to the closest panelled wall, run my hands along the wood, feeling for anything that might conceal a hidden compartment. I work every wall, high and low.

Twenty minutes later, I thank Mrs. Warner for her cooperation, trudge back to my car, sit inside while it warms enough to scrape snow off the windows. Did I say I miss doing this?

While I scrape, I try taking in the bigger picture. No tape means no evidence, no perp, no conviction. I get back into my car. Something is wrong.

A loud sloshing noise comes at me from behind. I glance over my left shoulder as a sanding truck passes. Sand mixed with salt spills out, covering the centreline. I smack the steering wheel. I missed my appointment to have studs put on my car.

I pull out my cell to call the shop. "Sorry I missed my appointment. Any chance you can take me now? Or tomorrow?"

"Apology accepted, Corporal. However, it doesn't clear the bays. They're full all day tomorrow, and so nope, there is no one available to change your tires. So, happy driving."

"I can pick them up, put them on myself."

"They should be balanced. Any of the shops will do it."

"Great. I'll be by later."

I stopped drinking the morning after Declan and Bronson died. I had no choice. The first taste of the day made me gag. The second caused my stomach to heave. The third had me racing for the toilet. By the time I spit up the fifth mouthful, my fog-induced thought processes finally kicked in. Alcohol and grieving didn't mix.

But how would I survive the utter anguish if I couldn't get drunk and stay drunk?

I grew up in the sixties, but I was in my early thirties before I had my first whiff of marijuana. The stench was disgusting. And sticking white powder up my nose wasn't an option.

But while it's true I couldn't eat and I couldn't drink, I was too cowardly to follow in Declan's footsteps. Suicide meant being brave, and that is something I've never been. Actually, I'm convinced others can smell my fear.

I think Killian smells it.

I watch him warm up his vehicle and drive away. The homey scent of cinnamon and vanilla on my hands and clothing seems at odds with my yearning for a stiff drink.

Leland was in Ottawa the day I found Declan hanging by a pulley in the garage, almost a year before he and Bronson died. I came rushing out of the garage as Bronson drove into the driveway. It was one of the few times he didn't argue with me when I asked for his help. While he grabbed Declan's legs and took pressure off the rope, I jumped into his car and pulled into the garage, and then climbed onto the hood and dislodged Declan from the noose while Bronson held him up. We didn't wait for an ambulance. We carried him to the car and drove to the emergency ward. When Declan regained consciousness, he said he'd been stringing the rope through pulleys so he could hoist the engine out of his car. His footing slipped. That is all he could remember. The police believed him. I believed him. I continued to believe him until Sophie spoke of her fears about that day.

Leland was right; I am a fool. Even the silly, empty-headed Sophie saw what I was too blind to notice. My son wanted to be dead. He wanted death so badly he shot and killed his own brother after almost causing the death of Meshango and her daughter, something I'm doomed to remember always.

I called Leland after I arrived home from the hospital that night. Bronson had gone out, so I was alone, shocked, and concerned about what could've happened. Leland wasn't at his Ottawa residence.

I called his office.

No one was there.

I made myself a drink, sat in Leland's study, and repeatedly pressed the redial button until he answered. One hour and twenty-two minutes later. "Where have you been?"

"Are you drunk, Sally? You know I won't talk to you when you're drunk."

"Declan's in the hospital." The alcohol had taken hold, and I felt strong and wilful, while outside my window dead yellow leaves whipped across our back yard.

Leland grunted. "What is going on this time?"

"He was working on his vehicle in the garage and accidentally hooked the rope around his neck. I found him hanging. Luckily, Bronson showed up and we were able to get him to the hospital."

"What did the doctor say?"

"They're keeping him overnight for observation, but they said he'll be okay."

"Then that's that, isn't it? Put the bottle away, Sally. Go to bed." He hung up.

I know for my own sake I must let go of these memories. I wipe tears from my eyes. It's not as if I don't want to.

Without further thought, I grab my keys, slip on my coat and boots, and head out to the garage to warm up my car. Twenty minutes later I'm at the mall. The stores are adorned with Christmas decorations. At least they're not playing carols at the moment. Christmas is still three weeks away. Closing in.

The fanfare of lights and tinsel and nativity scenes leaves me feeling hollow, as if my chest no longer holds my heart. Many of the families at my church have invited me for Christmas dinner. My sister Shirley expects me for the full week. My friends in Ottawa hope I'll consider travelling east. I wish I could sleep through the entire season.

The mall's corridors are packed. I wander aimlessly. Nothing catches my eye. The thought of going home to a big, empty house drives me onward, past the Sony Store, Telus Mobility, Big & Tall, and Lowes. I have money. I could buy stuff for the less fortunate. Bags, shoes, clothing, a multitude of colours and fabrics move past my view. Books. Jewellery. The entrance to Sears is soaked in perfumes. My eyes water. My feet keep moving. I turn the corner and head to the exit. I avoid eye contact. The last thing I want is for someone to recognize me and expect me to chitchat. Talk about what? The weather? "Ah, yes, it's cold outside. I wonder if it will ever stop snowing. Do you suppose we'll have a long winter? Yes, it's true, we did receive a bit of a reprieve this morning."

The sounds in the mall, ricocheting off the walls and ceilings, roar in my ears; murmurs, electronic reverberations, shuffling feet, laughter, somewhere a baby screams. Soon I'm in my car and leaving the parking lot because I'm stunned stupid as to what else I can do. I'd drive forever, to the ends of the earth, except it's winter and the roads are deadly.

I have no idea where I'm going.

At the north end of the mall parking lot is the liquor store. My signal light blinks before I realize I've switched it on. I slow down and pull in, find a parking space. My pulse races. What if someone recognizes me?

So what if they do. I'm entitled to shop wherever I like. Buying a bottle of cognac or brandy or vodka doesn't mean I'm a drunk.

My thoughts keep circling. My husband died recently. Am I even supposed to be out? I'm not sure of the protocol. When the boys died, Leland did my errands. It was six weeks before I ventured anywhere.

This time feels different.

I choose a twenty-sixer of vodka and grab a menu from the display. For all this woman knows, I'm planning a dinner party for important guests. Normally, rye whiskey is used in recipes, but vodka is odourless.

The store is quiet. I pay my money, wish her a Merry Christmas, and calmly walk out.

The phone is ringing when I exit my garage. I rush into the house. That desperate feeling sweeps over me again. Please, whoever you are—don't hang up. "Hello."

"May I speak with Mrs. Warner?"

"Speaking." I strain to recognize the woman's voice and catch my breath at the same time.

"Mrs. Warner, it's the medical centre. Your blood tests came in and the doctor would like to see you Monday morning."

I clutch my stomach. Monday morning? I've never been summoned to his office before. The blood work for my annual check-up was procedural. Though he was concerned about my health and how I was coping with losing my children and now

241

Leland's death, he never mentioned Digger.

"Monday isn't good for me." I don't usually leave the house on Mondays.

"It won't take long. How's eleven-thirty?"

"I'm not sure."

Why don't I insist that she tell me what's wrong?

"The doctor has a busy schedule, Mrs. Warner."

And I don't? "Yes, of course." I'm quick to hang up. The room spins. I sit. The dizziness passes.

Snow swirls past the breakfast window. When I was a child, I loved the snow. Remember that, I tell myself and stand. I imagine joy in my heart. I smile. Joy. Love. Happiness. I concentrate on these words.

Routine means everything to me now, and I take pleasure in little things. Like kicking my boots off in the closet instead of setting them down in an orderly fashion. Hanging up my coat on a hook, and setting the kettle to heat on the stove before putting my things away. Lately I've taken to using my good china teacups. Hiding them in the cabinet seems silly.

The telephone call keeps popping into my mind. Despite repeating the word "joy" to myself several times, the receptionist's abrupt manner still irritates me. There should be a law against putting patients through this. I've three days to worry.

I uncap the vodka and take a quick sip. My hand presses against my chest. I'm hoping that my sense of touch will discern if something's wrong. It could be anything. Cancer. Some black spot on my lung. Or a tumour the size of a baseball in my uterus. I hope it isn't a brain tumour. That would be a terrible way to die.

My tea is too strong.

I'm sweating.

My pulse sounds in my ears.

Is it true? Am I dying? Inside my head, there's an image of me surrounded by black nothingness. I'm having trouble breathing. I'm dizzy. The phone is...way over there.

I'm gasping so hard I can barely see to dial 911.

It's ringing.

I shiver.

Please help me, I'll say. Don't let me die. Death would be so final. So—I hang up.

Death would solve my problems.

With a flick of the switch the fireplace in the study burns. The heat feels soothing. Comforting. Irrational fear had made me vulnerable and freeze-dried my brain. Freeze-dried? I see myself reflected in Bronson's eyes. Him smiling. Me smiling. Laughing.

If only I had laughed while he was alive.

The house is a showcase of elegance and good taste. From the architecture to the extraneous details to the aesthetic experience. Chandeliers drip with crystals. Lustrous maple and walnut and mahogany panelling. Crown mouldings. A garden oasis outdoors—under all that snow. A dream home that any person would be thrilled to own.

The new Leland would sometimes complain that I was ungrateful when I asked him when he would be home. He said, "You don't know how lucky you are, Sally. You have the kind of life few ever obtain. Stop and look around. You have a lot to be grateful for."

I'm looking around, Leland.

Fire crackles.

Silent tears flow.

Why isn't Digger here?

The desk phone is in my hand, and I'm dialling the number without any thought. Sometimes it's better to just be.

Her phone's ringing. Then I remember that she teaches Fridays. Please be home.

"Hello."

"Brendell, it's Sally Warner."

"Mrs. Warner—hello. I meant to call you. I'm sorry about yesterday."

"I understand. No need to apologize. It was difficult for both of us. Oh, and it's Sally."

"Sally, how are you?"

The question chokes me up, and I'm embarrassed. "I think we should continue our conversation, if you're up to it?"

"Yes. I realized now that I need to talk to you as much for your sake as for mine."

"Are you free tonight?"

"Tonight?"

I've already decided if I have to beg, I will. Before I die I need to hear what she has to say. But mostly because Brendell Meshango is the only woman I know, the one person who would understand my secrets. She was my son's confidante. Who better to hear my sins? "Please."

"Of course. Tonight it is."

A big weight lifts off my chest. "Good."

"Where?"

"How about here?"

She stutters, "Oh. Umm..."

I'm close to laughing. To think I've actually unsettled the eloquent professor. "I have a nice fire going."

"I'd be happy to visit you at home. I just don't want to intrude upon your privacy. I wouldn't like to—actually sometimes I come on too—God, listen to me. I'm not making any sense."

My heart goes out to her. I've misjudged this woman, and I'm terribly sorry. She witnessed the deaths of my sons. I can't even imagine how horrible that must have been.

"Sally, are you still there?"

"Yes. Listen—if you don't want to do this, it's fine, but I'm not angry any more. I blamed you because I had to blame someone. I don't expect you to make the nightmares go away. You probably have enough nightmares of your own. I only..." I'm crying again. Damn.

"Sally, how's seven o'clock? I'll bring wine."

I wipe my nose on my sleeve rather disgustingly, and smile. "I'll bring cinnamon buns."

Brendell's laughter is reminiscent of the singer Shania Twain. The sound makes me ache to live long enough to learn how to laugh with such gusto. "Sounds like a plan." She laughs again. "We'll discuss Lionel Kearns' work, or author John Robert Colombo and his famous poem, and I quote: "Canadians...not great beauties. You will look long and hard for a Venus and Adonis..." She's laughing harder now, with utter delight and what I'm sure is a deep-seated need to find joy in life's every moment.

It doesn't matter. I've already decided this wise woman is what I need, this woman who experienced the worst life had to offer and still finds the heart to laugh at men I've never heard of.

Fingers of snow stretch and twirl across the winter blanket covering my yard. In the centre of the driveway a double eight appears, four feet tall, swirling magically like Tinker Bell's stardust. With no visible celestial beings, my yard lamps have the job of drawing the space around our house into an enchanting vision of mystical dancers.

What am I thinking! This isn't wonderland. Beneath the snow is decay. Decomposing leaves frozen in place until spring ripens their stench. Rotting insects, food for next year's swallows before many of them fly into my cleaned windows and break their necks. Smelly feces: compliments of neighbours who would never think to fence in their cats or dogs.

Someone took great pains to make winter look pristine. I know differently. Life is a lie. The only redeeming quality of life... something I have yet to recognize.

Will Brendell tell me when she arrives?

I picture her laughter filling the void in my home and feel strangely giddy. This is remarkable considering how many years it's been since I experienced joy of any kind. The last time? I'm struggling to remember...

Twelve years ago. Leland and I made plans to travel to northern Italy during his first parliamentary recess. I was so excited. Our suitcases were packed a full forty-eight hours before our flight departed out of Prince George. Our to-do list before we left lay on the bedside table. The newspaper was cancelled. Our mail was being held at the post office. The security company had been notified. Instead of the usual twice a week, the housekeeper was instructed to come Mondays, Wednesdays and Fridays; who knew what mess my boys could make. Yes, the best part of all, Leland and I were going alone.

I was categorizing my clothes—the next thing on my list—when Leland entered the bedroom. He had this stupid grin on his face, and I knew. He'd done something to crush my joy. I was afraid to ask until it occurred to me that there was time to rectify his mistake.

"You should hear your two brats. You'd think they were on

their way to the dentist." He swept a hand through his suitcase. He always did that prior to a trip to see if I'd forgotten anything.

"Leland, what have you done?"

"You'll need to check their luggage before we leave. And warn them that if they don't shut up, I'll duct tape their mouths closed. I don't care if everyone in the Vancouver Airport laughs at them."

"Please tell me they're not coming."

He scrunched his bushy eyebrows and drew his lips together, the way he always did when I stunned him with my stupidity. "For God's sake, Sally. Listen to yourself. You're talking about your own children."

Basking in equanimity, I said, "But, sweetheart." Saccharine-like goo glistened off my teeth, I'm sure. "I thought this was going to be our second honeymoon."

"Oh, for Christ's sake."

"You're never here, Leland. I'm with our sons day in and day out—I need a break."

He turned then and left the room. Over his shoulder he spat, "Get used to it. We're not leaving teenagers alone in this house to wreck the place."

Cold spreads like plastic wrap across my neck. I shiver and hug myself tightly. My thoughts wander back and forth between memories of our trip while I watch for Brendell's vehicle turn into my driveway.

What sorts of images are conjured up when one announces she's holidayed in Italy? Outdoor table tops covered with delectable foods. Breezy, sunny days. Antique ivory statues as tall as buildings. Clusters of freshly picked grapes so perfect you hesitate to touch them. Spectacular gardens. Or from fools such as me, descriptions of airy, romantic hotel rooms celebrated for their sheer scale and opulence.

I saw that and more. Sunsets deeply coloured in jewels of red, violets and purples. Long tattered clouds, reddening on the horizon then disappearing to expose the bluest of skies. Air soaked in olive oil and the scent of delphinium blue. Tempting, clear, simple flavours: Antipasto, *Brodo alle Mandorle e Funghi*, which turned out to be broth with mushrooms and almonds.

Quite sad that I can remember these names twelve years later. In particular, the night I sat alone, drank house wine, and ate a triple strawberry sundae with honey and almonds while my family exercised their right to avoid me.

Back in the kitchen, I stare up at the monitor. The remote is now wrapped in a tea towel inside the casserole dish in my pots and pan drawer. I retrieve it and switch channels. The outside cameras show a haze of snowflakes. I switch the scene back to the service entrance camera and notice that the yard lights have created apparitions across the front yard. The aroma of cinnamon and raisons seep out through the warming oven behind me. Digger's dish sits over in the corner in its usual spot. I had to stop myself three times today from filling it.

A tear slides down my cheek. My blurred gaze stays fixed on the monitor and the shadowy entrance of my home. Years ago I saw beautiful images in Bologna, Padova, and Venice. While my husband and sons would rise each morning and promptly disappear until dark. When Leland did show, he expected me to follow him to whatever museum or antiquity he felt like seeing on that particular day. We'd inevitably run into someone important, someone also accompanied by family. And when we were together as a family, we argued or sat sullenly ignoring each other. We never vacationed together again—something I was actually grateful for until it was too late.

At this moment I am filled with shame. In a heartbeat I would return to those days. I'd smile without hesitation from the pure joy of seeing them again. I'd be grateful for whatever time they were willing to give me. I'd remind Declan how proud he made us, how intelligent and gentle he'd become. I'd tell Bronson that giving him life was a wonderful moment in my life. Then I'd look at his smug expression and say, "I love you–simple as that—no strings attached."

Lights turn into my driveway. I gasp, take a deep breath, dry my eyes, and straighten my sweater, and then rush off to answer the front door.

The moving lights from underneath the eaves sweep across my circular driveway. Brendell climbs out of the passenger side of a black SUV, leans in, says something, and then shuts the door. She strolls towards my front door, carrying a bottle of wine by its neck. She is dressed in a long, black overcoat with the collar pulled up. The light from the house reflects off a string of Indian beads on the ankles of her fur-trimmed moccasins. They dangle as she walks like a model on a catwalk. The overall effect makes her seem taller. Actually, she is smaller than me. Yet, in her presence, I feel diminished.

As soon as she reaches the front door, the SUV begins to move. It passes my door and exits the yard via the circular driveway, and disappears down the road. The driver must be her boyfriend. Who else would wait until she reached the door? As if whatever demons that plague my home might attack her before she is safely inside? Not likely. The demons are inside the house, not outside.

I open the front door and instantly the cold astounds me. It's minus twenty. As she approaches, I smell the unmistakeable, scrumptious fragrance of vanilla chocolate.

"Brendell, hello. I'm so glad you're here. Thank you for coming." I can't help myself, and blurt, "You smell wonderful."

She laughs. "I brought dessert."

She shakes the snow from each moccasin. They're quality-made. The stitching is some of the finest I've ever seen; and I've been all over the world. I observe her face and feel ashamed. Most of my life I never equated being Native with elegance. I would hear the word and think crowded beer parlours on welfare day. I shudder in shame.

"Boy, is it freezing. That warm fire of yours sounds inviting. I've been drooling over the thought of hot cinnamon buns for hours." She hands me the wine. "Do you suppose red wine works best with cinnamon buns, or should I have brought white? Someone once told me it's white with white, but cinnamon buns are brown. Sort of." She laughs. "Maybe I should have brought beer?"

Is she making a joke?

Just in case, I laugh, too.

After she discards her moccasins, revealing grey knitted socks covering small feet, and I've hung her overcoat in the closet, she hands me a small package wrapped in white grape paper.

"Dessert. One of my students makes her own chocolates. Let's just say they're worth every mouthful and every added pound. But first, Sally, could we do a tour of your home? I'd love to see it."

"Sure." Her wrapped gift crackles in my hands.

She is wearing a casual outfit that looks adorable on her: thick, black leggings under a long, flowing, white silk shirt with the sleeves rolled to the middle of her forearms, front buttons undone to beyond the bust, exposing a purple-sequin tank beneath. Her skin looks stunning next to the colours. She walks beside me into the dining room, a room that until now I hadn't realized has the outside lights reflecting off the chandelier. It's magic the way the crystals sparkle without sound.

"Oh, so elegant," she says, and we move on.

Next, we tour the gathering room. With snow falling outside my museum-sized windows, the room takes on a private club atmosphere. Brendell, smelling like French chocolate, adds a wonderful aura to the room.

Onward, beneath the grand staircase to the study and living room. Brendell makes little "ooh" sounds. Then it's an about-turn to the staircase and up to the second floor. My house is beautiful, and I am reminded how fortunate I am to live here. Which is rather funny now, considering Leland often had to remind me.

"Oh, Sally. Your bedroom is incredible." She smiles at the tub and runs her hand over my Italian marble countertop.

I'm hoping she isn't lying and she really does like my room.

"Hope you drink champagne while you're soaking in it? This is a beautiful room. Next time I visit I'll bring you more chocolates. This place screams champagne and chocolates for those quiet moments. Please tell me you have a cleaning lady come in three times a week?"

"A crew—once a week."

"You're organized and tidy. Good for you." She sounds sincere. "Since meeting Gabriel I've tried not to throw a hissy-fit every time he hangs his shirt on the back of one of my dining room chairs."

I don't say, "My men used to do that, too." Instead, I lead her from the room towards Leland's bedroom. I'm glad she's asked for a tour. Now I can show her Leland's panic room. It feels good to finally tell someone. Not mentioning it to Corporal Killian made me feel bad. The key is exactly where it always is—in my sweater pocket. It warms in my hand as I approach the door. But suddenly something feels amiss. I stop and turn. Brendell stands fifteen feet back. The colour has drained from her cheeks, leaving her eyes with a dark radiance.

"Is that his room?"

"Yes."

She takes a step backward. "I can't go in."

"But?" If it's true and cancer is spreading through my body, I need to seek redemption and share this secret. "But don't you want to see?" Of course, I could be acting prematurely. What if there is no cancer?

"I mean I won't." She returns to the top of the landing and descends the staircase.

I catch up with her at the bottom, determined to tell her about the panic room over hot cinnamon buns fresh from the oven. Or not. Why spoil a nice evening? There is finally another woman in the house to talk to.

"Come into the kitchen and we'll feast on cinnamon rolls covered in a fattening and very thick icing."

Her tight grasp on my elbow stops me. "Sally, forgive me, but

I can't go in there either."

"Why?"

"It's a long story. My mother...I'm Native."

I nod and smile. "I know that. And it's wonderful. It wouldn't matter if you were purple with large patches of hair missing from your head."

She studies me for a moment and then bursts out laughing. The sound booms off the walls and ceiling. When she regains control, she says, "You don't understand. Your husband died in the kitchen."

"I know that, too."

She shakes her head. "No. That is not what I mean. I can't go into your kitchen because...he died in there. His spirit may still be there."

"It is not!"

I must look panicky because she pats my arm and says, "I'm sorry. I should explain. If his spirit is in there, that is not necessarily a bad thing. He's not haunting you, if that's what you're worried about."

Haunting? Would he do that?

"His imprint may still be hanging about to make sure you're okay. Sally, please don't be upset. I can't go in the kitchen because I'd rather not disturb his spirit. Can't we sit in your study? It's so cosy with the fire burning and the outside lights showing off the fresh snow. It's the perfect room to relax and get to know each other."

"I'll meet you there."

In the kitchen, I take a moment and wonder if Brendell is right. If so, should I say something? I laugh, stuff the napkins into my pocket, grip two wine glasses in my left hand, gather two plates of cinnamon buns in my right, and meet Brendell in the study. I had already positioned a small table between the two Tibeca chairs. I love my Tibeca chairs. I hope she likes them, too. She takes the glasses from me, and I set the plates, napkins, and forks down, and sit. She curls her legs beneath her. She's comfortable. A woman like her—and she's comfortable in my presence. Wow. I can feel myself beaming. Heat rises in my cheeks. I want to smile, but I don't want to come across as peculiar.

The flames from the gas fireplace reflect off the mahogany walls, and with the outside eaves lights, the snowflakes resemble goose down feathers from a duvet. For some reason that makes me think of the wine. I rush back to the kitchen for the corkscrew. I bring back a dish, unwrap the chocolates from my sweater pocket, and place them into the dish while Brendell pours the wine. I swirl, sniff, sip, and swallow, then look away and hope my surprise isn't evident. The wine is smooth. "This is nice wine."

"From Kelowna. Gabriel's brother has worked there for years and always brings us a few bottles when they visit. I hoped you'd like this one; it's one of my favourites."

I take another sip to prove my sincerity. "Delicious. Not the usual too-fruity or too-vinegary that I generally choose."

"It's a merlot. Smooth, eh? I think he said they store it in oak. If I remember correctly, they use dark fruit, blackberries, and vanilla. That is why I thought of chocolates."

I sip more. "I like that it's not too acidic or astringent, and it's more herbaceous than Cabernet Sauvignon."

Brendell's eyes grow large. She is impressed.

This small talk has worked. I'm feeling...I'm not sure what. At ease? We're simply two ladies comfortable together. Is there a word for that?

Brendell licks the icing off her fingers and plops a chocolate into her mouth, it settles into her cheek. She sucks on the chocolate and says, "I used to bake some when Zoë was little. Once she turned twelve and began fussing over her weight, she'd scream bloody murder if I so much as had a chocolate chip hiding in the refrigerator."

That is right, she raised a daughter. My heart aches with envy.

I've never seen anyone enjoy a chocolate this much. Watching her savour then chew the chocolate slowly leaves me jubilant. I'm so happy, I'm close to tears.

She pats her mouth with the napkin and shakes her head. "That is not to say Zoë was a screamer. It's just a metaphor. She's headstrong."

"She's less likely to be pushed around."

Brendell nods, but for a brief moment I see doubt in her expression.

"I never saw my parents argue," I tell her, pleased at how easy it is to share my secrets. "I've had time to reflect and I can't recall once hearing them raise their voices to each other. I know they had differences of opinion, but we never witnessed it. Most people would say, 'Aren't you lucky, Sally?' But am I? I married a domineering man and had no reference to fall back on when it came to justifying my thoughts or myself. He so often overwhelmed me that I literally went blank in his presence. It's no wonder he thought of me as stupid."

She blinks, and her irises contract. "I had the opposite problem. I was raised in a violent home, and I married a man who didn't know how to argue, let alone fight." She laughs. "He became a successful litigator." She laughs again.

In person, Brendell sounds even more like Shania Twain when she laughs. Because I adore Shania, I wonder if I should tell her? No, she'll think I'm ridiculous. "We all have our excess baggage to carry."

"Ain't that the truth?"

It's my turn to laugh, because even though Brendell was head of the English Department at the university for years, she's comfortable enough with herself to speak improper English. I'd be so afraid someone would criticize me.

"Chris, my ex-husband, and I are friends now. Zoë deserves as much. For years, I didn't respect him because he couldn't fight back. I'd learned early on to shout louder and push harder. I never stopped to consider he had his own way of dealing with stress."

"He's since remarried?"

She nods.

"Do you and his new wife get along?"

"I wasn't sure until last Christmas. We all went out for dinner—Gabriel and I, Zoe and Dennis, Chris and his wife—and at one point Chris got up to go to the washroom. As he was walking away, Tracy turned to me and whispered, "Isn't he just the yummiest man you've ever seen?"

"From then on I decided if she loved him enough not to notice the balding head or the middle-aged bulge, she was okay."

"That is nice."

She looks at me with compassion, not pity. "To suffer the tragedies you've been forced to suffer, Sally, I won't even venture to assume I understand. All this time...I knew you blamed yourself. I knew the repercussions were so painful you'd probably forgotten all the good you'd accomplished in your life."

I can feel my cheeks flush. "You've mistaken me for—"

"Despite what happened, Declan was a decent and kind and extremely intelligent man. And let's face it, until the last year, Bronson was a social butterfly who could charm a bear from a salmon run. Every time I saw him at the university he was with half a dozen friends, always enjoying himself, everyone with him laughing. I probably shouldn't say this—ah what the hell. We're being honest with each other...."

Part of me is afraid of what she's going to say next. Another part is desperate to hear it.

"I didn't like your husband, Sally. He was cruel and calculating, a bigot, a macho-pig. And—" she studies my face and frowns. "I've got a big mouth."

"Actually." I set my empty wine glass down. "I didn't like Leland either. Not back then."

We smile. Although, Brendell's smile seems sad.

"He's not why Declan had so much good in him."

"Declan is dead, Brendell."

"I know that. He was troubled. You did the best you could do. He—"

"His actions nearly took your daughter's life."

"I know. But he also helped me."

I frown. "Is there a word for victims who bond with their captor? Stockholm syndrome?" There is pain in her face.

"I don't know if it's safe to debate such things."

"Brendell, forgive me. I didn't mean to sound so righteous. I'm the one with the big mouth."

"It's okay."

"No. I am to blame. I stayed with Leland long after I realized what a horrible father he was. I stayed with him knowing he would ruin my children. They were like porcelain dolls. When he couldn't mould them into what he wanted, he broke them.

"I could tell you story after story of his brutality and illustrate in vivid detail how dysfunctional our family life was." Too much wine has eroded my armour. "You don't need to caress my fragile ego. I accept my responsibility. I married a man who I thought would protect me from my father. I need to make peace over that. But first, I need to make peace with you. I am so terribly ashamed at how badly I treated you after what you had to face."

"I hated Declan."

Her outburst stuns me, and realizing my mouth is gaping, I purse my lips and say, "Excuse me for a moment, please." I escape to the hallway washroom. I need time to prepare myself for what she'll say next.

"I hated him with a passion that scared the shit out of me," she says when I re-enter the room, before I have time to change the subject.

I sit.

"I wanted him dead. But, in the end, he changed my life. I grieve—I'm still grieving for him."

I sit up straight, suddenly anxious to hear every word.

"You can have your peace, Sally, if you would only realize I don't blame you for anything. You're not responsible. I know you didn't attend the inquiry. I'll bet you never read the newspapers or transcripts?"

"I couldn't." To disguise how close I am to weeping, I pretend there is something dry in my throat, cough, swallow, and then grin widely. I can feel my eyes brimming with tears. Please God, no more Mâtowak.

"I'm serious. It may sound odd, but Declan gave me back my life. When he shared his pain with me, he helped me see things differently. He made me understand I had choices. If events had been different, Bronson would have been charged and hospitalized. He was sick, and I think—no, I'm positive your husband's political aspirations drove him to ignore it."

She sets her drink aside, and I'm worried that she's going to reach out and touch me. I wet my lips and brace myself.

"You were out-numbered, Sally. Fighting a battle against all three of them was a battle you were destined to lose. Declan understood that. It was horrible for him when he realized he couldn't end his own life. He struggled with those failed attempts. There are gaps in his college transcripts with notes that say he was unable to attend due to personal matters. That was probably the beginning of his plan to kill himself. If you're wondering why you didn't know, it's because he made damn sure to hide it from you.

"He and Zoë were friends. She confided in him about our relationship, my background. He knew what my daughter meant to me. When he devised his plan, I think he believed it would be simple. He'd provoke me, pretend to endanger my daughter, and I would kill him to protect her. He didn't count on Bronson beating Jasmine Norris senseless and then kidnapping Zoë. After things got out of hand at my cabin in Cluculz Lake, Declan was forced into a situation he couldn't fix. He shot Bronson to save us. It all happened so fast. Bronson was out of control."

She reaches for her wine glass, takes a long drink, and sets the glass back on the table. The gas fireplace seems to have captured her attention. I'm wondering if she's thinking what I'm thinking, that by then Bronson had a taste of brutality and liked it.

I ask the only question I can. "How do you survive such a horrible ordeal?"

She folds her hands together and hugs them to her chest. "Good question."

I wait, anxious to know, anxious to wipe the image of Declan and Bronson alive one minute then dead the next.

She shrugs. "By remembering his courage."

"Courage?"

"When I refused to cooperate and shoot him, he found the courage he needed to end his own life. Sally, I know this is hard for you to hear. If the roles were reversed and it had been Zoe who died instead of Declan, I...I can't go there. But what you need to know, what I've hoped to tell you for months, is what Declan told me before he died. He said...'Please tell my mum that it's not her fault.'"

I'm crying hard now. Tears flow down my cheeks and drip off my chin. I'm crying because my son was a tortured soul and I was his mother—but couldn't save him. I'm crying because the pain in my heart is ripping a hole straight through my chest.

It's a while before I'm in control. Brendell has gone off and returned with a roll of toilet paper. I almost tell her there is a box of tissues in the kitchen until I remember she won't go in the kitchen. She hands me a long strip off the toilet paper roll while my sobs come close to sounding like hysterical laughter. She sits and picks up the remote. I blow my nose and, out of the corner of my eye, catch her turning the remote over this way and that, and then studying the room.

"The gas fireplace," I say through my sniffles.

"Huh?"

"It controls the temperature and height of the flames. There is even a button for sound effects."

"Shut up."

"If you press the middle button near the bottom, the sounds of wood crackling come out of the tiny speaker on the left of the fireplace."

"Oh, for goodness sakes, what will they think of next?"

"Press the right button and it will add more heat. Up at the top there is a button that says 'Sat'. Press it."

She does, and instantly "Stranger on the Shore" by Acker Bilk plays from the speakers inside the ceiling. It comes from the satellite radio.

"Nice."

One more deep breath and calm replaces my anxiety. I've regained my composure. I watch her musing over the remote and finally laugh with her. Another time, another place, we might have been friends. Maybe even best friends.

I'm about to tell her about the remotes for the kitchen monitor hidden in the casserole dish and the remote for the panic room when she says, "Want to know what I think someone should invent?"

I wish they could invent a way to reposition one's heart.

She holds up the roll of toilet paper. "Self-flushing toilet with edible toilet paper. That way you can snack while you sit, especially if you're left sitting for a long time."

I'm laughing so hard, salty tears pour down my face and into my mouth. I can't remember ever laughing this way. It's as if I've been set free. Mirth comes from deep down inside me. My belly shakes. My sides ache. I start snorting. My eyes feel as if my skull is swallowing them up.

Brendell laughs so hard she stops breathing. I lift my arm to smack her hard on the back, but she shakes her head and wards off the blow. Her small frame rocks the chair. Yes, it's actually teetering.

"I need a doctor." Her eyes grow wide and she sits back. "Damn, I forgot. They designed a toilet to flush after you lift off."

"Lift off?"

Now I'm roaring. In my imagination I've seen a rocket launch, the toilet flush, engines burn, bare-naked bum ascend and next—sky's the limit.

Brendell must realize what I'm thinking because she flings herself forward at the waist and convulses with cackles of laughter.

I stop. Her mention of a doctor reminds me of the telephone call from my doctor's receptionist. I'm full of disease or cancer or something equally deadly. I remember why I asked Brendell to my home tonight. I remember the panic room. "I'm scared."

Chest still heaving, she leans back, and wipes the tears from her eyes with both fists.

"Are you Catholic?" I ask.

The question puzzles her. Her eyebrows knit closely together. "Not anymore."

"Have you ever gone to confession?"

"I was forced to as a child." She pours more wine into our glasses.

I take a long sip. Warmth spreads from my stomach to my thoughts. When the wine is gone, I'll bring out vodka.

She shifts her body and turns to face me straight on.

"I need to tell someone—"

"No." Her eyes grow huge. "Don't." Light from the flames glistens off her lush, black hair.

"Don't?"

"Don't make me your priest."

I laugh. It's my way of soothing the tension. "I've upset you."

"I'm not upset." She glances at her watch.

"I've taken advantage of your hospitality."

"I'm at your house, eating your cinnamon buns, taking up

space in front of your fire," she points out.

"Yes, but you're helping me."

"I can't help you if you go there."

"There?"

"I'm not the one you should be speaking to about this. Visit a priest if you must."

Her behaviour is curious. Besides, I'm not Catholic. Going to see my pastor would be the last thing I'd do. "What is it that you think I have to confess?"

She brushes crumbs from her black leggings into her palm and drops them on her empty plate. "If this weren't so sad, I'd laugh. What is it about me that make people think I want to hear this stuff? Declan had the overpowering urge to tell me his secrets, and now his mother feels she needs to do the same?"

I'm stuck by how calm she sounds. She's not going to flip out and hurt me.

She shifts in her chair. "I'm living with a sergeant in the RCMP. I admire you, Sally. But I'm not risking my relationship with Gabriel. He'll know something's up. Anything you say to me I'll be forced to tell him. Don't put me in that position. Don't tell me your secrets. And for God's sake—don't tell me you shot and killed your husband even if the sick bastard deserved it."

Words catch in my throat.

"Stop looking at me like that. Listen to me...carefully. Don't tell anyone. Enjoy what's left of life. You deserve it."

I stutter while trying to find something to say, but honestly, I'm stunned stupid and speechless.

From the speakers the Rolling Stones sings "Under My Thumb". Brendell studies the contents of her glass, swirling the red wine gently while keeping her head low. The small lines around her mouth and eyes seem deeper. She looks tired, yet contemplative. I wonder how did this estranged woman came to mean so much to me. Her honesty and abruptness bring tears to my eyes. Not only does she think I murdered Leland, she believes he deserved to die and that I mustn't pay. Should I reach over and embrace her? No one has ever taken my side before.

Bob Dylan begins singing "Things Have Changed". The words resonate.

Brendell's still sitting with her legs tucked beneath her. I'm amazed her circulation hasn't cut off. Around her neck is an Inukshuk made of shards of jade native to British Columbia. Set against her dark skin and the purple tank top beneath her white silk shirt, pendant and gold chain glisten.

As the silence draws long I worry if I don't speak soon the spell will be broken, the spell she has over me. If I don't speak, will she vanish in front of my eyes? She shifts slightly and looks at the fire. Blue, red, mauve and azure flames reflect in her black irises. Without taking her eyes off the flames, she drinks from her glass. I choke over my gratitude; soundlessly—thank God. Her honesty terrifies me. I know whatever questions I ask, she'll tell me the truth. I'm not certain I can handle the truth. But I have to break the silence. How do you cope? I need to know, Brendell. I'm desperate to know.

"Would I be wrong," my voice cracks, "in saying that you've had a difficult life?"

One eyebrow lifts, and she shrugs.

"You're still here."

She nods as if I've confirmed what she already suspected.

"How?"

Lowering her head, she turns her chin and looks at me. Her expression is sad. I forgot to wipe my tears away. She stares at the spot where a tear has turned sticky on my cheek. I'm surprised my dry skin didn't absorb it.

"Sally, you have to let go of the guilt. Stay in the moment. Stop thinking about the future and refuse to dwell on the past."

"How?"

"Pinch yourself, smack your face, stomp your feet. Do whatever it takes to jolt yourself back to the present."

It feels as if I've just climbed out of the pits of hell. This woman can help me. "My therapist said something similar after my sons died. Now, when things become difficult I imagine there are blackberry bushes with their evil thorns springing up in front of me. But they can't hurt me. I'm wearing magical gloves, and I sweep them out of my way."

"That is an interesting concept. I'm surprised your therapist would have you associate healing with something as dangerous as blackberry thorns."

"The thorns and the gloves were my idea."

She gives me an "oh" look. Actually, it's more like an "ooh". "I'm not the one to discuss these matters with."

"But you survived. Who better to tell me what to do than someone who's made it?"

"What do you think you know about me, Sally?"

"Nothing. I mean, I've heard stuff."

"What stuff?"

"You were abused."

"Who told you that?"

"Leland."

"How did he know—Never mind."

"Don't be mad, Brendell."

She's quiet.

I feel sick. I can't bear the thought of losing her now that I feel a kinship with her.

She shifts in the chair and makes eye contact. "Every time you feel your mind going back to something painful, you pinch yourself and come back to the moment. Always the moment. In the moment nothing is ever wrong. Do you understand?"

I don't.

"I thought you would ask me specific questions. On the way over here, I had the answers all worked out." She straightens up.

She's waiting for me to say something. I'm afraid to speak. Tell me which questions to ask and I'll ask them.

"The truth is, I wanted Declan to die." Again she stops.

Is she waiting for me to object? How can I? I had often wished I'd win the lottery so I could leave Leland and the boys and run away.

"It wasn't until I understood that he wanted me to save him by killing him," she injects, her voice soft, "that I started caring about him." She fills her glass with wine, and then leans towards me.

I extend my glass closer while trying to find my voice. A sip of wine helps. "I'm sorry for what they did to you."

"It's not your fault."

"It is."

She shakes her head. "Declan thought if he pushed me hard enough, I'd fight back. I don't think he realized how scared I was. That time at my cabin, when he held me against my will, I thought he meant to kill me. I begged him to let me live. He asked why?"

"I don't understand." I press a hand to my chest for fear my heart would jump out. "When did he hold you against your will?"

"That's right, you weren't at the inquiry. Weeks before he died, he broke into my cabin and tied me up. He wanted me to give him a reason to spare my life. I was supposed to prove to him I was worthy to live."

I press a hand to my chest to force the sharp pain down. Without warning, I'm there, living her nightmare, fighting to convince Leland I deserve to live.

Did my sons rape her or her daughter? I'm afraid to ask.

She squeezes her eyes closed. "It was all a ruse. He hoped

259

to frighten me enough so when he chose the perfect time and place, I would take up arms against him. He hounded me for days. Called when I least expected it. Left photographs of Zoë and me on my pillow when I wasn't home.

"It was when his plan fell apart that we finally talked. I told him about my mother. He talked about his dad. I thought we bonded. When I begged him to remove the gun's barrel from against his temple, and he wouldn't, I got an idea. I thought if I could convince him I would shoot him, he'd give me the gun, and everything would be fine."

She looks over at me. Her eyes are desperate. She is close to crying.

"He was too smart for that. He told me to pick up Bronson's gun. He even lowered his to his lap and waited for me to make the first move. He said he was sorry for terrorizing me."

I make a move to rise. I can't hear anymore.

Brendell stands. Shakes her hands, arms, and legs as if to impede the effects of our conversation, as if shaking will erase everything. She studies my face, smiles, and then lifts her sleeve to expose her watch. "It was nice spending the evening with you."

"We could do this again."

"Yes."

I race off to the kitchen with our dirty dishes and return to find her in the receiving hall. The effect of the wine has me feeling mellow. I'm not her mother. If taking such a chance after three glasses of wine doesn't concern her, why should it concern me? She's the one sleeping with a policeman. And anyway, who would dare stop her? No one interested in their career, that is for certain. The image of some young constable insisting she take a breathalyser test makes me giggle to myself. Then a sharp cramp shoots up my chest. What am I thinking? I have to offer to call a cab.

"I'll call a cab, Brendell." I hand her a plastic container filled with cinnamon buns while looking to see where I left the telephone.

"No need." She texts something into her phone, and then slips it into her pocket. "My ride should be here soon." She touches my arm softly and distracts me from my visual search. "Stay with me while I wait. He shouldn't be long."

I motion her to the bench against the outside wall near the double doors. I placed the bench there for this reason, yet I don't think anyone has ever sat on it.

I sit first, then Brendell. Her right shoulder touches mine.

She turns slightly and looks out the window behind us. I look into her face. Her eyes are focused, clear, not dancing around as I'm sure mine are.

"Do you want me to stay?" she asks while watching outside.

"Thanks, but I'm okay."

My face feels warm. I reach up over my right shoulder and turn on the outside lights. The snow has stopped; the ground has a thick blanket covering. All the trees lining my property are frozen in white splendour. A beautiful sight. For the first time in a while, I feel appreciative.

Headlights pull into my driveway and stop outside the door.

We stand together. She squats down and tightens up her moccasins. I'm surprised she's not taller than me when she rises to her feet, without so much as a creak in her back. As she buttons her coat, I do my part and straighten her collar, and then reach for the doorknob. She faces me. Her dark eyes sparkle like black diamonds. In her hands is the container of cinnamon buns.

"Thank you, Sally. I'm sure Gabe will be thrilled to find a cinnamon bun in his lunch."

"Only one?" His name reminds me of something. "Before you go, may I ask one last question?"

"Sure."

It occurs to me now that I should have commented when she said she didn't want to know if I killed Leland. At the time silence was the best reaction. "Do you like Corporal Killian?"

Her eyes widen. She's surprised by my question.

"It's been a little over a week, and he still hasn't found Leland's killer. I want your honest opinion. Should I be speaking with Ottawa? Should someone with more experience be handling this case?"

Her dark eyes are intent on mine. "He's been in homicide a long time. I'm sure he's competent. What makes you think he isn't?"

"My dignity is all I have left. I have to stand up for Leland now."

She purses her lips and looks out at the black SUV. I've met all kinds of people in my lifetime, but never one so cautious.

Those dark intense eyes fix on me again. "He's personally responsible for catching The Butcher in Vancouver. Almost got himself killed while doing it. I don't know him well enough to have an opinion on his credentials, but he's widely respected and solemn about his job. Does it bother you because he's Native?"

"No. I'm surprised you would ask."

She shrugs.

"Have you met his wife? Is she contributing to the community? Doing her part to—"

"His wife is dead."

"Cancer?"

"No. She was murdered in Burnaby last year."

This revelation shakes me. I think back to the dull look in Corporal Killian's face. His empathy was real. "How?"

"She was stabbed multiple times in broad daylight. They found her next to her car in the Lougheed Mall parking lot."

"That is terrible."

She nods.

"Do you think his grief affects his job? Losing a spouse...well, it can affect your judgement. I know people. I could speak with the Attorney General. The Lieutenant Governor."

"I'm not the one to advise you about that, Sally. You should probably ask one of your friends in the Crown Prosecutor's office."

"You're right. Thank you." I mean that. I simply want Killian to stop hounding me. Although, I must admit I'm surprised she hasn't offered to ask her boyfriend. He is, after all, Killian's boss.

She hugs me. I stiffen. Not because it's an unpleasant experience, but because it's been so long since someone has done this without obligation. Still clinging to each other, we promise we'll have lunch one day soon. Whether we do or not doesn't matter. Though I do hope I hear from her again. Friends are precious and hard to come by.

Feeling comforted and suddenly calm, I exhale. She lets me go and steps back. Her scrutiny is intense and startling. She wants something. I search her face. What is it? She frowns at me.

Without thinking I blurt out, "Brendell, I would never repeat anything you tell me. Ever."

She looks startled and then close to tears. I won't be able to bear it if she cries. I try to think of something funny to say. There is nothing funny.

"I'll ask Gabriel about Killian and let you know later, okay?"

"Thank you."

"It's mostly me, Sally. I don't trust cops. Me being with Gabriel is..." She laughs, "a miracle. Because frankly, I think most of them aren't worth shit."

"Did they hurt you? I'm so sorry if they did." Part of me wants to shove her outside before I'm bawling again.

"Don't be sorry. Every bad thing that has ever happened

brought me to this moment. My life means something now."
With that she places her hands on each side of my face, smiles
warmly, and kisses my forehead.

I'm crying before she reaches the sidewalk.

Ten minutes before noon, sounds of boots hoofing it down the hallway echoes through the building as the meeting in the conference room of the detachment disbands. Thirty-seven task force members from District sweep pass the Homicide's glass double doors on their way to the side door exit. I look back at the door as the lead investigator stops to talk with Superintendent Malden, the visiting superintendent from E-Division in Vancouver, and Lacroix. The superintendent from E-Division says something. They all look at Lacroix, who shakes his head.

Their inanimate expressions and weary stances tell me that what transpired during the meeting did little to point towards a suspect in the hunt for the missing and murdered off Highway 16. Knowing the killer is free eats at my guts. But that's not what I'm waiting for. As soon as Malden and his guest return to Malden's office, I'll be summoned for the next meeting, to discuss the Warner case.

I dread revealing the lack of evidence, but I'm biting at the bit to hear what E-Division's superintendent knows of the investigation into Angie's murder. Do they really have the perp? Is the case solid? Have charges been filed?

Though it was yesterday, it feels like days since they telephoned to say they were making an arrest. Nobody's called. Should I ask for time off to fly down?

Before Warner's case, I'd fly down to Vancouver every six weeks and spend Saturday with the investigators. The rest of the time I poured over any new evidence they'd fax me. During the week I did my job, stayed away from the case, but Saturdays were different. Saturdays were for Angie.

All that changed after Warner was killed.

I pull out my phone, wondering if I had missed a call. There is nothing. I slip it back into my pocket, look over at my bosses. Lacroix finishes adding his opinion, passes my desk on the way to his office without speaking. Back at the door, Malden presses a hand to his guest's back, just short of shoving him, and, directs him towards his office. E-D's superintendent caught the early-bird to Prince George and is booked on the afternoon flight back. They have two hours tops. Then Malden will take the man for a long lunch and make sure he meets his plane on time.

Malden opens the door to his office door. The superintendent enters. Malden then signals for me to join them. I stand, straighten my tie, walk across the room, wonder for the umpteenth time what I'll say when the super from E-D asks the question: Who do you suspect killed Minister of National Defence Leland Warner (ret)?

Polite greetings are made, the usual small talk, then our visitor sits in the chair opposite Malden's desk. Malden sits behind his desk, gestures for me to take the chair next to our guest. I do, my body lax and uneasy. It's like I'm fighting a battle and both sides are winning. Damn, I'd like to be anywhere but here.

"Before we begin, Danny, I'll like to update you on your wife's case," the superintendent from E-D says.

I gaze into the man's luminous eyes, feel close to keeling over. Thank you, sir. Thank you!

"An arrest has been made."

My fingers dig into the arms of the chair.

"I know you've waited longer than necessary, and that is my fault. I told them I'd tell you in person."

"Thank you, sir."

"He confessed, Danny. Don't worry, his insanity plea won't hold up in court. The money he stole from your wife was later used for drugs. He'd been causing quite a stir in Burnaby: B & E's, assaults, all for money to buy drugs. When he ran out of funds, he bragged to his dealer."

"His dealer turned him in?"

"Not until he got himself caught in a sting operation. He gave our perp up during plea bargaining."

Of course he did. That is how it usually plays out.

"Doesn't matter how they caught him much because the evidence kept piling up. He eventually confessed. It was a savage crime, and the Crown will make certain he does life."

"The motive was money?"

He crosses one leg over the other. "Mrs. Killian wouldn't give up her purse. He said she told him to screw off."

Of course she did. She was annoyed with me for not showing up on time. She had no idea of the danger she was in.

"Good," Malden says, as if washing the detachment's hands of the case. "You can put it behind you now, Danny."

Put it behind me?

"How's the investigation into Minister Warner's case?" the

other man asks.

I'm still shocked over what Malden said. I'd like to jump across the desk and grab him by the throat. Put it behind me?

I meet my boss's heavily browed eyes, but feel no urgency to speak. I'm too consumed by the sudden tingling of warm skin filling my hand. Angie's. Slipping into mine so effortlessly that shivers travel up my arm, relaxing me. Like the first time, walking side by side, not touching. My fingers clutching hers gently. Later, open mouth loving. Smooth lips brushing over sweet tasting skin, feeling goose pimples, and—

My heart flutters, changes positions in my chest. Heart attack? Malden sees it. Not sure what it is, but he seems concerned. His eyes open wide. "Danny? You okay?"

I blink, her hand slips away. "Yes."

I turn to E-D's superintendent. "We're liking nobody for this murder, sir. There was no useable evidence at the scene. No leads since. We're no closer to solving this case then we were a week ago."

Contemplating my words, he lowers his eyes then looks at Malden. "We need to close this case."

"We know that." Malden's eyes shoot towards me.

I feel brave. "If you want Surrey to take over, I understand, sir."

E-D's superintendent shifts in his chair. "Surely you like somebody for this?"

I shake my head.

"Is this about Professor Meshango?"

Wow, now that definitely knocks my socks off. I shake my head. "No. She's not a suspect."

Later, as our guest finally exits, instead of following right away, Malden walks clear across the room, approaches my desk. He looks down at me while buttoning his overcoat. "It's Saturday. Take a break. Get something to eat."

I pull my palm away from my face and nod. "Yessir."

He gives me the same pitiful expression he's been showing me since Warner's murder. Nine days to be exact. He pulls leather gloves from his pockets, gestures towards the visiting superintendent. "You do understand the reason he showed up this morning was to save face?"

He slips on his gloves. I sit up straight. Is my anguish being mistaken for job insecurity?

E-Division's superintendent reiterated three times during our meeting that the purpose for his visit was strictly courtesy. He wasn't pulling rank. He was offering his services. "Solving

Warner's murder is a necessity if we want to send a message to the criminal elements across Canada."

Prior to the meeting's conclusion he told us, "Our Special Crime Unit is available if you need them."

Saying something like: *Tripping over each other might not be such a great idea*, didn't seem the right thing to add.

Malden's reply summed it nicely. "That is generous. We'll be sure to take you up on the offer if it comes to that."

Good reply. Probably why he gets the big bucks.

I would've said, "No need. We'll send the files to them."

"Your job is secure," Malden says. "Find Warner's shooter, Danny, and everything will be fine."

He leaves through the side door while his comment hangs in the air like the aftermath of a huge garlic burp. Is he saying, "Sorry, son, but there is nothing I can do to help. If you don't close Warner's case and fast, you'll be handing out speeding tickets to snowmobilers in Nunavut."?

Nunavut is a long way from Vancouver.

I sit for five minutes, too despondent to move. Finally, grinding my teeth because it stops me from cursing out loud, I tug on my outer boots, grab my coat, and am at the door when I hear my name.

"Hey, Danny?" Carrigan calls out. "Busy?"

"Going to grab something to eat. Then it's back to the paperwork. What's up?"

His eyes dart over his shoulder in Lacroix's direction, who is busy at one of the computers across the room.

Carrigan rubs his hands together and, scratches one palm. "It can wait." He tucks his chin into his chest.

Grateful, I nod my thanks, take a step through the door, then make a mistake of looking back over my shoulder. His expression is legible through the thick glass. He looks grimmer than I feel.

I re-enter the detachment. "I got a minute. What did you want to talk about?"

His brows shoot up. Big sigh. Now I'm not so sure I want to know.

He sidesteps away from the counter to the Wanted bulletin board in the corner. He glances towards the inner office. "Remember I told you we've been having some problems with our daughter?"

"Is she okay?"

She's sixteen, on a year's probation for doing something stupid one night at a concert. I don't know the particulars because frankly I don't want to know. Having no kids of my own, who am I to give advice?

"She's having issues." He rubs a palm over his short crop, checks again to make sure no one can hear. "You know how it is: cop's and clergy's kids. It's stressful at home. The wife don't appreciate me being gone more than I need to."

I glance at my watch, wondering if I should offer to go for a beer later to give him a chance to vent. I mean, it is Saturday.

"Sorry. I'm rambling, I know. That is not what I wanted to say exactly. Things got bad enough that we sent her down south for a bit. Found this wilderness outward bound program for troubled teens, sponsored by some members."

"Sorry to hear that, Stan."

He plants his feet firmly, looks at me square on. "Yeah, well, there were plenty of other cops' kids there. I can't name names, Danny, and I generally wouldn't pass along gossip, but I couldn't sleep last night, worrying and wondering."

This is not sounding good.

He glances again over his shoulder.

"Stan, maybe you should just say it."

"Okay." Deep breath.

Damn.

"She met this kid. His dad's high up at E-Division, a CO. This kid's a punk, Danny."

"Okay."

"When he found out my daughter was from here, he asked her stuff."

"Okay."

"About you." He checks again to see if anyone can overhear.

Who said ignorance is bliss? Probably an English poet. Meshango would know. I consider cutting Carrigan short to ask her, because right about now I'm thinking ignorance is bliss for a damn good reason.

"Even my daughter said this kid's a punk. Okay?"

"Okay."

"He asked her if you'd sobered up yet?" Carrigan blushes. "Said his old man was instrumental in getting you out of town after your wife died. Said you were considered one of the best investigators they had until then. He told my daughter everyone figured you'd end up eating your gun."

I don't blink. Carrigan looks like his guts are knotted.

"When the call about Warner being shot first came in, Lacroix called this kid's dad and requested the case be passed to Surrey. He was told in no uncertain terms to give it to you."

This doesn't actually surprise me. Of course, Lacroix figured I wasn't up for the job and only gave me the case because he was ordered. "Okay." I'm thinking a drink would go down well right about now.

"This kid said his dad told Lacroix if you didn't close Warner's case, he better find an opening for you way up north. He didn't care where. Just as long as there was no backlash."

Oh right. I'm Indian. Can't upset the equal rights whistle blowers.

"He's just some punk kid."

That is the problem. It's probably true. Where else would some little prick get such detailed info?

"Sorry, Danny."

"It's okay." I squeeze by him and head for the door.

"Oh, wait. I forgot. There was something else."

In a state of foggy denial, I stop, turn back, stoned-faced, I'm sure.

"Apparently, Lacroix didn't appreciate being told who to transfer and who to keep, and said as much. He told him he was more than satisfied with the job you were doing."

Stan must notice my duh expression because he grins. "But that ain't all. When he expressed his thoughts, he was told that if he didn't like the arrangement he could transfer with you." Again he must be able to read my expression because he adds, "I know. Weird, eh? Guess you got him in your corner after all."

I close my mouth. I feel like shaking my head like a dog. I'm not sure how I'm supposed to take this. I have a sudden image of Lacroix patting my back and saying, "Good doggie." I clench my jaw, squint, and force myself not to laugh. "I'll see you later."

I reach the door when a thought occurs to me. "Stan?"

"Yep?"

"Do you have a heated garage?"

When the boys were small, Leland and I attended our first Business Association's Annual Ball. It was during intermission for the live dinner theatre that my fantasy world came crashing to a halt. One of the newly married associate's wives was doing her part of hobnobbing with the boss's wife. Me.

I didn't mind. The attention was nice. I even reminded her, "Please, call me Sally."

I had spent a few moments describing our two beautiful sons Declan, four and Bronson, one. As I spoke, all eyes were upon my three-hundred-dollar gown. Being a wife and mother mattered, and you could hear it in my voice and see it in my mannerisms. A mere fifteen pounds from my goal weight, I looked competent and classy. My naturally blonde hair was thick and styled in the popular shoulder-length layered look of the day. Everything went well, great in fact. Until she asked that question. Do you know the one? The question that places your entire self-worth out there for everyone to soil.

"What do you do, Sally?"

I was about to say, "I'm a wife and mother, and loving every minute of it."

But Leland opened his big fat, ugly, stupid mouth. "Sally doesn't work."

The junior associate's wife graciously came to my rescue. "Certainly raising young boys is work?"

Her husband gawked at her as if to say, "Shut up, woman."

I was surprised no one else noticed. Or maybe they did.

While I smiled on the outside, inside my head I prayed: *Please, Leland, don't say anything else.*

No such luck.

"Right." He laughed, as if to soften the blow. "That is why billions of women all over North America have kids every day. Which is why some young uneducated immigrant takes over when most of you return to your fancy careers." Then he ducked, as if awaiting the blows.

The rest of the evening is a blur. Somebody turned up the air conditioner. Sharp pangs of cold air stung the back of my neck. I remember them staring at me with their pitiful expressions until they caught themselves and looked away.

"Ladies, tell me I'm wrong," Leland rebutted in his I'm-just-joking voice, aware of the awkwardness that had fallen over our table. The man wasn't a total imbecile.

I closed my mouth, searched the room as if intent on seeing something interesting and—now I know why I thought I'd seen Brendell before our first teacher-student conference, Declan's first semester at UNBC. She was there. Three tables over. Towards the centre of the room. The reason I noticed her was the sheer contrast of her person: a young, attractive Native woman sitting with the fair-haired and plain white folk. She was like a long stemmed rose in the midst of tired dandelions. An Indian Princess. Who would have guessed she'd become so important to my family? I shudder at the image of Brendell sitting next to Bronson when Declan shot him. She was inches away when his head...his blood—oh dear Lord. The image is God's ugliness.

I can't stop trembling. All this time and I never gave her ordeal with my sons any thought. I cared only of my suffering, my grief. What she must have seen, heard, felt at the hands of my sons—I can't imagine, though I should know. I owe it to her.

The transcripts.

I rush to the study. Despite it being late morning, a sudden overcast shrouds the room in shadows. I switch on the desk lamp. Under the Liberal offices heading in the phone book, I find the number and dial. After the usual niceties I state my request. By my tone, it's evident how important this is. No is not acceptable. Neither will a delay. I must read the transcripts before I die. Of course, I don't say this, but I imply urgency.

The shrewd politician on the phone says, "I'll have them hand delivered by this afternoon, Sally. Will that help?"

"Yes." I hang up.

The doorbell rings.

I avoid the front door by exiting the study into the hallway and race into the kitchen. The monitor shows Brendell. Quickly, I return to the front door.

"Brendell, hi." Behind her, blots of blue sky appear.

"I'm sorry to bother you, Sally, but I couldn't sleep last night. I feel bad about cutting you short, and after thinking about nothing else all night, I decided you're right. You need to confess."

"Excuse me?"

She stuffs her gloves into her pockets, rubs her hands together, and steps inside. "You wanted to tell me something important, but I wouldn't listen. I'm listening now."

"Brendell, what are you talking about?" I help her off with her coat and hang it in the closet; despite the sunshine the cloth feels cold to the touch.

I lead her towards the kitchen, then, remembering her superstition about Leland's spirit being stuck in the kitchen and his bedroom, I stop. "Let's go into the gathering room. I'll get us something hot to drink, then you can explain everything."

I show her into the gathering room and return to the kitchen. While I prepare our hot chocolates, I sneak a peek at Bredell across the way. I decide she's using this crazy story as pretence to return. I carry a tray with our steaming mugs, some jam busters, and a can of whipped crème to the gathering room, pleased she felt an excuse was necessary in order to visit me again.

She picks up her mug and takes a sip. I like my hot chocolate with whipped crème. Since she likes hers plain, will I appear indulgent?

We sit together on the sofa facing the back of the house. The only visible colour against the blue sky is white. Beside me, Brendell is quiet.

"How was your day, Brendell?"

Another quick sip of hot chocolate, she sets it down, and turns to face me. "Please, tell me what you were about to say last night. What was the secret?"

She means the panic room.

"I've thought about this carefully," she says while my eyes feel glued open. "I know last night I said I didn't want anything to jeopardize my relationship with Gabriel. That wasn't fair to you. You've suffered so much. I don't know how you hang on. But you're inspiring, and Sally, you're still a young woman. You can be happy. You do have a future. But you need to believe you deserve it."

"Brendell, you're sweet, but I wouldn't say that sixty is young."

"Please, let me finish." She reaches over and grasps my hands.

Her palms are warm and smooth. She's certainly not holding my hands tightly, but I feel strange. Heat races up my arms. I'm having problems listening. How can I pull my hands away without hurting her feelings?

She's saying, "...begged..."

My fingers cramp.

"...promised..."

Will she ever let go?

"...failed him."

What?

"Please let me help you. Let me do for you what I couldn't do for Declan."

I smile, but I don't know what she means. I should have listened.

"You deserve to be happy." She looks at me intently. Tiny, hairline wrinkles are visible at the edges of her eyes. The colour of her eyes reminds me of dark French chocolate, shiny, rich. True.

I smile again.

Her eyes moisten.

Is that a tear?

She frowns. "Please let me help you."

"You've already helped so much. I feel I should be the one helping you."

She lets go of me—a flush spreads across my face, targeting my cheeks. My throat glands hurt. Just as they did when I was a child and I'd blown up too many balloons. To escape this claustrophobic tight-hold, I look down. The skin on the top of my hands is taut over sharp bones. Old. I fold my arms across my chest and tuck both hands under my arm.

She's looking at me funny.

"I can't impose on you. You've already been too kind."

"Show me Leland's room."

"Now? But you said you couldn't go in there because—"

"I know what I said. I've thought about this carefully, and I was wrong not to help you."

I want her to leave. She's scaring me.

She stands up. "We'll pretend you're showing me your lovely home for the first time. We'll start in your husband's room." She extends her hand, indicating for me to lead the way.

I walk towards the curved staircase in the receiving hall. The morning's clouds have thinned again, allowing sunlight to lay like a carpet runner from one end of the room across to the other. We don't speak as we climb the stairs. Brendell is one step behind me. My hand slides along the top of the railing because I don't trust my legs. My knees wobble. Leland won't like me showing his room to her. But even as I think this I realize he's dead; he will never know. Still, going in there doesn't seem right. We reach the top landing. The key to his room is in my pocket. I slip my hand around it. In my left pocket is a small revolver. How did it get there? Where did it come from? I can't remember—

"Are you okay?" Her voice is soft and breezy, stirring the hairs on the back of my neck.

I grasp my fingers around the small revolver, coveting it. Leland's room has been closed to me since the day he died. There was no cause to go inside. I wonder if that is the reason I never mentioned the secret room to the police.

No. I don't think that is why.

Brendell is quiet, and I'm worried she might be holding her breath. His door looms before us. The key and gun are warm in my palms. The thought *release the gun* passes through my mind. I do.

I grip the doorknob, insert the key, and turn it. Click. The door whooshes open.

"Sally." My heart jumps. "Let's wait here a moment."

I push the door wide and an elegant, contemporary room mixed with Asian design opens before us. I'd nearly forgotten how sophisticated his space was.

"He liked nice things." I wonder what made me say that.

"It's lovely," she says behind me.

I stand perfectly still. Maybe if I give her a moment she'll get her fill and leave?

"What did you want to show me?"

"The panic room."

"As in the movie *Panic Room* with Jody Foster?"

"Yes."

"Where is it?"

"Behind that." I point to the wall mirror on the left, and then to the bedside table on the right. "The remote, in the drawer over there, opens the concealed door." I glance back to see her peeking over my shoulder; she's pale. "Do you want to see it?"

She hugs herself and leans back as if frightened I might force her. "Why are you telling me this?"

I'm about to say that Leland has private papers hidden in there. I'm not sure what else. I wanted her to see them and tell me it's okay not to tell the police. Nothing in there will affect their investigation.

I stop myself.

It's a lie.

"Sally?"

"I didn't tell the police about it."

I wait for her response while the skin on my arm itches. I remember now what I was thinking last night. I wanted to show her the room because I might be dying. But I can't tell her that. I don't want her pity. And what if I'm not dying?

I don't know what to do. I feel panicky.

"I have a doctor's appointment tomorrow."

"Sally, tomorrow's Sunday."

I have to wait two more days. I turn and look hard at her. What am I doing?

"Sally, have you been drinking?"

"It isn't even eleven o'clock in the morning."

"Did you kill your husband?"

A sharp pain shoots through my head. It's because I'm thinking too much. "Do you really believe I could do such a thing?" I rub my right temple and stuff my right hand in my pocket.

"If people knew what kind of marriage you had, they'd understand. He made your life miserable. Get this off your chest so you can have a future. Tell me what happened." Her eyes grow huge. "But for Christ's sake, don't tell the police. You've suffered enough." She touches my forearm. "Did you read 'Crime and Punishment' in college?"

I shrug.

"Written by Dostoyevsky."

"So?"

She stares at me. "Confess to me, Sally, right here and now, then let it go. It's the only way you can live in peace."

"In prison?"

"No, of course not."

I don't feel well. Trying to decipher what she's getting at is too much. I need some water. A chair. I'm worse than what she thinks. I let Leland destroy our children.

"Let's get out of here." She grips my arms and steers me out of the room.

"You don't want to see the panic room?"

"You need to lie down."

That is what I like about Brendell; she understands me.

I lie on my bed, and a soft throw blanket covers me. She sweeps the hair off my face. Shivers run down my neck. My mind clear, cognitively, I wonder if I've been sleeping. Then I worry, am I to die now? There is an acid taste in my mouth.

"How do you feel?"

I breathe deeply. "Could you please get me the waste paper basket from my bathroom? My stomach feels queasy."

She disappears.

I close my eyes...

"It's right beside you, Sally. Here, have a sip of water."

Her hand slides behind my neck. The water is sweet. I take two sips.

"Brendell, it's not my fault Leland is dead."

Her silence prompts me to open my eyes. She smiles at me like a sweet angel sent from God. I scan her dark eyes and decide there is nothing to fear. "You can look in his panic room if you like."

She shakes her head. "With my luck the door will close, locking me in, and you'll forget I'm in there, then goodness knows how many hours, days will pass before I'm found, wasted away, a shadow of my former self—" She inhales sharply and laughs.

I'd laugh with her, but I don't trust my stomach. My eyes close. I feel my body drifting.

* * *

Sounds of crinkling paper prompt me to open my eyes.

Brendell holds a large manila envelope. "This was delivered a few moments ago by messenger. I hope it's okay that I signed for it. I'll set it on your desk."

"Who's it from?"

"The MLA's office."

"Really? I'll look in a moment. You can set it at the end of my bed." I know I should remember something. "MLA? I wonder what they want."

"I don't know."

There is something off-sounding in her voice. "Brendell, are you all right?"

"I'm worried about you."

"Oh goodness, no need for that."

"Sometimes things happen that the mind can't cope with."

Is she waiting for me to add something? I don't know what that could be until I remember my sons. "That is true."

"Sally, I need you to tell me the truth. For your sake. Okay?"

"Yes, of course."

"I know it's not your fault your husband's dead."

"That is correct."

"Yes, that is correct. But that wasn't my question."

"Sorry."

"Don't be sorry." She tucks the comforter along my shoulders. I feel nurtured.

"You shot your husband, didn't you?"

Gastric acid rises in my throat, and I sit up fast with one hand covering my mouth. She's quick to realize what's happening and reaches for the waste paper basket. I hang over it and empty my stomach. The bile retches out of me, burning my throat, choking me. She holds my forehead in her palm.

I finish and flop back onto the bed. The room is darkening, and I pass out.

* * *

When I wake, Brendell has pulled the King Louis chair close to the bed and is sitting still with her eyes closed. It's overcast outside again. The lamp next to my bed casts a glaring light. I shield my eyes and squint at her. I'm amazed by life's twists. This woman I hated with such passion is now my friend.

But my new friend, my only friend, suspects I'm a murderer.

My hand moves under the comforter and covers the outline of the revolver in my sweater pocket. It's cold and hard, but fits surprisingly well in the contour of my hand. Did I take Leland's life? I imagine holding the gun, pointing it at him, and the expression on his face.

Yes, I think I did.

I have Warner's case files scattered across my kitchen table. I've read Mrs. Warner's file for the fifth time but I still can't concentrate. The last day Angie was alive keeps playing out over in my mind. The questions aren't new. I've gone through this stuff so many times. Like all those other times, the answers don't come, and the void grows larger.

If only...?

Why hadn't I...?

What if...?

How come...?

Why couldn't...?

The precise moment I was due to pick her up I was sitting across from my commanding officer; my staff sergeant sat in the chair next to me. This is the same commanding officer Carrigan was talking about. I'm sure of it. I was his pet project until I turned nuts after Angie's murder. Even now I remember how the clock on the wall above his chair ticked loudly as each minute passed. I sat there listening to them discussing my future, knowing if I didn't leave soon, I'd be late. I promised her that morning, but big things were at stake. Besides, my CO and staff sergeant kept talking. How could I interrupt to say I had to leave because my wife wanted to put our place up for sale? All this so I could put in for a transfer to a smaller, safer community outside the city limits—while they were doing their upmost to help my career? I mean, damn, she was talking about transferring north. To Ashcroft, Hope, or Penticton. How could I say that to these two men when they were telling me I had the opportunity of a lifetime? I was going places in the RCMP. They said I showed signs of being a top-notch investigator, they'd given it careful consideration, were willing and able to offer me a posting in the serious crime unit in Surrey. Nobody mentioned I was a minority, an Indian. And besides, what if there were no openings outside of the lower mainland?

Surrey's SCU is the headquarters for the Province. There was no limit to where an opportunity like this might take me. My career was on the rise. How could I say, "Sorry, gotta go?"

A typical Vancouver day: intermittent showers with gloomy grey skies. Although it was dull outside, inside that office things couldn't have been brighter. They smiled. I smiled. They laughed. I laughed. While somewhere across town Angie was telling a killer to screw off.

That morning she said, "I'm counting on you, Danny. How often do I ask you to do anything? I need you to do this one thing."

"Yeah, yeah," was all I'd said in return. The last words I'd said to her.

The last expression she saw on my face was me rolling my eyes.

For a glorious forty minutes, I listened to those two men compliment me on my work habits, my attention to detail, my citations. The Surrey Crime Unit was lucky to have me.

"Wait a minute." I laughed. "I need to speak with the wife. This is a great opportunity, but we always discuss things first."

Both men thought that was admirable.

I thanked them and left.

On my way to meet her, I heard the commotion over the radio. Something had happened at the east entrance of the mall near where I was to meet Angie. I didn't answer because I was in enough trouble, and no way could I offer to give crowd control assistance. Another patrol car could assist. But now I had an excuse for being late. Once she calmed down, I'd explain about the call; that would sooth her bad mood. After that I planned on spending the week chalking up brownie points before I mentioned we wouldn't be moving. As I pulled into the parking lot, I told myself to grow some balls. I was the man. My career was important. She married me for better or worse. She'd have to get used to the way things—That was when I saw the police cars, cops, and investigators taping off the perimeter. The coroner's van. I sensed something, but I pushed it back. I expected to see her nearby watching the scene, curious like any other civilian.

I push myself away from the kitchen table. Stand. Pace. I shouldn't think about that day. It never helps. I cross to the sink. It's because they've made an arrest. I'm about to get closure. Closure? The moment I saw her car across the way, driver's door open, policemen blocking...something on the ground. Camera flashes. Coroner kneeling. Me walking. Running. Yelling. Pulled back. Hands holding me tight. Screams—did I imagine a scream?

Think of something else.

I grab a drink of water from the tap, and drink long and slow. More than likely, I have two weeks to find Warner's killer. Then if nothing happens, they'll reassign the case. A move that wouldn't read well in my file.

"Do I look like I care?"

I sit back down at the table.

The night before Angie was stabbed to death, I found her in the sewing room, pinning a new hem on one of my uniform pants.

"Please show up on time tomorrow," she had said.

I had leaned against the doorjamb, ready to calm her fears. "I'll be there. But honestly, babe, I don't see what the rush is. If we wait until the end of June, we'd probably get more offers on the place. Families are more likely to buy after the school year's over."

"Danny, please. I need you to do this. I hate this city. I hate it with every inch of my being. I want out. Something bad is going to happen. We have to get out."

I squeeze my eyes shut, falling forward until my head hits the table, while my fist punches the underside...

The kitchen is still, quiet. Sunlight filters through the blinds; warm air shoots up through the floor vents while traffic resounded off the highway in the distance. I tremble. They've arrested Angie's killer. I'll take time off to attend the trial. No rush. It'll probably be months away. They usually are. Meanwhile, I'll go down and look him in the eye. Too bad we don't kill our killers. I'd sit on the other side of the glass and watch.

What's happening to me?

Nothing will bring her back. Arresting her killer changes nothing. She's still dead. A pile of ashes in a box in my living room.

Okay. Enough already.

I wipe my face on my sleeve, check the clock, and grab my phone. I dial my shrink's home number and count four rings.

"Danny, what's wrong?"

I hear the panic in his voice. He's a professional and trained not to show his concern. When he saw my name on his call display, he must have assumed the worst. And why not? I've never telephoned him before. "I'm fine."

"I said to call me if...Are you in trouble?"

"I need a favour."

"I told you I was here if you needed me, Danny. I meant it."

"Can I buy you breakfast in the morning?"

I put the question out there and hear dead air in return. He's probably wondering if this call changes things, if I'm pushing it to the next level. I hesitate to sooth his worries. But that is not nice. "It's not about me. I need help analysing a suspect."

"Don't you have analysis programs to help with that?"

"Yes."

"They're not helping?"

"No."

"Breakfast?"

"Unless you prefer to sleep in on Sundays. We could make it lunch."

"No, breakfast is fine. Where?"

"Tim Horton's, nine o'clock."

"I'll be there."

I hang up knowing he will. I put the report by the door.

In the aftermath of sleep, my empty King Louis chair leaves me feeling blue. Brendell is gone. I reach out to pat Digger before realizing he is buried in my garden.

My eyes tear up. I listen for sounds of Brendell. The silence intensifies the pain. If only I could relive the day. I made a mess of things. I generally make a mess of things. The first time I caught Leland cheating, I was on an errand for my church group when I spotted him and one of his floozies cuddled together at the bagel shop down the street from Leland's law firm, right out in the open. I drove to his office and waited for him. Forty-five minutes later, he strolled in. He was furious when I confronted him. He threatened to call mental health. He said they were preparing for an important case scheduled on the docket for later in the week and were certainly not fornicating in the middle of a restaurant as I claimed.

When I tried to articulate how I knew he was lying, he dialled her number and dared me to repeat my accusations.

Courage escaped me then as it escapes me now.

Brendell? Please come back.

My head hurts.

The clock says six. How can I be expected to wait until tomorrow to find out whether I'm dying? How cruel is that?

Too cruel.

I sit up and blood rushes to my head, so I close my eyes and wait. When I open them again, the dizziness is gone. I switch on the light and reach for the phone, filled with determination and enough anger to leave me fearless. As soon as I explain to the answering service who I am, she puts me through to the doctor. He's on duty at the hospital.

"Sally, how are you?"

"How am I? Robert, do you have any idea what you've put me through having your receptionist call me like that. No explanation, just that I must report to your office Monday morning? Do you have any idea what that feels like?"

"Well—"

"What did my tests show? And please don't torture me

further by insisting that I wait until tomorrow. I just buried my husband, have some pity."

"Sally, you know my receptionist isn't allowed to discuss your medical records over the phone. She's not a specialist. She's simply my receptionist. I know it seems unfair, but there are reasons we do things this way."

"You're not going to tell me. You're going to make me suffer another night. Why would you be so cruel?"

"Calm down, Sally. It's your cholesterol."

"My cholesterol?"

"It's too high. You need to come in so we can discuss immediate treatment."

"That sounds serious."

"It's not—well, it could be if left untreated. But with a good diet and some medication we'll balance those numbers, get that cholesterol down to a nice controllable four or thereabouts."

"What's it at now?"

"Nine-point-six."

I'm tempted to ask how high it can go before I should worry, but decide it's a senseless question. I'm going to fix this. "Thank you, Robert." I hang up. My face hurts because I'm grinning so widely.

I'm not dying. What a silly goose. Goodness, did I go on about things or what? I smack my leg and catch sight of a manila envelope at the end of my bed. I try to remember why the MLA would send me something.

Open the bloody thing, you stupid woman.

I slip my finger under the tab and rip.

The envelope contains transcripts of the enquiry into Declan's and Bronson's deaths. Now I remember calling and requesting them. How could I forget? I shake my head and start reading. The technical jargon makes my head hurt more. I flip the pages until I spot Brendell's name. I've reached the part where she testifies. I can hear Brendell's voice as I read; it's as if she's speaking to me.

"When Zoë didn't call, I knew something was wrong."

Something was wrong with my sons, and I never sensed it. I rub my eyes and continue reading.

"I found out that Bronson was at the airport when Zoë's plane arrived. No one would believe me when I said he'd taken Zoë. Declan wouldn't. Even the police said they couldn't help. I was on my way out the door to look for them when Declan showed up. He said Bronson contacted him, said Zoë was with him, and it was time to play their game. Their father had a hunter's cabin past Lejac, and Declan thought they were probably there.

"We never reached Lejac. We arrived at my Cluculz Lake cabin...and all hell broke loose."

"Could you elaborate, please, Professor Meshango?" his Honour asked.

"Bronson wanted Declan to revive my daughter so he could rape her."

I can't read this. I don't want to know what awful things my sons did to them.

But you owe it to her.

My eyes settle on the second paragraph. Brendell offered herself to Bronson.

I skim the text then throw the transcripts to the bed and fall back against my pillow. Brendell saved her daughter by offering herself, and Declan saved Brendell and Zoë by killing his brother.

Sobs rip from my throat. Tears flow. No sense stopping them. Mâtowak is who I am.

* * *

I feel the feather touch of the duvet on my cheek. My eyes blink slowly. Vision clears. I rise like a woman wearing a soaked mink coat and swing my legs over the side. Judging by the clock, it's early morning, still pitch black outside, but the yard lights turn on. I part the blinds in time to see a small deer bound across the crunchy snow in my front yard, over the ditch, and into the bush next to the house.

The phone is on my bedside table. I dial Brendell's number and listen to the rings while my fingernails dig into my palm. My gaze settles on the clock. It's after seven in the morning. It's a weekend, what if she's sleeping?

"Hello," she says, out-of-breath.

"It's me Sally."

"Are you okay?"

"I'm fine. I'm terribly sorry for bothering you this early. I dialled before thinking."

"It's fine, Sally. I'm usually up around five."

"Every day?"

"It's a curse." She laughs.

"I'm so sorry about yesterday."

"You have nothing to be sorry about."

"Oh, but I do. I did something stupid. I have this prescription, and I'm only supposed to take one in the morning." I'm such a liar.

"What prescription?"

"Something for my nerves."

"You mean Valium?"

I'm sinking deeper. "Uh, Wellbutrin, I believe. I was feeling pretty low yesterday, so I took six hundred milligrams and, oh dear, I acted badly. Please accept my apology, Brendell. You've been so kind, and I hate to imagine what you must be thinking of me."

"I would never judge you, Sally. I have no right to do so."

"Did you tell Sergeant Lacroix what happened?"

"No. What's discussed between us is none of his business, for obvious reasons."

She makes it sound as if I should know what that means. "You didn't tell him you suspect I shot Leland?"

"I've obviously put you through a terrible ordeal, and I'm sorry. Please forgive me."

"Oh, Brendell. You are such a dear girl."

She laughs. "It's been a while since anyone referred to me as a girl let alone dear."

I choke over my next words. "Did you tell Sergeant Lacroix about Leland's panic room?"

"No."

I cover the phone and take a deep breath.

"Please trust me, Sally. You have to stop focusing on the panic room. Because if you don't, it's going to haunt you forever. Do you understand?"

"Haunt me?"

"Let it go. Enjoy the rest of your life. Don't let bad memories ruin that."

We're both speechless for a moment, and I wonder if she's thinking about those last few minutes with Declan. I'm ashamed I doubted her and that I tried to justify Leland's role in their lives. He ruined our sons, and our sons almost ruined her. "Maybe I should talk to Corporal Killian about the panic room after my doctor's appointment tomorrow?"

"That's right, you mentioned your doctor yesterday. Are you sure you're okay?"

"I have high cholesterol. No more fried foods for me." I chuckle, but I can't remember the last time I had fried-anything.

The clock on my bedside table says it's already quarter after seven. "Brendell, I should go. I've got to get ready for church."

"Pray for me, Sally. And promise me something."

I'd crawl across a gravel road if she asked me. "What?"

"Don't tell the Corporal unless you feel you absolutely have to."

She's confusing me again. We say our good-byes and hang up. Now I'm left wondering if it is necessary to tell Killian about the panic room. Brendell doesn't think I should. What purpose would it serve? He'd be angry with me. They would all be.

"You failed me, Danny."

I feel strange, panicky. I beg her to forgive me. A man enters from the dining room. I know him. Angie doesn't move. She stares through me. It's too late; she'd lost her faith.

She gestures towards the man. "He stalked me, stabbed me. None of it would have happened, Danny, if you'd shown up like you promised."

"How do you find being dead?" the man asks.

Angie shrugs.

Scared and confused, I look over my left shoulder to the backdoor. I holler, "Let's go sledding."

Angie doesn't answer. The man stands motionless. A big grin. A sneer. A face I know.

Angie won't stop glaring at me.

I fly out of my chair, lunge at him, and grab for his throat. He smiles. I squeeze—hard, release one hand, dig into my pocket, pull out my cell, hold it up, scream, "Police—help me."

The man laughs. I punch him in the head with my phone. Behind him, Angie yells, "You let me down, Danny. You let me down."

I slam the phone into his head, harder and harder. His skull cracks, splits open, brain matter oozes out. I drop to my knees.

Angie yells, "You let me down."

I'm tired. So tired. The man slips out of my grasp. He stands behind me, leans over me. I struggle to stand. "What?" I ask him. It's Warner! Warner killed Angie. "You prick, I'll kill you."

He laughs. "You can't, stupid. I'm dead."

"I'm not," The Butcher says. "You can kill me instead."

Digger barks. His nose butts a ball towards me. He wants to play.

"Digger? Where'd you come from? Angie, where'd Digger come from?"

She shrugs. "I don't know. After I was stabbed to death, he showed up."

"Oh." I sit down at the kitchen table. Angie sets a bowl of hot porridge in front of me. She joins me. "What's it like being

287

dead?" I ask.

"Better," she says.

The Butcher coaxes Warner to join us. He does. He pours too much milk over his porridge and it overflows, spilling onto the table. Angie crosses the room to the sink, returns with a damp cloth. Digger licks the milk that spilled onto the floor.

"Try to be careful," she tells Warner. "And be nice."

Warner smiles. He picks up my gun, smashes it into her brain. The Butcher laughs.

I wake with a jerk. A second passes before I recognize the shouting, my own voice filling the dark bedroom, painting the walls with her blood, sobs that seem to reach right down into my guts, ripping at them.

Under a cold shower, I shake my head like a dog to wipe the images from my mind. Oddly, I feel calm, calmer than I have in a long time.

After two cups of coffee, I shave and, put on my suit. Fixing my tie at the dining room wall mirror, I turn, look through the window and out across the front yard. It didn't snow overnight but the temperature dropped and the perfectly sculpted blue spruces lining both sides of the street are frozen white. As are the shrubs and naked cherry trees scattered down the block. The eight inches of snow on all the rooftops looks like vanilla icing. On the steeper roofs, where the snow slips over the edges by a foot, it's fused in place. Still dark, some of the homes are lit up, and the street resembles a scene from a Norman Rockwell painting. The perfect place to raise kids.

I don't have kids, but I make a note to buy Christmas lights.

Thoughts of my nightmare sit at the back of my mind as I rinse my mug, clean off the counter. Every counselling session the shrink has urged me to share my feelings.

My feeling is: expressing fears and anxiety is bullshit.

"If you talk about your fears, Danny, they'll lose their power."

Bullshit. Talking doesn't fix anything. Action. That'll right what's wrong.

I use the remote to start my car. The weather report on Global News says the roads are dry, but I'll still stop and pick up the studs after I have breakfast with my shrink. Besides, the service manager has agreed to meet me there, unlock the doors, hand over tires on a Sunday. I don't show up and chances are I'll be in his bad book for the rest of my career.

I had a rough night, but on the plus side, my headache's gone, my back feels good. I swing my jacket over my head, slipping my arms into the sleeves in one smooth motion. My game is back. So is my mind-set. The dream—okay—nightmare was the release I needed.

I slip into my winter jacket, grab Mrs. Warner's file, and exit the house into the cold morning.

I arrive at Timmy's first, wait in my vehicle with the engine running. Less than five minutes later my shrink pulls in. I exit my vehicle and, wait for him at the door.

"Hope you didn't have to wait long," he says as I hold the door open.

"No."

He glances at his watch. "That's right, you're generally early."

Realizing he's made a joke, I chuckle, follow him inside. At the counter I wait as he orders a large bran muffin and a cup of tea. I look at him, at the muffin, wonder why I'm not surprised. I order my usual and pay the lady. He picks a table, takes the seat facing the window so I'm left facing the door. I think he's seen too many cop movies.

Mrs. Warner's file is snug in my briefcase sitting on the floor beside me. "I hope I don't need to tell you whatever is said is confidential?"

"No you don't need to tell me."

"If you should guess who I'm referring to, you'll keep it to yourself."

"Now you have me intrigued." He smiles.

This is serious shit, but recognizing the excitement in his eyes, I say again, "You'll keep it to yourself."

He loses the smile. "Of course."

"Person of interest: woman, approximately sixty years of age. Her father, an elementary teacher, changed jobs twice after two different parents accused him of molesting their children, one a boy nine years of age, the other a girl, seven-years-old. Lack of evidence and witnesses being under the age of ten, no charges were ever laid. What's the probability my suspect was also a victim?"

He sets his tea down. "Too little information to tell."

"Okay. When she was a kid, early nineteen-fifties, maternal grandparents fought for custody of her, her brother, and sister. They lost and soon afterwards the grandfather died of degenerative heart disease. The family had no contact with the grandmother for seven years until she fell ill and they took her in. That arrangement lasted four months, at which time she was placed in a home."

He doesn't offer conjecture, but gives me his full attention. The remainder of his muffin sits untouched on his plate.

"Suspect's brother, five years her senior, a continual disciplinary problem through junior high, quit school at fifteen, ran away from home. At seventeen, he lied about his age to join the Army. The father found out and had him discharged. As soon as he turned eighteen he went to the States and joined the Marines, did three tours in Vietnam. Committed suicide two days after the war ended. Told his buddy he couldn't go home and face his younger sisters. When asked why, he would say, 'They needed me and I ran away.'"

"Sounds like he escaped," my shrink says.

"The suspect met her husband at the University of Notre Dame. They married two years later, had two children. While it was rumoured he abused her and their children, it was never proven. The youngest grew up, beat a young woman savagely. She died in the hospital two days later. Soon afterwards the elder sibling killed the younger one, then himself.

"Is my suspect a living time bomb? Is she capable of murder?"

"Most definitely." He leans towards me. "I know what you're thinking, Danny. But be careful you don't risk more than your job to help her."

* * *

The shop manager is inside the building when I arrive. I back in, pop the hood on my trunk. He's rolling the tires to door when I enter.

"I appreciate you doing this."

He grunts, goes back for another tire. "Don't let these highways fool you. We got a warm front coming in, and right after that the temperature's going to drop. The roads will be deadly before tonight."

I nod my agreement, like I would know differently. I heave the last tire into the trunk. "Thanks again. Have a good day." As I'm leaving I hear another grunt in reply.

Heading out of the city on Yellowhead Highway I take note of the dark clouds ahead of me over College Heights. Once Warner's case is solved, I'll spend some time analysing Prince George's skies. Everybody else seems to be an expert in the weather, don't see why I can't be one, too.

It's not what I planned, my life in Prince George, but it's the life I've got. Mind-set intact, I make a promise to myself. I'm taking my life back. I'm heading up to Stan's to install my tires. When I'm finished, I'll go to the Warners' and find the evidence I need for a conviction. If she killed her husband, she needs to confess. Juries aren't without empathy. Once they hear the kind of husband he was, they'll go easy on her. She can't go around with that kind of guilt, because guilt can kill you.

Church begins at ten-thirty, and though I'm properly dressed and primped, there are still my keys, coat, scarf, and boots to gather. But I can't seem to get motivated. My mood has me sitting here at the breakfast table staring through the windows. Outside, chilly blue skies hold high cumulous clouds, while the ground is covered in untouched snow. Chickadees chirp, flickering from branch to branch, playing a game every child knows: catch me if you can.

A sense of gratitude overwhelms me, which is strange because there are dark secrets I've yet to face. When did I first confuse nightmares with real life? I sit here stranded like a seal out of water, wondering did I kill Leland. Or did I want him dead so badly my dream came true?

Reconstructing events of that day hasn't helped. Reality mixing so fluidly with my imagination has me assessing my sanity. The result leaves me agitated, teary, and morbidly drowsy. Instead of attending church, I should open Leland's panic room and discover what the truth is, or at best, whether I am episodically psychotic. I would open the room, except the prospect of knowing makes my blood run cold. Too bad mental exhaustion can't block the thoughts clawing at my brain. Is it any wonder eyelids laden with dreamlike skits close, and the same scene plays behind them like a movie stuck on replay?

Will Brendell forgive me for whatever I've done?

The morning of Leland's murder—Digger had a nightmare. I woke to his doggy cries and reached down to the bottom of the bed where I found his little body shaking. The digital clock showed six-thirty. I patted Digger and whispered, "It's okay. You're safe." Finally, he wagged his tail. One big stretch and he was on his feet, nudging my hand. I switched on my bedside lamp and knew then it was too late to go back to sleep. Donning bathrobe and slippers, I followed Digger downstairs to the garage door. In the wintertime, when the temperature dropped below minus ten Celsius, paper over a rubber mat on the cement floor saved Digger the trouble of going outside and risking frostbite to his paws. During the day, when the temperature reached minus one, we'd go for walks so he could do his business in the ditch. And no, I didn't carry a shovel and a bag. He was a small dog. His poops were no larger than a cat's.

But that morning I didn't feel like going for a walk. I was barely awake, and it was too cold to stand inside the garage with him, besides Digger preferred his privacy, so I waited by the door until he scratched to get in.

"Good boy," I said once he was finished. I gave him a doggy treat. We were on our way back up to my room when Leland appeared on the stairs.

"You're up early," he said.

"Digger had to pee."

"Are you going back to bed?"

"No." I lifted my nightgown to show him how pink my ankles were. "My legs are cold and I thought I'd get a pair of lounge bottoms on."

"I'll turn up the heat."

"I'll be down in a moment."

"I'll make coffee."

Mornings were always my favourite time of day. I loved the quiet. No phone calls, no traffic speeding past our house. It was too early for visitors. Even the crows had the good sense to stay in their nests until I had my morning coffee. I found some wool socks and thick lounge bottoms and returned downstairs to the wonderful aroma of coffee brewing. Leland had the newspaper opened on the breakfast table to the Sports pages. I took the Entertainment section from him and sat down with my first cup of coffee. I mentioned I wasn't hungry and would he mind fixing his own bagels this morning?

"Sure."

I left him to finish his paper and returned upstairs to shower and change. Thursdays, I volunteered at the United Way downtown. I had my clothes laid out on the bed, matching shoes and purse, and was preparing my toiletries for my shower when, through my open bedroom window, I heard a sound at the front of the house. Raspy breathing, rapid footsteps, metal jiggling like a chain.

I thought of going downstairs to investigate, but it was such a long trek that I waited.

Do I regret that now?

Of course.

I advanced forward, the distance expanding like a 3-D mirrored fantasy. When I finally reached the window and looked out, Digger had crossed the ditch to the road. I cried out for him to stop, pushed the window open wider, but the latch interfered. My fingers scratching at the glass as if that would get me outside. Digger—please stop!

His little body vanished into the bush in seconds.

Gasping, crying, my heart hurting, hands scratching at the glass...none of it would bring him back. None of my pleas or prayers would change the inescapable.

Is that what finally broke the thin string holding my sanity intact?

The next few moves must have attested to that. I grabbed my winter coat and boots from my closet and wore them over my dressing gown. I went down the stairs and straight out the front door. I didn't even have to go a block before I saw a car, a young man in bright jogging clothes, and...Digger.

Leland was still in the kitchen. He had no idea I'd even left. I went into the greenhouse without being noticed. The white plastic coveralls were stuffed in the cabinet, the long rubber gloves under the sink. Both items were intended for the young man due to paint my tool shed in the spring.

I went up to my room, dressed in minutes; my suit still lay flat on my bed for later when I would need to change. I covered my head with the shower cap from my last stay at a hotel.

It was easier to go out through the front door and walk around to the service entrance. How I knew it was still open didn't matter. Having already retrieved his unregistered gun from his panic room, I felt more like a stage extra than the bitter wife of a lawyer turned politician turned dog killer. I had my role to play, late or not. Fate had thrown me into the performance of a lifetime. I called him from the door. His face showed his initial shock. Eyes full of fear, until fear turned to confusion, denial, and finally terror. He backed up as far as he could go, the kitchen island forcing him to stop. "Why?" he asked, his voice pleading. Then it occurred to me that he was asking God, and who was I to answer? Besides, what was the point? The explanation would take too long. He had killed my spirit, my sons, and my dog.

But then something strange happened. Leland's expression calmed and he spoke with clarity and gentleness. "Aim for the head, Sally."

It's all a blur, the choices I faced that morning.

Now, fifteen minutes after ten, I know if I don't leave soon I'll be late. Heaviness weighs me onto the chair. My crowded mind wonders if my reconstruction is a fallacy. Moving towards the garage seems a step out of place. What did I do with the gun? I don't remember going back into the panic room. How did I, who knows so little of electronic surveillance equipment, manage to remember to destroy the video of me coming through the backdoor? Had watching all those CSI shows made me an expert? Remembering Leland's stunned expression those last few seconds makes me shiver.

How did Brendell know, when I can't even remember firing the gun?

I remember hating Leland, though. The sensation made me a giant.

Revenge. Retribution.

I'm contemplating attending service, thinking I might be a murderer, and if so, it's a matter of time before Killian discovers my secret and arrests me.

Buttoning up boots and overcoat takes seconds. Keys, gloves, and scarf, seconds more. After setting the alarm, I slip behind the wheel of my car when a thought occurs to me. What if the inevitable doesn't happen and Killian fails?

Snow lines the right-away on both sides of Highway 16. Gravel mixed with salt edges the snow-packed shoulders. Overhead the clear skies show a fading blue, while the highway seems relatively dry. Nevertheless, I drive with caution and avoid the ice patches. As I pass Mrs. Warner's turnoff, I note her road has been sanded and ploughed. Good. I'm dropping in on her after I leave Stan's. I've decided to push the investigation up a notch. Time to use the skills I'm supposed to be so good at and treat her as my prime suspect. If done right, I should know by day's end whether she's my shooter. For now, it's off to Stan's where I'll replace these bald tires with winter studs. Honestly, I'll feel better once that's done. I'm a cop. Having an accident because of worn tires won't sit well with Lacroix. Yes, I'm suddenly concerned with what he thinks.

Drops of rain land on my windshield. What's with that? It's warming up? Or is the weather about to kick my ass? I have no idea and that makes me wonder if I should take a night course in meteorology sooner than later.

I follow an SUV driving ten kilometres over the speed limit as far as Stan's road. The SUV takes a right at the first four-way stop sign, I continue through. The light rain turns heavy. If I don't gun it, I won't make the hill ahead. Do I dare? I tap the brakes. The car slides. I right it.

"Not now." I look up through my window to the black ominous cloud overhead. "Where the hell did you come from?"

I shift down, crest the hill. Only now that I've come up—I'm going down. Why don't they shave these hills? I proceed slowly, slide, straighten. I should have gone the roundabout way. I'm close though, turning around now would be stupid. Treacherous, in fact.

I smack the steering wheel. "Okay car, a few more miles and we're home free."

Out of nowhere—a downpour, full blast. Rain mixed with hail and snow splatters my window. I switch on the wipers, ease my foot off the gas. Good thing there is no traffic. The car slides. I swing the wheel hard, straighten the tires, and keep going. *Pull over, you idiot.* I'll turn into the next driveway, call Stan, ask him to call me a tow truck. Maybe I'm wrong about Mrs. Warner, too. Maybe the killer got away because I've been too stubborn to—a deer bounds across the road—I swerve out of the way. The car slides sideways. I steer into it. Too late. Shit, here comes the ditch. I swing the wheel right, my car goes left—spinning round and round. Out of my peripheral vision, a grey SUV skims by my window. Damn, that was close. They keep going. I stop dead.

I'm facing the opposite direction of where I was headed. My senses, alerted by the stillness, peak. Windshield blanketed in snow—it was raining a second ago.

Complete silence. The seatbelt holds me tight. A second passes before I trust the car has stopped on the edge of the shoulder. My head is spinning. Heart thumping. Somebody bangs on my window—*Sonofabitch!*

"Corporal Killian, are you okay?"

Lady, where in hell did you come from? I unwind my window. "Mrs. Warner? What are you doing here?"

She's visibly shaken. I came close to hitting her. "I drive a few of the elderly ladies home after church." Her warm breath mixes with the cold morning air stinging my face. "I'm on my last stop. Are you okay?"

"Oh sure." I smile. After all, I'm a cop, and everybody knows cops are expert drivers. Ha.

My breath turns to steam while snow coats Mrs. Warner's shoulders; the snow on her hat beads.

"Are you sure? Can you move your neck?"

I prove it by turning my head slowly right then left. Snow hits my face. "I'm good."

"I have to drive Ruth home. I'll stop on my way back."

"No reason to concern yourself. I'm sure I'll be gone by then. I'll drop by later to see you, if that is good with you?" If it isn't, I plan to anyway.

"Of course. Now, you're sure you're okay?"

I wave aside her worries. "I'm fine."

She looks reluctant to leave. I wind up my window; snow tries to fight its way through the glass. I smile at her, turn up the heat, switch the fan to full blast. She waves good-bye as she trots off to her vehicle parked across the road a short distance behind me. I watch in my side mirror until she and her friend disappear over the hill. I shove the door open, which takes some strength because of the angle of the car. I climb out and survey the damage.

The right front and back tires sit in deep crust-layered snow, but the left tires are firmly planted on the road.

I'll be on my way in no time.

I climb back in, turn down the fan, shift into drive, and rock the car forward. It spins in place. I shift into reverse, cut the tires so I won't sink deeper off the shoulder, rock back. The tires whine. Shift into drive, position my tires, rock forward, tires whine, shift, rock backwards, shift, rock forward, and whine.

I'm still rocking back and forth when Mrs. Warner returns. Her car is the only vehicle I've seen since she left. What are the odds of that? She pulls into the driveway up the road, treks back to where I'm still parked. I climb out of my car and check my cell phone reception. Weak.

"Don't dismay, Corporal Killian. If you like, I can steer while you push. You can't be expected to do both."

I smile. I'm like a fish out of water in this country, and she knows it. In fact, she's a lot smarter than she'd like me to believe. "Sure, that'll be great. I'll holler when I want you to step on the gas. Gradual pressure, okay?"

I pocket my phone, and wait for her to slip in behind the wheel. By the time I reach the back of the car, my hair and shoulders are wet. My winter coat is in the backseat. I find solid footing and test how much traction there is under my feet. I dig in, push, slip, land on my knees, get back up, and dig in again. The temperature hovers around minus two degrees Celsius. Drenched from my knees down, my trousers stiffen with cold.

"Okay, give it some gas."

I lean in and push. Tires whine. Car moves forward, rocks back. Forward, push, back, push, forward. I keep up the momentum. Forward, back. Slowly I feel it inch ahead, push, whine, push...it's back on the road. I brush the snow from my arms, shoulders, and head.

Mrs. Warner exits my car smiling widely. "I knew you could do it."

I grin.

"I hope you don't mind a little advice."

Hey, why not. She's my guardian angel.

"I'd replace these bald tires with winter studs. You really need studs in this country."

I almost laugh, but chances are she wouldn't get the joke and I'd end up hurting her feelings. "I'm actually on my way to a friend's place up the road to use his garage. I've got new studs in the trunk."

"There are several sharp corners ahead, not to mention a hill, and I don't think it's going to stop snowing any time soon. How far away is your friend?"

"A few kilometres."

"I'm right around the corner. Why don't you follow me home and use our garage?"

"That's nice of you, ma'am, but I don't want to intrude."

"You're no bother. Besides, you're soaked to the skin. If you don't get dry soon, you're liable to catch your death. Unless using our garage would violate some RCMP protocol."

I look closely to see if she's teasing. She has a point though. My teeth chatter.

"Leland's tools are just sitting there."

True. The image of their heated garage full of every conceivable tool imaginable makes the decision easier. Plus, it would be a good opportunity to push the investigation to the next level. "That's kind of you, Mrs. Warner. I appreciate it."

She looks relieved as she glances at my tires. "Good. If you don't mind, I'll follow you."

I brush off my windshield, then climb in. My frozen trousers crunch as I settle into place. I wait as she walks back to her car and, starts the engine. I shift into drive, move forward, test my brakes. This should be fun.

Once we arrive at the house. I pull in beside her husband's Mercedes. I leave enough room so I can work without threat of touching, denting, or scratching his car. The garage door closes behind Mrs. Warner, who pauses by the steps leading to her kitchen.

"I appreciate this, ma'am." I mean it.

"Why don't you let me take your suit jacket into the laundry room to dry. I have a wonderful machine where you hang something up and it's steamed and dried in no time. Honestly, it's wonderful."

"Thanks." I toss my outer coat into the backseat, then slip off my jacket, take it to her.

"Meanwhile, let's have a snack and a cup of tea. That should give you a chance for your hair and clothes to dry before you catch pneumonia."

I look back to the garage and almost say, "But it's heated," then realize I'm shivering.

"Working with damp clothes is a sure way to get sick," she says.

Because I'm learning it's best not to argue, I oblige and follow her into the kitchen. A few minutes later, we're sitting at the kitchen counter with tea and warm cinnamon buns. She slices an apple into wedges and garnishes my plate and hers. I raise a piece of the bun to my lips, savour the smell, pop the piece into my mouth, try not to drool.

Still not comfortable with silence, I ask, "How's it going?"

She takes a bite from her apple wedge. "What do you mean?"

"You've had a bad time and—"

"I'm fine. I've had to deal with death my entire life."

"I'm sorry to hear that, ma'am."

She looks at me with compassion, shakes her head, says, "You become numb until eventually little gets through."

"Is that how you feel?"

"Yes."

"You're being too tough on yourself."

"You don't know me."

"I can see you're a good person."

She doesn't look convinced. "You are a nice man."

I wipe sugar off my mouth. "Ever thought of volunteering at the crisis centre? A lot of people could benefit from what you've gone through."

She frowns.

"There are victims, Mrs. Warner, who could learn from you. You could help a lot of people."

She frowns. "Corporal...?"

"Ma'am?"

"Corporal, I can't help anyone. I know nothing."

"I don't believe that."

"It's true. I haven't learned from my mistakes. I'm not who you think I am."

A tired old woman who killed her husband because...? What set her off? What is it I'm missing? More importantly, can I do my job and still help her? I'm no shrink, but with a good lawyer she could probably get off on second-degree murder, especially if enough evidence is presented to show what kind of man Warner had been. Except, it might backfire. She said he changed. Then why did she kill him? Her dog died after Warner was shot. Her sons died two years ago. What drove her over the edge?

She moves suddenly, pushing her plate away and clapping her fingers together in a fake gesture of glee. Or is she applauding my efforts. "I get these morbid moments. They'll pass."

"Nothing to apologize for." I smile reassuringly. "Maybe it'd help if you got a puppy?"

Her expression shows instant distain.

"I know how painful it must have been to lose Digger the same day your husband died, but an animal will love you unconditionally."

Eyes downcast, she leans her elbows on the island, folds her hands together, presses them to her chin. At least she didn't see Digger hit by the car. The spot where Wickstrom said it happened was too far up the road for her to see from the house. Definitely a good thing. Witnessing her dog die might have pushed her over the edge for good.

She has grown quiet. I follow her eyes and look through the patio doors to her backyard, a winter wonderland. It occurs to me that I'm feeling hopeful myself for the first time in too long. I glimpse her face, question whether my mood is reflective, then switch back to the scene outside. Falling heavily, fat fluffs of snow lighten on the already twelve or more on the ground.

Does she feel hope, too?

She purses her lips and, glances at the sink of sticky baking dishes.

With the sweet taste of icing lingering on my tongue, I smooth the napkin and lay it beside the tea plate. It feels like she needs time alone. I should come back inside and check on her later. "Thanks for the food, ma'am. Your buns are delicious, the best I've ever tasted." She stares through me. "I should get back to putting those studs on my car." I gulp back the rest of my tea before slipping off the stool. Wait.

She blinks, focuses on my face, forces a smile. "Let me know when you're ready to leave. I'll put some warm buns in a paper bag for you."

I almost say, don't go to any bother...but I'm learning.

"Your timing this morning was great, showing up like that. Thanks."

"I hadn't planned on attending church this morning until the wife of one of our deacons let it be known they were having prayers for Leland."

"That was nice of them."

She nods, looks towards the window.

I leave her gazing out at a sudden streak of sunlight a foot wide running across the back yard. I go out the kitchen door to their garage.

Less than forty minutes later all four studs are on my car, and the bald ones are in the trunk. I stick my head in the kitchen hallway to check on her. I also need to piss. "May I use your washroom?"

I hear the hum of her fridge. I step into the hallway, listen at the washroom door, then enter the kitchen. Now would be a good opportunity to snoop, the excuse being I'm looking for a washroom. I imagine her saying, "There is a washroom right there, Corporal Killian."

Oops, forgot.

The kitchen's quiet. No Mrs. Warner. It's a huge house; she's got to be here somewhere.

In the upstairs guest bathroom, I do my business, wash my hands, wonder if anything's changed in the other rooms since our last search. I'll stay out of her room; she's probably in there. At the top of the landing, I head towards Warner's room. When I test the door handle, it turns. Interesting. All three times we searched the house before, we had to ask for the key.

I open the door as soundlessly as possible, enter Warner's room, and walk across to the bedside table. I slide open the left drawer, see papers I've already checked, and go to the right of the bed. As before, nothing but two remotes in the drawer. The second remote is probably an extra. I slide it closed, pick up Warner's phone, and hear Mrs. Warner's voice. Sounds like she's talking to one of the women from her church. The other woman says something about "God's Grace..." I set the phone down. The bedroom looks as if nothing has been disturbed. The dresser tops are untouched. The bathroom is spotless. I enter the library through the door next to his bathroom, find nothing different, step back into the bedroom. Eight large strides and I'm at the window. Outside it's still snowing heavily. Behind me, silence; nothing but my own pulse inside my head. I return to the bed, lift the phone receiver, and hear Mrs. Warner's voice.

I set the phone down gently, walk out onto the landing. The media room is straight ahead, I enter, walk to the back. Ten long strides. Back at the top of the landing, I listen. The furnace fan cuts in—I jump like a scared rabbit. Shaking my head, I re-enter Warner's bedroom, go through to the library. I count my large strides to the front window; eight—same as last time. I do the same trek on the landing to the media room. Ten steps. I do it again. My pulse hammers. In the middle of the room, I turn slowly, deliberately. Like a clue flashing across a blank screen, I picture the extra remote in the bedside table. I collect it, aim it at different angles in the room, grope my way along the wall, fingers rubbing every conceivable surface. The bloods pounds in my brain. I turn, catch my reflection in the wall mirror. My face is drained. I aim the remote at my image like a gun, whisper, "Use your brain, copper, or get the hell out of Dodge." I press a button. The mirror groans as it opens. A panic room.

The stale stink of blood assaults my nostrils as soon as I step inside. I cup a hand over my nose, and look for the source. The wall closest to the door at this end shows four monitors with views of the front door, back door, back yard, and inside the garage. I check the cupboards at the other end. In the bottom of the first drawer, a huge plastic bag. There is no mistaking the blood-stained white vinyl coveralls inside. I want to shout, I'm that happy. I was right. Sally killed her husband. I pull out rubber gloves from the drawer that could reach to her elbows. In the second drawer is a 9mm handgun wrapped in white tissue paper. I smell the faint odour of gunpowder residue at the barrel. I'm certain, once it's tested, this gun will prove to be the weapon that killed Warner. It's loaded. Her fingerprints may be on it.

Leaving everything as it is isn't an option. I have to get this evidence to the lab fast. I don't even have a camera. I open the cell phone. No signal. I snap several photographs.

From the rack in Warner's bathroom, I borrow a small hand towel. Back in the panic room, I wrap the gun, set it on the side table next to the bed, go back for the plastic bag filled with the coveralls, gloves, video tapes. I stand for a moment survey the panic room's space, looking for anything else I need to recover.

"You shouldn't have come in here," Sally Warner says behind my back.

My hand automatically touches the waistband of my trousers. "You shouldn't have."

I hear her crying, move my hand away from my gun. Best not to spook her. "Ma'am? I'm going to turn around. It's me, Corporal Killian. Mrs. Warner, you know me."

"You want me to get a new puppy, as if Digger never existed, as if his life meant nothing."

"I want you to have someone to love."

"I thought you were my friend."

I turn slowly. My eyes immediately settle on the small revolver in her hands, pointed at my chest. One of the first things they teach us is to never underestimate anybody, especially nice middle-aged ladies who have killed before. I raise both hands, see the tears rolling down her face. "I am your friend."

She shakes her head.

"We were bound to find this room. It's okay. I'll stay with you. I'll make sure they treat you proper. It'll be okay."

She continues to cry, shaking her head.

Maybe now might be a good time to remind her shooting a cop is a bad idea. "Let me help."

"You're just like him. I can't trust you."

"You can trust me. You know you can."

This is the first time I've had to look down the barrel of gun. I'd like to live to tell about it, but if I'm going to die, I'd like to know why.

"What happened the morning Digger died?"

"What difference does it make?"

"I'd like to know."

"How am I supposed to trust somebody who wants me to forgot about the only one who ever loved me? Digger."

"Put the gun down and we can talk. I'll tell you anything you want to know."

"Brendell said your wife is dead. Did you kill her?"

"What? No."

"Somebody stabbed her?"

"Yes." My voice cracks.

"Did you catch him?"

"No. But they have a suspect."

"They? Who are they? Where were you?"

She holds the small gun in both hands.

I wait for her to ask more questions while the weight of my arms grows heavier, like they're made of lead. But she doesn't ask; she's waiting for a response to the hardest question I've ever had to answer. "I'm not allow to work the case. They figure I'm too emotionally involved."

"So you do nothing?"

Damn it, no way am I letting her drag me down. "I didn't kill my wife. I'm not responsible."

The 9mm bobs slightly.

"They have a suspect."

Her eyes look like they're glazing over. "It wasn't until this morning that I remember what happened. I get mixed up."

I lower my arms four inches...five.

"Leland knew not to let Digger out. He knew if he left the door open that Digger would run. The last time it happened Digger was narrowly hit by a car right in front of our house. The time before that I saw a truck swerve and miss him by inches. He was all I had. As soon as he ran across the road, I knew he wouldn't make it. I went outside to search. Saw him...Leland didn't even know I'd gone. That is how observant he was. So full of himself. A pompous, evil father. A selfish, self-serving husband. Do you think such a man deserve to live?"

"Put the gun down, Mrs. Warner. I will help you." I lower my hands to my waist with my palms facing out. "I won't let anyone hurt you." Damn, I don't want to shoot her.

She smiles. Tears are still flowing. "I know they gave you a bad time over this case. But you proved you're better than they are. You solved Leland's murder."

I step forward. She's right, it will feel good to close the file. But I'm worried about her. Can she survive this? As if reading my mind, she steadies the gun.

"I'm sorry, but my arms are heavy. Do you mind?" I hang them to my sides. She looks strangely at peace. I step forward. A few more steps and I'll grab the gun. She uses one hand to wipe her face. I jump forward—

Ear-busting. Burning in chest. Pain. Can't breathe. Falling...

She weeps, covers her mouth with one hand. Says something. Can't hear. Eardrums—Blood...lots of blood...

She crouches. Sobs hard. Shouts, "...sorry...please...forgive..."

She's crying hard.

I don't want to die.

Distant chime. Strange sound. An angel gets her wings?

"Die, please," she pleads.

Sinking...

* * *

Blood. So much. Pooling on the floor around him.

The ringing in my ears hurts. Killian looks stunned, confused. I squat. What is it? He says something I can't make out. "Pardon?" I wipe the tears from my face. Should he be frowning like that? Is he in pain. Leland didn't frown.

The doorbell chimes. I straighten up, and my knees crack. Dizzy.

Doorbell chimes.

My lawyer?

Two steps backwards and I'm outside the panic room. As the door begins to close, I lower the gun to the floor and slide it through the opening before the mirror closes tight. The doorbell downstairs continues to chime. I don't rush. I can't. My legs are like rubber.

Hanging onto the railing, I descend the stairs. Across the foyer, on the other side of the front glass door I see someone standing under the entrance. I squint. Long black coat. Beaded moccasins. Short black hair.

Oh ...

Oh! How nice. It's my dear friend, Brendell.

I can't open the door fast enough. I have buns in the warming oven. I wonder if I should serve wine or hot chocolate. It may be too early for wine. Silly me, I'll ask.

"Brendell? What a nice surprise." I laugh. "Oops, my ears just popped, sorry for yelling."

She brushes the snow from her head and shoulders and stomps her boots. A strange-looking talisman dangles from her left hand.

"Sally, sorry to barge in, but I made up my mind, and I won't change it this time. I promise."

"Beg your pardon?"

"I've come to see your panic room." She hugs me, and then steps back. "This time I swear I won't leave until I do. In fact, let's go up right now." She steps by me and dashes up the stairs. "Come on, Sally, let's get this over with."

"Brendell, no dear. Let's go to the study. It's a perfect day for hot cocoa. We can dress it with brandy."

She's already at the top landing. "As soon as we check out the panic room and I perform a cleanse."

I hurry to catch up. "Honestly, dear, forget about it. There is no need, really. I'm fine. In fact, I haven't been better."

"It's okay, Sally, I've made up my mind."

I reach the top landing, gasping for air. Leland's door is ajar, and Brendell is inside. Oh dear, I forgot to lock his door—and now I suddenly feel faint. I'm not sure why, but something tells me...this is a bad idea.

"Brendell," I yell. "No—Please! Stop!"

At the open door I hesitate, lean against the doorframe, and listen. The swoosh of the panic door breaks the silence. I listen and wait for what feels like an eternity.

Finally...

"Sally, what have you done!"

I race into the room. Brendell is crouched beside Killian inside the panic room. He looks dead. She has blood on her hands. She's glaring at me. Why? What did I do? I didn't do anything. My heart's pounding. What do I do now? Ohmigosh! I search for the remote. I'll lock them in. I must protect myself. I grab the remote from the drawer and aim it at them.

Brendell stands up. "Wrong remote." She has something in her hand. Something in the other hand, too.

She's pointing a gun at me.

Help!

Heaven is dark.

Heaven is light.

No. Heaven is dark and light.

Alone.

No. A voice. Angie?

Eyelids...opening. Heaven? Is Meshango dead? She's smiling down on me. Strange.

Eyes closing.

Dark.

Rough voice. Lacroix. Dead, too?

Bright light.

"Wake up, Killian."

An order. I struggle. My chest. It hurts!

"Yes, you're alive." Lacroix's voice.

"Danny." Meshango's soft voice. "You're in the hospital. You were in a coma for six days. You're going to be all right. Do you remember what happened?"

Mrs. Warner shot me.

"Sally told them I shot you. When you're well enough, you'll need to give a statement."

"Mrs. Warner had gun residue on her hand and arm." Lacroix's voice. "That's why she's in the psyche ward."

"Yes, and she'll get the help she needs. Tell him about the other news," Dr. Meshango prompts.

"Your wife's killer plead guilty."

Sweet Jesus.

"Did you hear me, Killian?"

"Stop shouting. He hears you," Dr. Meshango says.

"You sure?"

"Tears. He's crying."

"He's not crying. He's smiling. Good—we can go home now."

THE END

About the Auhor

Joylene divides her time between Cluculz Lake BC, Canada and Bucerias, Nayarit, Mexico. When she isn't busy writing dark thrillers, conducting writer's workshops, providing editing services, or co-administrating for Insecure Writer's Support Group, she is a devoted wife and mother, and butler to felines Marbles and Shasta. Joylene has come full circle from her childhood of oral story telling days, compliments of her parents' endless tales.

CPSIA information can be obtained
at www.ICGtesting.com
Printed in the USA
LVOW11s1216280317
528747LV00001B/130/P